"What kind of woman are you?" Steve murmured.

"A woman who is her father's child," Savannah answered. "A Benedict, remember?"

"I remember." But she was far more than that. He'd heard it in her voice, seen it in the way she walked, the way she dressed. The way she looked at a man. That cool challenge in her silver eyes that made her a challenge herself.

Savannah "Hank" Benedict answered to a man's name, but any fool could see she was a hell of a woman. A woman any man would want. She would love with mind and heart, body and soul. Completely, without reservation. As completely as she fought.

Catching her hand in his, ignoring her gasp of surprise, he stroked her fingers. They were delicate, but he felt the strength there. Strength to fight the battles of her family and her ranch.

"Savannah Benedict," he murmured. "Woman extraordinaire. Enemy mine...."

Dear Reader,

The weather may be cooling off as fall approaches, but the reading's as hot as ever here at Silhouette Intimate Moments. And for our lead title this month I'm proud to present the first longer book from reader favorite BJ James. In *Broken Spurs* she's created a hero and heroine sure to live in your mind long after you've turned the last page.

Karen Leabo returns with *Midnight Confessions*, about a bounty hunter whose reward—love—turns out to be far different from what he'd expected. In *Bringing Benjy Home*, Kylie Brant matches a skeptical man with an intuitive woman, then sets them on the trail of a missing child. *Code Name: Daddy* is the newest Intimate Moments novel from Marilyn Tracy, who took a break to write for our Shadows line. It's a unique spin on the ever-popular "secret baby" plotline. And you won't want to miss *Michael's House*, Pat Warren's newest book for the line and part of her REUNION miniseries, which continues in Special Edition. Finally, in *Temporary Family* Sally Tyler Hayes creates the family of the title, then has you wishing as hard as they do to make the arrangement permanent.

Enjoy them all—and don't forget to come back next month for more of the best romance fiction around, right here in Silhouette Intimate Moments.

Leslie Wainger,
Senior Editor and Editorial Coordinator

Please address questions and book requests to:
Silhouette Reader Service
U.S.: 3010 Walden Ave., P.O. Box 1325, Buffalo, NY 14269
Canadian: P.O. Box 609, Fort Erie, Ont. L2A 5X3

BROKEN SPURS

BJ JAMES

Published by Silhouette Books

America's Publisher of Contemporary Romance

SILHOUETTE BOOKS

ISBN 0-373-07733-5

BROKEN SPURS

BJ JAMES

married her high school sweetheart straight out of college and soon found that books were delightful companions during her lonely nights as a doctor's wife. But she never dreamed she'd be more than a reader, never expected to be one of the blessed, letting her imagination soar, weaving magic of her own.

BJ has twice been honored by the Georgia Romance Writers with their prestigious Maggie Award for Best Short Contemporary Romance. She has also received the *Romantic Times* Critic's Choice Award.

Chapter 1

Dust lay heavy in the air. Dust and heat. Rosin and liniment. The whinny of horses. The pawing of bulls. Excitement. Adrenaline.

Incense of the rodeo.

The music.

The magic.

A ragged cheer rippled through an anxious crowd as one more fallen cowboy picked himself up from the dirt. Their rumbling ovation greeted the wave of his trampled hat. A signal that any injury was temporary, only to pride, a tender ego, and a bruised and dusty seat.

Applause dwindled, drifting into silence. Desultory laughter and conversation stuttered to a halt. Oblivious of the peculiar hush and grim-faced in failure, the next to last rider stumped from the arena in a sore and hobbling step. A pickup man, fearless savior of the bareback and saddle bronc cowboy, with no cowboy to save, herded a riderless bronc to the designated chute.

In the circle pounded to near concrete beneath its dressing of sand and sawdust, a rodeo clown jousted with another garbed in horns and tail, filling a bit of vacant space with comedy.

No one laughed.

This was the moment. Time, at last, for the event the dedicated, the true to the bone, rodeo fan awaited. The match of the rodeo, the match of the season—Steve Cody's ride on Shattered Dreams. In this specialized world of fierce individualism and sheer bullhead-edness with its touch of quiet arrogance, only the rare cowboy expected to stay his eight seconds aboard the volatile mare.

No one had.

Steve Cody could.

Neither friend nor fan nor cowboy doubted he could. If a rare streak of good luck held, he would.

Eager eyes searched for Steve and found him where he could always be found before a ride. Standing a few paces back from the arena, an arm draped over the top rail of a runway fence, head down, his thoughts turned inward. As he played and planned the ride in his mind, he was completely unaware of, completely untouched by the mood of the crowd and the screams of a brute of a horse that hated the chute only slightly less than she hated the men who tried to ride her.

"Let's rodeo."

The familiar drawl sliced through riveted concentration. Drawing a long, calm breath, he turned and stepped away from the fence. A crooked smile curled his lips, a tug drew his hat firmly over his forehead. Shattered Dreams waited.

Fringe fluttered at the edge of leather chaps, dulled and roweled spurs spun and jingled over worn boot heels as he took the short walk to the longest eight seconds of his life.

A quick check of back cinch and stirrup length, a cautious mount, a tight grip on the swells of the saddle, a tighter grip on the rope with its hand hold carefully marked, and all that's left is to ride. Cool eyed and controlled, Steve nodded. The chute gate burst open, a horse filled with fear and hate exploded into the arena.

In eight brutal seconds, when Charlie Cowboy scooped him from the bowed back of a screaming, maddened whirling dervish, the rodeo knew they'd seen a ride to remember. The ride of a champion whose dogged bad luck had surely changed.

Eight seconds more and a tired horse stumbled, a cinch broke. Steve tumbled with Charlie beneath the pounding hooves of the horse that hated men. As the announcer blurted a call for help, a silent crowd watched in helpless horror and cursed a lady called Luck.

Chapter 2

He was awake.

Totally, unremittingly awake. His eyelids lifted abruptly, like the shutter of a camera. Eyes, narrowed and staring, focused on nothing as murky shapes swam in and out of the nebula of an odorous gray haze hovering over his bed.

Bed? Tanned and chafed fingers crumpled the sheet at his waist. Why the devil was he in bed? Why was he alone, and why in this place?

This place? A frown pulled at the rigid muscles of his face. Where was he? Why? The questions sang in his brain, a monotonous litany without answers.

He meant to turn his head, to search out something real, something of recognizable substance, to orient himself. That was his intention, until the barest move sent a bolt of pain rocketing through his head like an ax. An ax, he was certain, determined to cleave his skull in half.

His head spun, his stomach lurched. Sweat beaded his forehead as he clutched the sheet in a savage grip. "Where?" he muttered grimly. "Why?"

He had to think, had to remember. Thinking hurt almost as much as moving, but he'd hurt before and survived. With burning gaze fixed and nerves straining with effort, he probed the darkness of the void in his mind.

"Where? Why?" The words became his anchor, his lodestar, the channel to remembering.

Sweat ran in rivulets now, over his bare torso, soaking coarse sheets. Tendons in his neck pulled taut, his jaw rippled over clenched teeth. The ax in his skull hacked out a tom-tom rhythm. Slowly, with monumental effort and by sheer will etched in pain, his senses began to clear. Silence became the silence of dawn. The gray haze coalesced into tiles of a ceiling discolored with age. Cloying scents permeating every shallow breath were the stench of medicines. Brutally starched sheets at peril in his tortured grasp were cold, unyielding linens of one more hospital bed.

"Okay, that answers where." His voice was rough from disuse, an alien sound echoing hollowly in the empty room. Drawing a long, cautious breath, he risked a subtle turn of his head and discovered a whole new collection of aches. A lovely accompaniment for the timpani of the murderous ax.

A familiar pain in his shoulder sparked a glimmer of memory. In a flashback of quickening ingrained responses, he was in the chute, aboard the devil mare. Sunlight burning down on a dusty arena glinted off scarred and battered rails of the claustrophobic cage. The band of his Stetson lay like a weighted circle low over his forehead. His shirt clung damply to his back, his palms were wet, his throat dry. In an aura of deadly calm, a thousand pounds of savage horse flesh bunched between his thighs. Ready. Waiting for his nod.

Waiting to be rid of him.

"She threw me." He lifted a hand to his hair in bitter thoughtlessness but stopped short of the habitual gesture, short of discovering bandages swathed his head, as he reconsidered in deference to the ax. Grimacing, he lowered his hand gingerly to his waist. "She did it." The sheet crumpled again in a convulsive grasp. "The bitch of a horse threw me."

Another fragment of recall nagged at him, scratched at his concentration, and almost clicked into place. He tensed, a startled growl rumbled in his throat as his straining mind caught and clung to the lingering remnant. His frown turned thoughtful, the killing grip eased, as softly he muttered, "Or did she?"

As if all that were needed was this small light in the void, memories suddenly assaulted him. They came fast, furiously, flashing before his eyes in fractured, disjointed snatches. He could find no order in them, no reason, no solace in their mayhem.

Squeezing his eyes shut, he sought the darkness again. Warding off confusion, he concentrated on the pain. Controlling it, exorcising it from his thoughts, he pushed each separate entity of it to the back of his mind as he'd done most of his life. Bit by bit he relaxed. Soothed by the comfort of old habits, he wondered how long he'd slept, and if he could again.

Once more the void enticed, reaching for him. Gratefully, he drifted into it, letting it draw him down, deeper into its numbing calm, deeper into peace. Deeper into security.

Calm. Security. Luxury for a man who had known little.

Solace.

The scream came without warning, bursting through the darkness. Rimmed by fire, a nightmare thundered out of his memory. A maddened beast tearing his arms from their sockets. Fighting, rearing, slashing hooves flying. Pounding. Crushing.

"Charlie!"

Bolting upright, wide-awake and shivering, his own scream reverberated in his head. Again and again, it echoed through the canyons of his mind, the agony of it leeching away the little left of his strength. As he crumpled, weak and weary, back to the bed, he heard footsteps racing down the darkened hall.

He closed his eyes again and waited.

"Mr. Cody?" A cool hand touched his arm. "Are you awake, Mr. Cody?"

"Yes." The word, borne on a new wave of pain, was barely audible.

"Are you in pain?"

"Yes. No!" Steve caught a shuddering breath. "It's passing."

"I'll call Dr. Hayworth."

"Wait." Catching her comforting hand, wondering if she was as lovely as her voice, he turned his head the little distance needed to see her. "What the hell?"

Two shadowy figures dressed in white, half merged, half separate, leaned over him in the brightening light of dawn. "Two," he whispered. "Why are there two of you?"

Brenda Crowley had been a nurse for thirty years, half of them in neurology. Years of practice and instinct told her Steve Cody needed answers more immediately than his physician needed to be informed that his comatose patient had roused. Folding his hand more securely in her own, she offered substance and truth. "You have double vision, Mr. Cody. Don't be alarmed, it was to be expected with injuries such as yours. But it's also expected to clear."

"Injuries such as mine?"

"You have a head injury."

"How? When?"

His grip threatened the bones in her hand, Brenda Crowley didn't flinch. "A horse trampled you, a week ago."

"I don't remember." His voice faded as he struggled again to penetrate the void. "God help me! I can't remember."

"Shh..." She soothed the tension she heard in him. "You wouldn't, but that, too, was expected. You've been unconscious since you were brought in."

"A week?" He couldn't comprehend the time span.

"Seven days exactly."

"Seven?" It made no sense to thoughts as blurred as his vision.

"For some, maybe even most, it might've been longer." Brenda offered encouragement. "But your friend insists you can't be counted like most. He's been here every day, all day, vowing Steve Cody is one tough cowboy, too tough to die. And a hero in the bargain."

"Friend?" Steve searched for a name, a face.

"He calls himself Charlie Cowboy."

"Charlie!" Assailed again by a deluge of unexpected memories of dust and terror, and blood, Steve struggled to rise. The gentle pressure of the nurse's hand on his chest stopped him.

"You aren't quite up to tripping down the hall searching for him, young man. Anyway, he isn't here. Yet."

"Where is he? How is he? Is he—"

"He's fine. Hale and hearty. More hale and hearty than you are at the moment. Except for a few fading bruises and a broken rib," she amended. "But you can see that for yourself. He'll be here the minute visiting hours start, as he has been every day. Then he'll stay, until someone shoos him away to get some rest. Between times, he'll tell anyone who'll listen that he's here on this good earth, alive to see his first grandchild, because you saved his life, and he owes you one."

The sweat on Steve's body turned cold. The image of Charlie lying beneath the hooves of a frenzied horse bent on death and destruction seared his mind. But Charlie hadn't died. Steve didn't know how, but he hadn't. "I doubt it happened quite like he tells it. Even if it did, the ratio would be one to a hundred or more. If either of us is indebted to the other, I owe him."

"Well, now, that isn't for me to judge. How you and Mr. Cowboy keep score is strictly between the two of you."

Steve laughed, a low, gleeful chortle. If it hurt, he didn't care, Charlie was alive. He was alive. That's all that mattered.

"I said something funny?" Brenda drawled, marveling that her patient could speak and even laugh. Though he was a man for whom pain was a way of life, she suspected his headache must be beyond bearing.

"I've heard Charlie called a lot of names by the ladies, occasionally even Charlie Abramson, his real name. But never Mr. Cowboy, and not by one as beautiful."

"Ahh, a sure sign of recovery—the blarney begins." Brenda stepped away from the bed, smiling down at the roughly handsome cowboy who had beaten the odds. He was a long way from recovery, and how much he might accomplish was questionable. But he'd taken the first doubtful step. He was awake, when no one had been sure he ever would be again.

"If you're certain there's nothing you need, and if you'll promise not to go running off down the hall the minute my back is turned, I need to check in with your doctor, Mr. Cody. He really shouldn't be the last to know that he has another miracle in the making."

"All I need is answers, and I assume the doctor will take care of them." Steve tried for a smile that didn't quite work. "Go make your call, and have no fear. This miracle, if that's what I am, has no intention of tripping down any halls."

"That's what I like, a cooperative patient. Now, if you need anything, anything at all, there's a bell at your side. If you call, ask for Brenda Crowley, and I'll be here before you know it." Her name was on the tag clipped to her breast pocket, but she knew he couldn't read it. It would be some time before he read anything. Squeezing his hand one more time, she hurried to the door.

"Crowley."

She paused, waiting.

"I meant what I said, double vision doesn't keep me from seeing that you're beautiful."

"And old enough to be your mother," she quipped, and was grateful he couldn't see her blush.

"So? Who said mothers couldn't be beautiful?" Thoughtfully he added, "Mine was."

"I would've bet on it." She was smiling again as she opened the door, believing he meant every word, and understanding the charisma that made Steve Cody a champion in tragedy, as well as triumph. "Rest now, if you can. You'll have a busy morning ahead of you. Not the least of which will be Mr. Cowboy."

The door closed behind her with a muffled thud. Steve lay as he had before, starkly still, staring at the ceiling. "You don't owe me anything," he murmured. "Not a thing, Mr. Cowboy."

Then he laughed, and somewhere deep inside, he knew he should be thankful he was alive to feel the hurt.

"Steve?"

"Hey! Charlie!" Steve lifted a hand, moving as little as possible. In the course of the morning and the battery of tests to which Dr. Hayworth had subjected him, vertigo had been added to a growing list of symptoms.

"You all right?" Charlie curled his own knotted and callused hand around Steve's.

"If I'm not, I'm getting there."

"I told 'em you would."

"How about you?"

Charlie moved to the foot of the bed, in range of Steve's vision. "A broke rib, or two. Some bruises. They tell me you're seeing double, so I'm only half as beat up as I look, and only a particle as ugly." He spun his hat nervously, threading the brim through his palms.

"I can see you fine, Charlie," Steve said quietly, his fingers straying to the patch over his eye. "There's only one of you when I wear this. Nurse Crowley says I look more like a train robber than a cowboy right now."

Charlie Abramson didn't laugh. It was too soon, too much lay ahead for Steve. "You don't remember the rodeo, what happened?"

"It's coming back in bits and pieces."

"But you don't remember what you did."

"No, but it doesn't matter."

"Does to me," Charlie declared vehemently. "Lord knows, what happened to you in a glancing blow was bad enough, but for me it would have been a direct hit. That bronc would've put my lights out if you hadn't shielded me."

"Where would I be if you hadn't lifted me off a few hundred saddle broncs intent on putting my lights out, Charlie?"

"It ain't the same. Picking cowboys off broncs is my job. Getting kicked in the head ain't yours."

"Charlie, let it go. If it makes you feel any better, we'll count it even."

"Can't," the older man insisted stubbornly. "What are your plans?" he asked in an abrupt change. "What are you going to do when you get out of the hospital?"

A look passed between them, and Steve realized that his old friend knew Steve Cody, the hard luck kid, wouldn't ride the rodeo circuit again. His luck seemed to have changed for a while. He'd never ridden better, or luckier, and the elusive national championship was nearly his. Then, in one disastrously placed hoof, it all slipped away, and he'd spent his life chasing a dream lost forever. His father's dream, sacrificed for his ailing wife and growing son.

Steve fought back a wave of grief. One more painful than the sum of all the physical battering. His mother had gone first, then his father, and now the dream, the focus of his life. He felt unanchored and adrift, and more lonely than he'd ever been.

"I don't know, Charlie. I've been thinking about the ranch. You know, that distant goal for someday. Maybe it's time to stop talking and make it reality."

"Maybe," Charlie agreed noncommittally.

"Horses," Steve mused, for the first time squarely facing a future without the rodeo. "I'd like to raise horses. The prize money's been good this year—maybe I'll take what's left after this and find that perfect tract of land. Nothing big, but good grass and sweet water, and after that some good breeding stock. The Cody horse, bred and trained by Steve Cody." Steve grinned at the weathered cowboy. "Has a nice ring, don't you think?"

"If there's any prize money left," Charlie groused. The hat spun, work worn fingers worried nervously at the soiled brim. He didn't like being the bearer of bad news. The only way he knew to deal with it was to say what he had to say flat out, no frills, no sugarcoating. "Angie was here."

"Angie?" Steve's grin faltered. "My lovely not quite ex-wife?"

"You know another Angie?"

"No. Maybe that's my one stroke of luck in this." Angie, a lovely woman, indeed. Once he'd thought he loved her, now he knew he'd married her out of loneliness in the long, desolate days after his father's death. She'd married him for the fame and fortune she thought an up-and-coming bronc rider could give her, but she hadn't reckoned with Steve Cody's renowned bad luck. When she did, she'd left him, taking half of all he had as compensation for her disappointment. "What did she want? Did she come prepared to celebrate my wake?"

"Maybe."

"I'd be lying if I said I was sorry to disappoint her again."

Charlie stared glumly at him.

"That was a joke, Charlie."

"She might've been disappointed, expecting to line her pockets with the life-insurance money, but she didn't leave empty-handed. She claimed half your winnings, Steve." The hat brim crumpled in his fist. "She skipped nearly a year ago, then you get your shot at the big time, collect the biggest prize money you've ever won, and just like that she waltzes back. She was all set to play the dutiful wife of the national champ if you survived, but she preferred the grieving widow. Then the doc gave her the facts and she couldn't skedaddle fast enough. Hell," the grizzled cowboy growled, "even the weight in her pockets couldn't slow her down. Said she had it coming."

Steve was silent for a while. Too silent, as he put a surge of bitter disappointment behind him. "She did," he said quietly, at last. "The law says her rightful share is half. Maybe she deserved it too."

"For what?" Charlie exploded. As far as he was concerned, if Steve Cody had one single character fault, it was that he was too willing to see both sides of an argument, too forgiving.

"She stuck by me through some lean times."

"Less than a year by my calculations. And every time you landed in a hospital or was hurt, was she by your side? Nooo..." He drawled the word in utter disgust. "She was out dancing and partying with someone who hadn't tangled with a bronc and wasn't stove up."

Steve had no answer for Charlie. He couldn't deny the accusation, and he didn't want to get into another discussion. Angie was out of his life, and maybe it was worth half of all he ever hoped to have to keep it that way. "Things could be worse, Charlie. The doctor assures me I'll recover, but it's going to be a long haul."

"A long, expensive haul," Charlie interjected. "And breeding stock don't come cheap."

"So, when I get out, I'll take what's left and buy land. The stock can come later."

Charlie knew there would be precious little left, even for land. Steve had been years clearing the debt accumulated during his mother's chronic illness, then his father's. Now he had his own to contend with. "You're thirty, Steve. How long are you going to have to wait?"

"A little while." At Charlie's accusing look, he shrugged and admitted, "All right, quite a while."

"Seems like you got a problem."

"Seems like," Steve agreed.

"Well, now, I got me a problem too." Charlie laid his hat at the foot of the bed to scratch at the paper tucked in the pocket of his shirt. "In a way our problems sorta jive. We can each solve our own problem by helping the other."

"What's wrong, Charlie?"

"You know I got a daughter." He paused for Steve's nod, then rushed on. "She came along late in my life, and we ain't been exactly close since her momma left me. But lately we've mended our fences. She's got a little one coming now. Her ma's been gone a few years, and her husband ain't got a family, so she thinks it's real important the little tyke has a grandpa. Seeing as this was my last year to rodeo, she's asked me to come live closer to her."

"Hey, that's not a problem, that's great! You do get along with them, don't you?"

"Sure, sure." Charlie frowned and scratched his head. "But you see, I got this other problem. I got this ranch, had it for years. Good grass, better water, a natural canyon perfect for horses. Always thought I'd go back, now I know I won't. I was in a study what to do with it, then it come to me. You could take it off my hands. If I was to sign it over to you, I could go on down to California without a care."

"Ranch? You've never talked about a ranch."

"A man don't talk about everything."

Steve shifted carefully in the bed, and waited for the wave of vertigo to subside. "I can't let you sign it over to me. I could look at it, and maybe we could make a deal and I could buy your land."

"You ain't got enough money to buy my ranch."

"Then you should sell it to someone else."

"Nope." Charlie shook his head. "It's a fine parcel of land. I only left it 'cause Sarah's momma was so unhappy there. When she skipped out on me anyway, I just didn't have the heart to go back. Leastwise, not at first. I joined the rodeo, then one year piled on another, and another. And here I am, too late and too old. I always pictured a good horse ranch there, but I ain't going to sell it to just anybody. It's gotta be somebody who'll love it, work hard, and take care of it." He shrugged. "That kinda person don't grow on trees."

"You can find someone, Charlie."

"Already have." Charlie slipped a folded paper from his pocket. "Already solved my problem. There's some paperwork you'll have to see to, but it's a done deal. You got yourself a ranch."

Steve was staggered by the older man's generosity. "No." He turned his head cautiously. "I can't let you do this."

"You can't stop me."

"You don't owe me anything, Charlie."

"Maybe not, but you sure as hell owe me. You saved my life, now you owe me what it takes to make it a good one." He tossed the deed onto the bed. "That means taking the ranch off my hands."

"Charlie, no."

"Hey, it won't be all belly high grass and sweet water. The land's been lying like open range for so long, some folks consider it just that. They won't take kindly to your coming. So you got a little trouble on your hands. But I ain't seen much trouble you couldn't handle. Go to it, boy. Make the ranch what I always wanted it to be. I'd count it a favor."

Grinning, he plucked his hat from the bed and settled it firmly over his brow. Instantly he looked more at ease, more natural. More like the old Charlie. "We'll talk some more later. I'll tell you about the ranch and your neighbors, especially your closest neighbor. It'll take half a day just to tell you what an ornery son of a bitch Jake Benedict can be on his best days. Right now my daughter's taking me out to lunch." Charlie tilted his hat to a rakish angle and laughed. "Do I look spiffy enough to go to lunch with a beautiful woman?"

"You look fine, Charlie. In fact, you look downright handsome. Any woman would be proud to be seen with you."

This time the laughter erupted from him. Laughter so deep, it could have come from his toes. "Then I'll see you later." The folded deed lay on the bed. "Think about this while I'm gone."

"I don't have to think, I'm not taking your land."

"Hey! Who said you had a choice? You owe me, remember." As if an invisible weight had lifted from his shoulders, the best pickup man in the rodeo strolled from Steve Cody's room.

"I won't," Steve muttered when he was alone. "I won't take your ranch." Leaning back against a stack of pillows, he stared at the familiar ceiling. If the doctor was right, he had a long haul ahead. He had to concentrate on himself. Charlie made it sound as if he were choosing the one man he trusted to realize an old cowboy's dream.

"I've spent one lifetime chasing another man's dream. I won't again."

Exhausted, determined, he put Charlie's ranch from his mind. But as he drifted, seeking the thoughtless limbo, it wouldn't stay put.

Horses.

A natural canyon.

"No."

Belly-high grass.

Pure, sweet water.

"I can't."

Another man's dream.

"I won't."

But this time a dream that matched his own.

There could be no limbo, no peace, for as Steve's heart waged one battle, his mind and body faced another. Head thrown back on his brace of pillows, he turned his one-eyed stare from the too familiar ceiling. Gray, the color of melancholy. He could lose himself in it if he allowed it. Instead, he forced his tortured thoughts to the future.

Would he be doomed to see the world in twos for the remainder of his life? Would the headaches and transitory weakness plague him forever? Would he grip a rein in his left hand again? By the grace of God, therapy and hard work, would his condition resolve?

If it didn't, what would become of him? And even if it did, what then?

All he'd known since he was a kid was ranching and the rodeo. With the rodeo and most of his earnings gone, what would be left for a ranch? Would he ever have his own dream? Or was he doomed to serve first as proxy, then as cowhand for hire?

"Sure, a one handed cowhand." His pained and bitter laugh splintered the sepulchral silence.

He stifled a groan as a wave of agony washed over him, blinding him. As it began to overpower him, one by one the fingers of his fisted hand unfolded. Sliding over the sheet as with a will of their own they found the deed. Sighing, Steve crumpled it in his palm.

"A partnership, Charlie," he muttered through clenched teeth. "Your land, my labor."

The pain was too much. The void reached for him. As he consigned himself gratefully to its sanctuary, there was sorrow in his hoarse whisper. "Half a dream."

Chapter 3

"**M**r. Cody!"

Steve paused at the foot of the courthouse steps, wheeling around in surprise. No one in Silverton knew him. No one until a half hour ago, and then only the clerk who registered his deed and brand. Could there be a problem with the papers? Some hitch that would keep the Broken Spur of Sunrise Canyon from becoming reality? Scanning past a number of cowboys and secretaries sharing lunch in the shady courtyard, he saw no one who resembled the lady in question. Puzzled, but relieved, deciding he was mistaken, he turned away.

Shrugging the incident aside, he threaded his way through the courtyard. Laughter and gossipy chatter drifted about him, but no one looked up. No one spoke. Crossing a small garden clustered around a bronze commemorating the American cowboy and his horse, he stepped into the flow of foot traffic on the sidewalk. Hesitating at the curb, exasperated by the prickling need to turn back for one last look, he shook his head at his folly.

No one had called his name. The harried clerk was too busy and a bit too plump to come tripping down the steps after him. At any rate, her voice was high-pitched and anxious, edging into squeaky. The voice he heard was low, a sultry contralto.

"The voice you imagined, Cody. Face it," he muttered in a wry undertone. Next he would be seeing things. But if he did, at least it wouldn't be in duplicate, and he would recognize it. His recovery had taken many long and costly months, but it was complete. The rodeo was all he'd really lost.

Which was why he was in Silverton recording a deed on the day of the spring stock show and auction.

In Silverton, an old and bustling small town that had preserved the look and feel of a turn of the century Western village. Where no one knew him, he reminded himself as he crossed the narrow street.

"Mr. Cody."

Or did they?

This time there was no question of mistake or imagination. Stopping in front of the general store, he spun about again, wondering who the hell wanted him and why. His gaze flitted over the procession of ranchers and cowboys and their ladies, shedding winter's doldrums, dressed in their best for the festivities of the show. He searched among them for a face even vaguely familiar. Perhaps someone from a rodeo, somewhere, sometime.

At first glance there was nothing, no one seemed unduly interested in him. No one fit the commanding voice with its lilting Southern drawl.

That one drew a rueful chuckle. What bit of nonsense prompted him to think he could recognize her from the sound of her voice?

He was damning the vagaries of a bruised brain when the loosely formed band of revelers scattered and he caught sight of her. A woman not quite like the rest. Smaller, leaner, weathered and darker, a single braid lying over her shoulder like a gleaming rope.

He was a stranger to her, yet he hadn't a doubt it was she who had called to him.

He'd never seen her before, anytime, anywhere, but he knew her, and he liked what he saw. As she sidestepped a cluster of rowdy children with graceful ease and moved toward him in an unhurried, unbroken, ground-eating stride, he liked it very well.

In total disregard for the finery surrounding her, she wore a work shirt and Wranglers drawn over worn leather boots. A man's belt cinched her waist, and a vintage Stetson rode low over her forehead, shading her face. Beneath its curled brim, her gaze was riveted on him.

Strollers brushed by, but Steve hardly noticed. He was engrossed and intrigued, and more than a little curious. He waited, letting the rest of the revelers of Silverton pass him by, as she closed the distance between them.

It gave him an edge, letting her come to him.

Just for an instant he was startled at the turn of thought and wondered if he would ever have the edge with her. Then there was no time to ponder it, for she was there, before him, her head tilted fractionally to look up at him. A captivating woman, not beautiful, but striking, with a look of challenge in eyes as pale as silver.

"I'd like to speak with you, Mr. Cody."

He hadn't been wrong. The voice suited her down to the last softly drawled word. Quiet words, refined, with a hint of arrogance and tempered steel. "Well, ma'am," he matched his tone to hers, the drawl, the arrogance, the steel. "I'd like to oblige you, but I don't think we have anything to talk about."

Her silver gaze turned frosty. "I think we do."

Questioning what she had to say that merited stopping him on the sidewalk, and wondering why she was so hostile, he chose to hear her out. But on his terms, and to his advantage. "Suit yourself, lady." He let his gaze drift to her mouth in a long, thoughtful look. Long enough and thoughtful enough to wear away a bit of the lofty confidence. "Speak."

Stung by his unconcern, and unsettled by a gaze as dark and unfathomable as midnight, she drew herself even more erect. In her boots she stood a regal five-four that barely topped his shoulder. A feathery brow lifted as regally. "I would have preferred someplace more private."

Steve's grin was slow and wicked. He was enjoying himself more than he had in months. Looking down at her, hardly an armful dressed like a cowhand with the frosty expression of a queen, he couldn't resist teasing. "Well, now, don't tell me this is an Arizona pickup."

"I beg your pardon!" The frost deepened.

"Do you?" With the thumb of a loosely fisted hand, he tilted his hat from his forehead. In a drawl more pronounced, he murmured lazily, "I'm a Texan, ma'am, and, lord, I do hate to make a woman beg."

"I beg your pardon!" she blurted out of angry habit, then caught a stuttering breath at the unfortunate repetition.

As a flush of color stained her cheeks, a nerve fluttered at her temple. Wondering if it was a gauge of her temper, Steve pushed his advantage. "All right, if you insist, in your case I'll make an exception, Mrs...." Glancing down at fingers he already knew were bare, he amended, "Or Miss?"

"It's Miss," she snapped, just managing to rein in her irritation.

The slightest inclination of his head acknowledged her control, and he decided to test it. "All right, if you insist, in your case I'll make an exception, Miss..." His brow wrinkled in a broad parody of innocent curiosity as he paused for another answer.

"Benedict," she filled in the blank again with strained grace. "Hank Benedict, from The Rafter B."

"Hank? Miss Hank?" Steve mused with a grimace. "A pity."

"Don't trouble yourself, Mr. Cody." The advantage of surprise had slipped away. She didn't know how, but she wasn't ready to fold. "I don't need your pity, not for my name, nor for anything."

Sliding his hat back another notch, concealing his surprise that the Benedicts had made their move so soon, he lounged against the porch railing at his back. His look traveled the length of her once more, leisurely seeking out the womanliness beneath the rough clothes. A condemning growl that held no shred of teasing rumbled in his throat as he returned his gaze to hers. "Let me guess. Jake Benedict, ruler of the Benedict empire, wanted sons. Strong sons, to carry on his work and his name. When there was only one child, a daughter, he turned her into the next best thing."

"Jake?" Her eyes narrowed speculatively at his use of her father's name. "You've done your homework, I see."

"No homework needed." He shrugged a shoulder in a deprecating gesture. "Say the name Silverton and someone's sure to come back with Jake Benedict. A free association, like saddle tramps and broncs. Doesn't take a genius to figure he's the most powerful man around. The sort who would turn his only daughter into his right hand man."

The caustic observation should have been an insult, but something in his tone took the sting from it. Another time, she would have taken her cue from his face, but not now. It was too difficult to judge his expression as she looked from unrelieved brilliance into the shade of the jutting roof of the store. Calculated, no doubt, to give himself another advantage. A move so natural it was second nature. A wily move, a wily foe. She wondered if, like Jake, he played a fiendish game of chess.

Whatever game he was playing now, he was good. But so was she. Pleasantly, with a trace of irony, she observed evenly, "If you're telling me that as a woman raised to be her father's son I'm a dime-a-dozen cliché, then consider, also, my company."

Two fingers brushed the brim of his hat indolently. One cliché saluting another. "Touché."

"French, Mr. Cody?" A hint of the South was in the drawl again. Hooking her thumbs in the back pockets of her jeans, with narrowed eyes, she probed the shadows. "Is that the extent of your bilingual skill, or is there more?"

"A phrase or two. Enough that I can order from a menu." At her look of doubtful mockery, he smiled. "Even a dime-a-dozen rodeo has-been climbs out of his dusty cliché once in a while, Miss Benedict."

A flash of amusement sparkled in her eyes, warming the frost a bit. With a minute inclination of her head, she acknowledged it was her turn to concede a point in what had become a guarded fencing match.

Their gazes met for a moment, adversaries, acknowledging and respecting the worthiness of an opponent.

An acquaintance of the Benedicts walked by, halted, watched curiously, then moved on reluctantly.

Hank hadn't acknowledged the man, indeed, had hardly noticed him. But because of the minor intrusion into her riveted concentration, she was abruptly and acutely aware of other watchful stares. She realized that the news of Steve Cody's arrival had certainly leaked from the courthouse. Concetta had managed a discreet call from the registrar's office, sending a runner to the corrals with the news for Hank first.

That small act of friendship would have strained the discretion of the benevolent busybody. And like any gossip too good to keep, once the news was broken, it would spread like wildfire. By now, anyone in Silverton who wasn't deaf, or asleep, already knew or would know soon just exactly who this rangy black haired cowboy was.

Conversation on street corners were common in Silverton. Conversations between a Benedict and the new owner of Sunrise Canyon were not.

Half turning, she looked down the crowded walkway, her mind churning. This encounter was ill-advised. A tactical error that would require a temporary mending of fences. But how?

Surprised by her withdrawal, Steve watched her. In this stolen moment, allowing himself a very masculine appreciation of a woman, not his adversary. He found he liked her. He liked her spirit, and the challenge she offered. He liked her body, shapely and compact, yet gracefully lean, with small breasts rising with each breath. He liked her profile, the tilted nose, the stubborn chin, the way her lashes swept her cheeks as she struggled with herself, or with him. He liked her hair, rich and dark, with sunlight striking shimmering cinnamon in its depths. He wondered how long it would be freed from the braid, how thick, how silky. How it would feel in his hands, sliding through his fingers. And how sweet the caress of it drifting over his body.

Remembering she was a Benedict, never forgetting she was a woman, he watched her, thinking impossible things, feeling the rush of impossible desire.

"I am my father's son, Miss Benedict," he said softly, turning his mind to the issue. "I know what it's like to spend a lifetime trying to be something I couldn't be. Trying to give a man I loved something he couldn't have."

The sympathy she heard in his words rankled. The last thing she wanted from this man was sympathy. Her chin lifted, the challenge returned. "No, Mr. Cody, you don't know." She'd striven all her life to be a Benedict. As a Benedict, she'd play the cards she'd drawn. "This wasn't the place for this discussion, but there's no help for it now."

In this abstruse shift, an inexplicable mood vanished. They were adversaries again. In feigned nonchalance, he waited for Hank Benedict to come to the point. "Your choice, lady," he reminded. "Your discussion."

In a clipped voice, she snapped, "Are you always this insufferable?"

His mouth tilted in a restrained smile. "Are you always this imperious?"

As color rushed to her cheeks again, Steve relented. "All right, Miss Benedict, you look like a busy woman, so let me save you some time." Pushing away from the rail, he stood, looking down at her. "The Broken Spur isn't for sale. Now or in the future."

Steve felt a deep respect, tempered by regret. Respect for this woman who would fight him, valiantly, defiantly, to the end of her strength. Regret that she wouldn't admit there needn't be a battle at all. For one mad moment, he was tempted to offer a compromise. Wisdom predicated on Benedict history and the seething look in her fascinating eyes warned it would be thrown back in his teeth.

"I'll be bringing in my stock soon." Annoyed with his moment of weakness, he spoke curtly. "I'd appreciate it if you'd send a couple of your hands over to round up the cattle you've been grazing in the canyon. If there's no one you can spare, I'll be obliged to herd them out myself.''

"*You'll* herd my cattle out?" Hank glared up at him, holding desperately to a control that threatened to slip away.

"Your choice again."

"Rafter B cattle have been grazing that land for twenty years. You can't just waltz in and take possession, then tell us to get out."

"I can, Benedict. I just did. You have two weeks to move every horse and cow wearing the Rafter B brand off the Broken Spur."

"None of this would be necessary if you'd listen to our offer. It's generous and more than the land is worth."

"More than it's worth to you, maybe, but not to me. This is more than a ranch, it's a dream. There's not enough money in all the Benedict coffers to buy a man's dreams."

"That's absurd!" A door closed, footsteps crossed a wooden porch, paused, then clattered down the steps. Hank was too indignant now to care who witnessed her encounter with this stubborn interloper.

"Is it?" Steve asked mildly. "Tell me why."

"Everything has a price," she snapped. "Even dreams."

"Not mine."

"Listen to me. . . ."

"No." Steve wrapped her braid around his palm, drawing her closer. "You listen. You don't need my land, Benedict, you have more than you can use. Without the canyon, you may have to cull your herd, or drive them farther and stretch more fence. But beyond that inconvenience," he wrapped the braid another loop around his hand, tugging it not ungently to emphasize his point, "you don't need it."

"Need doesn't enter into it. My father *wants* the canyon." The calm she sought escaped her. Even in anger she was aware of the strength of his hand and the heat of his wrist as it rested against the slope of her breast. She wanted to move away from his touch, but wouldn't give him the satisfaction of struggling to be free.

Lifting her chin a haughty inch, she stared up at him, seeing him more clearly from close range. The inescapable eyes she thought were black were darkest brown, flecked with gold. She saw now that he was pale for a cowboy. A paler half-moon scar curved over his temple, then disappeared into his hairline. A reminder of tragedy. As was the shirt that clung to his shoulders and chest a little too loosely.

He'd been ill, grievously injured in a rodeo mishap. She'd read of it in the news months ago. Gazing at the grainy photograph of a handsome cowboy with an engaging grin, she'd sympathized with his misfortune. It would've been too incredible to imagine that one day his misfortune would pit them against each other in a battle that promised no easy solution.

No solution? she wondered. Perhaps it was there all along, in the truth.

"You're right," she admitted, trying a new course. "We don't need it, at least not geographically. My father has been ill for several years, since then he's been even more obsessed with the canyon and the grazing land around it. He wants it badly."

"Why?" Steve asked, bluntly. "Because it sits squarely within the boundaries of the Rafter B? Another man's land, a blight in the middle of the map of all his holdings?"

"That's why, exactly. He wants the boundaries to be completely intact. You speak of dreams, that's been his dream all his life. The one dream he couldn't have." There was compassion, not malice, when she said softly, "You know what it's like to want something that badly, to almost have it, then lose it.

"You almost had the national championship, and you would've if it weren't for a stroke of bad luck. Doesn't it rankle? After all the years of grueling work and pain, don't you ache for that buckle? Wouldn't you like to hold it in your hand, knowing it's yours? *Yours,* Mr. Cody. Your dream. Just as my father had a dream, until first Charlie Abramson, then you, were his bad luck."

Steve stared down at her, still holding her braid. Not pulling, simply holding. "That was quite a speech," he said, releasing her. It wasn't simply a speech. He knew every word came from her heart, and that she meant no hurt to him. But something perverse in him wouldn't let him accept it. "I hate to pop your bubble, but the championship was my father's dream. The Broken Spur is mine.

"I won't be selling, Miss Benedict. Not to anyone, for any reason."

"There's other land...."

"No," he said so quietly she hardly heard, but only a fool wouldn't have sensed the unshakable resolve, the edge of danger. "Not for me. And no one, not you, not your father, or anyone will take it from me. If Jake Benedict wanted his land intact, he should have thought twice before buying up all the ranches beyond the canyon."

"He was convinced Charlie would sell one day."

"Then he didn't know Charlie. Just as you don't know me. But you will, maybe better than you'd like. I'm here to stay. Save us both a lot of misery, accept it." Twinges of pain had begun to flicker behind his eyes like muted lightning, a warning of one of the rare headaches that still plagued him. He hadn't much time, in a matter of minutes he would be half blind with it. Parking was at a premium because of the sale, and his truck was blocks away. If he didn't leave soon, it might as well be miles.

"If you refuse our offer, you'll have only yourself to blame for the consequences." The minute she said the words, she wanted to recall them. She wanted to apologize as he stood like an image turned to stone. Only his eyes seemed alive, their feverish darkness stared at her from a face that seemed grimmer and paler.

"Threats, Benedict?" A thin, humorless smile quirked at a corner of his mouth. "Have we come to that at last?"

"No!" With a jerk of her head, she searched for a way to make him understand she spoke of misery and heartache, as he had. But how did one explain an unfortunate choice of words?

His smile didn't change. "It sounded like a threat."

"No, please." She laid a hand on his bare arm beneath the turned back sleeves. He was shaking, and even in the early afternoon heat, his skin was cold and clammy. Startled, she looked up at him, drowning in unexpected concern. Her fingers tightened over his arm. "Is something wrong?"

"I'm fine," he snapped, damning the luck that she should discover his weakness.

"But you're shaking!"

A lie wouldn't work, she was too sharp for it, so he settled for half truths. "It's nothing, just the lingering effects of an old injury. I'll be okay in a second."

"What can I do? There's a doctor in the next block."

He laughed, a guttural growl meant to be mocking. "Threatening me in one breath, offering help in the next? What sort of woman are you?"

"A woman who is her father's son," she said mildly. "A Benedict, remember?"

"Yes." The word resounded in his head, and the ax wreaked its havoc. There were two of her. There would be two of everything until the headache subsided. His doctors has given them a fancy medical term for a name. Then explained the involvement of the optic nerves, that there would be no lasting damage. The attacks would gradually decrease over a period of a few months, then sub-

side completely. It had been months, and they were decreasing, bu
even if this one lasted less than the course of the last one, a hellisl
couple of hours lay ahead.

"I remember," he managed. But she was more than that sim
plistic summation. Far more. He'd heard it in her voice and seen i
at first glance. In the way she walked, the way she dressed. The wa
she looked at a man. That cool challenge in her silver eyes, tha
made her a challenge herself.

She answered to a man's name, but he would have to have wors
than double vision not to see there was a hell of a woman beneatl
the rough clothes. A woman any man would want.

She would love with mind and heart, body and soul. Com
pletely, without reservation. As completely as she fought.

Catching her hand in his, he took it from his arm. Her finger
were slender and tapered, the nails even but short. There were cal
luses on her palms. And blisters—new calluses in the making. He
bones were delicate, but he felt the tensile strength. Strength to figh
the battles of Jake Benedict and the Rafter B.

With his thumb he stroked a roughened ridge at the base of he
fingers. The skin was tough, but once it would have been raw and
bleeding, the pain excruciating. Only time, more work, more in
jury and more healing had formed this protective shroud. Time and
pain.

"Savannah Benedict," he murmured. "Woman extraordinaire
Enemy mine."

Ignoring her gasp of surprise, he released her reluctantly. He wa
pushing the time frame, he had to go.

"How do you know my name?"

"Shh . . ." He stroked her lips, stopping the tumble of words
discovering he liked the feel of her mouth, moist and startled, un
der his fingertips. "It's no mystery, and I'm far from clairvoyant
Charlie might've left Sunrise Canyon twenty years ago, but he neve
forgot you. A solemn nine-year-old with freckles and braids, wh
slipped away to the canyon to play with his daughter, or tag behin
him, when the battle over her made the Rafter B too uncomfort
able."

As her silver gaze clouded with the burden of old memories, he
saw only guilt for her own shortcomings in her quest to be botl
daughter and son. The innocent clay of a strong-willed mother and
a despotic father. A tough kid, who had no concept of how tougl
she was, who loved both mother and father without reservation.

"Nine," he murmured, seeing the child she'd been in the woman she'd become. "With the makings of a lady a man couldn't forget, even then."

Something flickered in her eyes, a response too quick, too vital, escaped her guarded control. Vulnerability beneath the iron, stirring needs and desires he hadn't known in too long to remember.

"You were right, the street isn't the place for this." His voice was hoarse, little more than a whisper. Silenced for a moment, the thudding rhythm of the headache returned with a vengeance. Backing away, he smiled and touched the brim of his hat with one finger. A rogue's salute, a rogue's pale lipped smile.

"We'll meet again, Savannah."

He was a half-dozen strides away before she realized he was really leaving. "Wait!" she called after him. "Mr. Cody!"

He didn't turn, didn't acknowledge her.

"If you would just..." Her voice faltered. Pleading came hard to a Benedict, and she wouldn't. Not for anything. Not even for her father. Never with this arrogant man.

Bitterly, she watched his strategic retreat, only just beginning to wonder if it were more than strategic. Though his back was straight, his head up and his shoulders back, there was something unnatural about his step. The easy cowboy gait was gone. He moved as if he were walking on ice—a man on shifting ground, desperately unsure of his footing.

He'd been pale, the pallor of weathered skin locked away from the sun for too long. Hospital pallor that turned even paler. He'd dismissed it as nothing, an irritation, a stubbornly persistent side effect of the injury that ended his rodeo career. One small last hurdle in his recovery, he would have her believe.

"But I don't." She took a step after him, then began to hurry. "Mr. Cody!"

He neither turned nor hesitated. For a moment, with concentrated effort, his step was surer. But only a moment.

"Wait."

Nothing. He might've been deaf.

Giving no thought to propriety, she raced to him. Catching his arm she stopped him. "Please." Her voice broke a bit as a gaze as dark and empty as a starless night turned to her, staring at her, through her, seeming not to see her at all. "Mr. Cody...Steve." She felt helpless, lost, pinioned by unseeing eyes.

Never looking down, he took her hand from his arm. His fingers laced through hers, his thumb stroked over a callused palm.

"Another time, Savannah Benedict. Another battleground, then neither of us will walk away until it's finished."

Releasing her, he turned without another word, resuming his cautious odyssey to his truck. Spine straight, head up, step determined, but no surer.

Hank Benedict let him go. The enigmatic new owner of Sunrise Canyon was a man unto himself, who wanted nothing from her at any cost. But there was much she wanted from him, and she would have it.

"We'll meet again," she mused as he reached a dusty nondescript truck and half crawled, half fell into it. "Then we'll see what price the dream."

The door to the truck thudded hollowly. A sound too faint to distinguish if she hadn't been watching and listening for it. After what seemed too long a time, the truck backed from its parking place and moved slowly down the street.

Truck and driver were soon lost in traffic. Still looking in the direction he'd taken, she imagined the rest of his journey. The dusty, meandering road, the awesome landscape. Spring was her favorite season, the canyon was never prettier than in spring. She wondered if he would notice. Or if he truly cared.

"Dreams," she mused. "But whose? Yours, or Jake Benedict's?" Smiling grimly, she took up the gauntlet. "We shall see, Steve Cody. Oh, yes, we shall see. You and I."

"Sis." A familiar hand touched her shoulder, drawing her from thoughts and promises. "Jake wants you."

Her smile faded as she looked up at Sandy Gannon. "Something wrong?"

"Naw," Sandy pulled a Stetson of indeterminate age lower over his forehead. "Just being his usual impatient self."

"The sale doesn't start for an hour yet."

"I know that." Ambling along beside her, he headed back toward the tents and temporary corrals erected especially for the sale. "There's a stallion he wants you to look at."

"We've looked at what's offered ten times over." She was only stating fact, not complaining.

"This one ain't offered."

"Jake wants me to look at a stallion that isn't for sale?"

"The stockman claims not. Says he only transported the critter up here for a friend."

Hank stopped dead center of the walk. "A friend named Cody?"

"Would be my guess." Weathered creases fanned from Sandy's eyes as he squinted down at her. He was fourteen years younger than Jake Benedict, an integral part of her life and the ranch. Though he'd claimed to be eighteen, he was a day shy of fifteen, a runaway and a drifter, when he'd ridden into the fledgling operation looking for work. Nearly thirty-five years later he was still around, and the Rafter B had become a sprawling territory.

For most of those years Sandy had been top hand, helping Jake Benedict get what he wanted, and then more. The Benedicts were his family, and along the way he'd served as mediator, conscience, friend and confidant.

He'd never taken sides in the conflict over her. Never calling her Hank, nor Savannah, only sis. And she wondered now, as she had so many times before, how she would have survived without him.

"What do you make of this?" She looked up at him, making a mental note to remind him he needed a haircut. A permanent condition for Sandy, a handsome man of absolutely no conceit. "Jake has expounded endlessly on this, but you've said nothing."

"Well, now, I'd say it looks like the boy means business. This horse ranch just might come to pass."

"One horse doesn't make a ranch," Hank observed mildly.

"This one makes a helluva good start."

No one was more intuitive or more knowledgeable in judging horses than Sandy. His skill had been as instrumental in building the Rafter B as Jake's business acumen. "He's that good, huh?"

"Better."

"So which way to the wonder horse?"

Taking her arm, Sandy guided her away from the corrals toward a cluster of horse trailers. "Jake's got a tussle on his hands this time, sis. Together, horse and man comprise a genuine threat. Bullheaded determination, topnotch horseman, topnotch horse." With a sly glance at her, he added laconically, "Handsome pair."

The remark elicited only a mild nod. She was accustomed to Sandy's innate wisdom stated in the mixed vernaculars of cowhand and self-taught scholar. However it was stated, she couldn't deny that Steve Cody projected a certain handsome charm. And no one in his right mind would argue Sandy's call on horseflesh.

"A real handsome cowboy." He slanted another look at her. "'Cept for that minute when Cody looked like he swallowed his chaw."

"Swallowed his... He didn't..." She returned his look in surprise, then laughed and prodded him with her arm. "You're teasing."

"Just checking."

"To see if I've been around cows and horses so long I don't know a good-looking man when I see one?"

Sandy grinned. "Something like that."

"I'm a Benedict, Sandy. Not blind."

"Can amount to the same thing, sometimes."

"Not this time." They walked for a while, her hand resting naturally in the crook of his arm. "You were watching when Cody and I were speaking."

"Just waiting for the two of you to lay down the ground rules." He patted her hand. "Minding my manners like your momma taught me. You know, not interrupting, not eating my peas with my knife, not—"

"He was pale." She stopped the teasing rhyme and verse she'd heard countless times.

"Took a hell of a knock is why. Lucky he's so hardheaded, or his skull would've caved in, instead of just denting. He'll be okay. His doctors wouldn't have let him out of the hospital otherwise."

"You sound positive."

"I am. Charlie told me."

"Charlie Abramson?"

"The very same."

"You've kept in touch all this time?"

"Yep. Same as I did with you those years you went south."

"As you still do with Mother."

"Yep." Sandy made no other comment about Camilla Benedict. He'd said little since the day she left the Rafter B with her daughter eleven years before.

"How is she?"

"Sassy." He grinned. "Beautiful and sassy. After all this time Georgia ain't sure what hit it."

"She decided not to marry the count."

"I know. Was never an option. Not so long as she's still married to your daddy."

"There's always divorce."

"Not for Camilla," Sandy said succinctly. "Not from Jake."

Lapsing into the comfortable silence of longtime companions, they drank in the sights and sounds of the stockmen's camp. In an effort to keep her thoughts from Steve Cody, Hank concentrated on

Sandy. He'd been in love with her mother more than half his life. When Camilla Benedict was a lonely, neglected bride, Savannah suspected she might have responded.

But Sandy was too fond of Jake and too honorable. So he settled for becoming the word of wisdom, their rock when he was needed.

A horse whinnied, the cry reaching across the meadow. A reminder of the battle ahead.

"Sis." Sandy drew her up short. His blue eyes were worried. "I've never gone against Jake Benedict in my life. He might be an ornery bastard and a greedy one, but he's always been reasonable."

"You don't think he is this time?"

"Steve Cody deserves a chance. With this stallion and a lot of hard work, he just might make a go of the Broken Spur. He should be left alone. Dammit! The Benedicts have enough land without coveting his."

"Have you said as much to Jake?"

"A hundred times in the last two weeks."

"He didn't listen."

"Does he ever?"

"Then he won't listen to me, either, Sandy. So what would you have me do?"

"Just be careful, don't get hurt. Stay clear of the fracas if you can. Jake won't win this time. If I'm right, and Cody stays, I've a feeling you're going to have a choice to make."

"I'm a Benedict, Sandy. Win or lose." The stallion whinnied again, a reminder. "Jake's waiting."

When she walked on, Sandy let her go. He wouldn't argue any more, but he wouldn't back away. He'd seen Steve Cody—how he looked at her, even as he stood pat. A bronc rider down on his luck, but a man who wouldn't fold at the first sight of Benedict money. A man strong enough for Savannah.

Jake Benedict and the Rafter B.

Steve Cody and the Broken Spur.

Father, or lover.

Sandy Gannon was betting against the odds, that one day, perhaps a day not so far away, that would be the choice Savannah Henrietta Benedict must face.

Chapter 4

Steve laid the digger aside, hefted the next to last post from a dwindling stack, set it, filled in the dirt, tamped it. Then, breaking the flow of the systematic routine, he stepped back, tired but pleased, regarding the result of his labor.

The new corral was almost finished. As strong and sturdy as the original, soon all it would lack was the stock. The barn was in passable shape, the house livable. Both structures in better repair than he expected after the twenty years the place had been abandoned.

The house was most surprising. No one would call it a mansion with its lack of common conveniences, but it was well constructed, and the Spartan, handmade furniture comfortable enough for his needs. Aside from a few cobwebs and a thin film of dust, Charlie and his family might have walked away only yesterday.

He'd wondered about the relative order and the attention given to minute details of its repair. Each evident in a shingle here, a board there; a hinge or window sash, newer, shinier, fresher than the original. All of it a puzzle without an answer.

In the end he'd dismissed it as the work of a wandering, luckless cowboy who found shelter from time to time in the canyon. One from the old school, who lived by an ancient code, repaying an absentee owner with a bit of handiwork. It was a custom not uncommon in the wilds of Texas—work for hospitality or shelter—a drifter offering secondhand gratitude by leaving a line shack or lean-to in a welcoming state for the next wayfarer.

No wayfarer could've been more grateful than Steven Cody. His trip from Silverton had been rocky. A trek across Benedict land, taking longer than the four hours he expected. The moon had been rising when the truck finally rattled around the last turn to begin the descent into the canyon.

A shaft of moonlight lit his way. In burnished half-light, half-crazed from the aftermath of crippling pain, he'd seen a land like none he'd ever known. A wonderland, a land of promise.

The heart of the Broken Spur.

He didn't remember much of the journey before that moment, and little after. Only that the stream had been his guide, a ribbon of sparkling silver, leading him home. In his feverish mind, the canyon seemed to be waiting for him. For Steven Cody, welcoming him home.

He'd climbed the roughhewn steps and crossed the porch with a sense of déjà vu. That inherent awareness that he'd come full circle, returning after a long sojourn, to what he was meant to be. The creaks and groans of wood beneath his steps were familiar. As he lifted the leather strap that served as latch, curious scents of must and roses wafting from the interior of the tiny house were exquisite perfume.

The narrow bunk with a mattress of straw had been like a gift. When he'd crawled into it, shedding only hat and boots, it was the scent of roses that soothed him. As he let himself drift into the sleep his body and mind demanded, the ripple of water became his siren's song.

His last coherent thoughts, half dream, half reality, were of a stream of silver. As silver as liquid moonlight. Sparkling silver, the color of Hank Benedict's challenging eyes.

Grass and water, roses and silver, he'd mused on the edge of oblivion, wondering how could this not be paradise?

"Paradise," he murmured now, looking out over the canyon floor. There was no moonlight to paint mystical pictures, no headache to cloud his judgment, and still spring's new crop of grass was bright and succulent. The stream, even more brilliant in the sunlight, was clear and deep, approaching flood stage from the runoff of winter's melting snow. The cattle that grazed within his sight were sleek and fat, their brand the brand of the Rafter B.

Four days into the third week, and no one had come to herd the cattle from the canyon. A nagging reminder that even in paradise there were serpents.

Sliding off his gloves, he tucked them in a back pocket and reached for his canteen. The water was hot and tinny, but no less quenching than if it were cool and fresh. Like a child with a wonderful surprise, he kept remembering this water was his. The land it flowed through was his. Every inch of it. There was no partnership, no sharing. Sunrise Canyon and the Broken Spur belonged to Steve alone. Charlie would have it no other way.

Savoring the last drop from the canteen, he took his gloves from his belt. Slipping them on again, with his mind far from the chore at hand, he decided he would give the Rafter B three more days. Two weeks more than promised, in the spirit of neighborliness. A last-ditch effort for peace.

Thirst slaked, taking up the digger he attacked the ground with renewed vigor. In a short time the last post was set, the last rails up. The corral was done. For days on end, he'd labored from sunup to sundown, digging, straining, sweating, a definite change from his last months in rehab. He'd loved every minute and every aching muscle of it. Even the return trip into Silverton for the supplies he needed had been a pleasure. Half expecting a hassle, he'd crossed Benedict range cautiously, but no one had approached him. No one had challenged his legal privilege of right-of-way. Finally, ignoring the bump and scrape of the poor road, he'd given himself up to the transient softness only spring could lend to the stark beauty of this land.

Too beautiful to be true.

As the day was drawing to an end, he was in a mood to celebrate. With the sweetest water on earth he would drink a toast to the satisfaction of a job well done, to spring, to new beginnings.

Laughing to himself, he crossed to the low bank of the stream. Crouching at the water's edge, he scooped up a handful, sipping from his palm, letting it spill down his arm and over his chest. Tossing his hat aside, he splashed his face and head. The water was cool and refreshing, offering relief from the waning heat of the day. He'd discovered the stream was always cool, always refreshing. As if it rushed along too swiftly for the heat of the sun to catch it.

Chuckling at his flight of fancy, he shook his head. Coal black hair flattened by sweat and the stricture of the Stetson began springing into curls over his forehead, dripping beads of water down his face and into his eyes. Fingers raked impatiently through the black mane tamed it for a time. Drying his eyes with a swipe of a shirtsleeve over his face, he looked to the horizon to judge the time.

"Well, hello," he said softly, catching sight of a horse and rider, poised at the distant rim of the western wall of the canyon. "Who might you be?"

Squinting into the glare of the setting sun, Steve waited for some greeting. The hearty hale of a curious cowboy, a neighbor come to call. Perhaps a drifter passing through. There was nothing, only a waiting, watchful silence.

"Not the friendly sort, huh?" Rising cautiously, aware that he was well within rifle range and a perfect target, he lifted his head to meet a stare he couldn't see. "A canny one, too, aren't you? Keeping the light at your back."

Moving carefully, Steve began to circle toward a copse of trees. Oddly, he didn't feel he would need protection, but it never hurt to cover all the options. "Brazen." Still moving, he plucked his hat from the ground. "You know I see you, and you don't care."

This strange visitor might've been carved of stone. Neither horse nor rider moved.

The horse would be a handsome one, Steve judged. He could see at a glance that it was big for a cow horse. Not even distance could hide that it was powerfully formed and trained to stand, awaiting the next command.

The rider was another matter, with nothing distinguishable. A mystery.

"Who are you? What do you want?" Steve wondered, half aloud, half to himself. "What do you gain from watching?" He'd reached the edge of the grove of aspen, inches from sanctuary. His fists clenched in a rush of anger, at himself for the defensive move, at the shadowed figure for standing immutable, untouched by his muttered harangue.

"You want to see? Come down, take a close look, I've nothing to hide." His voice turned guttural, yet never rose above the singsong whisper. "Come down! Or maybe I'll come up."

As if the horseman sensed the turn in Steve's mood, a slight tug of the reins wheeled his mount around. In a prancing step, eager to run, the horse raced away.

Echoes of hooves striking stone filtered to the canyon floor, then faded. Steve was alone again. A small breeze rippled his drying hair, the sun burned the tender flesh of the scar at his temple and cheek. He hardly noticed.

A bird called from the foliage of the aspen. A calf bawled for its mother. Thoughtfully he tapped his hat against his thigh in a cloud of dust. Settling it at its customary angle over his forehead, he listened to the lowing response to the calf's demand, wondering if his mysterious visitor was such a mystery after all.

His gaze lifted to the west, to the rim he knew would be deserted. "Scouting the enemy, are you? Wondering if I'm as good as my word?" His lips quirked. "Three days, Benedict," he promised as the sun dipped below the rim, leaving the canyon in shadow. "Three days and you'll see."

Hank pushed back her chair and reached for her hat. The day was wasting. If she started now, she could ride to the east range and back before sundown.

"Going somewhere?" Jake Benedict asked grumpily from his position at the head of the table.

"Thought I'd take a ride over by the old Jordan place." Standing by her chair, she tossed down her napkin and lifted a glass of iced tea for one more sip. Watching her father over the rim of the crystal goblet, she explained. "Sandy says a couple of heifers grazing there will be dropping calves soon. One looks to have two."

"Late for calves," he commented tersely, giving it the sound of an accusation.

"Some," Hank returned mildly, refusing to accept the blame for caprices of nature and a busy bull. Ice and crystal rang in bell-like tones as she set the glass down. One of many enduring customs brought to the Rafter B by her mother was lunch, served promptly at twelve-thirty, with a full complement of crystal and linens, whether there were a dozen at the table, or one. In the hotter months, the delicately minted tea replaced strong and bitter chuckwagon coffee prevalent at every other meal and in between.

Customs of a Southern aristocrat, that Jake complained of intemperately, yet they still survived, more than a decade after Camilla Neal Benedict had returned to the South.

"You should eat more." Jake groused, taking another tack in his quest for a fight.

"So should you."

"I would, if I was riding the range." The answer was matter-of-fact, with only a tinge of the bitterness Jake Benedict felt at being trapped in a wheelchair or chained to a walker for four years.

Hank didn't remind him that stubborn pride was as much the culprit as the series of strokes that left him with partial paralysis, and interrupted her second year in the school of law at the University of Georgia. In typical Jake Benedict fashion, he'd refused therapy, determined that he would recoup lost strength and agility on his own.

He had not. Oddly, and at odds with the man he'd been, though he fought the daily battles, he truly hadn't the heart for it.

"Maybe I'll have Bonita pack a snack." Hank ventured, giving her father the parting shot he needed. "If there's no trouble with the cattle, maybe Sandy will join me for high tea by the Jordan Oaks."

"High tea!" Jake snorted as a scowl deepened lines in his weatherworn skin. "Dammit all, you sound just like your mother."

"Thank you." She was smiling as she set the chair in its place. "I'll count that a compliment, though we both know it isn't true."

"Is, too, dammit." His retort sounded like nothing so much as a querulous child.

"Is not." Hank was laughing as she laid a hand on his stooped shoulder and leaned to kiss the minute bald spot just beginning to show in the thick thatch of his graying hair. Despite the petulance of illness and his nearly sixty-four years, he was still a man of commanding presence. "We both know that if Mother were here, or if I were truly like her, you'd be scolded for cursing at the table."

A quick squeeze of his shoulder, a covert look of regret for what a proud, often obscenely arrogant man had lost, and she was crossing to the door.

"Hey!" Ever the one to have the last word, Jake called after her, "You forgot your tea party. You wouldn't want to go to the Jordans' without it."

Hank didn't turn. Acknowledging this last parting shot with a wave and a wiggle of her fingers, she stepped through the door onto the veranda. They both knew she wouldn't be asking Bonita to pack the snack. The small, plump woman so much like her daughter, Concetta, had more than she could handle in taking care of the house, the meals. And Jake, when he would let her.

In a loose limbed stride, Hank covered the distance between house and barn quickly. She'd spent the morning cooped up in her office, pouring over the ledgers. A necessary evil, but one she liked little. After the enforced imprisonment, she was anxious to get away.

"Good day, Miss Benedict, ma'am."

Startled by the formality of the greeting, she looked up and found the fresh young face of the newest hand grinning up from the stack of saddles and bridles Sandy had given him to repair and clean.

"Good day, Jeffie," she replied, wondering how long it would be before he became familiar enough to call her Hank, as most of the other hands did.

"Going for a ride, ma'am?"

She nodded, without breaking stride. "To the Jordan place."

"To check the new calves?" There was a wistful note in the young voice. Like all the eager, starry-eyed kids from the villages and farms nearby, he'd come to the fabled ranch to be a cowboy riding the range, roping and branding. Certainly, he hadn't planned on spending his days with saddle soap and neat's-foot oil.

Jeffie was beginning as all novice cowhands began on the Rafter B. Before Sandy was through, he would understand completely that a cowboy's equipment could make or break him. The day might come when it would mean his life.

Smiling, remembering when she'd spent her days exactly as Jeffie Cade, and as disgustedly, she entered the barn. The scents of hay, oiled leather and horses assailed her. Familiar scents, as much a part of her life now as her beating heart.

For a number of years, more than six if she counted, her life had been perfume and lace, the courtroom her destiny. Classrooms and books had filled her days, the excitement of learning conquering a restlessness the dryasdust ledgers of the ranch could not. She'd played at being a Southern belle, the strong, gentle sort of woman the Neal women of Savannah had always been. She'd enjoyed every minute, lived it to the fullest, but she couldn't go back.

Those years were priceless. She wouldn't change them, but she *wouldn't* go back. The ranch was where she belonged. She'd known and understood four years ago, in that first moment when she'd stepped again onto Arizona soil.

The Rafter B was her destiny. She knew it every morning when she crawled, aching and still a little weary, from her solitary bed. She knew it at the end of every taxing day as she drifted into sleep, too tired to dream. She knew it every aggravating and exhilarating moment in between. But never more than now.

Stables lined the corridor of the barn. Most were empty at this time of day. Still cooped in his stall, Black Jack would be wild to escape, to run. But no worse than she.

He was waiting for her, nose twitching, body quivering, as eager as a puppy. "Missed me, did you?" Laughing while he nibbled at her shirt pocket, she curled her arms around his massive neck and rested her cheek against his sleek coat.

Drawing away after a moment, she eyed the horse with mock sternness. "You think you deserve a peace offering?"

The horse nibbled at her pocket.

"So do I." In a practiced routine, she extracted three sugar cubes from her pocket. "An extra one today," she said, laughing again as the horse snuffled them from her palm. "Because I owe you."

"Is he always that gentle, or just with you?" The voice came without warning from a little distance away.

Hank whirled around, puzzled. No one should be here. Not at this hour, not on a busy day. Her sight still hampered by the change from sunlight to shade, she probed the dusky corners of the barn.

He materialized slowly, long, lean, with heart-lurching familiarity. An easy smile tilted his lips. "Cody!" Stifling a startled gasp, she demanded, "What the devil are you doing here?"

Ignoring her question, Steve pushed away from a stable gate, coming to his full height. "He looks like a brute, but he purrs like a kitten for you."

"How did you get here?" Anger flared, for allowing herself to be taken unaware, for the rush of her pulse. "What do you want?"

"Does everything and everyone on this ranch purr beneath your hand, Miss Benedict, ma'am?" He took a step closer, still smiling down at her. "Jeffie surely does. I think I would."

Taking refuge in routine, and to buy some time, Hank reached for a halter that swung from a hook by the stall. As her fingers closed over the braided leather, she brought it to her side. "All right." She drew a calming breath. "We'll start again. What are you doing here?"

"Persistent," Steve mused, his smile never altering. "Like a bulldog that takes hold and won't let go." His gaze slid down her, liking the fit of her jeans and shirt as much as he had on the street of Silverton. "Prettiest bulldog I've ever seen."

Before she could snap back a comment, he laughed softly, delighted by the flash of fury that darkened her eyes to stormy gray. "For the sake of peace," he drawled, "and to save time..."

"You're really into saving time, aren't you, Cody?" she interjected in scornful sarcasm. "The best way to do that is to take our offer for the canyon. You will, you know, sooner or later, so why not sooner? Make it easier on yourself."

Brushing the interruption aside as if he hadn't heard, he continued as before. "We'll take your questions from the top. What I'm doing here is waiting for you. I got here on horseback. Jeffie isn't much of a watchdog, he grinned and waved when I rode in."

"He's new, not familiar with who belongs here and who doesn't. But he'll learn." Hank bristled, defending the newest hand.

"I'm sure he will." Steve deliberately held her gaze. "Considering his teacher."

"Sandy will be his teacher, as will several others." A toss of her head sent the braid tumbling from her shoulder. She glared up at him. "Cut to the chase, Cody. What do you want?"

"I'm discovering I want a lot of things, Miss Benedict, ma'am," he answered softly.

Hank resented the lurch of her heart, a woman's response to an attractive man. It had been years since any man had made her feel this keening, breathless awareness. She hadn't allowed it. She wouldn't now. Drawing herself to her fullest height, with her head at a regal angle, she stared coolly back at him. "I have work to do, and you're wasting my time. And don't call me ma'am."

"Riding over to the Jordan place?"

"Exactly."

"A neighbor?" Steve didn't recall Charlie mentioning any ranchers by that name.

"A section of the Rafter B," Hank retorted. "If you heard that part of my conversation with Jeffie, you know I'm riding out to check on new calves. I would hardly do that on another ranch."

"Hardly." He understood then that the Jordan place was one of Jake Benedict's acquisitions. He wondered if every one gobbled up by the land hungry rancher was still called by the name of the luckless past owner. "While you're out, you might want to check the cattle in the small holding pasture nearest Sunrise Canyon."

"We have no cattle in that pasture."

"You do now, seventeen head."

"You moved our cattle from the canyon!"

Steve shrugged. "Just saving you time and aggravation."

"There you go again, saving me time." If leather could break, the bridle would have shattered in her palm.

"It seemed the neighborly thing to do. Just as taking your cattle from my grass when I asked would have been." He touched her cheek, drawing his finger down the satiny curve of it. "Did you forget, Miss Benedict, ma'am?"

"I didn't forget." Her teeth were clenched with the need to jerk away from his familiar touch. No response was her best defense against the flicker of tension that had nothing to do with anger.

"Somehow I didn't think you did."

"Good, then we understand each other." Hank stepped away, giving herself room to breathe.

"You're mistaken there. You don't understand me at all. I meant what I said, about the cattle and the Broken Spur."

"Moving cattle is one thing. Running a successful horse ranch is quite another." Dismissing him, as well as his ambition, she opened the door to Black Jack's stall and led him out. He was a massive stallion, his sleek bulk filled the corridor, making it too small, too close.

"Horses have been my life," Steve reminded her, running an appreciative hand over the stallion's flank.

"Riding horses has been your life." Rising on tiptoe, Hank slipped the bridle over Black Jack's head, expertly, with a minimum of effort. Patting the horse affectionately, she turned back to Steve. "Judging and breeding them is not the same."

"Not the same for a broken down rodeo has-been, you mean."

"No, Mr. Cody, I mean for anyone. I fly a plane, and I fly it well, but I don't build them. I wouldn't presume to think I could." She reached for the blanket and saddle lying on a shelf by the stall, but he was faster. He made quick work of saddling the horse. Quicker than she could have. In a guarded glance, she saw there was no bravado in the act, no macho condescension. He'd simply reacted with an old-fashioned chivalry he wore well and naturally.

The saddle was heavy, and Black Jack was tall. Saddling him was a stretch no one else seemed to notice. Or perhaps they wouldn't allow themselves to notice, because by unspoken agreement, it was what she wanted. She pulled her own weight with no concessions. It could be no other way. Even so, the small gallantry unsettled her, leaving her at a loss.

"My guess would be that you could. Build an airplane, that is, if you set your mind to it." He continued to stroke the stallion, but his attention was riveted on her. "I doubt there's little you can't do, if you set that stubborn Benedict mind to it. But you don't offer me the same confidence."

"I've seen too many operations go down here. Shoestring operations with grandiose expectations, lost from lack of expertise and funds and most of all, dedication."

"Lucky for them, there was always Jake Benedict," Steve observed with a hint of steel in his mild tone. "Jake Benedict, with more acres than a cactus has spines, watching and waiting to take the land off their hands."

The remark stung. She'd heard it before, whispered behind shielding hands, with a more vicious twist. "He never took what wasn't offered and never for less than fair market price."

"Everything always had a price, except the one that mattered most." Steve's jaw tightened, but there was no change in his voice. "Charlie must have been a burr under his saddle all these years."

"Jake wanted Sunrise Canyon," she admitted levelly, despite the flush that gleamed over her cheeks. "He never stopped hoping the day might come when Charlie would sell."

"Then I came instead, with the deed signed and recorded, and no more willing to sell than Charlie."

"You will." Her tone lent more conviction to her prediction than she felt.

"You sound like a broken record, Miss Benedict, ma'am. I'm beginning to wonder who you're trying to convince. Does the lady protest too much?"

The gold in his brown gaze was lost in the shade of the barn, but she knew it was there. The eyes of a playful predator, looking into the mind of his quarry, seeing too much, understanding too much.

She'd dismissed him as a thrill seeker. A daredevil with a grandiose vision. One who would lack staying power as he grew weary with the demands of the desert and bored with the never-ending routine, the abiding solitude. She'd seen it many times, and expected it again. Lulled by the assumption, she'd underestimated him. She wouldn't again.

"My, my." Clucking her tongue and shaking her head she drawled, "You are a learned man, indeed. First schoolbook French, and now the bard."

"Hidden talents." A subtle shift that could hardly be defined as a move brought his body closer to hers. "There are others."

"If I were a gambler, I'd bet on it," she returned blandly. Through a drift of lowered lashes, she looked at him. She couldn't avoid looking at him as he blocked her path from the barn. He was still lean, but with an overlay of hardened muscle on his rangy frame. The sickly telltale pallor had darkened to a glow of healthy color that had no tales to tell. His time on the ranch had been good for him, yet all the evidence of his recent ordeal hadn't faded. It was there in the bracketing lines softened only a little by his lazy smile. And in the haunted wariness of a strong and virile man who found himself at the mercy of factors he couldn't control.

She suspected the pain always came with little warning, with no regard for place or time, without clemency in its crippling attack.

Though he'd smiled there on the streets of Silverton, dismissing it, offering an offhand explanation, before it was done he was nearly blinded by it. He coped, with bitter acceptance, but had not escaped unmarked by the powerful hatred strong and passionate men harbored for even a moment of helplessness.

She knew of secret battles and their toll. She tried not to see them every day in Jake.

Jake Benedict. Steve Cody. Men from different places, at different times in their lives, yet so much alike. Strong men, silent in their grim battle against the enduring effects of physical catastrophe. For whom, perhaps for the first time, the clock and age were as significant as strength.

At sixty-three, time and age were Jake's enemy. Each day's struggle leached away a little more of his strength, a little more hope. While, with the tenacity and vigor of youth, this man grew even more dynamic.

Steel tempered by the fires of hard luck and disappointment, had grown stronger with each challenge, making Steve Cody a disturbing and dangerous man. Dangerous, indeed.

Lashes sweeping from her cheeks, her eyes wide, she stared into the face of the man who challenged and enticed. A man of courage, and conviction. In another time, another place, she admitted with uncompromising Benedict honesty, a man she would want.

"All through?" Steve asked softly.

"What?" A frown gathered on her face as she cast about for the thread of conversation.

"Ready to place your bet?"

Remembering, she nodded abruptly. "If I were a gambler."

"Which you aren't?"

"I'm not a lot of things, Mr. Cody." Gathering her wits, she appended quiet words with a quiet rebuke. "You've delivered your message and made your point. We'll see to the cattle. Now, if you'll excuse me, I'm a trifle too busy to stand around speculating on hidden talents and listening to fractured Shakespeare."

When she turned to the stallion, Steve captured her braid as it swung over her shoulder. A tug turned her back to him. "The way I hear it, you're always busy. Too busy for anything but the ranch."

"Been listening to gossip, have you?" Once before he'd held her like this. Once before his wrist had brushed over her breast. She *would* ignore the warmth that stirred like a blush in her.

"I needed supplies." Steve shrugged noncommittally. "The townsfolk are friendly." Because he couldn't resist, he looped the braid tighter across his palm. A rope of silk, soft against his flesh, binding her to him. His voice dropped to a husky murmur, his eyes glittered with amber fire. The back of his knuckles brushed the tip of her breast. "Have you ever cut your hair?"

"You're trespassing, Cody."

An eloquent shrug dismissed her accusation. "The gates were open. There were no signs of welcome, but none warned that trespassers would be shot."

Hank would have none of his innocent, teasing pretense of misunderstanding. Her voice was as quiet as before, deceptively quiet. "Is that your good hand?"

"You've been reading old news from old newspapers." Steve grinned as he released her braid. "Both my hands are good hands."

Hank found her face captured in the curl of his palms before she could dodge away. "Take your hands away."

"Why, Miss Benedict, ma'am, I'm just showing you I have two good hands." His thumb raked over her mouth. A mouth that was soft and warm, and delightfully alluring even in contempt.

Hank's teeth were clinched, her flashing glance was glacial. "Move both your *good* hands, while they're still good."

"Careful, you'll have me believing none of these red-blooded cowboys ever touches you."

Her fingers closed around his wrists in a strong, surprising grip as she took his unresisting hands from her face. "No man does," she said succinctly, her words clipped and as cold as her gaze. "Our riders understand that working for the Rafter B means exactly that, work. I'm not part of the package, I never have been, I never will be. Anyone that wants to stay understands, and never forgets."

His brows arched, he wondered what in hell they were talking about. "No man . . ." he began, then broke off. This wasn't the question to ask, not here. With his sardonic smile carefully in place, he infused his tone with amused incredulity, "Never?"

"Never." Hank brushed past him, neither caring nor concerned with what he thought. With the practice of a lifetime, she swung into the saddle. Black Jack pranced to the side, eager to be off and running as reward for his patience. Quieting him with the pressure of her knees, she leaned forward in a relaxed crouch, folding her arms over the pommel of the saddle. More at ease with distance between them, she allowed herself a small taunting smile. "Don't let the gate hit you in the butt as you leave, Cody. And don't come back until you're ready to sell."

Steve's hand flashed out, catching the collar of her shirt, drawing her face-to-face. "You're pretty sure of yourself and your men, aren't you?"

"Sure enough."

"Maybe you shouldn't be. Maybe you should be more careful. Maybe you aren't a lot of things, but there's one thing that's damn sure, you're a woman. You might forget, but you can bet your last Benedict dollar your wranglers don't." With his free hand he stroked the startled curve of her lips, a sensation he never tired of. "Neither do I."

Hank jerked away. Wheeling Black Jack around, she held the stallion barely in check, keeping him on the edge, controlling him as much with her mind as her body. "You're wrong on the first count, Cody. And the second doesn't matter."

With a subtle tap of her heels, Black Jack lurched into a run. "Remember what I said about the gate, Cody," she called as he raced from the barn after her. "Don't hurry back."

She rode like a cossack, on a creature that was more wild beast than horse. As one they thundered through the empty corral, taking the fence in a flying leap, spooking Belle, the mare he'd ground hitched by a sycamore. Bending forward, arm outstretched, Hank snagged the mare's dangling reins. For a furlong they raced side by side, the coal-black stallion with his well seated rider, and Belle.

Blue Belle, named for his mother's favorite flower, his best hope to carry the first Cody horse. Too valuable to risk in a headlong gallop. Steve's shrill whistle stopped the mare short, dragging the reins from her captor's hand.

Black Jack danced to a halt, rearing and prancing, while Hank Benedict laughed and waved. "Neat trick, Cody. I thought you might enjoy a stroll. See the countryside while you can." As the mare trotted back to him, the stallion whirled and turned in quivering excitement. A strong hand brought him around again.

"Remember your butt, and don't hurry back." With a final salute, she was off.

Vaulting the corral fence and catching up his horse, Steve watched her out of sight. A woman, only fools and boys could ever forget it.

Stepping into the saddle, he turned Belle toward Sunrise Canyon. "See you around, Miss Benedict." Two fingers brushed the brim of his hat. "Miss Benedict, *ma'am*."

Chapter 5

The horse approached in a steady gait. The rider, a grizzled man with a whipcord build, slouched comfortably in the saddle.

Steve looped the stallion's reins over a rail and waited under a cloudless sky. His visitor was in no hurry, not the least perturbed by his curious scrutiny. He rode well, whoever he was. More part of the horse than rider, as only a man who knew horses and spent a lifetime in the saddle could be.

Dust ruffled under glinting hooves. Small stones clattered with a dull ring. At an hour after full daylight the sun was beginning to scorch. If he was aware of dust or heat this desert traveler didn't show it.

Drawing to a halt at the corral fence, he studied the barn, the house, a roll of barbed wire. Nodding his approval of work done and to be done, he shifted his attention to Steve and the stallion. Reins held loosely at his fingertips, he leaned an elbow on the pommel of his saddle. A small smile settled over his spare, handsome features. "Howdy."

Steve nodded a greeting, reaching out to soothe the stallion shying nervously at the unfamiliar voice.

"Quite a piece of horseflesh you got there."

Steve didn't take his hand from the horse. "He'll do."

The traveler chuckled at the understatement. "A mite nervous."

"A mite."

"Been cooped up too much of late."

Steve only nodded again.

"Not good for man or beast." A gaze that lost none of its intensity in its paleness settled on Steve, noting the tensile power in a frame still a little too thin. "Not good atall, being cooped up."

"No."

The potent gaze turned again to the stallion. "Good lines. Strong. Be a good breeder when he settles down to it, you reckon?"

"I reckon," Steve answered the question that needed no answer. What he reckoned was that this laconic man had forgotten more than he would ever know about horses.

The traveler looked up at the sky, squinting into the glare of the sun. "Got us a hot one."

"It'll get hotter."

The man with the pale eyes chuckled. "I reckon so."

Steve said nothing, leaving the next move in this game of verbal chess to his uninvited guest.

"I 'spect you wouldn't begrudge a man a drink of sweet water out of the stream."

"I 'spect I wouldn't." Moving away from the stallion, Steve gestured an invitation to dismount.

"I ain't much of a walking man." In a practiced and graceful swing of a long leg, the older man swung down. Bracing his hands at his waist he arched his back, his eye twinkling as if he were making a secret admission. "But, damn! it feels good to step out of the saddle every now and again."

"There's cool water in the house," Steve offered with an easy hospitality. He liked this straightforward man instinctively. He liked everything about him.

"Naw." The quiet refusal accompanied a shake of the rider's head sending silver-tipped hair drifting over his collar. "Directly from the stream is good enough." Laughing softly, he declared, "More than good enough. It's how I like it."

Shoulder to shoulder, in unspoken consensus, they crossed to a worn path leading to the stream. One was taller and older, the other broader and younger, but, in silent rapport, the same.

Tossing his hat aside, kneeling by the stream, the traveler sipped from his cupped hand, then poured another over his head. "Lordy, that feels good." Another shake of his head sent water flying in a shining arc from his mane of gray. "Sweetest water in the land."

"You should know," Steve observed amiably.

Squatting as he was, with a wrist draped over his knee, the older man squinted up at him. "Figured you'd see the brand."

"Figured you meant for me to."

"Ain't no sneak in my makeup." Brushing back a dripping lock and snatching up his Stetson, he stood to face Steve, waiting for a tacit judgment.

"That's something the townsfolk would agree on, when they speak of the foreman of the Rafter B." Were he to recite it, the list of descriptions would be long, and mostly kind. Steve had discovered the majority of people liked Sandy Gannon as much as they didn't like Jake Benedict. "Granted, you didn't sneak, but I wonder why you're here." Steve's eyes narrowed, considering the most likely reason. "A quick study for your boss? The rim wasn't close enough for spying?"

"Didn't come to spy." Sandy Gannon took no offense. "No need for it. I knew what you'd do without looking."

"Because it was what you would do?"

"Maybe that, and what Charlie told me."

"Then the lady who spends her evenings on the west rim didn't send you?"

"The lady on the—" Sandy broke off, chuckling. "Had company, have you?"

"Long-distance company. She seems mighty interested in what I'm doing."

Sandy regarded the western rim. "That's a powerful long way, even for your young eyes. Are you sure it's her?"

"Who else would it be?"

"Be easier to tell you who it ain't."

"Jake Benedict can't ride."

"That's the list." Sandy nodded. "But you could take your pick of just about anybody else it could be."

"I have taken my pick."

"You may be right. The canyon has been one of her favorite places since she was a pup."

"Like it is her father's?"

"Not exactly." Sandy offered no other explanation. "I imagine you're wondering what I'm doing here, if not spying."

Steve noticed the subtle, smoothing shift in the foreman's speech. Gannon had the reputation of a straight shooter, but he wasn't above playing roles when it suited.

Taking a pair of gloves from a hip pocket, Sandy drew them on. Flexing his fingers in the soft leather he glanced back at Steve, as if all his wondering should be resolved. "Well?"

"Well, what?"

The foreman looked at him, the pitying look one reserved for dumb creatures and dense men. "Let's get started. The day ain't going to get any younger or any cooler."

For the first time, Steve was taken by surprise. "What the devil are you talking about?"

Another long, pitying look swept from Steve to the field at his back. "I'm talking about a field that needs fencing and wire that needs stringing. Ain't it sunk in yet I've come to help?"

"Come to help—?"

"Stretching wire is the devil's own chore, next to impossible for a man alone."

"So, I'm to believe you came to help? Jake Benedict wants to add my land to the Rafter B, and his foreman comes to help?"

"Something like that." Standing at ease, Sandy respected Steve's skepticism. He would have dismissed the young man as a naive fool, if he hadn't questioned. "I punch cows for Jake Benedict and count him a friend, but my conscience is my own. I follow where it leads, even when it parts company with Jake."

"He would understand that?" Steve couldn't quite comprehend a relationship of this sort. Not with the mighty owner of the Rafter B. It went against all he'd heard of the ironhanded Jake Benedict, but not, he admitted, of Sandy Gannon. "You really believe he would?"

"Has for well-nigh thirty years. Why would he change now?"

"Given the circumstances, it doesn't make a lot of sense."

"Maybe I'm worth the trouble I cause," Sandy suggested genially. A mischievous grin crinkled crow's-feet at the corner of his eyes. "Or maybe I'm just handy when he's in a mood for a fracas."

Steve laughed, the sudden sweep of tension flowing out of him. "A helluva fracas it would be, I gather."

"Can be. Has been."

"I won't ask who wins, or how many times you've been fired."

"I hold my own," Sandy replied in his succinct fashion. "Been hired one more time than fired." Dropping his hat back on his drying hair, he observed dryly. "Less'n you want a baked horse, I'd put that stallion out of the sun. Soon as you do, we can get to that wire."

"Will you tell Jake?"

"If he asks."

Steve nodded, gleaning a new perception of the rare friendship that existed between Jake Benedict and Sandy Gannon. He wondered how good a friend the foreman had been to the father's daughter. After a considering moment, he drew a long, quiet breath. "I'll put Gitano away."

The simple sentence cemented a burgeoning bond of trust without fanfare. The smile of recognition that passed between them was as binding as a handshake.

Sandy accepted the confidence easily, as if it were a natural happening for two cautious strangers to trust so completely, so quickly. They were simpatico, men of the same breed. Western men. In his usual mild manner he tucked this rare prize away. It would never be discussed, nor would it be forgotten. "Gitano." His attention returned to the corral and the stallion standing hipshot in the sun. "Spanish, is he?"

Steve nodded. "Gitano Magnifico, by way of Mexico and Texas."

"Good horse breeders, the Spanish."

"Some of them."

"This one was."

"A bit given to fits of misjudgment."

"Didn't recognize what he had? That how you got the stallion?"

Steve nodded.

"Magnificent Gypsy." Sandy grinned at the extravagant name. "You give the horse that title?"

"The breeder's blind daughter. Everyone else called him Sapo."

"Toad," Sandy translated. "Ugly colt, I reckon."

"The ugliest."

"This girl, she saw with her heart when others were blinded by sight." Sandy pronounced this bit of poetic wisdom with no trace of pretension.

"She loved him. They were..." Steve looked to the sky, his gaze ranging as his mind ranged, searching for the word that would describe the bond between a blind child and a horse too ugly for more than the glue factory.

"Simpatico," Sandy supplied quietly.

Steve's gaze returned to Sandy. His look was long, contemplative. "Yes."

"Her father saw with his eyes, she with her heart, and you with both."

"Maybe."

"No maybe to it." Sandy wouldn't accept the dismissal. "Every now and then one comes along," he mused, studying the magnificent horse grown from an ugly, ungainly colt. "You got a good eye, boy." He looked again at Steve, a sustained, judging look. "A good eye and a damn good heart."

"Luck." Steve shrugged away the tribute.

"The day I believe that is the day I kick myself for standing here. Speaking of standing, time's awasting, the thermometer's rising. I'll see to my own mount." A jerk of his head indicated bare posts waiting like solitary sentinels for the wire that would unite them, completing a holding lot for horses yet to be. "Meet you there."

His mind reeling, perplexed yet strangely gratified, Steve watched the retreating back of the foreman of the Rafter B. His coming made no sense, until one understood the man. Sandy Gannon rode for the brand, but his principles were his own.

Sandy was unrolling a wickedly coiling strand of wire when Steve went to attend to Gitano. As he grained and watered the stallion, his thoughts turned to Jake Benedict. He wondered curiously what qualities there were about him that he commanded the loyalties of a man the caliber of Sandy Gannon for more than thirty years.

A mystery, he concluded as he went to join Sandy. One time would unravel.

The sun was hovering over the western rim before Sandy Gannon swung into the saddle and sat looking down at Steve. They were worn and dehydrated, but the holding pen was complete, the wire taut and secure. Its barbs gleaming in the light. "A good day's work."

"Would've been longer working alone," Steve admitted. "I'm not sure how I can repay you."

"Dealing fair with the girl will be payment enough. Fair," Sandy emphasized. "No more, no less. Agreed?"

"Agreed," Steve answered.

"Your word on it?"

"That and more." Steve stepped closer, his hand extended.

"Good enough." Sandy leaned down, callused palm touched callused palm briefly but firmly.

Steve stepped away, feeling the pull of tired muscles, the sting of countless salt encrusted cuts. "Thanks, Sandy."

"One more thing." Reins dangled from a lax hand, the horse shifted its weight impatiently but stood in place. Sandy's riveting gaze didn't stray from Steve. "I ride for the brand. When there's trouble, that's where I stand."

"I know."

"Just so we're clear on it."

"I wouldn't expect anything else."

Sandy nodded, the matter was settled. "There's a sale up toward Sedona. Private. Fancier shindig than Silverton's, nothing near as big, but good." Taking a sweat dampened fold of fine vellum from his shirt pocket, he tossed it to Steve. Pulling the reins tighter, he straightened in the saddle. "Several good fillies offered, one worth a look-see. A sleeper, like the Spanish stallion. Good match for him. My guess is he'd sire mighty fine colts out of her."

A tap of his heel sent his mount dancing, ready to run, waiting the final signal. "Look to see you there."

A two fingered tip of his hat and a grin, and he let the horse go, leaving Steve in a boil of dust turned to haze in the canted light of the setting sun. The paper clutched in his fist was an engraved invitation. A simple map had been sketched on the back, beneath the map the name of the filly.

Lorelei.

There was a festive atmosphere about the ranch. Sales at the J Bar R were always as much reflection of Jubal Redmond's celebration of life as business.

Tables were scattered in random order over the tiled terrace and an immaculate lawn. Champagne flowed as liberally as the fountain in a small courtyard. A chef in a white coat and tall hat tended a massive spit turning over a smoldering pit. The scent of roasting meat and piquant spices was everywhere. Blending with the balm of newly clipped grass drying in the sun, mingling with the perfume of masses of imported flowers arranged in immense urns.

White fences, more fitting for Jubal's native Kentucky than Arizona, were immaculate with a fresh coat of whitewash. The lawn, a product of an extravagant sprinkler system and an astonishing supply of water, was as lush as bluegrass in spring.

Above the strumming guitars of strolling musicians, Jubal's hearty laughter rose, rich and deep, and often. He was laughing as he bent to greet his oldest friend in Arizona.

"Jake, you old horse thief!" A beefy hand rested on Jake's frail shoulder. A flicker of concern flitted over Jubal's face at the moment of contact but was hidden by his jovial tone. "Have you come to snatch up all my fine pretties to improve the equine bloodline of the Rafter B?''

Unbearably pale in the formal Western attire Jubal's galas required, Jake scowled and gripped the arms of his motorized chair. "The day a Benedict needs a fancy Redmond nag will be a sad day. I came because Hank insisted." Allowing his ramrod posture to relax a fraction, he chuckled. "And for some of that French perfume you call champagne.''

Jubal laughed, but the look slanted at Sandy was tinged with sadness at the fragility he saw and heard. The enduring friendship had always thrived on a little bristle; over the years of rare contact, both reveled in the haggling immensely. "You called it something a little less kind in the past. But I'll have you know," Jubal bellowed in a tone the uninitiated would think rude and angry, "this perfume cost every cent of three dollars a bottle."

Spinning his massive weight lightly on the balls of his feet, in a deft move and with as much aplomb as he'd lied, he snagged three brimming glasses from a tray carried by a passing waiter. Without spilling a drop, he presented one to Jake, one to Sandy, keeping the last for himself.

"To life, to love and three dollar wine." Touching his glass to Jake's, he chuckled his own joke. Anyone who knew Jubal knew his tastes ran to expensive wines, expensive women and expensive horses. In reverse order.

Sipping heartily from his glass, he looked out over the small, select crowd groomed to the hilt and ready to charm or be charmed. "The lovely Savannah is here? And she didn't come to kiss me hello?''

Before either Jake or Sandy could answer, he waved a hand impatiently. "I know. Or I should after all these years. She went straight to the stables. More interested in my pretties than in me."

"The day she ain't more interested in a horse than a Redmond will be a sad day for the Benedicts." A half glass of wine, quaffed without proper reverence for its superb quality, and the sheer joy of the verbal jousting put a spot of color in Jake's face, the hint of an old irascibility in his voice.

Sandy drank from a fragile glass, as always, content to listen to the repartee that would escalate as the day progressed.

"There's a young man here, a rather quiet and intriguing new guest, as intensely interested in this crop as she." A black brow tinged with gray lifted as Jubal turned his attention in Sandy's direction. "The young man who arrived with your invitation, as a matter of fact."

"What young man would that be?" Hank's voice drifted over Jubal's shoulder.

"Savannah, my love!" As he turned, Jubal's great arms were enveloping her, sending her hat tumbling over the grass. From his great height of nearly seven feet, he bent to kiss her gustily on the top of her head. Holding her at arm's length, he looked her up and down as critically as he would one of his pretties. Appreciating as always, as only a connoisseur of women could, her sense of style.

With unabashed joy, his vivid blue-gray gaze roamed over her, noting the perfect fit of a creamy leather jacket bound in brown, the demure blouse revealing only a seductive ruffle of silky cream at her throat and wrists. And a riding skirt of matching brown that clung with tantalizing faith to her hips before falling away into the full split that stopped just inches below the tops of polished brown boots. A neutral palette enhancing a stunning, virginal beauty.

With her hair coiled in a heavy knot at her nape, Savannah Benedict was the epitome of sophisticated perfection. Artless, aloof perfection that warned, *Don't touch,* even as it filled every randy young buck in sight with the smoldering urge to disobey.

Some not so young, Jubal mused as he smiled and wished he were thirty years younger. "Lord! It's been too long since I've seen you." Exercising his prerogative as old friend and ersatz uncle, he kissed her again. "How long has it been?"

"A year," Hank said dryly. "You missed Silverton in the spring, remember?" Refusing to be deterred, she asked again, "What young man?"

"You look more and more like your mother." Jubal realized all over again that she hadn't a clue of the effect she had on men. The respect she commanded that held them at arm's length even as they ached for her. Cocking his head, he regarded her closer, recognizing her mother's influence. Softly, he murmured, "Maybe prettier."

"Thank you, Jubal." Returning to the point of interest as she was released from another bearish embrace, she insisted, "What young man?"

"Why this young man, of course." Jubal pointed inelegantly over her shoulder. "I assume you know him."

Hank turned, harboring not one single doubt of the identity of the mysterious guest. Her cold silver gaze collided with one dark as a moonless sky.

Steve smiled, tugged the brim of his hat in classic Western greeting and with a gallant half bow, offered her fallen hat. "Miss Benedict." As she snatched it from him, he added softly, "Ma'am."

Jubal regarded the exchange thoughtfully, cognizant of the crackling tension in Hank's unexpected response. A very recognizable and familiar tension. After all, he couldn't have spent the first quarter of his adult life pursuing and seducing women, and the latter quarter being pursued in hopes of seduction, without firsthand knowledge. Silver winged brows, as much his trademark as his size and gusto, lifted in speculation. "I see . . . ahh . . ." The suggestive pause ended in a wicked drawl. "I see you two know each other."

"We've met." Without turning her glacial stare to Sandy, she said pointedly, "But I didn't realize some of us knew him so well."

Sandy said nothing. There would be time later for explanations.

"I wonder if someone could enlighten me," Jake groused irritably. "What the devil is the problem?"

"Not what, Jake," Hank responded tersely. "Who."

"All right, who the devil, then?"

"Jubal's interesting guest." A flick of her wrist directed her father's attention to Steve. "Steve Cody."

"Cody?" The slump lifted from Jake's shoulders, the tremor left his voice. A gaze dulled by boredom sparkled with angry fire. He was Jake Benedict, as he hadn't been in a long time. "Cody!" He barked the name. "The squatter in Sunrise Canyon."

Steve offered his hand. "Steve Cody," he corrected, standing tall, perfectly in tune in dress and manner with his surroundings. "Legal and rightful owner of Sunrise Canyon."

"Legal and rightful aren't always the same, young man." A heated flush spread over Jake's neck and face. Eyes as cold with silvery disdain as his daughter's stared back at Steve. Pointedly he tightened his grip of the arms of his chair. "We made a good offer."

"No, sir," Steve interrupted, not unkindly. As if the slight had gone unnoticed, he tucked his fingers in the pocket of his narrow trousers. "No offer was made."

Jake's head swiveled toward Hank with an accusing scowl. "You said you had a discussion."

"We did," she answered levelly.

"Then what the hell did you discuss? The time of day? The weather? Silver-plated buckles and the ro-day-o?" The last was thick with sarcasm. "You going soft on me, girl?"

Even as he bit back an oath, Sandy shot Jubal a look. A nearly indiscernible shake of his head warned the massive Redmond to stay out of the fray.

"I'm not going soft." Hank stood her ground, making no excuses.

"What, then?" Jake demanded.

Before she could defend herself, Steve spoke in a low voice. "She tried."

Jake didn't look away from Hank. "From the day she could walk, she's been taught to get done what she tried."

"Yeah, well," Steve shrugged negligently, the shoulders of his short, fitted jacket pulled tautly over newly added breadth. "So was I, but it doesn't always work that way. Your daughter didn't make your offer, because I wouldn't listen. Before you go off half-cocked again, there's something else you'd better understand. I wouldn't have listened if it had been you, or anyone else."

Jake made a derogatory sound.

"I wouldn't listen because there's no need. The canyon and its land has no price tag. It isn't for sale." Steve's pleasantly conversational tone only made his resolve more unquestionable. "I've told your daughter, now I'm telling you. I see no reason we can't coexist on friendly terms."

"There's one." Twirling the glass in his long-fingered grasp, Jake watched the rise and fall of the pale liquid. After a moment he looked up, smiling smugly into Steve's narrowed gaze. "You have to be in the canyon to coexist, and you'll be gone before snow flies over the mountains."

Steve laughed in amusement. As a waiter walked by he took two glasses from a tray as easily as Jubal had. One he handed to a startled Hank, the other he lifted to his lips. After one small sip he held the glass casually before him, his gaze ranging to the horizon. "It's easy for a man to learn to like this country. The space, the sky, the land itself." Shifting only slightly, he included Sandy in his evaluation. "The men." His glass lifted in a silent toast to Jubal. "The hospitality."

Jubal nodded his acknowledgment.

Silence spun out, Steve stared into his glass much as Jake had done. When he lifted his head and his glass again, it was to continue his tribute. "To the men, the hospitality. The women, the extraordinary women."

His gaze touched Hank's briefly. "I'll be here when the snow flies." He made a promise, to Hank and to himself. "Before I'm through, the Broken Spur will have the best horses in the South-west." He faced Jake, addressing him squarely, shoulders back, stance wide and confident. "I'll still be here when they carry you feetfirst from the Rafter B. Because some things are without price.

"I have one such thing, Jake Benedict. You have another." Draining his glass, he set it on a small table. "Sandy, thank you for the invitation. And you, Mr. Redmond, for allowing me to stay. Now, if you'll excuse me, I'd like another look at the horses. Gentlemen." The farewell was accompanied by a brief nod as he turned to Hank. "Miss Benedict, ma'am, would you like to join me? To argue the finer points of Mr. Redmond's pretties?"

Taking her glass from her he set it on the table by his own. Giving her no chance to demur, he led her from the small group.

"Well, hell!" Jubal Redmond blew out an explosive breath. "The kid has guts."

"More than he has sense," Jake drawled. Flashing an angry look and a promise of more to come, he spun his chair, giving his back to Sandy. "I need fresh air. That stinking stuff Maeve Montgomery calls perfume would smell better than present company."

Scorn hovered in his wake as he wheeled away, the chair rolling over the smooth lawn as if it were fine wood. Jubal waited until Jake was surrounded by a crowd before turning to regard Sandy critically. "You've stirred a can of worms."

"Could be." Sandy set his glass aside and tucked his thumbs in his belt. "You saw how he was when he got here."

Jubal nodded. "Defeated. Old. My God! I never thought I would see either in Jake Benedict."

"Look at him now."

"I know. You've given him another battle. One he understands." Jubal looked away from Jake, who spoke with Maeve Montgomery with more animation than he had since the strokes made an invalid of him. "You think that while he's fighting one, he'll inadvertently win the most important one?"

"Who knows?" Sandy jerked a shoulder.

"He needed a cause, a reason to live," Jubal surmised astutely. "You created it."

"Charlie created it, by sending the boy to the canyon. I just helped the inevitable along."

"He isn't really a boy, you know."

"Better than most."

"He knows horses. I heard gossip about the Spanish stallion. Sounds like the best stud to come into these parts in a while."

"He is." Sandy scuffed a heel in the grass, catching himself short of leaving a divot in the perfect lawn. "I've seen him."

Jubal snagged another glass of champagne, but Sandy waved the waiter away. "In Silverton, then again when you were stringing wire in the canyon?"

"Yep. Cody told you about the wire, I take it."

"He did. Said he didn't suppose it was a secret. What does Jake say about your helping Cody?"

"Ain't said nothing yet."

"But he will, as soon as he hears it. What then?"

"He asks, I'll answer."

"You're going to be fired again," Jubal predicted.

"More than likely," Sandy agreed.

"How many times have you been fired over the years?"

Sandy grinned, squinting at the sun as if the answer lay in the sky. "Never counted, but I'd put it near a hundred. Twice some years, three times in others. Once a half-dozen."

"One day it's going to take and be for real. The Rafter B has been your life for too long, what would you do without it?"

"Hadn't thought much on it," the foreman admitted. "Mosey on to another ranch, I guess. Or start my own."

"There's a job here for you, anytime you want it."

"Thanks."

Leaning back against a terrace balustrade, they watched the crowd in companionable silence. An aging multimillionaire playboy who had come to the desert to die and lived instead; a rawboned cowhand who'd never had much more than the fabled cowboy salary: "forty and found." Friends.

"What about the other two?" Jubal asked after a while.

Sandy chuckled and scratched his chin. "Imagine they're fighting about now. Why else do you think she'd go so agreeably, but for the opportunity to tear a strip off him?"

"And later?"

"I'd say later is in the making now."

Jubal nodded, and returned to watching the crowd. "Out of war, peace and love." Then, in an abrupt change of subject, he asked, "Heard from Camilla lately?"

"Couple of weeks ago."

"She planning to marry the duke?"

"He was a count, but naw, she won't marry him."

"Think she'll come back?"

There was no hesitation in Sandy. "When the time's right."

"Is that part of your plan?"

"Maybe."

Jubal quenched a monumental thirst caused by conversation with another glass of champagne. Sandy waved the waiter away again.

Steve and Hank strolled into distant view, leaving one stable for another. "He knows horses."

Sandy nodded a laconic agreement.

"I'm going to offer him Lorelei." Jubal cast a sly glance at the foreman. "That's why you sent him, isn't it?"

Sandy didn't admit or deny the suggestion. Jubal was famous for choosing a special horse and offering it to a preferred buyer, for an astronomical price, or nearly nothing, as the mood struck him.

Jubal sipped and sighed. "What will Savannah say?"

"She'll be mad for a lot of reasons," Sandy predicted. "Being bested by him, the main one. She'll be hurt and disappointed, too. She's had her heart set on Lorelei since we saw her last year."

"I don't want to hurt her."

"She'll get past it. She's learned to get past a lot."

Laughter rumbled deep in Jubal Redmond's mammoth chest. "Looks like the children have discovered the identity of our mystery guest."

Across the lawn, by a pristine stable, a gaggle of children surrounded Steve. As he signed napkins, hats and collars of shirts, he reached out more than once to keep Hank Benedict from wandering from his side.

"He knows his horses," Jubal observed again.

This time, as the waiter made another pass Sandy took a tulip stem filled to the brink with Jubal's "cheap" champagne. "Knows'em like an Apache knows the desert."

"Knows his woman, too."

"Hasn't admitted it yet. It's gonna take some time before either of them will."

"There's going to be bad blood." Jubal's mild warning didn't mask his worry.

"Has to be."

Jubal's gaze narrowed critically, considering. "You figure it has to get worse before it can get better?"

"You know Jake, what he's like when he wants something. What would it take to make him change his mind, admit he's wrong?"

An exasperated grunt burst from Jubal. "Something drastic! In nearly a quarter of a century, I've never known him to change his mind."

"Would losing his canyon and his daughter be drastic enough?"

"Do you think it will come to that?"

"Look." Sandy gestured with his glass, returning Jubal's attention to the corral by the stable.

"They're arguing."

"Yep. Up close and personal. Real close, real personal." A pleased grin spread over Sandy's face.

"He can't take his eyes off her." Jubal chortled.

"A strong man for a strong woman."

"You got it backwards, Sandy. A strong woman for a strong man."

"Backwards, frontwards," Sandy dismissed the importance of order. Lounging against the balustrade, he laughed a pleased laugh. "Any direction," the grin grew, "it looks like it might be love."

Chapter 6

"What the devil are you doing here?" Hank spoke through clenched teeth even as she smiled a greeting in return to one called across the way. The smile was warm and natural. The smile of a woman completely at ease, enjoying a stroll over Jubal Redmond's manicured grounds.

Only Steve knew the effort it required. As he walked by her side, his shoulder nearly touching her, his gaze ranging over her, only he could see the taut defensiveness. Only he felt the seething anger in the burning rake of her eyes.

Witch eyes. Eyes that enchanted, mesmerized. Eyes he couldn't escape, and couldn't forget.

When he looked down at her that first day on the teeming street of Silverton, he'd felt himself falling, slipping over the edge, tumbling Stetson over boots into the well of their silver depths. He'd dismissed it later, when he could think again. He spent days telling himself it was the strangeness of his mood, part of the fugue that presaged the crippling headaches.

He'd dismissed the silver eyes with hidden shadows in their steady gaze, but they wouldn't stay dismissed. They were always with him, waiting. In the abstracting repetition of his grueling labor, she was there, filling his thoughts. In his dreams the haunting gaze beguiled, seduced.

Witch eyes.

He'd been burned in the past, enough to stay away, to live th insular life the ranch offered. Passive resistance was the answer t Jake Benedict's greed; it was an impotent greed that couldn't touc him. The Broken Spur was legally and morally his. If it failed, th fault would lie at his door. But he'd waited too long and paid to dearly for this to fail, and he wouldn't. So long as he tended his ow business and remained indifferent to the enemy. This he knew an understood in every waking moment and every conscious thought

Yet Hank was there in unguarded moments, drawing him back A mystery, a need. One to resolve. One to exorcise.

Why had he come today? He wanted to believe he'd come to in vestigate the promise of an exceptional horse. Intrigued only by horse with the name of a siren. But when he'd looked again into tha silver gaze, he knew he'd been drawn to Jubal Redmond's by th woman he couldn't forget.

"Don't play the strong silent type." There was scorn in her voice and a smile too perfect on her face. "Why are you here?"

"Why, Miss Benedict, ma'am . . ." Putting total truth aside, h matched his step and his smile to hers. "I'm here for the same rea son you are, to see the Redmond horses. Perhaps to buy. For all th trappings, selling horses is the purpose, isn't it?"

"That's where you're wrong. Horses are Jubal's passion and th focal point of the sale. But what you've seen today is much mor than that. As an outsider you wouldn't understand, but the rest o us do. I've known Jubal most of my life, and in that time he's bee a friend, and a good one."

She didn't slow her pace, or hurry, as she paused in her story o Jubal Redmond. Steve walked beside her, sensing there was more

A hummingbird chittered irritably. A butterfly danced from flower to flower, fluttering wings a flash of color. A dog barked. / horse whickered. Hank didn't notice.

Jubal's joyful bellow burbling across the lawn coaxed her from silence. "Jubal's laugh, it says more of his zest for living than an words. Yet it hasn't always been so. Longer ago than I can remem ber, he came to the desert to die. And die badly."

Before Steve could comment, she shook her head, warding off th obvious. "I know any death is bad, but for Jubal, what he face was the worst. There was no hope for more than a matter o months, so to spare those who knew and loved him, he came here But because he's Jubal, he didn't stop fighting. When the pro jected time of his death arrived, he decided he didn't feel like dying that day, or that week, or that month. He decided to live instead.

"Six months became a year. One year became two. Two became three. Each a gift, cause for celebration. And he grew stronger. There were more doctors, more tests to determine what changed the course of his illness. The benign but inoperable tumor that threatened to destroy his brain, promising to rob him of every human dignity, was gone. No one knows how, or why, only that it is. Jubal calls it his desert miracle.

"That's why I'm here," she finished. "To celebrate Jubal and the life the desert gave him."

"Yet you went to the stables before you did to him."

"Yes," Hank answered almost pleasantly, finding it difficult to nurture an anger that seemed petty compared to Jubal's trials. "He would have been disappointed had I not."

"Then you aren't really interested in Redmond's horses."

"I didn't say that." The sting crept back into the rebuke. "Any breeder would be interested in what Jubal has to offer."

"Sorry, Miss Benedict, ma'am. I took what you said about going to the stables first to be something you did to humor Redmond."

"Think again." Anger flared before she could control it. Anger turned inward for letting Steve Cody rile her as no man had. "Don't assume, Cody. Neither for me, nor about me."

"No, ma'am." Steve struggled to look properly regretful. Failing miserably, he abandoned the effort, grinning with an innocence never intended to be believed.

Hank seethed, the desire to slap the handsome face becoming a dire need. Curling her fingers into a tight fist, she returned her look stonily to the front, concentrating on their destination, the stable and the horses.

With a sudden shriek and a spate of giggles, a group of small children engulfed them. Joining hands they danced in a circle, teasing, begging for autographs. As they broke away, exhibiting his name on every conceivable surface, Steve took Hank's arm instinctively as a small boy and a puppy tumbled happily into her path.

"Don't touch me, and don't call me ma'am again." Though she didn't jerk away, the demand was a hiss under her breath as she waved in response to a childish chorus of goodbyes. "Let me go. I'm not going to fall on my face in the midst of Jubal's marvelous lawn because a puppy trips me up. And I'm not falling for the chival-

rous routine. Bowing and scraping will get you an aching back and
a raw ego. Nothing more.''

Steve continued to hold her arm, secure in his assumption that she
wouldn't make any sudden or angry moves to draw undue attention to their difficulties. He kept his hand on her, not out of need
or even courtesy, but because he'd discovered in earlier encounters
that he liked to touch her. As much as he liked the color that
brightened her face when she was angry and the sparkle in her eyes
when something surprised her.

Now that he'd finally met the infamous Jake Benedict, he discovered he admired her strength and respected her cool-headed
composure under fire. A lesser woman would have shrunk from
Jake's unwarranted attack, but she'd challenged him, refusing to
buckle under his caustic and unfair remarks. She'd done it with little fanfare and the skill of long practice.

"Your dad can be pretty hard on you," he commented, laughter
giving way to somber concern. "Not always justly."

"Whether he is or he isn't, just or not, what he does and says to
me is my affair. It's something I can handle. Next time, if there is a
next time, stay out of it."

His hand rested lightly at her elbow, his fingers circled her arm.
She let him lead her past a cluster of ranchers who stood apart,
smoking and arguing the merits of this horse or that. Her smile felt
wooden as their conversation stuttered to a halt and all eyes turned
toward them.

Though she hadn't a doubt the gossips had spread the word of her
companion with the speed of smoke signals, she refused to confirm suspicion by avoiding introductions. The momentary pride she
might have taken in the accomplishment was dashed when several
of the ranchers nodded a particular greeting to Steve, calling him by
name.

"I didn't mean to interfere with your dad," Steve continued
amiably when that gauntlet had been run. "I thought I could help."

"I don't need your help."

"Everyone needs help, now and again. Even a Benedict."

"I don't." She stepped through the entrance of the stables. "Not
yours."

"Your smile is slipping. Someone's liable to guess we're knee
deep in a quarrel." Wondering who but an original of Jubal's caliber would decorate even such modern and pristine stables as these,
he drew her to a halt within the tenuous privacy of a potted palm.
From smaller pots clustered among ferns, gardenias and jasmine

sent up their fragrances. A remembrance of sunny Southern days and moonlit nights, recalling the soft lilt he sometimes heard in her voice.

He moved a step closer. "The gossips might decide we're having a lovers' tiff."

With exaggerated determination, she peeled his fingers from her arm, putting distance between them. "If you'll notice, we're alone. But even the most illogical gossips couldn't get it that wrong."

The stables were, indeed, deserted. Steve closed the distance she'd just put between them, hemming her in the curving wedge of palm and plants. "It would be illogical not to consider it a possibility."

"Sure!" Denying an insidious awareness of his lean and rangy body nearly touching hers, she lifted her head to stare into his dark, dancing eyes. "Jake Benedict's daughter and the squatter from Sunrise Canyon? A likely pair."

"Stranger things happen." He wouldn't argue the contemptuous name. Not when there were other things to think of. Not when his fingers tingled with the need to stroke the curve of her cheek, learning the textures of her skin. Nor when he barely controlled an irresistible longing to drag the pins from her hair, to watch it drift in a bright fall over her shoulders and breasts. "If it happened, a number of problems could be solved."

A capricious breeze swept through the wide door, tickling palm leaves, casting a mosaic of light and shadow over her. In the shout of hothouse perfumes, a whispered fragrance drifted to him. Her fragrance. Wild flowers and roses, subtle, demure. Maddening.

"Our problems will best be solved when you come to your senses." She remembered children scattering in every direction, eager to show his prized signature. "You're a star, not a rancher. Go back to the rodeo. You don't belong here, you never will."

"Won't I?" A finger under her chin tilted her face to his. "Why are you so desperate for me to go? What are you afraid of?"

"I'm not afraid of anything." She wanted to move away from his touch, away from his probing scrutiny, but her pride wouldn't allow it. "My father wants Sunrise Canyon, I intend to do all that I can to see that he finally has it. That's the beginning and end of it."

"Is it?" With his body shielding her from the chance of probing curiosity, succumbing to desire, he stroked her cheek with a roughened knuckle. "Have you deceived yourself into believing what began between us in Silverton can be ended so easily?"

Her hand jerked, her nails drove into tendon and flesh. "I'm not one of your buckle bunnies. I won't swoon at your touch or fall into

your bed. All that began in Silverton was war." Flinging his hand
from her, her heated gaze turned icy. "When it's finished, you'll be
gone, and Sunrise Canyon will be part of the Rafter B, as it always
should have been."

"How do you propose to accomplish what Jake Benedict couldn't
in all these years?" He should have felt the heat of her anger, but
all he could think was how magnificent she was.

"Fairly," Hank shot back. "At your own game."

"Horses?"

"Is there another reason we would be standing in a stable?"

Steve could think of several. "Are you making this a formal
challenge?"

"Why not?"

"My horses against yours?"

Hank nodded.

"What criteria? What time limit?"

"The best-trained horse, bringing the best money, the Silverton
sale," she answered succinctly. "A little less than a year from now."
Stepping past him as if the matter had been decided, she amended
with an edge of scorn, "Unless you're gone by the time snow flies
over the mountains, as Jake predicted."

"I'll be here, Benedict."

Hank laughed and continued toward the stalls. "We'll see."

Taking two long steps and reaching out for her, Steve brought her
back. "I'll be here," he repeated in a tight voice. "I don't give up
easily, so don't count on winning by default. Don't count on winning at all." The planes of his face were sharp, his eyes were cool
and appraising, yet his mouth curled in a grim smile. "What are the
stakes?"

"We set our own." His hands were heavy on her shoulders as she
cocked a brow at him, waiting for his agreement.

"For you, Sunrise Canyon deeded to the Rafter B, naturally."

"For a fair price. I won't cheat before I win, or after."

"If I win?" Steve asked.

"You won't."

"For the sake of argument, let's say I might," he persisted
"What then?"

Hank shrugged out of his grasp with some of her confidence
sheared away in the face of his. "Your choice." She hadn't considered losing, or what he would gain by winning. "My horse?"

"I don't think so," Steve said thoughtfully, giving her challenge
the respect it merited, weighing alternatives. "Why would I want the

second best horse if I had the best?" Simply to see the proud lift of her chin, he ventured, "I will have the best, you know."

"You won't." This stubborn bravado took some effort, she wasn't so sure of herself, nor of him. She hadn't stopped to think that Sandy had seen more than a washed-up bronc rider in Steve Cody. He wouldn't be attending Jubal Redmond's sale on Sandy's secondhand invitation if there wasn't more.

Then there was Jubal. In all his good humor, he suffered fools and insincerity poorly. Yet he was impressed by the interloper. In reckless challenge she hadn't accounted for the possibility that she wouldn't win. Now she knew she must, if only half seriously. "If you don't want the horse, then, perhaps, the money?"

Steve pretended to weigh the choice. "The canyon for the price of a second-best horse? Not quite an equitable gamble."

"What then?" Hank grew weary of the verbal jousting. "Name your prize. Anything short of the Rafter B."

"Anything?"

Fury trembled on the brink of erupting. "Isn't that what I just said?"

Steve let his solemn gaze sweep over her, slowly, lazily, before settling again on her face. "Your word on it?"

"Of course you have my word," Hank snapped. "I assumed that was understood."

"You aren't a very good gambler, are you, Benedict? Gamblers never assume."

"This is a sure thing, not a gamble."

"Maybe. But in the way of all good gamblers, and as you suggested earlier that I mustn't, neither of us should assume anything. Not when the stakes are so high."

"Name your prize, Cody." As she watched the hard edges smooth from his face, and a spark of laughter dance fleetingly into his eyes, Hank knew she'd been drawn into a trap. "Name it!"

Her voice slipped from the low, smoky range that had made Steve wonder if she ever sang the blues. Standing only inches away, he watched her, taking in every nuance of her irritation and frustration and, for once, uncertainty.

Color flagged her cheeks. Her breasts rose and fell beneath the clinging silk of her blouse as she struggled for composure. Light spilled though the door in the ever changing cant of the sun, her hair drew fire from it. There had never been a woman more alive, more desirable.

"Name it, damn you!" She'd been maneuvered into a corner, and with the exclusion of the Rafter B, had given him virtual carte blanche in setting her risk in this wager. "Name it and be done with it!"

"You."

She wasn't sure she'd heard right, certain someone had come into the stables, with pieces of a separate conversation preceding them. Blankly, she stood shocked and startled, realizing there was no one else. No one else had spoken. "What did you say?"

"I said, you, Savannah," his voice remained softly resolute. "I want you."

She shook her head, more to clear it than to deny. Her body trembled, her heart tripped. "No!"

Steve flung his hat aside, his arm snaked out. His hand cupped the back of her head, sending her hat falling after his as he drew her to him. "Yes." Their bodies touched, the curving bounty of hers yielding to the hard planes of his. "You." He stared down into silver turned stormy. "And this."

He meant it to be a teasing kiss, part of the game he played. He knew he wanted her. Consciously and subconsciously, he'd known it for a long while. Yet he didn't expect the intensity of the rush of desire that rocked him as his mouth closed over hers. Nor that he would be so hungry for her that it hurt. With her smothered cry warm on his cheek and her body taut and hard, yet lush and giving against him, there was more than the simple, physical need stirring deep inside him. His cradling hand stilled her head, keeping her lips locked to his, parting them, exploring the velvet beyond. In his last coherent thought, he knew that nothing between them would ever be simple.

Through slitted eyes he saw the flutter of her lashes and felt their sensuous caress. After the first shocked gasp and taut jerk of her head, she didn't struggle. She endured. Passive resistance, his own weapon of choice. But even then she felt good, the heat, the contours and textures, the natural sweetness, the elemental womanliness.

Savannah. Guileless enchantress, who seduced simply by being.

A challenge. But not for here, not now.

Releasing her, he backed away. She only looked at him, her eyes darker than he'd ever seen them, her mouth swollen from his kiss. With a will of its own, his hand returned to her face, his palm curving around her cheek. His thumb glided over her full lower lip, stroking, soothing. And, God help him, he wanted to kiss her again

"You, Savannah," he repeated hoarsely. "I want you."

She didn't move from his touch, didn't look away from his gaze black with passion. "Never, so long as you live, you son of a—"

"Lady." He stopped her with a word. His fingers slipped from her face to her nape, burrowing beneath the coil of her hair, grasping her tightly, but not hurting. "Whatever I've been, whatever I become, I will always be the son of a lady."

Because nothing in the world could have stopped him, he leaned to brush her mouth with his. Her response was a ragged denial and a flutter of lashes as her eyes closed. Then, in a sudden, reluctant quickening, a subtle change, a hushed nuance...an answering passion. Smoldering, sensual. As unfathomable as elusive. Exquisite.

"Forever is a measure of time too brief for lovers," he whispered in a shattered breath, "and never has no meaning."

With tender constraint he kissed each eyelid, watching as they lifted, as unfocused confusion became the riveted fury he expected. Lifting his hands from her, he stepped back.

"Quoting bad poets now, Cody?" She was a figure carved of ice. Only her lips moved, and her throat, forming each word precisely for the smoky, bluesy voice. And he found even the warp of scorn tantalizing on her lips.

"A poetess," he corrected in a tender tone she hardly heard. "A lady, who suffered the worst of a terrifying death with the grace of an angel."

Silence unraveled between them, a thread broken only by Steve. "I called her Mother."

Spinning on the flat heel of his boot, he turned from the quick, stricken look on her face. From the need to take her back into his arms. Catching up his hat, settling it in the way of lifelong habit over the ruffled wave of his shining hair, he left her while he could.

Hank watched him go, off balance, a little ashamed. He'd kissed her and teased her, but had never been cruel.

"Just cocky as hell." With a swipe of her sleeve, she scrubbed the memory of his mouth from hers, striving to rekindle a vacillating indignation.

"Broken down has-been bronc rider." She began the enumeration of his shortcomings in an undertone, her voice rising with each. When she reached 'lecher' and 'squatter,' the words were half a decibel short of a shout. "Touch me again and I'll break your hands."

Steve was past the entrance, but on that one he turned to her. He stood indolently in the sun, half his face shaded by the brim of his hat, one hand on his narrow hip, the band of his handsomely tailored jacket touching his wrist. "Welshing on a debt already, Benedict?"

"You haven't won yet!"

"Yet?" His dark brows rose in a parody of surprise. "Feeling the pressure so soon? Having doubts? A while ago you were so sure."

Her chin assumed that familiar regal angle. A pulse thrummed an uneven rhythm beneath the tanned skin at the hollow of her throat. Every gesture declared she would fight him each step of the way. "Nothing's changed."

Delighted by her spirit, Steve fell a little more under her spell. "Nothing, *yet.*"

Nothing, he amended silently, until she was in his arms.

"You'll lose, Cody. You always have, when it counted."

His lazy look moved over her again, lingering, touching. "Not this time." His voice held the promise of things better left to sultry nights and erotic dreams. "Not when the prize is paradise."

"You're a fool, Steve Cody," Hank drawled with all the contemptuous mockery she could muster.

"Am I?"

"It won't happen."

"Won't it?" A tilt of his head revealed the intensity in his smoldering black gaze. "You'll see," he promised in a low, husky voice. "And when you come to me, you'll know that what began weeks ago could end no other way."

"No."

Steve heard the tremor beneath the strength of her defiance and remembered a moment when he kissed her. A wild and heady ripple of time, ended even as it began. A mercuric nuance of passion so sensual it nearly brought him to his knees. A flicker of response so exquisite a kiss meant to tease left him ravenous and aching for more.

"You kissed me just now. For the space of a heartbeat you met me halfway, with no reservations and the dissension between us forgotten. Deny it if you will, but we both know." His voice never rose above a husky, longing whisper. "God help us, Benedict, now we know."

"There is no we!" She was shaking and barely able to conceal it. "There will never be. And God help *you* if you ever touch me again."

"When I touch you, really touch you, Savannah, it will be because you want me to."

Hank drew a long, grating breath, and still it was not enough, as impotent fury snatched the strength from her lungs. Holding herself perfectly erect, making the most of every scant inch, she looked at him through the cold fires of disdain. "I've heard enough. I'm going to check the horses before the sale begins. You can go to hell."

"I did, but now that I'm back, I think I'll stay." His fingers brushed his hat in the westerner's gallant salute. "Be seeing you around, Miss Benedict, ma'am."

He left her abruptly. Watching him, her body clenched, and rigid, with a look of bewilderment stealing over her face, she found herself admiring the lean, lithe body, the rare, fluid step.

Steve Cody was a handsome man of unexpected depth and perception, with pain hidden in his teasing laugh. Instinct told her it was more than physical, and far worse. In spite of her indignation, she watched him, and wondered.

"I won't do this! I don't care who you are, what you are, or why, you son of a—" She couldn't finish the slur. Insult shriveled in her throat as she recalled the pride and sorrow when he spoke of the lady he called Mother.

"Damn you, Steve Cody." She wanted an enemy who would stay an enemy. One of hard, unblurred lines, with no tenderness and no saving grace. She needed that. It made the battle easier.

Concentrating on putting him from her mind, she ran full tilt into a solid chest. The arms that gripped her, restoring her balance, held her a little too tightly, releasing her reluctantly. And then only when she pushed away.

"Ransome!" Ransome Lawter was tall and lean, and pretty. A ladies' man. The only cowboy on the Rafter B with whom she was not completely at ease. He always watched her, his gaze appraising, sexual speculation clearly written on his face. Yet in the two years he and his brother had worked for her, he'd never done anything to merit a reprimand. Finally, she'd shrugged his interest aside, attributing it to the predatory nature of a born womanizer, and a man too pretty for his own good. Yet reservation lingered, and she found his touch unpleasant. Resisting the urge to brush the memory of it from her arms, she asked, "What are you doing here?"

"Don't worry, Miss Benedict. I'm not crashing the party. I'm here with Sally Pickette, as her guest." His hard look swept over

Hank, dwelling on the flush of her cheeks before settling on the softness of her mouth.

Hank felt the burn of a blush as she wondered how much he'd seen and what he'd heard. "How long have you been here?"

"Not long." Ransome lifted his eyes, following the path Steve had taken. "Long enough. I can see that it doesn't happen again."

Hank was startled by his cold rage. "What are you talking about?"

"Cody." A look seething with an emotion she couldn't fathom returned to her. "Wallie and I can make certain he never touches you again."

"That's enough, Ransome." Hank did not like his proprietary presumption, nor the added threat of his hulking, nearly silent brother. "Steve Cody isn't your concern."

"He put his hands on you."

"That's my business," she said, cutting him short. "You were hired to ride for the brand, not to be my keeper."

"I could help."

"I don't need your help." Stepping back another pace, she looked past him. They were alone. She moved away another step, not really sure why she needed the distance between them. "I think you should go back to Sally. She's sure to be wondering where you are by now."

Ransome clamped his perfect teeth over a belligerent comment as he struggled to accept her veiled command. "You're right, she will be. And since I'm not needed here . . ."

"You aren't." Hank was annoyed, past caring about bruised male egos. She felt no regret for her bluntness as Ransome stalked back the way he'd come. He stepped through the back door and into the empty corral before she relaxed.

It was not easy to put Ransome from her thoughts. She recognized him for a ladies' man to whom women of all ages were fair game. During the time he'd worked for the Rafter B, he'd left a string of broken and bruised hearts scattered across the countryside. It seemed to rankle more each day that hers was not one of them. Yet when she questioned the wisdom of keeping him on at the ranch, there were never concrete grounds for dismissal. For all his weaknesses, he was one of the best with cattle.

Hank worried about Sally, the daughter of a rancher whose spread bordered the Rafter B on the north. She was young and spoiled. But, given Ransome's notoriety, hopefully not so naive.

A bell chimed. A warning the formality of Jubal's sale would begin in five minutes. Abandoning her intention to have one last look at the stock, Hank hurried from the building and crossed the lawn, searching the congregating crowd for Jake and Sandy.

"That's it," Jake declared as the auctioneer laid down his gavel. He was tired and relieved to have done with the pomp and ceremony Jubal instilled in the event. "That's the last one."

"It can't be," Hank protested.

"Check the list, sis, they're all accounted for."

"No, Sandy. The unlisted ones, Jubal's special horses . . ."

"There are none this year," he told her.

"I don't know why Jubal has to go through all this fancy folderol, anyway," Jake groused. "Why can't he just parade the animals out here, say this is what I have, what will you give me? A straightforward sale, and be done with it."

Hank didn't exactly ignore her father, but she'd heard the complaint so many times she knew it verbatim, verse and chorus. "Jubal said there would be one special horse."

"Jubal said," Sandy reminded her, "but he didn't promise. You know as well as I do, that's why his special horses are never listed. He can pull them if the mood strikes. His horses, his prerogative."

"And damned eccentric," Jake put in.

"Isn't that why you like him, Jake?" Sandy rebuked mildly. "Would he be half so interesting if he weren't exactly what he is?"

"Hell, no!"

"At the same time he wouldn't be half so frustrating, either." Hank snapped. "Not by a long shot."

Sandy only shrugged. He knew Hank had come to the sale with her heart set on acquiring Lorelei, the best three-year-old to come through the chutes in some time. He knew that in one of his whimsical gestures Jubal had withdrawn the horse from the sale. He knew why.

"Jubal has decided who will have Lorelei," Hank remarked, before Sandy could comment. When the foreman was silent, she studied him critically. "He has, hasn't he?"

Sandy nodded, with no recourse but the truth.

"Do I know the lucky new owner?"

Sandy hesitated. "You know him."

Following the direction of his gaze, Hank found herself looking across the sales arena, straight into Steve Cody's steady gaze. "The squatter."

As if he read her lips, or her mind, or simply anticipated her reaction, Steve smiled and bowed his head in a rueful gesture, before turning back to Jubal.

"Did he know, Sandy?" she asked, after a moment.

"Not until the sale began."

"How did it happen?"

"Cody's a good stockman. A few minutes in his company and Jubal recognized just how good. You know our distinguished host likes to place his special 'pretties' with the best."

"Bull!" Jake decided to join the discussion. "He's a ro-day-o bum. All he knows about horses is how to keep the seat of his pants in the saddle. Leastwise, part of the time. He knows how to con people pretty good, too. Jubal, for one." A glare caught Sandy. "Present company, for another. You brought him here. Now he's snatched the best of sale away, and right under our noses."

"Jubal made the decision," Sandy addressed father and daughter with an unshakable calm. "But I'm responsible for his being here. I couldn't deny that if I wanted to, and I don't want to. He's a hard worker who's had a run of bad luck. I'd like to see him have a fighting chance to make a go of the Broken Spur. If he does, he deserves to keep the canyon. If he doesn't, then your victory will be earned, and all the better."

"Whose side are you on, anyway?" Jake demanded.

"I ride for the brand, but I live with my conscience." Sandy kept his cool before Jake's heated interrogation. "Anytime you don't like the way I do it, you can tell me to pack up my bedroll and ride out." He looked from Jake to Hank, including her in his proposal. "I have before, I can again."

Sandy fell silent, waiting for their decision.

"Who the hell said anything about packing any bedrolls?" Jake put in gruffly. "And anytime I can't best some young whippersnapper, wheelchair or no wheelchair, is the day I know I'm over the hill. Hell, it's those old he-coons who used to own the canyon that I couldn't corner."

"Sis?" Sandy looked to Hank, his blue gaze probing hers.

Hank said nothing, instead she slipped her arm through his, and smiled.

Sighing, Sandy patted her hand in his fatherly fashion. "Sorry about the horse. I expected Jubal would like Cody, what I didn't expect was how much."

"No one could anticipate Jubal." Or Steve Cody, she was discovering.

Their contention resolved for a time, Jake sat morosely watching as Jubal petted and stoked Lorelei in preparation for turning her over to Steve.

"What are the terms of their agreement on the horse?" Hank inquired as the horse pranced and danced, her blue-black coat glittering under the lowering sun.

"Only Jubal and Cody know." The foreman's answer was spare.

"She's beautiful."

"Yep," Sandy agreed. "He'll do well with her."

Hank knew the odds had just tipped in Steve's favor. A sobering turn of events, requiring thought and careful consideration. "It's time we went back to the Rafter B."

Time to gird for the battle of her life.

After their goodbyes, as they retraced their path over the lawn, a pair of dark, sad eyes watched them go.

From a secret place a second pair watched. Green eyes, glittering with jealous hate.

Chapter 7

"Easy, girl. Ho. I'm not going to hurt you." Steve raked his fingers down the flank of the skittish mare and stroked her hip. His crooning voice calmed her. As he took her through each new step, into each new area of her training, he moved carefully.

Lorelei had proved to be everything Jubal Redmond promised. Quick, responsive and, once she learned to trust Steve, a pet. Even when she shied away from unfamiliar paraphernalia, she was arching her neck to nuzzle at him. Her lips nibbling at his shirt, a whicker, like a purr, rumbling in her throat.

Carefully, with measured caution, Steve never forced her to go where she wasn't ready to go, never pushed when she was tired or fear threatened to slide into terror. He worked with her twice each day. First in the early morning hours before the temperature soared. Then, again, in the last of the day when the scorching heat abated and the sun had not quite set.

As in all things, he never asked as much of the horse as of himself.

"You can rest soon. You've earned it." He continued stroking the quivering horse, teaching her that his hand would be firm, but never hurtful. Dragging his palms down her hip and hock to the tapered foreleg that seemed much too frail to bear her magnificent form, he knelt in the dust of the corral, examining critical tendons, hooves and shoes.

As he worked, more labor of love than chore, he looked neither to the western rim of the canyon nor to the patch of scrubby foliage that had overgrown an ancient path the base of the mesa.

"No company today." His voice never rose above a croon. It mattered little what he said to the horse in the lullaby that couched no commands. Familiarity was the key, and trust, as Steve trained with methods that were his own. Leading her into the barn and her stall, he attended the routine duties that marked the end of another grueling day. As he worked to settle the mare for the night, and made a final check on the other horses that comprised his growing herd, his mind was filled with thoughts of the rider who came without warning, watched from the vantage of the rim, then left as quietly.

Quiet. The land was steeped in it as he crossed in falling darkness to the cabin. Even the soft rhythmic throb of the gas generator that would provide heated running water and an hour or so of light did not penetrate the hush that sifted through the night like liquid velvet. The distant ululating cry of a solitary coyote echoing through the canyon only accentuated its depth.

It should have been lonely for Steve, but he'd never felt so alive, nor so content. After years of wandering as footloose and rootless as tumbleweed, with the next rodeo and the next buckle dictating the direction of his life, he had come home.

A home worth fighting to keep.

His steps were weary and halting, their sound muffled as he climbed the weathered boards of the steps leading to the porch. Each new day and each new challenge brought its degree of renewed strength. Muscles that once protested unaccustomed repetition were striated power. His grip was surer, raw and weeping blisters hardened into protective calluses. He rose each day before the sun. Each day he demanded more of himself, and each day a body and brain once grievously injured responded.

While days slipped into weeks and weeks into months, as he drove himself, doing the work of two, half a man became whole. One by one, difficulties fell away, weakness became strength. And in the greatest gift of recovery, the crippling headaches diminished, then ceased.

He was weary, but there was fulfillment in his weariness, a sense of accomplishment and satisfaction. Pausing for a moment, leaning on a newly constructed balustrade, he recounted his blessing and looked out at the cloistered land.

The moon was full, a perfect burnished pearl climbing the car opy of a cloudless blue-black sky. Stars marching in glittering fo mation seemed impossibly near. A night breeze weaved throug cottonwoods, the tumbling stream splashed and chuckled ove polished stone. Somewhere, tucked away for the night in its nest c sticks, a mourning dove muttered a low lament. Adding its ow harmony, a poor-will called and called again, to be answered b another.

Music of the canyon rising from a well of ancient and abiding s lence.

In reverence he listened, raising his face to the kiss of the breez that swirled over the canyon floor, breathing in its captured fr grance. The scent of leaf and grass, of wild flowers and lingerin sunlight teased him, recalling a memory and a whispered name.

As he pushed away from the rail to seek rest and peace for bod and mind, his gaze was drawn to the western rim, where empt purple shadows gathered in the first of night. His chest rose in long held sigh, yearning stirred. An impossible need.

"Savannah."

Crouching deep in the saddle, with her braid whipping about he Hank dodged a low hanging limb of a tree without slowing Blac Jack's eager pace. In her rush to escape the claustrophobic con fines of the ranch house, her hat had been forgotten. It was just a well, for it would only be lost in this mad dash. She hadn't given th stallion a good run in more than a week, and he flew now, as if h wanted to catch the wind. His excitement was infectious as she ben lower still and gave him his head.

Black Jack was as surefooted as a mountain goat; he knew thi part of the range, perhaps better than she. There was no need t hold him back, nor to care what trails he chose. Giving herself u to the pure joy of a rare and precious freedom, she rode with reck less abandon. As she hadn't ridden since she was a young tombo certain of her invincibility. A naive girl, convinced that as surely a she could master any horse on the ranch, as surely as she rode lik a hussar, once her life was her own nothing and no one could eve rule her again.

With dust boiling from Black Jack's heels and her laughter trail ing behind her, she didn't dwell on frustrations or the disappoint ments of shattered fantasies. She was happy and unfettered, one with the horse, going with him where he would.

Black Jack sailed over fences and small crevices, and each time he was rewarded with his mistress's laughter. Hank would wonder later if she truly hadn't noticed where his trail was taking her. And in her truthful way she would deal with it, but now her surprise was no less real when the ground fell away and the stallion came to a rearing halt. As he pulled and chafed against the bit, eager to turn and run again, Hank stared down on Sunrise Canyon.

Confused by her distraction, the stallion tossed his head and paced, his hooves dangerously close to the crumbling edge. The bunching of his massive muscles warned too late of his panic.

There was no warning as a figure moved swiftly from a cluster of junipers, darting between flailing hooves and the looming brink of the precipice. A strong brown hand caught at the reins, arching the horse's powerful neck, drawing his head down, dragging him back.

"Whoa, boy." A deep voice soothed the frightened animal, as a powerful grip held him in place on surer ground. "Easy. Easy. You don't want to do anything foolish." With each crooning word the massive head fought the reins a little less, muted squeals of terror ceased. As the stallion stood quietly at last, Steve Cody's heaving chest rose in fury, his seething black stare fastened on Hank. "A kinder judgment than I can make of you."

Before she could do more than right herself in the saddle, he moved past the horse's head, his free hand shot out to catch her wrist in a punishing grip. "What the devil do you think you're doing?" His voice never changed, but in his pale face the lines and planes were grim. "If you're hellbent on committing suicide, by God, do it somewhere else."

"Let go." A twist of her wrist failed to break his hold. Her eyes narrowed, her teeth clamped over an angry outburst. As coolly as she could she restated her demand. "I said, let me go."

"Not until you tell me what this mad dash was about." With stone faced care he avoided any mention of the few surreal seconds he'd fought to keep horse and rider from pitching into the canyon. The image of her clinging to the saddle while the ledge crumbled beneath thrashing hooves was too vivid. The abject fear that clawed at him was too raw. A silent cry, his cry, ripped from his lungs only to freeze in terror in his throat, echoed too endlessly in his mind.

"Damn you!" Fear spilled out in an angry rush. "Damn you to hell, Savannah Benedict!" Only his tight grip kept his fingers from trembling on her arm. "If you don't give a penny and change about

yourself, think of what you might have done to the horse. He could
have snapped a leg in a heartbeat.''

"But he didn't," Hank snarled back, her own fury serving as
defense for moments of chaos too swift and terrible for the mind to
hold.

"No, he didn't." The admission was a low growl. "And he
cleared a strand of barbed wire that would have gutted him if he'd
been a half foot lower." And Steve's heart had threatened to burst
from his chest as he watched helplessly from the vantage of a small
tower of stone that rose above the trees lining the rim of the canyon. "What did or didn't happen doesn't make it any less dangerous."

Black Jack had cleared the barbs more times than Hank could
remember, and raced across the range as often. She didn't offer any
defense, she saw no reason for it. "I don't need you to tell me how
to ride, Cody."

"Maybe not." He would concede that she rode like few he'd ever
seen. If he hadn't been so terrified for her, he would have admired
the way she sat the saddle, her lovely body moving in graceful con-
cert with the powerful pounding of the stallion's hooves. If he
wasn't struggling so desperately with his own anger now, he would
be delighted by the threatening storm that seethed in her silver gaze.
"What you need is someone who's man enough to shake some sense
into you."

Hank dismissed the remark with a contemptuous laugh. Instead
of grappling to free herself from his grasp, she leaned nearer, di-
recting the focus from herself. "I suppose you just happened to be
skulking in the bushes today."

"I don't skulk, Benedict. But it was no coincidence that I was
here when you rode in. I knew you would come."

"Ah, you're clairvoyant!" There was an edge of wry amusement in her tone. "Lucky you. When this is over and you've lost the
canyon, you should consider buying a crystal ball and setting up
shop."

"I won't be losing the canyon, or buying a crystal ball," he muttered through gritted teeth. "I wouldn't need to be clairvoyant to
know you'd come. If not today, then tomorrow, or the next day.
Always at sundown."

Hank shook her head in a slow, pitying motion. "I hate to wreck
your arrogant little illusions, but it was Black Jack who chose the
trail. I only came along for the ride."

Steve turned his attention to the horse, stroking the whiskered muzzle with the reins looped over the back of his fist. When he stopped, Black Jack abandoned his usual wariness, butting Steve's shoulder hard enough to move him forward a step.

His sudden smile a flash of white in the weathered darkness of his face, Steve resumed the light, leisurely stroke the stallion begged. The smile faded, but lingered in his eyes as he returned his gaze to Hank's. "Horses. Creatures of habit." Without releasing her, his hand shifted over her wrist, the tips of his fingers measuring the furious rush of her pulse. "Black Jack came to the rim out of habit. Because he'd been here so often before."

Hank didn't dispute what she couldn't. She looked down at him in silence, stoking her anger, willing herself not to care that he knew by the erratic beat of her heart the power he wielded. "So," she drawled, "you hid in the bushes to spy."

Nervy, he mused, allowing his gaze to slide from the willful tilt of her chin and down the slender column of her neck. Letting her feel the weight of his study, he traced the path of a droplet of perspiration that trickled from the base of her throat, then disappeared into the clinging cleavage of her shirt. "No." He let his look climb slowly back to hers. "I came to catch a spy."

"You flatter yourself, Cody," she snapped, the angle of her chin not easing by even a fraction.

"Do I?"

"I have no interest in you, and no need to spy."

His mouth tilted at one corner. The gliding pressure of his fingers at her wrist recorded its pulsing leap. "Don't you?"

Hank was incensed that he blocked her at every turn, that his hand on her arm was gentle, yet as binding as a steel band. It didn't help that she found her nemesis so attractive, nor that in other circumstances she would have liked him, even felt a certain kinship with him. "I told you once before that I'm not one of your buckle bunnies. I come to the rim because it's one of my favorite places, certainly not to stand gazing longingly down at you."

Steve laughed, a hearty, pleasing rumble that would melt stone. Black Jack responded by tossing his head and shifting his stance. Steve held him fast and stood his own ground as Hank's knee and thigh brushed his chest. The heat of her body sent shards of need burning through him like a brand. Need that banked and smoldering fury couldn't restrain.

"It never crossed my mind that you were sitting up here lusting after a broken down has-been rodeo bronc rider, Benedict. But I have to admit I'm pleased it crossed yours."

"I wouldn't be too pleased, if I were you." She stared down with a look that dared any commentary on flags of color that burned her cheeks and turned her eyes the color of wintry moonlight.

"Wouldn't dream of it." In ill concealed amusement he explained, "I didn't dream of it. I assumed you were simply spying on the competition."

"Competition?" Hank was truly puzzled as her mind groped with the lightning changes in him.

"Sure. You don't expect me to think you weren't curious about my method of training horses and the progress I've made?" His hold slipped from her wrist to her palm, the pad of his thumb swept slowly over the line of calluses left by years of sawing reins and demanding labor. They were graceful hands, delicate and well shaped. Better suited for more elegant pursuits—playing a piano, strumming a guitar . . . caressing a man, inflaming him with their tantalizing touch.

"We have a wager." His voice roughened, deepened. "We both have a lot to win, or a lot to lose."

Her hand convulsed in his. A harsh breath grated through her teeth. She pulled her hand away, and this time he let her go, his fingers curling instead around the pommel of her saddle. "Have you forgotten what's at stake if you lose, Savannah?"

"I haven't forgotten anything."

"Is that why you come here? Do you sit on the rim, brooding, thinking of the day when I call your bet?"

Caught in the web of spiraling emotions, Hank stared down at him, discovering that eyes that had seemed black were truly, richly brown, but shades darker than flecks of gold reflecting in the light. The scar, once a whitely sullen reminder of all he'd lost, had darkened and tightened. As it curved over forehead and cheek before disappearing into the fringe of unruly waves visible beneath the band of his Stetson, it had become a symbol of strength. The mark of a warrior. A man who would fight to keep what was rightfully his and revel in the fortunes of victory.

But not this time. Straightening in the saddle with a snap of her spine, infusing her voice with all the disdain she could muster, she said evenly, "You're a dreamer, Cody. And you're a loser."

"Am I?" One brow lifted over narrowed eyes, the angle of his lips never changed.

Hank gave an abrupt inclination of her head. "When the chips are down."

His gaze searched hers, holding it, probing its depths, before gliding over her, lingering lazily with undisguised admiration at every intriguing curve and hollow. "Ah, but you *do* forget. The chips were never quite so beguiling before. What's a silver buckle compared to a woman like you? One who promises paradise with every move and a taste of honey with every smile."

A trill of sound that could have been honest laughter or derision burst from her. "I was wrong, Cody. You're not a dreamer." Her drawl held that haunting hint of the South he'd heard before. "You're a fool. I promise you hell, not paradise. Venom, not honey."

"If I win."

"You won't."

"But you're not quite so sure anymore, or you wouldn't be here, would you, Savannah?"

"Lord love a duck!" She laughed, a pretty, smoky note, as false as her icy smile. "Are you deaf? I just told you it was Black Jack who chose this path..."

"And you came along for the ride," Steve finished for her. The withering look she slanted at him only sent his blood pressure off the scale. *God help me,* he thought, this is more than I wanted. With the sun at her back, its light marking every regal line of her body in fire, she was magnificent. Haughty and willful, and stubborn to the end. Standing her ground, when the ground was crumbling beneath her feet.

Was it a tactic she learned from Jake, or the only weapon a very young, untried Savannah had possessed to use against him? "Is this how you looked? Is this what it was like for you?"

"What?" A frown scored her brow as she lost the thread of his conversation again.

"Is this how you looked when you were caught with your hand in the cookie jar? Proud and regal, so unwavering, and so innocent. Even with cookie crumbs here." With his thumb he retraced the curve of her upper lip and tugged at the enticing fullness of the lower.

A second too late, Hank turned her head away, refusing to acknowledge the quiver of sensation that began deep in the pit of her stomach, then, as quickly, threatened to become an avalanche. He was the enemy. He had to stay the enemy. If she couldn't keep that perspective, it would be so easy to fall under his spell, forgetting everything but the strange longing he could quicken with a touch. A response, she had already learned, so powerful it wove itself into and through anger, until there was nothing left of it. Nothing but the wanting.

She'd walked among men, worked with them, lived the life they lived. Yet this was new to her. No man frustrated or bested her at every turn as he had. Only Steve Cody made her feel as she did now.

"No." She didn't realize she'd spoken aloud, she knew only that she couldn't let this happen. The next step would be falling in love, the surrender of that part of herself she kept inviolate. A vulnerability she couldn't risk. "I can't do this."

Hearing the utter panic in her, fearing another wild, reckless ride, Steve caught the reins tighter before she snatched at them to wheel the stallion around. Holding fast, he refused to give ground, refused to let her run.

Settling the horse with a low command, he reached for her, turning her face to him. "What can't you do, sweetheart?"

"Let me go!"

"Not until you tell what's bothering you." The grin had long disappeared, his eyes were still, bottomless. "Why did you ride across the range as if the devil himself were chasing you?"

"That's none of your business." She couldn't bear the intensity she saw, the caring.

"I'm making it my business."

"Don't." She stared out over the land her father coveted.

"Too late, Savannah." The name she heard so little was a low, sweet sound falling from his lips. A caress as tangible as his hand at her face. "Far too late."

"We're enemies," she reminded him tensely. "I've sworn to do everything in my power to see that you lose what you want most in the world." With each word her voice grew huskier, lower. "So why do you care?"

"This." Steve hooked a palm around her nape, drawing her down to him. "This is why I care."

"No," Hank cried, but in no more than a desperate whisper.

"Yes."

His mouth barely touched her. His lips only sipped at the rich promise of hers. But the gentle contact was enough that he felt the soft, unwilling tremor of yielding, enough that he heard the slow, shuddering sigh of a lost battle.

Giving her one last choice, he turned his mouth from hers, drawing away just enough to stare once again into the tortured

storm of her silver eyes. Relinquishing his token captivity, his hand
slid from her nape, returning to her cheek, then traced a path
downward, as light as a whisper, as undemanding. Circling the
slender column of her throat, his fingertips swept over the fragile
flesh. One by one they plundered the hollow pulsing beneath their
touch. One by one they curled into his palm, until his shaking, fisted
hand fell away.

Withdrawing, he released the reins. Black Jack was free, she
could run or stay.

Holding her, keeping her only with his gaze, he waited.

She stared down at him, her breasts rising with the ragged rhythm
of each hard drawn breath. Her mind was reeling and her body
trembled. All her life her loyalties had been clear-cut, above challenge. But neither rigorous training nor the harsh existence in which
danger was a constant, and survival and success were measured by
the same unwavering rules, had prepared her for a time like this.
When nothing was as it should be.

She had no concept of danger that threatened the intrinsic val-
ues of her life, nor an enemy who looked at her with naked need.
There was no defense when his lips were soft and clever, and his kiss
sweet and wild.

In the aftermath of Jubal's celebration, she'd spent days convincing herself the frisson of response stirred by a stolen kiss was
shock and anger, not passion. She wanted to believe it now, but
twice judged shattered lie.

With brutal Benedict honesty she admitted that it was neither
shock nor anger that swept every coherent thought from her mind.
The inescapable truth was that Steve Cody's touch left her weak and
confused, with age-old loyalties forgotten. His kiss kindled desire,
leaving her yearning for more.

With only his mesmerizing look he kept her when she should fly.

She wanted to go. Common sense demanded she should. Looking to the reins dangling over Black Jack's massive neck, she willed
herself to take them up, to dash like mad to safety and sanity.

A thundering heart that cared nothing for safety and sanity said
no.

She was pale, her eyes dark and brooding in the pallor, when she
turned again to him. Her thoughts, her struggle, were written on her
face, and in her melancholy cry.

"Steve."

Damning himself and Jake Benedict, Steve lifted her from the
saddle. She was nearly weightless in his arms. As he let her body

slide the length of his, he realized that in the weeks since he'd come to the canyon, she'd grown smaller, and for all her tenacious strength there was a fragility in her slenderness. There were shadows and fine lines drawn on her face, left by restless fatigue. An accepted condition, more often than not, in ranch life. One he discovered he loathed when it was Savannah who wore the bruise of sleeplessness beneath her eyes.

Regarding her silently, he drew a knuckle over the faint blue marks, as if with tenderness he could erase them. "Savannah." Her name was a hushed, strangled sigh as his lips followed the path his tender touch had taken. "Sweet Savannah."

Drawing her closer, bending to her, his mouth dipped to hers. She was pliant and quiet in his arms, her lips were warm but unyielding. He kissed her long and hard, with a building passion, decimating every faltering denial. With the last falling around her like a broken chalice, uttering a sigh of longing and need she opened to him, yielding more than her lips as his tongue teased and stroked, demanding entry.

Lost in the plunging, rhythmic caress, her breath grew shallow. Banked fires that smoldered white-hot burst into hotter flames. Amid a wild, smothered cry, her palms skipped over his chest, to his throat, to his nape, clasping the crisp waves that fell too long and shaggy over the collar of his shirt. Holding him, needlessly keeping him where he wanted to be, like an unskilled wanton she lured him deeper into the rich, dark secrets of her kiss.

No woman in his life had ever been like Savannah Benedict. None so elusive, yet so innocently provocative. None was so magnificent an opponent, nor surrendered so completely.

He wanted her. So badly it was frightening—for himself, for her.

"Savannah." Catching her wrists, his clasp curling about them like manacles, he drew them to his chest. In husky reverence as she looked up at him, he confessed. "Sweet Savannah, I didn't know."

"That you could do this to me?" She moved away the little distance his embrace would allow. The tips of her breasts still brushed his chest with each agitated word; as she swayed unconsciously, the line of her thigh was only inches from his. An exquisite intimacy hovering on the brink. An impossible taste of Eden, neither unremembered nor redeemed, bittersweet for having been.

Her eyes were smoky, bleak with the first of innocence lost. "You can't be blamed for this, not alone. You couldn't know that with a touch and a kiss, I would forget this is all part of a high stakes game and respond as if it were real."

Steve had no answer for her, he wasn't sure what had happened himself. He knew he wanted her, as any virile, red-blooded man would want her. But was this more than a game? More than sexual conquest?

Had she touched his heart, or was it only that she was a woman beyond his experience? "I don't want to hurt you." That much he believed was true. "I don't want either of us to be hurt."

"I know." Her smile was filled with regret. "But one of us will be. We must. It was in the cards from the first."

"Why?" Steve demanded flatly. "Why can't Jake Benedict be content with what he has?"

Hank shook her head thoughtfully. "Only Jake can answer that. I've never really known. Perhaps he lost the canyon when he was bested in a deal. Maybe it's truly that it sits within the border of the Rafter B—something that isn't his, something beyond his control, eluding him for years. A terrible prospect for a man who controls everyone and everything around him."

"Everyone except the women in his life," Steve suggested.

"In one way or another, he controls us, as well."

"Only because you let him."

"Does it matter how or why? If we do what he expects and demands, it's still control. When he had his stroke and needed me, I left law school without a backward look, and came home where he wanted me."

"Have you ever regretted coming back, Savannah?"

"No. I understand now that this is where I belong. Where Jake Benedict's daughter has always belonged." Her tone changed, her husky voice grew pensive. "But sometimes..." Shrugging away from his embrace, she abandoned a mental quest for words that evaded her. "Sometimes I wonder."

Feeling incredibly lost without the heat of her body against his, catching her braid he coiled it around his hand. Fascinated by its soft shimmer, letting it slide like a silken rope through his palm, he barely resisted a consuming urge to draw her back into his arms. "Would you come back?"

"Would I come back? An odd way to phrase it." She lifted her head, studying him curiously. "Do you mean to Savannah, or the university?"

"Either. Both." *To my arms, to begin again what can't end until we resolve it.* The words rang hollowly in his mind, words better left unsaid for now. "Savannah." He spoke of the city, wondering if there was significance in the name. "Is that where you studied?"

"I lived there for a while, with my mother's family. I share its name in remembrance of her childhood there, but I studied in Athens. At the University of Georgia." She smiled absently as she recalled another time, another life. "As it turned out, it amounted to a prolonged sabbatical from the ranch."

That explained the hint of the South he heard in her speech, and the elegant gentility she never quite succeeded in hiding with her rough wrangler's clothing. "My mother was born in Charleston," he heard himself saying. "My father met her there when he served a short stint in the navy."

Hank was surprised at this fragment of information. Not that his mother was a South Carolinian, but that he offered it at all. Steve Cody said little about himself. "Did you visit Charleston with her?"

"Once," he answered succinctly, not venturing the explanation that it was in search of a second opinion to refute the diagnosis of a terrible illness. A death sentence that would be carried out by degrees, levying a slow and agonizing mental imprisonment with its cruel irony. A sentence most abhorrent, but one with which all of many consultants would finally concur.

"I was nine," he said as the first silence of sunset began to envelop them. "Just nine, but I never forgot what it was like."

"Then you know it's beautiful, but a whole different world. I understand now that Jake knew better than I where I belonged, and why."

"You'd just begun law school?"

"I was only a week short of completing the second year."

"But you hated it."

"Of course I didn't. I loved every minute of it. Every facet, even the driest facts."

"Then tell me what Jake knew better than you?"

"I told you, he knew I belonged in the West, not the South."

"Something you weren't capable of discovering for yourself?" Before she could lash out at the innuendo, he pushed on, "Or was it something having a law degree would have prevented?"

"You're being ridiculous."

"Then you would have come back to the ranch, no matter what?"

"Eventually."

"Eventually. That means later, rather than sooner?"

"Perhaps," Hank conceded, wondering where he was taking this.

Steve picked his hat from the ground where it had fallen, unnoticed, long ago. Turning the brim in his hand, watching dust drift from it in a cloud, he muttered an uncomplimentary judgment of selfish and ambitious men like Jake Benedict. "Maybe you'd better explain to me again what prompted Jake to call you home, Savannah."

"Can you not look at Jake and see he needed me?"

"Why?" Steve asked bluntly.

"To run the Rafter B."

"Sandy couldn't?"

"Of course he could!" Stepping blindly into a skillfully laid trap, Hank hurried to defend her foreman. "There's nothing on the Rafter B Sandy can't handle."

"And no reason for Jake to call you home when he did. He used his illness, playing on your love and sympathy to get what he wanted. He's doing it now. Using his health as leverage, and you as his intermediary to get what he wants." He clasped her shoulders in emphasis. "We don't have to do this, Savannah. We don't have to fight."

Hank backed away from him, shaking her head as she went. "You don't understand. You don't know what it's like to watch a strong, virile man waste away. You don't know how it feels to see an insightful mind trapped in a crippled body. If you did, you'd understand that I'd do anything to make him even a little happier.

"If that means winning our wager and the canyon," her voice thinned, "then I'll do anything I can to win it for him."

"Anything?"

"Anything."

"I'll remember that." From arm's length, he brushed a stray tendril from her face, letting his fingers follow the line of her jaw to her chin. With a knuckle, he traced the undercurve of her full lower lip, catching his breath when the soft flesh trembled beneath his touch. "Will you remember this?"

"I'll remember." She wouldn't deny what had happened between them. "But don't make the mistake of thinking it changes anything."

Her warning given, she backed away, stopping only when she felt Black Jack at her back. With a quick turn and a step into the stirrup, she vaulted into the saddle. "Coming here was a mistake. I won't say I'm sorry, but none of this should have happened."

A rush of tears threatened, she fought them back and tried not to see how handsome he was.

In three steps he could have her out of the saddle and back in his arms. But he stood his ground, understanding Savannah more than she knew.

"I won't come again."

"I know." A smile curled the corners of his mouth, yet left his eyes untouched. "Jake wanted sons. He's luckier than he knows, having a daughter like you."

Hank's eyes glittered brilliantly an instant before she launched the stallion into a full gallop. Dust churned thickly beneath mighty hooves, and soon it was all that marked their passage.

Steve waited until she disappeared. Then, accompanied by the memory of the gentle lady for whom he would have sacrificed anything, he retraced the hidden path to the floor of the canyon.

Chapter 8

The last of a blood red sun slipped below the horizon. In less than a minute from the time it touched the earth, bathing the land in infinite shades of fire, it was gone. Long shadows pooling in sooty puddles grew longer, thinner, fading to purple. Then blue, then gray. Blending with an encompassing darkness, rising up to embrace the fall of twilight.

Sundown. Time of illusion. When the stark beauty of a stark land became a sensuous play of ever changing textures. When there was languor in a natural calm, when a breathless hush that was muted sound, never its absence, grew deeper still.

A light switched on, turning a bunkhouse window into a tiny beacon guiding the tardy and the weary to their beds. Muffled laughter drifted from sheltering shadows, while cigarette smoke wove a lazy thread through lingering scents of the day. From a little distance away a guitar played. A low and unfettered strum, a soothing, tuneless melody.

Serenity, the hard won reward at the end of a fruitful day. One that escaped Savannah Henrietta Benedict as she paced the veranda that swept the length and breadth of the sprawling ranch house.

She'd paid her dues to the day. First to begin, logging her fair share in the saddle, collecting her portion of dust, earning her quota of secret aches. Last to ride in, last to topple gracelessly from the saddle, stumbling on protesting legs to the stable.

Her relief and gratitude were beyond measure when Jeffie dashed to take her mount from her, offering his services with the blushing gallantry of an adolescent crush. Now, an hour later, dust and aches sluiced away by a steamy shower, the dazed exhaustion had been blunted. But nagging concerns that scratched at her mind remained, compelling this restless rambling.

She paced, absorbed, on the ragged edge. Oblivious to the coming night, to music and laughter. Unaware of the quiet step at her back.

"Savannah."

With a strangled response, she whirled, her freshly washed hair flying damply about her before falling again to her waist. One hand curled at the furious lurch of her heart, the other clawed at a banister for support. "What—"

The question faltered on her lips as Bonita stepped through the doorway leading from the kitchen. This gently determined intruder was small and pleasantly plump, a woman with the dark hair and dusky skin of her Mexican-Indian heritage. A graceful lady who moved with a step more suited to dancing than keeping house or cooking. A face avouching the acclaim of her name was scored with lines of distress the erratic light of a lantern couldn't erase.

"What is it, Bonita? Is it Jake?" Hank's tone was sharp with alarm. "Has something happened to Jake?"

"All is well with Señor Jake," Bonita assured with an implacable poise. "He plays chess with Sandy."

Alarm quieted. Worry that was a constant companion slipped into its secret hideaway, to sleep again its light sleep, waiting to wake another time. A captured breath whispered from Hank, her tone gentled. "If all is well, then why the frown?"

"You, Savannah Benedict." The handsome woman crossed her arms over generous breasts, her scowl unrelenting. "You make me frown."

Hank laughed, an expression of relief more than humor. In her distraction she'd forgotten Bonita always called her Savannah when displeased with her. Apparently her displeasure was monumental this time. "Oh, dear, what have I done now?"

"It's what you haven't done, and what your momma is going to say to me when she sees what I've let happen to her daughter."

"What I haven't done?" Hank was puzzled by Bonita's oblique scolding. "If I haven't done something, why would you be blamed?'' There was no need to add it was unlikely Camilla Neal Benedict would be seeing her daughter, or Bonita, in the immediate future.

"Look at you!" In a imperious gesture Bonita directed Hank's attention to herself. "You do the rough work harder and longer than ever before. You do not sleep. You sit without speaking, with your head somewhere else." A grave note in her voice, Bonita intoned Hank's cardinal sin. "And no matter what I cook to tempt your appetite, you eat less and less. I watch you disappear in mind and body, of course I worry, and sometimes I wonder if it is the sickness.''

"The sickness?" The housekeeper pronounced it as if it were an epidemic, yet Hank had heard nothing of it. The ranch hands and their families, always notoriously healthy, were healthy still. "What on earth are you talking about? Everyone on the ranch is fine and dandy, including me. Especially me. No fever, no chills." Hank held out her arms. A token gesture, for below the turned back sleeves of her shirt, only her wrists and forearms were visible, the sun darkened flesh darkened more by the dim light. "No rash."

"Ha!" Bonita tossed her head and stamped her foot. "I speak of a fever of the heart, not the body. Of longing and passion, not chills and rash."

"Fever of the—" Hank broke off with a laugh. "Oh, Bonnie, who is there here to give me a fever of the heart?"

"There are those who would like to, but none who has. This I know. So I think I am mistaken, then I remember the papers."

With her laughter lingering, Hank leaned against a railing, waiting for the rest of Bonita's lecture.

"When I remember them, at first I am relieved. Then, when I think on it some more, I worry again. First you wither away to almost nothing, then the little that's left will be torn between them." Black brows arched like cathedrals, accentuating lines that marked a broad, patrician forehead. "Ay, yi, yi! What will become of you?"

Another sweeping gesture, another frown, and the little woman lapsed into Spanish. Eloquent verbal hand wringing, in a torrent pouring from her so swiftly it would have been unintelligible to any but the most fluent.

"Bonita." Hank caught a fluttering hand, clasping it closely. "You aren't making sense. What papers? I will be torn? By whom?"

The question spurred another torrent of Spanish, as rapid as the first. Hank knew the language, she spoke it with moderate facility. But this was beyond her. "English, Bonnie," she said, soothing the agitated woman. "English, please."

When Bonita fell silent, catching her breath in great gasping breaths, Hank asked again, "What papers?"

"The newspapers!" Bonita's disdain was one reserved for the thick headed. "The old and yellow ones with the face of the handsome man on them. The papers you should know by heart."

Back copies of the newspaper stories on Steve Cody. The original had arrived at the ranch and had been read when current, then dismissed. Until she'd realized the charismatic, tragic rodeo star and the squatter of Sunrise Canyon were one and the same. A friend from college who worked with a news service managed to scrounge them from somewhere, sending originals rather than copies.

"Bonnie, the newspapers have nothing to do with my distraction or my appetite. But you're right," Hank admitted. "I have been working harder than ever. I'm just tired and jumpy. It happens." She meant to placate the little woman. "And though we're mostly too obstinate to admit it, even to a Benedict."

Bonita made a derisive sound, her ever arching brows threatened to lift to the sleek, smooth line of her tightly coiffed hair. "You've worked hard before, and managed to eat and sleep."

"This time is different. This time there's more at stake."

"Your heart."

"The canyon."

"The canyon! Always the canyon! Is it worth this?" Bonita demanded.

"It is to Jake."

"And to you?" Flashing eyes studied Hank critically. "Is it worth it to you, Savannah?"

Savannah. Steve had called her Savannah. She wanted to think that explained why her startled thoughts had been of him when Bonita called to her through the gathering darkness. But, again, an unyielding honesty would let her believe nothing but the truth. And the inescapable truth was that in a short time he had become a part of the fabric of her life.

Releasing Bonita, Hank stared over the cloistered land. Her restless mind was a morass of strange longings and niggling doubts.

Muttering annoyance at Jake, and men at large, Bonita touched Hank's shoulder and stroked her drying hair. "Only you can say, Savannah. Only you can judge its worth."

"No." Hank's shoulders rose and fell in a dejected sigh.

"Yes!"

"But I don't know, Bonita."

"You will." The housekeeper spoke with an assurance based on years of watching the youngest Benedict ply her strength and fair-minded vision.

Bonita Sanchez had come to the Rafter B only a matter of months before Camilla returned to the South, taking her teenage daughter with her. A short time, but more than was needed to see the battle waged over the young girl, the veritable tug-of-war that pulled her first one way and then another. Enough to see the young Savannah handled situations and herself with a dignity and maturity far surpassing her age. Indeed, she'd thrived on the duality of her life, becoming the best she could be in her roles as Jake's top hand cum substitute son and Camilla's elegant and accomplished daughter.

"History," the small woman grumbled. "It does repeat itself."

But the young girl torn between mother and father was a woman now. A strong woman, and for all her inexperience in matters of the heart, the lessons of youth made her a wise one. "When the time comes, you will know which choices are yours, and which you must make."

"If it comes to that, *if* the final choice is mine, no matter which I make, someone will be hurt." Hank didn't look away from the fading color reflected on the eastern horizon.

"That's life. You should know it well, for you've made such choices before. When you left the ranch to go south with Camilla, Señor Jake was hurt. When he needed you to return to the ranch, it hurt to leave your studies. And though she always knew you would leave her someday, it hurt Camilla to lose you so soon, to see your studies cut short, and to live with the knowledge that the law degree you wanted so much would never be." Bonita paused and shrugged. "Choices. They hurt. We survive."

"Survival isn't always enough."

"True, it isn't always enough." With a touch Bonita turned the younger woman to face her. "This time you must be selfish. You must do something you've never done before, choose the path that's best for you."

"What's best for the Rafter B and Jake is best for me," Hank declared with new conviction. "This is merely a lot of speculation, based on a few sleepless nights and a lost appetite."

"Based on the reason for the sleeplessness and..."

"Only because, for once, I have doubts about what Jake wants," Hank cut short the housekeeper's contention. "Steve Cody's had his share of bad luck, the Broken Spur is his chance to turn it around. What right do Jake and I have to try to spoil that chance, simply because Jake wants the borders of the Rafter B intact?"

"I can't answer, Savannah. I know what I think, no more."

"What you think is that we should let the man be. Give him his chance without complicating the matter," Hank supplied for her.

"Do you want me to say yes to ease your own guilt for the same feelings?" Bonita cocked her head, watching Hank like a curious bird. "Would you feel less disloyal to Señor Jake if someone else shared your view? If so, then yes, I think the Benedicts have enough. Enough land, enough success, enough prestige, and some should be left for those that deserve it."

Hank nodded almost absently. "Sandy does too. So does Jubal. Neither of them has actually spelled it out, but there are little things they've said, things they've done."

"You don't seem disturbed by this defection."

"It isn't defection. When the chips are down, Sandy rides for the brand, and Jubal is a friend." *When the chips are down.* The words echoed in Hank's mind.

When the chips were down the gamble would be over. Someone would win, someone would lose. She had no concept of what might follow. No idea where she would stand.

As quickly as the latter thought arose, she put it aside. "I'm a Benedict. Like Sandy, when the chips are down, I ride for the brand."

"Even with a fever of the heart?" Bonita drew a breath, waiting for her answer. "You would turn your back on passion?"

"There is no fever, Bonita. And certainly no passion. What you've seen is an attack of conscience. If I can persuade Jake to back off, give Cody some time to prove himself or to fail…" Hank left the thought hanging. After a moment, as if she'd regained a lost thread of conversation, she added, "If he fails, then Jake will have his wish later rather than sooner."

"If he succeeds?" Bonita posed the other side of the proposition.

"Then he succeeds, and that's all there is to it. The canyon has never been a lawful part of the Rafter B, and as you said, we survived. Jake survived. God and his health willing, he will again."

"And you, Savannah?"

"I'll be fine. I *am* fine. No fever." She laughed, and didn't know the melodic note rang hollowly in the night. "No rash. And Hank, not Savannah, will go on as she did before."

"You're sure?" Bonita regarded her steadily.

"Very." Hank's smile was small, but real. "Thanks for caring, it helps knowing that you do, and that you understand."

"There are some things left from dinner in the warming oven." With the trenchant instincts of a mother hen, the housekeeper suggested hopefully, "I could set them out before I leave."

"Thank you, but no. Maybe later." Though Bonita was an excellent cook, Hank knew the food would not be eaten.

"Will you sleep?"

"Yes." Another white lie, for peace of mind for her self-appointed guardian.

"Then I'll say good-night." There was skepticism laden in the closure, but Hank's mild assurances left Bonita no other recourse.

"Good night, Bonita."

The housekeeper's footsteps had fallen silent, and her swishing skirts disappeared around a corner as Hank turned away. There was silence again, and now unrelieved darkness. Lost in her unsettled thoughts, she faced the east and Sunrise Canyon.

From the shadow of a tree at the edge of the walk, green eyes stared at the veranda and the woman bathed in the pale light of the lantern. Hungry eyes. Angry eyes. The eyes of a man filled with lust.

The watcher was so still, creatures of the night had long since taken up their nocturne. In the midst of their song, he did not move, even his breathing was too shallow to be detected. But beneath his stillness, his mind was alive with hate and hate filled plans.

The woman he coveted crossed to the lantern, bending to it, with the light radiant on her face. His chest jerked in a breath drawn in a ragged groan. He made no other move, no other sound, as he lapsed again into stillness. When the veranda was dark and the rustle of her footsteps echoed over the stone, he waited. His silent breath quickened once more at the muted thud of the door snapping shut and the grate of the lock sliding into place.

Sleepy laughter drifted from the bunkhouse, making the night seem lonelier, the veranda emptier. He did not move. Like a predator checking the wind, he lifted his head, staring, waiting, as he had many nights before. Waiting for the light to spill from her bedroom window.

The glass was curtained. Hank was only a vague moving shadow against it. But in his mind there was more.

When the single square was dark, and the ranch house descended into a final hush, he moved away. His face was bathed in sweat, his body shook. In a voice hoarse from the lust of his imagining, he muttered a single word. A hateful name. "Cody."

Steve was whistling as he walked from the ranch house to the stables. In the paling dawn the day was still cool, with only an underlying hint of the heat that was to come.

His tread was steady on the familiar path. His mind filled with the order of his routine as he stepped through the open door of the stables. A horse whickered, then tramped restlessly in its stall. Lorelei.

Breathing in the pleasant scent of hay, Steve chuckled. "Eager to get started, are you? Can I take that to mean you're not going to turn mulish on me today?"

The mare was gleaming ebony, rippling darkness moving within the pearly shades, dancing and pacing nervously along the borders of her small stall. Steve considered lighting the lantern, then dismissed the thought. Electricity for the stables was on his list of improvements, but that was for someday in a far distant future. And who knew when someday and the money would come? Anyway, he liked the softness of the morning, the gradual changes he would miss in the sudden switching on of a light.

He moved away to begin his chores, then turned back. Something about Lorelei disturbed him. She seemed uneasy rather than eager. Stepping to the door of the stall, he reached out to scratch the favorite spot along her jaw. She shied away, nostrils flaring, eyes rolling and white.

"Ho, girl. Easy. What's wrong? Something bothering you?" Disturbed, Steve looked around. With the exception of Lorelei, the stables were quiet. Too quiet? Puzzled, he looked again. Nothing, he thought, and was on the verge of attributing Lorelei's low-keyed frenzy to an aberrant mood when a blur of color caught his attention. Blue. Pale blue, where there should be none. The sleeve of a shirt. "What the—"

He was rounding to face a rushing flurry of scuffled sound when massive arms closed around him from the back, dragging his own arms behind him. Hands clamped like vises over his wrists as a form burst from the next empty stall. The blur of blue registered only a millisecond before a brutal backhand snapped his head aside. A second followed. Then another, and another, each sickening thud accompanied by a guttural grunt of satisfaction.

Shock and reality coalescing, Steve fought to pull free. Calling on every part of his regained strength, he strained against a cage of bone and flesh. The binding clinch was impervious, the long, ape-like arms as relentless as steel. He was trapped, at the mercy of faceless marauders.

Who? Why?

In his helplessness, the questions reverberated in his mind. Concentrating on answers, he reverted instinctively to old habits. Pain and anger were pushed to the back of his mind. Nothing mattered so much as the riveting resolve to know these men as more than a collection of perceptions. More than the Ape and Blue Shirt.

Reeling and groggy, with every blow he struggled to focus on the man in blue. Paying for each desperate effort with ever more vicious retaliation. Fists pummeled his body, low and hard, brutally smashing at bone, bruising soft tissue. On and on.

Time crawled.

Seconds were hours. Minutes, an eternity. Steve struggled stubbornly against unjust odds. Until he conceded, at last, this was a fight he couldn't win, that his only hope was to survive.

A man who spent a lifetime living by his wits, who walked away from broncs he couldn't ride, not in defeat, but with a resolve to have his day, accepted the inevitable. His body went slack. His mind closed down, silencing the echoing questions. Waning consciousness stuttered briefly, then snuffed out.

The frenzied beating continued. In maniacal rage there was no mercy for the battered and bloodied man who was dead weight in his captor's arms.

"Enough!" The deep voice boomed through the hastening morning. "Stop. No more."

"Like hell!" the smaller of the men snarled. "Not til I teach the son of a bitch to keep away from her."

"I said stop!" The command, spurred by alarm, climbed a decibel above the frightened thrashing of stabled horses. "I said I'd help you rough Cody up a little to warn him off, but I won't be party to beating him to death."

"You're in this now, too deep to back out." The labored retort was punctuated by a solid, jolting blow.

"I said no!" Letting Steve crumple to the ground in an inert heap, the massive hands that had held him shot out, closing around a blue clad arm raised to strike again. "I won't let you do this. Not again."

"You can't stop me."

The grip that could break a bone as easily as a match stem tightened savagely. "I just did."

"What if he saw our faces? He could have recognized us." Blue Shirt was wheedling, coaxing the simpler man to his view.

"He didn't." The stolid answer rang with rare conviction.

"You don't know that, and we can't take the chance. We can't just leave him."

"I can." The massive man turned his back on his brother and only friend and walked away.

"Wait." The call was a command, in a tone that expected obedience. The broad back neither flinched nor hesitated in the retreat from the stables. Command turned to a whine. "You can't ride out now."

"I can." Leading his horse from the far side of the barn, the huge man stepped into a saddle that barely contained his bulk. "I am," he growled with a new finality. He walked the bay a little distance away, then eased into a steady trot.

Staring after him, stunned belligerence withering, Blue Shirt found a new direction for his rage. But not before he finished what he'd begun. First he opened the stall that held Lorelei, swinging the gate wide. Then he returned to his victim. Kneeling, he caught Steve by the hair, bringing a swollen and bleeding face to his to whisper a final warning. "A message from the lady, squatter. Clear out, or next time will be worse."

Dropping Steve's head, Blue Shirt stood and backed away. With a snarled curse and a parting kick, he raced to his own horse. Wheeling the animal in a neck breaking circle, he whipped it into a furious race after the bay.

The thunder of hooves faded, after a while the stables were silent. The frightened horses had ceased their agitated clamor when Steve moaned and stirred. Lightning ricocheted off the walls of his skull, leaving a steady thud of agony in its wake. He lay as he was, not daring to move, not sure where he was, or what had happened. All he knew was that he was alive, and as the thudding in his skull became a familiar, mind jarring timpani, he wasn't so sure that was good.

Forcing himself to take stock, he realized his face was stiff and sore and his ribs ached nearly as much as his head. His eyes were swollen, he felt the taut, pulsing pressure in blood filled tissue. When he strove to blink away the dirt and grit clinging to his eyelids, a red haze clouded his vision. When he tried again, he realized his lashes were heavy and clotted.

With a grim frown and a set jaw, he wedged his arms beneath him and tumbled on his back. Bare rafters loomed over him, solid shapes floating in a hazy mist.

"Here we go again." Steve hardly knew he'd spoken as pain dredged old memories from his mind.

He knew a horse hadn't kicked him, but he also knew he was on the verge of another concussion. With a sense of déjà vu and gritted teeth, he made himself sit erect. Arms clasped about his middle, he held himself tightly, closing out the punishing pain. He'd been in enough serious fist fights to recognize the pattern, and knew the damage to look for. Probing fingers skimmed clumsily but gingerly over his ribs, drawing a careful sigh and a nod from him.

"Nothing broken." The determination was slurred through cracked and puffy lips, in a voice made hoarse by the hacking edge of a hand to his throat. In a flash of memory, he saw the slashing hand, a blue cuff fastened at the wrist. A disembodied arm, with no substance behind it, no identity. But he knew the vagaries of a rattled brain, and couldn't trouble himself with it now. His immediate concern was physical. His hands brushed over his ribs again, this time more firmly. Wincing at his own thoroughness, he finally sighed and relaxed. "Bruised. Maybe cracked, but not displaced."

With that assurance he began the torturous climb to his knees. The third time was the charm. Cold sweat beading his face and running in rivulets down his body, he knelt there in a scattering of hay and dust, body hunched and swaying like an ancient cripple. Wondering why he tried, yet knowing that he must, he reached out, locked his fingers around a supporting column and dragged himself to his feet. Ignoring the nausea that churned at the back of his throat, he took a tottering step. Pausing tiredly, drawing a long, slow, careful breath, he took another step. Then another, and another.

Setting his sights on the open door of the stable, and the path that would lead to the house, he staggered along. Bending to the pain, arms clutching it close, he forgot all but the need to put one foot in front of the other. No step was too small, and every inch an accomplishment that brought the rictus of a gaunt grin to his lips. After a time that to Steve was eternal, his labored steps brought him to his first goal. Half falling, half walking, he passed through the roughhewn portal, clinging to it only long enough to get his bearings. Flinching from the blast of light, he stumbled on.

The ground was uneven, heat rose from it in waves, clawing at him, sucking the breath from wounded lungs. He grew dizzier, his vision worsened. No effort could wipe away the fog, yet he tried, pushing himself blindly on, until his legs refused.

Head down, swaying like a broken willow, he knew he wouldn't make it to the house. A sweet and poignant yearning welled within him. As his body ached for the succor of his makeshift bed, his mind longed for the haunting scent of roses. The soothing ambience that seemed as much an integral part of the house as shingle and board.

"Roses." The sound, more groan than word, whispered from his lips. "Imagining." He blinked at the darkness that reached for him, muttering, "Only imagining."

Like broken springs, his knees buckled, rocks ground into flesh and bone as he knelt in the sun. Lifting his face to the great white ball, feeling its fire, he knew he had to get up. He had to go on. He tried to rise. Once, twice. Again. He couldn't.

"Tired." Shoulders that had gained new breadth bowed under an invisible weight. His head rocked in a slow rhythm, side to side. Denial. But of what, he'd forgotten. "So tired."

Even in forgetting, he meant to sit only long enough to gather his thoughts and recoup his strength. "Rest." He tried to nod. "Only a minute."

He didn't know that before the words were finished, he crumpled into a heap, his face in the earth, dust stirring in fits and starts with each erratic respiration. In his delirious memory a pair of worn boots paced before him at eye level, a curious star carved in one heel winked and laughed at him. Hot breath touched his ear, burning, spewing hate.

A message from the lady . . .

His hand curled, loose soil sifted through his fingers, then he was still, lying beneath the burning sun. "No."

Hank hurried across the veranda and down the steps. A meeting with Jake had run long, and she was getting a late start. She would have to push herself and her horse if she was going to check the herd on the north range and return before dark. The truck would make quicker work of it, but this roughest range would beat her black and blue the first mile. Unless she was hauling back a calf, she rarely took any of the ranch vehicles, preferring the freedom of the saddle.

Busy with her plans, she didn't see Jeffie until she collided with him at the entrance of the barn. "Whoa!" Catching his arm, she righted herself. "Where's the fire?"

"Fire?" Jeffie snatched his battered hat from his head, clutching it hard against his chest. "There ain't no fire, Miss Benedict, ma'am."

"You could have fooled me, the way you came barreling out of there."

"Jeez, did I hurt you?" If he crushed the hat any flatter, it could serve as the Frisbee at the next ranch barbecue.

"I'm not hurt," Hank assured him. "But I have to wonder what demon was on your heels to send you galloping at such a headlong pace."

"No demons. Nossir. I mean no ma'am." The boy backed away, ducking his head as he went. "No demons atall."

The boy was babbling, his eyes were troubled. "What is it, Jeffie?" Hank rested a concerned hand on his shoulder. "You seem upset. Is there something I can help you with?"

"No! Yes." The boy backed away another pace. He looked as if he would bolt at the slightest provocation. Miserably he ducked his head even lower. The hat curled in his palms. "I don't know what to do."

In a hasty decision, Hank determined the herd could wait. The boy's distress was becoming palpable. She couldn't walk away from him, leaving him so troubled. "Jeffie." She took the mutilated hat from him, dropping it on a peg that held a bridle, as well. "Come with me."

Taking his hand, she marched with him into the small room that once served as the foreman's office. Sandy had seldom been in residence in the past, and never after Jake's strokes. In their aftermath, and with the consequential disabilities, all ranch operations had been moved to the house.

Settling the boy in a chair, Hank sat across from him. "Now," she began like a schoolmarm. "Suppose you tell me what has you in such a state."

Jeffie shook his head as he stared down at his knees. His palms rubbed rhythmically over the tops of the bony protrusions.

"Jeffie." Hank caught a hand in hers, stilling it, waiting for him to look at her. When he lifted his bleak gaze, she realized with a start that he was far younger than he claimed. A boy, with his head full of dreams, in the body of a man.

From the look of him, his dream had just turned into a nightmare. "There's nothing you can't tell me, you know."

He hesitated, not sure what he should say. When Hank simply waited, her hand quiet over his, the dam burst, a torrent of broken words and disjointed phrases tumbled out. "They were fighting. I heard 'em."

"Who was fighting?"

"They rode out long before dawn, creepy like, walking their horses like they didn't want anyone to see them. I was sleeping in the loft." A flush spread over pale cheeks. "I like it in the loft, I used to sleep there most nights when I was home."

A telling remark, one that would bear further concern. Perhaps it held the key to why a boy large in body, but young in years, sat before her trying to cope with something beyond him.

"When they came back later in the morning, I was working with the saddles. They started arguing in the corral, accusing each other, saying terrible things." A pink tongue licked nervously at dry lips. "They ambushed him and beat him, and left him. Maybe he's dead." He looked away from Hank, unable to hold her shocked gaze. "Now that I've told, they'll kill me too."

Dread gripped Hank with a cold hand. "Who, Jeffie?"

"Rance and Wallie." Ransome Lawter and his brother, Wallace.

Wallie and I can make certain he never touches you again. The remembered threat splintered through her calm demeanor. Cold dread turned frigid. "Steve."

His name was a low moan that snapped Jeffie's bleak stare to her. "Yes, ma'am."

"Why? When?" Hank was on her feet, her mind racing furiously. "Where is he?"

"They jumped him in the barn at the Broken Spur and left him there."

"What else did they say? No!" She shook her head. "Never mind. It doesn't matter now. Turn the mare in the corral and saddle Black Jack for me."

Jeffie jumped from his chair, eager to help. "I'll go with you."

"No. See to the horses, you've done enough already." Before the boy exited the office, Hank was rummaging through a cabinet of first aid supplies always kept near the stable for the common injuries incurred there. But what injuries would Steve have? Would anything help? She considered taking the utility truck, then discarded the idea. Horseback would be faster. There were caverns and small crevasses she would have to drive around. Black Jack could jump them.

Slinging a small bag of supplies over her shoulder, she went to find Jeffie and her horse.

Black Jack was saddled and eager to run. Hank noted this youngest of cowhands had taken a minute to fill and tie a canteen to her saddle. Her rifle was in its scabbard. "Thanks, Jeff." Patting his shoulder, she smiled encouragingly. "Don't worry, you handled this well. I think you're going to be a hand the Rafter B can be proud to call one of its own."

Stepping in the saddle, she secured the bag, checked the canteen and the rifle. "Call the doctor in Silverton. Tell him to meet me at the Broken Spur." Leaning down she met the boy's gaze, and was gratified to see that it was utterly calm. "Warn him it may be urgent."

She didn't wait for an answer as she spurred Black Jack into a breakneck run. The stallion was in top form, and her desperate mood was contagious. From the first leaping start he gave her all he had. Hank's only challenge was staying in the saddle in a ride that promised to be one that made all others seem tame.

Black Jack picked his way down the last precarious turn of the nearly vertical trail from the top of the mesa, and Hank scanned the grounds of the Broken Spur. She saw the horse first, standing head down in the sun, as if she grazed where there was only hard packed earth. Lorelei. But why was she free? Hank wondered. Why not in the corral, or her stable?

As Black Jack gained the confident footing of level ground and broke into a gallop, the mare tossed her head, but stood. The shadow huddled at her hooves didn't move.

"Steve." Before the stallion slid to a halt, Hank was swinging from the saddle. One step and she was on her knees, her fingertips at the pulse at his throat.

"He's alive, Black Jack! Thank God! He's alive!"

There were tears in her eyes as she buried her face in her hands.

Chapter 9

*R*oses.

He was caught in a drift of the scent of roses. A faint whisper of fragrance, as delicate as the touch that stroked him. As elusive as the sounds that washed over him like a lazy summer tide. He heard the pad of a quiet footstep, the muffled drone of voices without faces and words without context.

Familiar words in an unfamiliar place. All part of an exotic dream.

"Dust," he croaked through lips too stiff to move. In his dreams there should be dust, the roar of the rodeo, the tramp of horses.

Horses!

He needed to see to the horses.

The compelling need leaped into his thoughts out of the senseless ramble. He had no idea what horses, or where, but out of longstanding habit, he knew he must go to them. Somehow, somewhere.

"Horses," he muttered, struggling to rise, trying in vain to see through eyes that would barely open. "Have to see to the horses."

The voices of his dream fell silent, and above the labored gasps of his efforts he heard the rush of footsteps. An angel's footsteps, light, airy, weightless in their hurry. Hands touched him, an angel's hands, warming his bared chest as their comforting pressure eased him back.

A quiet voice murmured, "Rest, be still. You needn't worry about the horses, they're in good hands."

"Who—?" He lost the thought as he waited for a stabbing pain in his side to subside.

"Who took care of them?" the voice in his imagination supplied. "I did, of course."

It made no sense. When did angels become stable hands? He tried to sit up. "My job."

"It was your job." He was eased back, carefully, firmly, unable to offer even token resistance. "For the next little while, it will be mine."

"Mine," he insisted, certain he'd lost his mind. That the touch was not real, that he argued with himself.

"You can't."

"Yess . . ." Steve growled through hard-bitten teeth. "I can."

"All right, be bullheaded. I suppose you wouldn't be who and what you are if you weren't."

The soothing touch of his dream angel lifted away. He lay silent and oddly unanchored, enveloped in a gray darkness broken by shards of moving light glimmering through tiny slits between swollen eyelids.

"Show me." The voice never altered, but there was a taunting dare in its coaxing tone. "Come on, prove it. Show me now."

She had backed away, he heard her step, the change in the direction of her words, but he couldn't see that the hands of the woman who was more than a dream were raised and ready.

Ignoring the pain, he jolted forward. A costly inroad on his conviction, yet he wouldn't give up. He couldn't. Arms hugged against his sides, he waited until a wave of nausea passed. Every move hurt, every effort drew sweat to his brow, but from long experience, he knew the first move was the killer. The worst was over.

Sliding his legs over the side of the bed, he shifted, planted his feet on the floor, and lurched to a standing position. His body felt too long, too ungainly, as if there were more than the fraction short of six feet of him.

"I can do this." He fought down another surge of nausea, and took a shuffling step. "I can."

"Of course you can, Cody," the melodic voice agreed as his knees buckled and arms too slender for their valor closed around him, breaking his fall. "Just . . . not . . . yet."

They went down together, her back slapping the unadorned floor, her body cushioning his. Both lay still, Steve from the draining of the last of his stamina, she from the shock of the fall emptying lungs of that small, precious, priming flow of oxygen. Deflated tissues sealed and clung, defeating her silent, unmoving struggle. Yet she held him, her fingers curling around his shoulders and in his hair, wrapping him in her strength even as she endured the slow easing of the breathless paralysis.

Steve was conscious, but inert, a boneless, powerless form weighing her down. Though his respiration was shallow, there was an evenness in it, the warmth of his breath whispered over the slope of her breast with an assuring rhythm. His skin was clammy, but a fingertip at the pulse at his temple ascertained that his heart was staunch and steady. Relief brought a great gasping sigh to her lips, her chest lifted, drawing much needed oxygen to starved blood.

As if she woke him from a long sleep, Steve stirred, his body clenched, his head turned, his lips brushed yielding, fragrant flesh.

Roses, but not a dream. A flesh and blood woman.

Reeling away, he pulled from her arms. Disgust masked the excruciating punishment he inflicted on himself. The flare of angry disbelief widening the swollen slits of his eyes. "You."

"Steve, don't." She reached for him, but he jerked away, his momentum bringing him to his knees.

"Damn you!" His face was pale, his body weaved drunkenly beyond her touch. He tried to catch the edge of the bed to gain his feet, his fingers missed the sturdy frame and closed over rough linen, dragging it down to him. In his helplessness a bleak, bitter twist of his mouth tore at split lips. A drop of blood, trickled down his chin, with the last of adrenaline-borne willpower, he wiped it away.

He stared at his hand, at the blood. His pain was more than physical, as he lifted his poor gaze to hers. "Why, Benedict?" He shook his head, perhaps to clear his thoughts, perhaps to deny what he must ask. "Why like this? Did winning mean so much?"

His head drooped, a shuddering groan racked his body, his shoulders bowed. Darkness hovered at the edges of his vision, spiraling down around him, bringing with it oblivion. One last conscious cry tore from him as he toppled forward, one last muttered word as he was embraced again by the arms of the woman he believed had betrayed him. "Why?"

Hank caught him, holding him as she lowered him to the floor. "No." She leaned over him, stroking his hair from his battered face. "Winning would never mean this much."

He was hungry. The tantalizing aroma of cooking meat went straight from his nostrils to his stomach, reminding that he'd had only coffee before going to the barn.

The barn! Memories flooded over him. Images flashed through his mind too swiftly to be defined, but he knew. With undeniable clarity he knew everything, from the first scream of the horses to the healing, soothing touch of the woman.

"Benedict." He opened his eyes, flinching only a little from the sudden bright burst. Lying in a tangle of cotton sheets, he let recognition of his surroundings seep in, orienting himself.

The Broken Spur. He was home, in his own bed. A pot hung on a hook in the open fireplace. Vapors bearing the rich, mouth-watering scent billowed above it as a lone tongue of fire leaped from smoldering embers to lick at the sooty base. With studied care he turned his head, probing the rest of the room. All was in order, every surface shone, far more than from the haphazard ministrations of a solitary man.

A woman's touch.

"Benedict," he called again. There was no answer, and no place to hide in the single room of the small ranch house. He was alone, but only for the moment. She was here, somewhere. He knew it as surely as he knew he must find her and confront her with what she'd done.

A promise easier to make than to keep, he discovered five minutes later. He stood by his bed, naked, finding no trace of the clothing he'd worn, and with little hope of reaching the shelf that held fresh shirts and jeans. Not when his trembling legs threatened to dump him on his backside on a floor that lurched and bucked like a sailor's nightmare. Still, he had to try. A stumbling, lunging step sent him headlong into a wall. Not the way he intended to go, but he was grateful for the support.

He was inching along, pale as death, clawing at its rough surface with one hand, clutching a makeshift chair with the other, when the latch lifted, the door opened, and Hank Benedict stepped through it.

"Ahh," she observed casually, as if he were hale and hearty and fully clothed. "I see you're awake."

Steve didn't answer. He was too busy biting back the sickness that threatened when he turned too quickly to acknowledge the obvious.

In his watchful, brooding silence, Hank crossed to the hearth, adding the wood she carried to the stack at its edge. When she turned her arms were folded over her breasts, her hidden hands were clasped against the urge to offer a shoulder to lean on. Steve Cody was a strong, proud man who suffered his own weakness with neither reason nor grace. He wouldn't welcome help. Especially from her.

So she kept her distance while her concerned and practiced study marked the sheen of sweat glistening on his face and shoulders, and running in rivulets down his abdomen. In the days of her unstinting care she'd become intimately acquainted with every rough-hewn feature and every craggy line of his face. Learning, in familiarity, to distinguish bruise from the shadow of fatigue, gaunt lines of pain from the etchings of natural expression. With that hard won perception she saw shadows darker than any bruise staining the tender tissues beneath the brush of his lower lashes, and frustration more painful than pain itself.

He was a fierce and wounded warrior in dire need of venting his fury. A bewildered creature who would lash out with dark satisfaction at any who would comfort him.

Holding his bleak, hard stare, with the compassion in her own tucked carefully away, she let her lips tilt in a wry smile and offered a hand to bite. "Well, now," she drawled, "are you planning to climb that wall, or are you holding it up?"

Steve's head snapped back, his eyes narrowed, anger flashed in them. "Cute," he snarled, only a trace of weakness in his voice. His grip threatened the makeshift chair that supported his full weight. As his ill humor found its quarry, he cared not one whit that the flimsy slatted back succeeded poorly in shielding his nakedness. "Almost as cute as the friends you sent to call."

"They weren't my friends." She held his gaze, refusing to shy away from the indictment. "I didn't send them."

"You expect me to believe that?"

"Yes."

A simple answer. Direct, with no equivocation, and more convincing than any argument. But it would take far more proof before Steve believed. "One of them wore a boot with a star on the heel."

"I wear a boot with a star on the heel," Hank said. "Does that mean I'm one of the culprits?"

"It means you ride for the Rafter B, as they do." Steve hadn't known until this second that he'd recognized the star as one sported by nearly all the cowhands who worked for Jake Benedict and his daughter.

"As they did," she corrected simply. "But not anymore."

"Sure." The jeer was a coarse insult, branding her a liar.

Hank looked down at her boot, at the star visible on the scuffed and scarred heel. Years ago, when Sandy carved the original in her boot heel, a teasing gesture commemorating the breaking of her first horse for the Rafter B, she'd never guessed that it would become a respected tradition. Nor did she expect that each new hand would wear a star when he broke his first horse for the ranch, carving it proudly in the heel of each new pair of boots. She hadn't expected any of the mystique about the silly symbol, nor that it would be zealously coveted by the likes of Jeffie, who had yet to win the right to wear one. Most of all, she never thought something so innocuous would one day be a source of incrimination.

"I haven't tried to deny their guilt. I won't deny our mistake in hiring them." She stood her ground under his hard, cold stare, asking no quarter, as the import of what she'd said penetrated the haze of pain and anger that dulled his mind.

"You know who they are." The remark was the final accusation, more trenchant in its softness than a shout. "You've known from the first."

"Not from the first." Hank's response was clipped, a refusal of blame. When misjudgment of men and their principles was a crime, she would readily plead guilty. Until then, she would not stand accused of more. "I knew within a short time, but after the fact, not before."

"Ah, I see, a revelation." Steve mocked. Goaded.

Smothering an oath, Hank reminded herself he was hurt and felt betrayed, and had every reason to be hostile. "Jeffie sleeps in the barn loft some nights. He was there when Ransome and Wallace Lawter saddled up and rode out before dawn. He was there when they returned. Apparently Wallace suffered an attack of conscience. He and Ransome quarreled and fought. Jeffie heard it all."

"Then he came to you."

"He was frightened and hardly knew what to do at first, but yes, he came to me."

The fierce black stare never altered. "And you came to me."

"Yes."

Steve's thoughts ranged. Ransome Lawter, a preening, strutting braggart, and Wallie, the brute. They fit his impression of the men who ambushed him. Their names had been offered with the willingness of one with nothing to hide. "I hadn't quite worked out who they were, but I would have, in time."

"You think I gave you their names to cover my own guilt?"

"They ride for the Rafter B. They take their orders from you."

"Not in this." A thread of steel crept into her smoky voice. "No one at the ranch could ever condone this. Neither Jake, nor Sandy, nor I. Perhaps it bears saying again that because we couldn't, the Lawters no longer ride for us."

"Maybe they do." He refused her the slightest concession. "Maybe they don't. A moot question at this point, wouldn't you say?"

"Steve." She spread her hands in an imploring gesture. "Can you truly say you think I would be capable of this?"

"Lady, I don't know what you're capable of doing. At the moment, I don't care. But you gotta admit one thing." He scoured her with focused fury. "It's one hell of a way to win a bet."

"I wouldn't. I couldn't. What can I say? What can I do to make you believe me?"

"There's nothing that will change what I believe, or undo the damage that's been done." He risked a tiny, derisive bow. "You win, Miss Benedict, ma'am. There's no chance in hell I can meet the terms of our wager. When the snow flies over the mountains, the canyon will finally be part of the Rafter B."

Calling on every shred of his waning strength, he forced himself to relinquish the support of the chair. Standing rigidly straight despite the stitch in his side, he met her pained expression coldly. "If you're all through looking, I'd be obliged if you'd fetch my pants."

"Certainly." Smarting from his accusations, but denying herself the satisfaction of explaining to him that after three days of caring for him, there was little about his body that was unfamiliar to her, she crossed to the shelf. Riffling through the stacks, she selected a freshly laundered pair of undershorts, faded jeans and a shirt. Returning to him, she kept her gaze carefully riveted on his face. "Will you need help?"

Steve snatched the clothing from her, regretting his folly when the undershorts fell at his feet. He didn't stand a chance of retrieving the garment without pitching on his face.

"I don't need your damnable help," he growled, covering his mounting humiliation with a resurgence of vitriolic humor. "After nearly thirty years of dressing myself, I think I can manage now."

"Have it your way." She meant to leave him caught in his own arrogant dilemma, but her tender heart wouldn't let her be that callous, even to a man who thought so wrongly of her. "Here." Eyes averted, she scooped up the shorts, offering them with her fingertips. "You'll need these—to keep the jeans from chafing the newest scar on your saddle-worn backside."

"Newest scar? My back—" He snatched the shorts from her, his face set in a scowl. "What the devil are you jabbering about?"

"You figure it out, Mr. Rodeo Star. While you're figuring, ask yourself who took care of you these past three days. Have you wondered who fed you? Who bathed you?"

"Three days?"

"Exactly." Tender heart or not, Hank took a certain satisfaction in his shocked response. "I assure you, there's little need for modesty at this late date."

"You've been here for three days?"

"Sandy came by with the doctor the first day."

"Sandy and the doctor," Steve parroted. "But only on the first day."

"Don't worry, Dr. Bonner is a good man and an excellent diagnostician. He checked you over pretty thoroughly, then conferred with the doctors who treated you last. He'll be back in a day or two, to see how you are. Until then, the good news is that most of the trauma to your head was strictly cosmetic. So, there was no fear of severe concussion, even with your history. Your ribs are badly bruised, but not broken. The worst of it is a bruised kidney. Which means you won't be riding broncs or training wild horses for some time."

"Let me see if I have this straight. I didn't have a concussion, but I've been out of it for three days."

"Right. Given your hardheaded disposition, it was suggested by the medics who treated you before that it would be wise to keep you sedated for a time."

"For a time, but not for so long."

"No one expected you would react as you did, nor that the mildest sedative would put you out for days."

"During which time I was at your mercy."

"There was no one else, Cody."

A brow arched, a new ache announced itself. "You undressed me?"

"Down to the last stitch."

"And, of course, you washed me."

"Every inch."

Resenting his own helplessness, he closed his eyes, trying to recall the intimacy. There was no inkling of recollection. Yet when he looked again into her clear eyed gaze, he knew. He might doubt her word regarding the attack, but not in this.

"Then I suppose it is a bit late for modesty."

"A bit." She stifled a smile at the understatement.

"I trust you won't mind if I choose not to continue au naturel for the little time you remain here," he drawled, willing that she find something to do, someplace to go, before his treacherous legs finally buckled on him.

"I don't mind at all." She knew he wanted her to leave. Modesty aside, after his brusque declaration of his ability to dress himself, he wouldn't want her hanging about witnessing the struggle. She understood. She understood all of it very well. Yet something perverse in her, perhaps the same demon that prompted her to mention a most strategically placed scar, prompted her to stay.

Going to the hearth, she busied herself with the stew, stirring, tasting, pronouncing it almost ready. Next she attended the fire, noting that, even kept to little more than embers, it generated an uncomfortable heat. Soon the room, which was already stifling, would be unbearable. In the days before, when the temperature soared, she'd used water directly from the stream to bathe him and cool him.

She wanted to laugh when she considered what a brawl bathing him would be now. The laughter in her thoughts still lingered on her lips when she turned and found him watching her.

"You're enjoying this, aren't you?"

"I beg your pardon?" She hung the spoon she'd used to stir the stew on a hook embedded in the stone fireplace. In a move intended to be nonchalant but that became unconsciously seductive as it drew her shirt taut over small, firm breasts, she brushed a loose tendril of hair from her forehead with the back of her hand. "I have no idea what you mean."

"Like hell!" His grip on the chair cracked a thin slat, threatening to drive a splinter into his palm. "You like puttering around so virtuously, while I stand here buck naked wondering when my knees will finally buckle, dumping my bare butt and my last shred of pride at your feet."

"Oh, I doubt that." Hank made no pretense at diplomacy. "Considering your insufferable arrogance, I suspect you're a long way from your last shred of pride."

"Point taken," Steve growled. "You can go now."

"Really? You're absolutely certain you don't need help? Considering buckling knees and such."

"I'll be fine once I make it back to the bed, not to sleep or rest, but get into my clothes. I do recover quickly."

"Hobble away from one nightmare and straight to another, no matter the cost. That's your creed, isn't it?"

"Bucked, trampled, and in the saddle again. It's all a bronc rider knows." Steve remembered other times, other hardships. "We live it every day in all we do. And we live it better alone." Quietly, he insisted, "You really can go now."

In a gathering of strength, a confident but pensive smile flitted over his hammered face. And Hank understood the mystique of the rodeo cowboy, Western hero in spurs and boots, and Stetson with the proper curl. The lonely, wounded gladiator, fiercely individual, with an unbelievable threshold for pain. Even higher for confidence, and more for sheer bullheadedness. He lived for the challenge, that rush of adrenaline, and believed he could do anything. If not today, then tomorrow. If not tomorrow—someday.

Through it all, her cowboy hero smiled his wicked smile.

"I'll give you a while." She was surprised that her voice was rough, and her step a little unsteady. At the door, with her hand on the latch, she paused. "For the record, you aren't the first cowboy I've tended or seen naked. I doubt you'll be the last."

Giving the offhand remark a moment to sink in, she opened the door and stepped through. Glancing back at him, she added, "Take as long as you need. When you're dressed, we'll discuss your recovery—and when I'll be leaving."

The door banged shut, and Steve was left to face the punishing fulfillment of his foolhardy boast.

It was the combination of heat, fatigue, and claustrophobia that drove him from the house. After the ordeal of dressing, his original intention had been to rest and recoup. When he stepped onto the porch, he realized what he really needed was to move, to rebuild his stamina, not lie about stoking his weakness with inaction.

Sunlight hit him in the face, full blast, as he descended the steps in his new old man's pace. By its angle he calculated the time, discovering it was just coming on to noon, when he could have sworn the day was almost done.

"How time does fly, when I'm having fun." Yeah, three whole days of it had flown by, and what great fun. But he wouldn't dwell on what was done and couldn't be changed. When a horse bucked him, he couldn't undo it, but he could damn sure see that it didn't buck him again. As he would see that he never spent another three days suffering the dubious charity of a Benedict.

Bracing his shoulders and breathing shallowly, he set himself for the harrowing adventure of finding her and sending her on her way to the Rafter B.

Crossing to the barn and the empty corral proved to be quite another ordeal. As much because he'd been bedridden for too long as from his injuries. Both difficulties he could correct. Ducking into the barn, he was grateful for the relative cool of its shady walls. He'd found heat and cool were always relative in Arizona—relative to the day, the season, the situation.

A short tour of the stalls proved all horses but one were still in their stalls. With practiced eyes, he saw they'd been well tended in his absence. Gitano pranced and tossed his head as he passed by. Blue Belle nudged his shoulder and nibbled at his hand. Someone had been lavishing them with attention, maybe petting them, and the barn was cleaner than he would have left it.

Nothing was amiss but the absentees.

"Lorelei." Steve passed a hand over the top rail of her empty stall. It didn't take a mastermind to know that where he found the horse he would find Hank Benedict.

"Hank," he muttered. A tomboy's name, incongruous and ill-fitting. A name from childhood that suited the woman no better than the garments of a child. A name as graceless as she was graceful, as ugly as she was lovely. As prosaic as she was intriguing.

Intriguing. She was more than that. More than graceful or lovely. More than alluring and captivating. She set his head spinning, his blood scalding. He wanted her when he'd first seen her on the street in Silverton, even with his head threatening to come apart. He wanted her when they wrangled and wagered over horses and land. He'd kissed her, and walked away from Jubal's sale with Lorelei, the horse she wanted—and he wanted *her.*

He wanted her when she rode like a cossack across the range. At the rim of the canyon, only the grace of God kept him from dragging her from her black devil of a stallion, and proving to her that she wanted him, as well.

He'd mistaken lust for love once and paid dearly. He wouldn't make the same mistake again, but hadn't he paid anyway?

And still he wanted her. Every inch of her. So badly that even when she was most annoying and he most angry, a secret part of him longed to reach out and bury his hands in her hair to drag her to him.

He wanted her now. So much he didn't care what she was, or what she'd done.

"This is crazy." He leaned his head on the stall door. "I must be losing my mind."

"Steve!" There was panic in Hank's voice as she called his name, yet the hand that clasped his shoulder was gentle. "What are you doing here?"

Dropping Lorelei's reins, with the question spilling from her she dodged beneath his arms to stand within their circle, facing him. Her eyes were huge, their gaze raced over his face. "I heard you cry out. Are you all right?"

Fighting the effects of another sudden move, he made himself stand rigidly erect. "I'm fine, Benedict. Fine and dandy."

When he would have turned from her scrutiny, she caught his arms, keeping him close. "Are you?"

"Yes, damn you. At least I will be, when you take the hint and go home. I don't need anyone."

"You don't need anyone!" Fear sparked her temper when she wanted to be peaceful. "You have five horses back there to tend. A half-wild stallion and two mares to breed, and two to train. A one-way trip from the ranch house turns you paler than snow and so weak a kitten could knock you down with the lash of its tail, and you think you don't need anyone?"

"No." He wanted to pull away from her grasp, but she was wrong, it wouldn't need the lash of a kitten's tail to send him to his knees, were it not for her steadying hand.

"No, you don't think you need anyone?" She leaned closer, and the scent of roses drifted from her hair. "Or no, you don't need me?"

"You," he managed as his head began to pound. "I don't need you."

"Tough!" She released him and backed away until her shoulders touched the gate of the stall. "I'm what you got. In fact, I'm *all* you've got."

Steve was elated he was still standing; better still, when the head-ache began its song and dance in earnest, the dizziness ceased. A surge of adrenaline, that exhilarating lift of mind and spirit that could make or break a rider or a man as it spurred him to do the impossible, bolstered his strength and his confidence.

"Go away, Benedict. You won the bet by default, but my carnal instincts don't seem to understand. So, go, dammit," he ground each word out, as if it were a separate entity. "Go, if you know what's best for you."

"What about what's best for you?"

"What's best for me is that you leave before I..."

"Before you do what?" Her head lifted, her chin jutted as she threw down the gauntlet he couldn't resist.

"This." His fingers threaded through her loosely bound hair, his gaze locked with hers. Her eyes were sparkling silver, mist over the mountains, smoke on a rainy day, and so beautiful he could lose himself in them. Her step was halting, but not resisting, when the gentlest pressure drew her to him. His head tilted, his breath mingled with hers. "Before I do this."

His mouth closed over hers as she started to move. It was hardly more than an impression, and he never knew if the momentum would have brought her to him, or away. When their lips touched, he forgot everything, except that her kiss was all he thought it would be. All he wanted it to be.

Soft.

Sweet wasn't the word, but he knew no other.

Satin.

Strength beneath fragility.

Passion.

The wanton within the lady.

Caught in the mystery of her, he felt her arms slide to his shoulders, then his neck, her breasts pressed against his chest. All the world seemed to spin in a fathomless wonderland. And he was lost in all of her.

The day was hot and growing hotter. Horses stamped and shifted, waiting patiently to be taken to pasture. The scent of hay and dust and horses was borne on heated air. But for Steve there was only the scent of roses and the lithe body that curled into his as if it were fashioned for only him.

Hank meant to evade, to step away. She told herself it was the stall against her back, the close quarters, his arms lifting at her sides that stopped her. She told herself that her fingers meant to tug him away, not caress him. When her mouth opened to his demand, her mind whispered that she only meant to speak her denial.

When he released her, staring down at her, grim faced and bleak, as if he hated her and himself, she wanted to believe, tried to believe she was glad. Yet when he cursed her and drew her back into his arms, she went willingly, clinging to him as roles reversed and he was the stronger.

"Damn you, Benedict. Damn you, damn you." His voice was harsh, the words soft. As his lips brushed over her hair, her face, her throat, he chanted a rite of loathing, and in it she heard, but did not comprehend, the fierce need that was ripping him apart. The need he wanted desperately to deny.

"This is foolish!"

"Don't. Don't say anything." As if he would assure her compliance, he skimmed a finger over her lips. His gaze followed its path, tracing the arch and curve it traced. Mesmerized, thirsting, he couldn't turn away as smoldering desire reached its flash point, exploding in white heat, pushing him to the edge. His last shred of reason decimated.

"Damn us both." His hand was an iron band at her nape, drawing her swiftly, brutally, to him. The thrusting collision of his long, rigid body against her yielding softness brought a cry that was lost in the crush of his kiss.

He kissed her as he'd never kissed a woman, savagely, with a punishing thoroughness that left no doubt of his anguish.

Hank's head spun with the swiftness of his move, her body burned from the heat of his. Passion she'd kept in check for years slipped its traces, racing beyond its careful boundaries. Shattering every rule by which she lived, every law of survival. With no will of her own, commanded by emotion and longing she knew little of, she opened to him, taking as he took, as ruthlessly. As a woman takes.

She reveled in newfound freedom, in the joy of holding and being held. She drew in the scent of him. Leather and soap. The soap with which she'd bathed the wonderfully masculine body that caressed her now with its touch. Her soap, and it seemed right that it be so. And with it she drank in the heady taste of him.

"Steve," she murmured, his name on her lips caressing his. Then, abruptly, he was reeling drunkenly away.

Color leached from his face, his eyes were black, burning pits as the last of the adrenaline left him weaker for the false surge of strength. He swayed on his feet, his respiration shallow. But when she reached out to steady him, his hand shot out, closing brutally over her wrist.

"Don't touch me. Hate me or love me, but don't touch me. Not now."

She stared up at him, probing the closed expression, but saw only agony and bitterness. "All right." A fraction at a time, she pulled from his grip. "I won't touch you."

Stepping past him, she caught up Lorelei's reins and led her to her stall. Beneath his scalding stare she unsaddled the mare and saw to her needs and closed the gate, stepping past him once more.

"What the hell do you think you're doing, and where are you going?" he demanded, turning gingerly in her direction.

Hank continued to walk, barely glanced over her shoulder. "I'm hungry. By the time I put together a batch of fry bread, the stew should be ready. After that, I'm taking your horses to pasture.

"I'm here for the duration, Cody," she said staunchly and quietly. "Like it or not."

Heart pounding, her compassionate soul bleeding for him, she left him to wallow in the dilemma of hardheaded pride.

Chapter 10

"More stew?"

"No."

"Fry bread?"

"No."

From her seat across the table, as close as she'd been allowed for days, Hank watched Steve toy with the last of his food. In the weak glow of the lamp, lit to stave off the encroaching shadows of evening, the changes in him were evident. In a week and two days, the unconscious stoop in his posture had overcorrected with a bent toward military perfection. Swollen tissues shrank, bruises faded, the gaunt and hollow look had vanished from his face. The stolid cynicism of his expression never changed.

"Refill?" She lifted the dented coffee pot half filled with the awesomely bitter brew he preferred morning and evening, no matter the climate.

"No." Then, reluctantly, "Thanks."

She set the pot down. Apparently another thing not due for change was the monosyllabic growls that greeted every overture. "Then, if you're through, I'll clear the table before I bed down the horses."

As she reached for his plate, he stopped her. Fingers cuffing her wrist, he turned her arm, examining the flesh where once a bruise had circled the small bones like a bracelet. The forbidden memory, the kiss, the desire, waited always in the deepest part of his mind. Waited to exert its mastery. He pushed it away, banishing it from mind and heart. And it grew a little stronger, nattering at the edges of his control, wearing it away.

But it hadn't won yet.

His hold relaxed, but kept her. "How long do you intend to continue this farce?"

"What farce is that?" Settling back, she waited for the rebuke that had been days in coming.

"You know what I mean." He dropped her arm, regretting the impulse that drove him to touch her.

"I'm afraid I don't."

Afraid! Steve wondered if she was afraid of anything. Either angry man or wild beast, or act of God.

Hank's arm lay where he dropped it, only inches from his as he pushed his cup away. With the slightest move she could cover his hand with hers, lace her fingers through his, and know the heady experience of their strength. "If you're referring to my cooking, I never claimed to be capable of better than range fare. Bonita does the cooking at the house. If you're sick to death of stew and bread alternating with bread and stew, I could ask her to pack a basket of her best dishes. Now that you're better, we could have a picnic down by the stream."

Lurching from his chair, arms braced on the table on either side of her, he glowered down. "I don't want any blasted baskets, and considering that I stand to lose the Broken Spur, the last thing I'm in the mood for is a picnic. What I *want* is for you to cut the pretense and get out of here. Then I can get on with my life and you with yours."

"You can't do that." She kept her unruffled poise, completely unintimidated by his show of temper. "Neither can I."

"What the hell!" He shoved away from her, then, as quickly, moved back. "What does it take to get it through your thick skull that I don't want you here? I don't need you."

Same song, second verse. Or was it the third? Maybe the fourth? Leaning back in her chair, her hands as still as marble on the table, her braid lying like a heavy weight over her shoulder and breast, she strove to keep her voice steady. "Perhaps my skull isn't as thick as you think. I'm perfectly aware that you don't want me here. It would take a fool not to know. But it takes a bigger fool not to know the last is a lie. No matter how much you rant and rave, nor how insulting you become, we both know you need me. You need me most desperately.''

"All bets are off, remember."

"Exactly."

"Then why would I need you?" he jeered.

"To train the horses you hope to sell in the spring."

"I can train my own, thank you."

"No, Cody," she contradicted matter-of-factly. "You can't. To try could be suicide."

"This isn't the first bruised kidney I've had. It won't be the last."

"I know your history. The medical bulletins were pretty specific last time. The newspapers printed them verbatim, leaving nothing to conjecture. Another injury this soon after one so serious is courting disaster. You have to be careful. To quote Dr. Bonner, that means no riding more strenuous than a slow walk for the next couple of weeks."

Steve shook his head adamantly. "My schedule won't permit that."

"I'm aware of that."

"Since you know so much, then I suppose you know that even without our wager, I have to have two good horses ready for the sale. And they have to be good enough to take top dollar."

"Payment on the mortgage you made on this place, to have the funds for Gitano," Hank filled in the gaps succinctly. The stallion had been a steal in terms of value, yet still commanded a considerable price.

Steve's expression grew harder, the flare of his temper turned him white lipped. "How the devil did you know that? Have you been snooping into my private papers?"

The accusation scrapped Hank's tenuous hold on her own temper, bringing her to her feet. "I don't snoop," she snapped. "Any more than I hire thugs to disable my opponents."

"That remains to be seen."

"One thing that doesn't remain to be seen is that you're a stubborn, insufferable idiot."

A cold grimace quirked his mouth. "Then go. Don't suffer."

Hank bit her tongue, willing her temper to cool. Staring down at her hands, she realized they were clenched. One by one, she forced her fingers to uncurl, and with each a bit of tension uncoiled. Implacable and unshakable reason returned before she dared face him again.

"For the last time, I hired no one to hurt you, and I haven't snooped. What I know of your situation, I heard in three days of your worried ramblings." She wouldn't mention Angie, the name she heard over and over in those ramblings, nor the anguish it caused. She couldn't deny being curious, but this was the time to make a final stand, not for asking questions.

"Lastly," she declared emphatically, "no matter how many scenes such as this you instigate, I'm here for the duration. Your horses will go to the sale in Silverton, and I guarantee they'll be the best trained horses there."

"Who will train them?" he goaded, knowing the answer.

"I will." Her reply was succinct, as if he'd asked a perfectly legitimate question for the first time.

"How?"

"My way." She picked up her plate, intending to take it to the sink, where a pan of water waited. Instead, she set it back down with a bang and headed for the door.

"Where the hell do you think you're going now?"

Her hands were on her hips, her chin jutted at a telling angle. "Did your mother ever wash your mouth out with soap?"

"No."

"She should have."

"She couldn't." Sidestepping another question, he repeated his own. "Where are you going?"

The unguarded sadness at the mention of his mother hadn't been lost on Hank. She'd spent hours studying that face, learning every feature and every nuance, even the closed, unfathomable look that defeated her. Perhaps in defense of the unthinking indiscretion, it was the insular control that looked back at her now.

"I'm going to the barn." Her reply lost the heat of her anger as she wondered what heartache she'd inflicted. "To make the most of what daylight is left. If I hurry, I can take a short turn with the small bay—another step in meeting the obligations of the job I signed on to do."

"You didn't sign on," he flung at her. "You barged in."

"Maybe I did, and maybe you should be thankful for it." She tucked her thumbs in her back pockets, a move that pulled her belt snug, making mockery of the masculine clothing her work demanded. Hardly aware that his piercing gaze ranged over her, she continued her lesson in propriety. "There are others you should thank, as well. Most of all, Jeffie, for having the courage to tell what he'd heard. It wasn't an easy thing for a kid to risk the retribution of the likes of Ransome and Wallie Lawter. Considering what they did to you, can you even imagine what they would do to keep him quiet?''

"I can imagine.'' The anger he'd hurled at her became cold, quiet rage.

Hank fought back a shiver. In three blunt words she heard danger, and saw what he could become. In a more charitable mood, she would have felt sympathy for the Lawter brothers when their paths crossed Steve Cody's.

"Who else?''

"I beg your pardon?'' Hank had lost the point of her lecture.

"You said there were others I should thank.''

"Lorelei.''

By habit a brow arched, this time without causing a wince. "I should be grateful to a horse?''

"Stranger things have been known to happen. If her stall door hadn't been left open, if curiosity hadn't drawn her to you, and if loyalty hadn't kept her with you, shielding you from the brunt of the sun, you would have been badly burned by the time I arrived.''

"On the back of your black devil, no doubt.''

"Black Jack is a little wild, but I've never thought of him as a devil.'' She wouldn't argue even that point. "He's our fastest horse, with the surest foot.''

"For racing across open range, as if the devil were after you instead of under you.''

"Across the range was the quickest way. There was no time to waste.''

Steve's frown deepened as he remembered another ride. "Then I should be doubly thankful. First that you came, then that you arrived in one piece.''

"There was no danger. I knew the way, every dip and swell. I told you before that I've crossed that particular section of the range many times.'' Perhaps not quite so hurriedly, nor in such reckless abandon, she admitted, but it served no purpose that Steve should know. "You misjudge the ride.''

"I've witnessed a part of it once, and I know what I saw.'' He looked into her clear, silver eyes, and wondered if her conscience was as clear. But why would she risk her neck to come to his aid if she'd ordered the ambush? The only answer that made any sense was that she hadn't. The thought turned every accusation he'd leveled at her into a sieve. Yet he wasn't ready to believe. Not for a while.

Raking an impatient hand through his hair, he stared at her, searching for proof. The definitive proof that lay in trust he wasn't ready to give. "I suppose I owe you a debt of gratitude."

Hank nodded, wary of this sudden change. "Maybe."

"How do you suggest I repay you?"

"Stay out of my way, let me do the job I came to do."

"That's all?"

"That's all. Unless you can see your way clear to doing the dishes." She was pleased with the idea, and with imagining the virile cowboy doing the mundane chores of housekeeping. "Sure, why not? Do the dishes, if you know how."

"I know how." Steve almost smiled at her small revenge. "I've done a dish or two in my time."

"Good. That means I can get to the horses that much sooner."

"A splendid idea. I'll finish up here and be along later to watch."

He'd caught her off balance with another lightning change. "Just like that? It's settled?"

The brow arched again. "Just like that."

"You're joking."

"I don't joke about horses or dishes, Benedict." He kept a bland expression on his face.

"Serious business, huh?"

"Very."

Not sure what to make of this new attitude, Hank decided not to question it. Flipping the latch, she stepped to the porch and into twilight. As the door closed, she was glancing over her shoulder, watching him curiously.

Steve was smiling as he cleared the table, his first real smile in days. There was more than one way to skin a cat, he decided. Or, better yet, more than one way to to catch a foxy lady.

At the sink, as he washed and rinsed their meager dishes, through a window that afforded a perfect view, he watched her work, completely, skillfully, wonderfully as one with the horse.

Beautiful.

"Now," he muttered under his breath, the brief and rare smile forgotten. "All I have to do is make sure I don't get caught."

"Ho! Ho! Good girl." Hank leaned forward in the saddle, raked her hand down the mare's bowed neck, petting and stroking her until she settled down. "Good girl. Easy does it."

Steve watched from the fence, so engrossed in the woman and the horse and the intricate move they were practicing, he forgot to feel like excess baggage. After days of watching, he knew this low, comforting monotone by heart. The same familiar words chanted endlessly, until the bewildered animal began to understand what it was she asked of it, and understood approval. For this reason, Steve knew the guiding hand would be firm, the signals clear, but the breathy song would never be sharp or impatient. This rider would never ask more of the horse than it was ready to give.

A second maneuver was not added until the first was accomplished with relative comfort that became second nature. As natural for the horse as the switch of its tail.

Then, and only then, the new exercise would be introduced, the same patient method employed. When the horse was ready, the two were integrated. Hours of more practice followed, until the horse responded to knee and hand signals, segueing from one task into another, quickly and competently.

When she was completely satisfied the horse was ready, she introduced it to yet another technique. And the patiently repetitive routine began all over again.

He'd watched her, admiration and approval grudging at first. Now he simply enjoyed.

"Good girl!" A pat accompanied the approval. "That's it."

The lilting praise marked the end of the morning's session, and Steve found himself waiting for the moment Hank Benedict would swing from the saddle, turning to him as she slipped her gloves from her hands. He didn't realize that he stood with his breath caught in his throat as he waited for her smile.

"This one's a lady, and she's going to be something." Hank tossed the words over her shoulder as she dismounted. Standing by the horse, she kept her back to him, one hand resting on the pommel of the saddle, the other stroking and petting. "One of the best."

"Yes," Steve muttered, his attention focused on the woman. With her head barely level with the saddle, and her braid tumbling down her back, she seemed far too small and fragile to hold such complete command over a creature nearly ten times her size and strength. Yet when she turned, worn jeans clinging to narrow hips and booted heels buried firmly in the dust, a look of sheer joy on her face, he knew size and strength were the least of it.

"Good morning." She offered the belated greeting with the smile for which he'd waited.

"Good morning," he responded.

And it was.

Looping the reins over the saddle, Hank left the horse to rest as she approached the fence. "How are you?"

"Better. I managed to put on my pants this morning without cussing once."

Hank laughed. A low, deep chuckle that made him think again of blues and smoke and silver eyes.

"That's progress, more than I expected." A hint of mischief glinted from the shade of the brim of her Stetson. "The part about the language I mean. But," she sighed in mock regret and touched his arm briefly, "give me time, and I'll do something that will set you off."

She was teasing. They hadn't quarreled in days. Their war had slowly evolved into an armed truce, the truce to conditional acceptance, and that to harmony that sprang from respect.

He did respect her, for her skill and dedication. No one could watch her work, or listen to her as she went about her chores...his chores...and not respect her. Each day it became more difficult to hold an unswerving belief in her complicity with the Lawters.

"You started early today." He'd heard her drive in as first light played over the eastern rim of the canyon.

In the beginning, when his injuries were still rawly painful, she stayed over. Spreading her bedroll on the floor each night, she curled on her side and drifted off as easily as if his cabin were a line shack and he just another of the many cowhands she'd slept beside in the common occurrences of running a ranch. As he improved in body and became more irascible in spirit, she declared him well on the road to recovery. Citing his restlessness and ill temper as proof that what he suffered from most seriously was a flaming case of male ego, she returned to her own ranch, to her own bed.

From that day, she never stayed over again. Instead, she came to the Broken Spur early each day, and left late. And not even the promise of a wing footed stallion standing at stud would have made him admit that he missed her. He would not admit that the small house was suddenly a rambling hall, and the nights were long and too quiet. Nor that when morning came, as he gulped the first coffee of the day alone, walls that seemed too distant in the darkness began to shrink, closing in on him.

Trapped by four walls and the vagaries of his own mind, he caught himself inhaling the remembered scent of roses, wishing he could turn thought to reality and she would be there. It was then he called himself forty kinds of fool, and tried to resurrect his suspicions.

It became her habit to drive when she came so early. It was her habit, as well, to cut the engine, letting the range scarred, stripped down army jeep that was nearly as adept as Black Jack in going where it shouldn't rattle to as quiet a halt as it could. He knew she hoped she wouldn't disturb him.

She never succeeded, and he never told her that she hadn't.

"The mare did so well yesterday, I was eager to put her through her paces this morning." Resting a booted foot on a rail and pushing back her hat, she looked at him over the top of the corral, letting her scrutiny rove over his face, taking in every detail. "How are you, really?"

"I won't be turning cartwheels for a while, but I'm fine, Benedict. Recovering right on schedule."

His schedule, maybe, but rapid for mere man. Yet today there was something different about him. A frown gathered, her head cocked, as if the angle gave her a truer perspective. "You seem tired. Better, yes, but tired."

"Restless night," he admitted, without considering his answer.

Hank was instantly alarmed, grasping his arm as if she probed for fever or telegraphed pain. "What's wrong?" It took all her effort not to brush back his hat, to stroke his forehead, to judge and answer for herself.

"Hey." Steve covered her hand with his. "Slow down. A restless night means exactly that. A restless night—no more. If you want the truth, I think it's cabin fever, or maybe canyon fever would be a better analogy."

He decided that was a fair description of his mood. Cabin fever, from the walls that closed in when she was not with him. Canyon fever, from the inactivity the Lawters had forced upon him.

"A good day's work," he said with emphasis, "and I'd sleep like a baby."

"You're sure? That's all it is?"

"Positive."

"Then maybe we should do something about it." She moved beyond reach, but the subtle awareness of all that he was remained with her. "What would you say to a ride? The mare is ready to be put through her paces outside the corral, and that's our agenda for the day. We're going to take it slow, no mad galloping or jumping fences. On a chance that you might consider accompanying us, I spoke to Dr. Bonner last night. He gives the green light, so long as you're careful." She was suddenly flustered. "That is, if you'd like to go. If you want to go."

"Maybe." It was his turn to tease, for a ride was exactly what he needed. Even one taken at a sedate pace.

"Have you had breakfast?"

"Just coffee."

"Good, then you're in for a treat. In case I had to tempt you into the saddle, Bonita made up a thermos of her coffee and a fresh batch of bear sign. If I know her, there will be a few other delicacies in the basket, as well."

"Stew and fry bread?" he ventured.

"Possibly." She smiled at the sly reference to her meager culinary expertise. "But not likely. Jake's a meat and potatoes man, and so is Sandy. When she gets a crack at someone new, Bonnie likes to show off a little. About the only thing I can guarantee we won't have is baked Alaska."

"Because of the heat." Steve suggested the obvious.

Hank shook her head, her smile becoming a grin. "Because it goes to waste when there's Bonnie's best bear sign."

"Ahh, of course, Bonnie's Best Bear Sign. Sounds like something out of one of the old dime novels, with cowboys riding miles and fighting duels over a can of peaches and a handful of sign." The sugary concoction, somewhat like the modern day doughnut, was truly legend in the old West. One that lived on.

"Wouldn't be unheard of even today. When you try one, you'll see." With laughter trailing behind her, Hank returned to the mare. Checking the cinch, she drew it tighter, readying for the rougher terrain ahead. "I'll saddle Blue Belle, and get the basket," she said with more composure than was true. "When you're ready, we'll go."

The trail she chose was an easy one if ridden wisely, and one she'd ridden often as a child. Over the years it had been overgrown by scrub, narrowing to a one horse path. The terrain was uneven, but with no insurmountable ground. The mare, who had no official name yet, moved with an effortlessness that promised great things.

Hank guided her around a fallen rock that seemed to have no immediate point of origin, then urged her over a clutter of detritus and was doubly gratified when she took the crossing as well as solid ground.

"Good girl." Hank petted the mare before she looked back at Steve. "You have the makings of an excellent mountain horse in this one. She walks like her sire or dam might have been part mountain goat."

"Sorry, all horse. Both of them." Steve fell silent again as he jogged along in her back trail, too contented to enter into discussion. She'd guided him to a part of the canyon he'd had time to afford only cursory exploration. Repairs to the house and stables, and then the fencing had filled his days, leaving time for little else.

"A good mountain horse would bring a tidy sum. Especially one as good as this. Other than Black Jack, I've never seen a horse that showed such early promise." She led the mare through an intricate turn, then, with a tap of her knees and a cluck of her tongue, urged the animal up a narrow incline. At the top of a rise she stopped, waiting for Steve and Blue Belle to catch up.

When he drew along side her, she turned her attention from the floor of the canyon, waiting for him to speak, to make some comment about the land, the ride, or surefooted horses. Yet he didn't seem to feel the need for comment or conversation. In fact, he was so self-involved and caught up in his own thoughts, she wondered if he'd heard the last at all. Indeed, was he even minimally aware she was at his side?

She'd entertained high hopes for the ride. That it would cheer him and appease his restlessness, and lead the way to laying the last of his doubts to rest. Now she had to admit she'd accomplished the opposite, as he sank deeper into thought.

"She needs a name." To assure that he attended her, Hank touched his shoulder, brushing blue-black hair in dire need of cutting. The contact left her fingertips tingling and her throat dry. Resentfully she wondered why he must have that effect on her, when he scarcely knew she was in the world. "The horse," she explained, and wondered why. "One as good as she needs to be called something other than girl, or horse."

"Why?" he asked flatly.

"Because she's a fine animal, and when I finish with her training, she'll be a fine cow horse," Hank said in a low voice, her eyes molten silver, her thigh skimming along his as Blue Belle tossed her head and stamped her feet impatiently. "Better than fine," she snapped as a current of unexpected longing for things she couldn't have, and wouldn't admit she wanted, rocketed through her. "Damn fine! Dammit!"

A spur to the mare's side set the animal into a rocking gallop. Dust spurted from her hooves like umber smoke as Hank rode deep in the saddle, one wanting to run as much as the other. As the trail descended sharply, twisting and turning, brush thickened, thriving in the protective shade of canyon walls. And with the difficulty, her anger, hasty but short-lived, abated.

In only a little time, she was sawing on the reins, pulling the reluctant mare to a halt. The trail at this point was too narrow to turn. Resting her hand on her thigh, the thigh that had brushed his, she shifted in the saddle to look back.

The trail was deserted. He wasn't there.

Panic played like a trip-hammer on her nerves, her throat convulsed. Visions of Steve sprawled in some crazy twist of the trail danced in macabre vignettes before her eyes. Deep in the horrors guilt heaped upon her, she hardly believed what she saw as he rounded one last turn, horse and rider plodding along.

Relief flowed through her like wine, sweet and intoxicating. She wanted to apologize, but there was too much between them for mere apology. Too much and too little . . . Too much anger and distrust. Too little understanding and forgiveness.

Hank waited though bleak eyes as he kept Belle at a safe, deliberate pace, and his wandering gaze on the land around him. When he drew closer, with a flick of her reins she urged her mount into a walk as deliberate.

The remainder of the ride was as uneventful as silent. Under a dome of blue sky, they wound their way through mesquite and patches of golden grass. The stunted oaks the trail bypassed grew fewer, giving way to cottonwoods as the path grew wider and far more worn, suggesting the approach of a riparian habitat. In the dusty hush, the steady, muffled clop of shod horses was only amplified by the whistle of a kingbird catching an insect on the wing. Far above, from an unchanging sky, the hunting cry of a hawk rained down as it wheeled and soared, riding an invisible tide.

Once, a cat too large to be a pet gone wild loped across their path so swiftly the horses had no time to do more than balk and whicker nervously.

"Jaguarundi!" Hank called out, just loudly enough to be heard. "They range out of Mexico, but only rarely. It might be years before you see another. Or never."

Steve made a note to watch the horses closer. Like Hank, he thought the cat's appearance was a rare happening, and likely no threat to the stock, but it behooved a rancher to be always cautious.

A last gooseneck turn threaded through a pass so narrow his knees brushed before the rugged walls opened to a small jeweled vista. The hush of the trail became the music of the faint tumble of water, and the jaguarundi was forgotten.

She had led him to a secret place he would have been a long time discovering. An arroyo more than a canyon. A place where few people had ever been, and only one in a long while.

"This is where you came when you rode across the range." In his mind he saw a child, hair wild and flying, riding as only she could.

"Charlie brought me here when I was very young. He said it was my place, a haven to come to when—" Breaking off, she shook her head.

"When things got too rough at the ranch," he finished for her.

"Then," she admitted. "And other times." She didn't ask what more he knew of her life than she and Charlie had told him. She didn't ask how. Silverton was a small town. Its gossips weren't always accurate, but they were always busy, and a new ear was an exciting challenge. "I don't come here much anymore."

Dismounting as she did, sensing the shift of her mood, Steve said nothing as he took the reins from her, looping them together over the limb of a cottonwood. Giving her the privacy of the moment, he moved away. His critical inspection ranged over the unexpected *ciénega*. Though it was scarcely a true marshland, the Spanish name seemed to fit.

The arroyo was a tiny world painted in varying intensities and hues of every color of the spectrum. There was the yellow of the sun, the reds of the land blending to browns. Blues, beginning clear and pristine in the perfect sky of a perfect day, descended to shades of purple in cloistered shadows, and blue-black in a small reflecting pool. And all of it dressed in green, rich and light and dark. A gift of the earth and the sky.

Steve had never wanted to paint, had never even thought to covet that talent. But now he understood the driving force behind it, the joy of sharing.

As he looked to the woman who had lived in his thoughts and his dreams for weeks, he understood even more. Savannah Henrietta Benedict was many things. A woman of strength and substance with threads of compassion and honor running deep in the fabric of her being.

She was Jake Benedict's surrogate son, Camilla Benedict's daughter and her own woman in one. And neither would ever compromise the principles that guided her.

Drawing a shuddering breath, Steve closed his eyes, his fists clenched, then unclenched, as something inside him cast off its painful bindings, soaring like the hawk, exhilarated and unshackled.

"Savannah," he murmured when he could breathe again. "The lady. My lady."

When he opened his eyes, the sun was brighter, the sky bluer. In the whisper of trickling water and the rustle of leaves there was respite.

Crossing the clearing to the small bright patch where she knelt, laying out the banquet prepared by the venerable Bonita, he caught her arm. Bringing her to her feet, he drew her to him, holding her in the circle of his embrace.

Her gaze was level, but puzzled and wary. When he stroked her cheek, trailing the back of his knuckles over fine, fragrant skin, she didn't move away.

"We'll call her The Lady."

Hank accepted the name without comment, as if her singular conversation had been only a little time ago. His choice couldn't have been more perfect for the mare with her quick intelligence, her sure and delicate step.

"Thank you," he said softly. "For everything, and this."

She stared up at him, silver eyes catching the gold of the sun. Radiant eyes. She felt no need to remind him the arroyo was his, part of Sunrise Canyon and the Broken Spur. No need to remind him she was the enemy, for in the darkness of his eyes she saw redemption.

Her heart was too full for words, too full for laughter or tears. In the end she simply nodded.

"Yes," Steve whispered, apropos of nothing and everything. Binding her braid about his hand, he brought her closer, drawing her head to his chest. His heart was soft thunder beneath her cheek as he held her.

In a land of color and light, magic and miracle, with a woman like no other in his arms, he wondered where this moment would take them.

Chapter 11

The corrals and temporary holding pens were blaring sound and feverish turmoil. To the uninitiated it would have been unremitting carnage, chaos with hope of only chaotic results. To one who understood the branding and separating of stock, there was order in the bedlam, credible and efficient, born of habit and instinct.

In the choking, blinding whirl of dust, in desiccating heat, each hand had a job and knew it well. Each job named its skill.

Ropers roped. Flankers and rastlers, working in teams, flanked and wrestled calves and yearlings down. Iron men branded, wielding the white-hot iron with consummate skill. Markers, plying needles and knives, marked, inoculated, castrated.

There were new and more modern methods for some, but Jake was a man who resisted progress. Even more since his strokes.

In the middle of a corral, Hank worked the iron, the stench of blood and burning hair stinging her nose and eyes as much as the sweat that soaked the band of her hat and trickled down her face. Minding the fire, the heated iron, the depth of the brand, she was too focused to know when Jake Benedict propelled his chair from the veranda, bumping over timeworn ruts, halting at the fence nearest her.

"Well," his voice lifted, with effort, above the noise and commotion. His hands were folded in his lap, his Stetson tilted over his forehead to block out the slant of the morning sun. "I see you deigned to join us today in this little endeavor."

Swiping a sleeve across her eyes, she looked up from a calf. "Yes, sir," she agreed. "For a number of years now."

Jake stiffened at the rejoinder. "I thought maybe you'd stay out on the range this year, since you've taken such a liking to it."

"No." The iron sizzled, the calf bawled and struggled as she signaled its release.

"Makes a man wonder, seeing as how you're gone more than home, lately. Maybe we should see about putting in a few conveniences in whatever line shack you've taken to camping out in." Jake was irritable, spoiling for a fight.

"Thanks, Sandy," Hank murmured in an aside, smoothly relinquishing her station to the foreman, who came to relieve her. Flexing cramped fingers as she walked, she approached the fence. The old-fashioned wheelchair was big and bulky, Jake Benedict was a tall man, and at the moment, his disability did not keep him from holding himself straight and proud. Having inherited none of his massive, rawboned frame, as she leaned a shoulder on a rail, the disparity in their heights was only minimal. "I'm here, Jake."

"Yes," her father admitted, the thirst for a battle still stirring his blood. "You're always here when you're needed."

"There's nowhere else I'd rather be." She did not point out that her nights away from the ranch had ended. She was up early, and late to return, but she'd been home each night for days. The reminder would only be wasted, and no improvement of his disposition.

Since his strokes, it was always the same when the ranch itself was busy. When he couldn't escape the reality of his helplessness, nor what it had done to her life. Hank understood that it was the ambivalence of resentment and guilt that drove him to seek her out, to vent the anger he felt for himself and the fates that put him in the chair.

Sliding off her gloves, she tucked them in her belt and ducked under a rail. "I'm glad you came down." She leaned on his shoulder. "The hands always work hard, but they put an extra effort into it when you're watching. Impressing Jake Benedict ranks right up there with wearing the Benedict star."

Jake startled her by laughing; it was a deep, natural sound that drew looks of surprise from those hands familiar with his moods. "You're nearly as good at evading an issue as your mother. You're not in her class yet, mind you, but you're getting there." His smile widened as he reminisced. "But, lordy, when she didn't want to evade, she put up one hell of a fight." He touched her hand as it lay over his shoulder. "You're like her in that, too."

Hank laughed and tugged the brim of his hat. "I'll count that as a compliment."

Resettling himself, he shrugged and blinked, as men uncomfortable with emotion were wont to do. "Was meant as such." Then, as if the first admission required reinforcement, "It surely was."

Hank crouched quietly at his feet, poignantly certain that Jake Benedict missed his wife more than he would say. Perhaps more than he knew. Clasping his hand only briefly she smiled up at him, then turned to watch the melee, sharing a moment that was rare between father and daughter.

A half hour later, when Bonita bore down on them wearing an anxious frown, Jake was exhausted by the heat and noise and his own conflict. Though she knew he would go to his grave denying it, Hank saw he was relieved when the small, plump woman scurried away, muttering about heat and sunstroke as she rushed him back to the shaded veranda.

"He's having a hard time." His place taken by yet another, Sandy stood a pace behind her, whipcord tough, with worry in his piercing eyes. "It gets harder every year, and this is the worst."

"Because of my absences?" Hank spoke her own worry.

"No, sis, you can't take the blame for this one." The foreman, who had been as much her father as Jake, squeezed her arm reassuringly. "This year, more than ever, he sees his life slipping away, and the days in the chair become more intolerable."

"He uses the walker in the house. He could use it more."

"He could," Sandy agreed. "But, as much as he hates it, he'd rather sit in that damnable chair with his stubborn vanity intact than let the hands see him stumble and stagger around with a metal cage bracketing his legs."

"Pride!" Hank spat the word as if it were an abomination.

"Benedict pride," Sandy drawled. "Seems to me you've inherited your share, and some from the Neals to boot. Considering the way you've been running yourself to a frazzle and all, making up for something you had nothing to do with."

"The Lawters worked for us." She wouldn't insult Sandy by pretending she didn't understand where he was going with his sly lecture. "Ransome had the crazy idea he should protect me from Steve." She kept her tone at a normal pitch, certain the bleat and bawl of cattle would insure she wouldn't be overheard. "Mis-

guided as they were, what they did, they did in our name. For me."
Her mouth curled in loathing. "In my book that lays part of the
blame at my door."

"Then I suggest you read your 'book' again. Dammit, sis, there's
enough trouble for each of us to have our share, no need to ask for
more." It hadn't escaped the wily foreman's notice that she re-
ferred to the newest tenant of Sunrise Canyon by his first name, and
real friendly like. "You can't hold yourself responsible for what a
couple of idiots choose to do."

Refusing debate, she took another course. "If the situation were
reversed, what would you do in my place, Sandy?"

"A moot question. It isn't reversed, and I'm not in your place."

"But if you were?"

He looked away, unwilling to meet the challenge in her gaze.
Tapping the top rail of the corral, he studied the wood too intently.

"If you felt even remotely responsible, what would you do?"

"Aw, hell!" He turned, eyes like lasers meeting hers. "The same
damn thing you're doing—train his horses and make sure they were
the best at the Silverton sale."

"Yes," Hank said, pleased and vindicated. "You would."

"It's a mite different."

"Because I'm a woman?" Before he could agree or deny, she
rushed on, assuming an all too familiar fighting stance. "That never
cut any slack before, why should it now?"

"You're tired, sis." Abandoning one indefensible course, he addressed another. "Burning yourself up, and Jake's suspicious. I
don't know how much longer I can cover for you."

"I know." Covering for her had never been discussed. Hank
simply trusted that he would. As Sandy always had, supporting her
in what she did, her buffer against the world. No questions, no
judgments. "Jake thinks I've been spending my time at a line shack,
working the herd. Would it be off the mark to think you're responsible?"

The handsome, graying man shrugged. "He assumed."

"And you didn't correct him."

"Seemed for the best, for both or you."

A calf escaped a rope, and in the confusion banged into a fence.
There was bedlam in the corral. Short-lived, and brought quickly
under control, but pointedly reminding that all hands were needed.

"We'd best get back to it." The rangy foreman climbed the fence.
Swinging a leg over, he sat astride the top rail looking down at her.
"You gonna take a ride later today?"

"If we finish up here."

"Mind some company?"

"I'd like some company. Our friend would, too, I suspect." A grin crinkled her eyes. "He's bound to be ready for a change of faces."

"Well, now," Sandy drawled, slipping with ease into his untutored cowhand persona. "I don't know if I'd be too sure of that. The boy ain't a fool, you know." A chuckle drifted down to Hank. "Truth be told, he ain't exactly a boy, either. Is he, now?"

Hank ignored the sly teasing with the aplomb taught her by her mother. And for once she was grateful for the red dust that streaked her face, hiding the flush his observation prompted. Unaware of how much she looked like the girl who'd spent most of her young life struggling with priorities, she asked with an artless candor, "You like him, don't you, Sandy?"

"I surely do, saw he had sand the minute I laid eyes on him." His voice was kind as he recognized sentiments she wasn't quite ready to put into words. "I 'spect that makes two of us."

"Maybe." Scaling the fence, Hank swung over and dropped to the ground inside the corral.

Sandy climbed down to walk with her to the branding site.

Calves bawled, milling around them. Yearlings bucked and kicked. Red dust churned under hooves and boots, bearing the heat of scorched earth, plastering itself on everyone and everything.

Branding! Misery marked by sweat. Grim, grueling, gratifying. Every man with his work, separate, yet dependent on another. Out of pandemonium, order. Out of teamwork, trust, and truth, the measure of men and a woman.

A far cry from a courtroom, but judge and jury for Hank Benedict.

Iron in hand, ready to work again, she paused, smiling ruefully up at Sandy. "Yeah," she admitted to him, to herself. "I 'spect it does make two of us."

"She's a natural."

"Yep." Sandy pushed his Stetson back a notch, and shifted a sprig of hay from one corner of his mouth to the other. "Took to horses like cactus to rain."

"She's tired."

"Can't argue that." Catching the hay between thumb and forefinger, squinting at it in a gesture reminiscent of a reformed smoker, the foreman tossed it away. "You do two jobs, you get tired."

"My point exactly." Steve turned from the corral where Hank put The Lady through her paces. His dark look settled on Sandy Gannon, the man who knew her far better than he. "And another reason I'm glad you came with her today. Help me convince her she doesn't have to do this."

"Can't."

"Yes, you can," Steve insisted. "She respects your opinion, and if any man can make her listen to reason, it's you."

"*If* any man can. That's the key," the older man explained. "And no man can."

"Sandy..."

"I tried already."

"And?"

Sandy pushed his hat back another notch. "You see where she is." With keen regard, he studied Steve. "I'll ask you the same question she asked me. In the same circumstance, what would you do?"

Steve considered his answer, even when there was no need. His response was long in coming, and reluctant. "Exactly what she has."

"Right."

"It's different."

The foreman laughed, wondering if it was just the Western man, or all men, who were steeped in the same arrogance. "I tried that one too. She reminded me in no uncertain terms that being a woman never cut her any slack before. She doesn't expect it now."

Steve had no difficulty imagining that particular scene. "So what do I do?"

"You leave her alone, son. Let her do what she has to do." A pointing finger charged Steve to understand. "Remember, this is as much for herself as it is for you."

Steve accepted the inevitable. Then, taking up another worry as he put one aside, "What happens when Jake finds out his daughter is aiding and abetting the squatter from Sunrise Canyon?"

In a moment of silence, Hank's assuring singsong drifted to them. As smoothly as if she'd been performing the tasks for years, The Lady responded to every command. She seemed eager to please the soft spoken rider who never asked more than she was capable of giving.

Watching a horse and rider so in tune was an extraordinary sight. One more confirmation of the mettle of the woman.

Steve had begun to think his question wouldn't be answered, when Sandy responded thoughtfully, "What she does about you and Jake is her bridge to cross, and she will, in her own way, when she comes to it."

"Just like that?" Steve was disturbed that this man who had been virtually a part of the Benedict family would dismiss a possible disaster as cavalierly. And disaster it would be, he had no doubt.

"She's a helluva woman, and a Benedict in the bargain." Sandy's tone was unperturbed, but his eyes were as penetrating as a blade of blue steel. "She's been in the middle before and come out with the best of two worlds. If you're half the man Charlie thinks you are, maybe she can again."

"Charlie?" Steve had the feeling he'd missed something, somewhere along the way. Something important. "What does Charlie have to do with any of this?"

"Is this a private conversation," Hank asked from a pace away. "Or can anyone join in?"

"Sis!" Sandy turned to her. "When did you finish up?"

"Long enough ago that The Lady and Lorelei are bedded down for the night, and the other chores are done. The way you two were going at it, I could've shifted the barn off its foundation and you wouldn't notice."

Her gloves were tucked in her belt. When the branding had been done, a bath and a change of clothes rid her of the evidence of her work. But neither soap and water nor the fresh, bright blue of her shirt could erase proof of its rigors.

Her eyes were heavy-lidded with fatigue, her smile was strained. The too perfect bearing betrayed how difficult it was to stand at all.

The curse, not quite smothered by the clench of Steve's lips, was bitterly explicit. Only a flashing look of warning from Sandy kept him from sweeping her into his arms, taking her to his bed and forcing her to rest. The look and the certainty the foreman was right, that she would fight him, worsening her desperate condition by denying it, kept him still.

He couldn't make her rest, but he could keep her off the half-wild stallion when she was too wasted to stay in the saddle. "It's time you called it a day. Get in the truck, I'll drive you home."

"I rode in." She bristled at his peremptory tone. "I'll ride out, when I choose, and under my own steam."

"You're mistaken, Benedict." Steve moved from the fence to stand squarely in her path. "You've run out of choices and steam. Get in the truck."

"Cody!"

"Stay out of this, Sandy," Steve snapped without taking his hard stare from Hank. "This discussion is between the lady and me."

"That's where you're wrong, there's nothing between us. Nothing! What I do, when and how, is not and never will be open to discussion!" She was turning aside, moving toward the stream where Black Jack grazed and paced. "Let's go home, Sandy. The way we came."

"Dammit, Benedict!" Flaring temper and remembered fear got the best of proper intentions, after all. With an iron grip Steve caught her wrist, wrenching her around and back. She was in his arms, and he was spinning away from Sandy before either could react.

"Cody!" Hank and Sandy spoke in unison, but it was the foreman's voice that carried the threat.

"What the hell do you think you're doing?" Sandy took a step, pausing only when Steve turned back.

"I'm taking her home, Gannon." Smoldering black eyes met the arctic chill of blue. "Where you should have kept her today, if you had to hog tie her."

"I'm the foreman, she's the boss." One look at Steve's face, and Sandy understood the anguish and frustration of a man backed into a corner by his own helplessness, and the impact of contradicting emotions. The man was at war with himself. "She gives the orders," he said in a tone turned benign. "Not me."

Hank stirred tautly in Steve's arms. Her protests were low and commanding, but he didn't hear her as he snarled again at Sandy. "She may be the boss, but you're a hell of a sight bigger."

He didn't wait for an answer as he stalked to his truck. The door was flung open and she was tucked safely inside when he faced the foreman again. "You can tether the horses to the truck and ride in with us, or you can get back under your own steam."

The invitation was less than gracious, and Sandy responded in kind. "I'll bring the horses along in my own good time."

"Fine!" Steve slammed one door, stalked around the truck and ripped open another. When he climbed in Hank was sitting rigid and erect, fighting the threatening tremor of rage. "Don't say it." He leveled a finger at her. "Don't say one word."

Throwing the truck in gear, showering loose earth beneath his wheels, he spun into the road.

"Stop the truck, Steve!" Hank demanded over the roar of the engine and flying dirt.

"No." He kept his glowering stare on the road.

"Stop it now!"

"Be quiet, or else."

"Or else!" Her voice crackled with anger. "Or else what?"

"This." Brakes locked, tires skidded, the truck spun right in a perfect one hundred and eighty degree reversal. Before it stopped rocking he was reaching for her, dragging her to him. "Or else this. This, dammit! Always this."

She opened her mouth in a protest lost as his closed over it.

The first kiss was ruthless. A passionate punishment for what she'd done to herself, for making him care. A reckoning with his own vulnerabilities.

The second was honest. The admission of who she was, what she was, and how important every part had become to him.

The third, when her hands barely brushed his chest—neither keeping him nor pushing him away—was desire. The need to hold her, shield her. The hunger to touch her, filling every lost and solitary part of soul and heart with the excitement and wonder she brought him.

Hank neither resisted nor fought him. Instead, she forced herself to simply endure. Holding herself fastidiously aloof, she pretended her heart didn't flutter in her chest like a caged bird longing to be free. Denied that she liked the feel of him under her hands. Clung, as to a lifeline, to the memory of outrage even as it vanished in smoke.

When his mouth gentled, slanting and teasing, smoke became fire and her battle was lost. Her breath grew ragged and her skin softly flushed with dew as passion ignited. A shattered sound vibrated in her throat as she met his kiss, reveling in the scent of him, the taste, the textures. The seductive maleness.

God help her, she'd forgotten. Forgotten how it could be with a man. Forgotten how it was to walk the tightrope between lust and love. The exhilaration, the yearning, the beautiful madness. The danger.

Sensation built upon sensation, and then yet another. A feast, too much, too rich. The slow heat of passion that knew no ebb, too exquisite to bear, too beguiling to deny.

As her body throbbed with desire . . . sang with it . . . ached with it . . . she wondered how she could forget what she'd never known.

"Never," she murmured into his kiss, and her body trembled with the joy of him.

As she trembled, so did he, meeting the sultry demands of her kiss, drinking in the fire of her passion. Until the most ancient and primal needs swept away the discipline of mind and body. With unanswered torment clawing at him, and the last bit of reason spinning nearly out of reach, a small, still voice whispered, stop.

Stop? How could he? When she was so warm and pliant in his arms, how could he? Yet the whispers would not be quiet. Would not be silent.

Calling back the anger that would keep him sane, making it his lifeline, he backed away. Slowly, regretfully, with every ounce of will left to him.

Her lashes fluttered, and in her bewildered gaze he saw the fragility, the faltering strength. The cost of her day. Touching her throat, trailing the back of his fingers over the vulnerable flesh, he vowed not to contest her stubborn course, but to make it better.

"Steve…" Grappling through the fog of fatigue, she strained to regain her composure.

"No." He stopped her with a fingertip at her lips, wishing he could kiss her again, but certain he dared not. What he had to say required a cool head and thoughts tightly marshaled.

Hank stared up at him, not quite sure what had happened. All she understood was that he was angry. He was always angry with her. A circumstance that threatened to become a perpetual state. Yet in anger, he kissed her, one emotion seemed to spark the other.

It made no sense. Yet, in the back of her restless mind, a vague and elusive thought insisted that if she would only consider carefully, it made perfect sense. Later, she decided. Later, when her mind was clearer, when she wasn't so befuddled by weariness and the intoxicating aftermath of his touch. Perhaps then she might decipher the irresistible mystery and mystique of Steve Cody.

"Later," she promised herself.

"Not later," Steve insisted, giving the wrong interpretation to her muttered promise. "Now! You'll listen to me now, Benedict."

"Listen?" Suddenly, she was more than exhausted, as the surge of adrenaline dissipated, taking with it a part of her reserve. Indignant with herself for what she considered weakness, and with him for more reasons than she could count or comprehend, she turned turmoil and warring emotion back at him. "Listen. Listen! All I ever do is listen, and all that you ever say is angry."

"That isn't quite the case," he continued firmly in the face of her outburst. "But we won't debate the point." He waited, holding her heated stare, giving no ground. When she sighed wearily, looking down and away, for once defeated in a battle of wills, he lifted her face with a touch that refused to let her retreat again. "Tonight we lay down some ground rules.

"Ground rules!" She sounded like a magpie. "We don't need rules."

"If you're going to train the horses, we do."

"Oh yeah? Such as?"

"Such as you don't put in two days work in one at the Rafter B, then come to the Broken Spur. You don't drive yourself so hard. When there's something I can do to help," the grave line of his mouth hardened, "something you and Dr. Bonner agree is allowed, you let me do it. When you're tired, you say so." He tilted her face, absorbing the effects of a day already imprinted on his mind. "You say so, do you hear?"

"I hear! I hear!" Hank snapped, straining to break free.

"Okay." He took his hands away, holding them upright in a peaceful gesture. Sliding back under the steering wheel, he gripped the leather-bound circle tightly. "That's it. That's the list. Is there anything there you can't live with?"

Hank drew a long, considering breath. "No, I suppose your ground rules are pretty sensible." Then, surprising herself, she added, "More sensible than I've been. I expected more."

Encouraged by her compliance, he risked another point. "There is one more I would have tacked on, but I figured it would shoot down the rest."

"Must be pretty impossible."

A grim smile left his eyes untouched. "Impossible for you."

"Try me." She challenged.

"Black Jack."

"Let me guess." A gesture stopped him before he could say more. "You want me to stop riding him across the range."

"Yes."

"You're right." She leaned back, closing her eyes. "That would blow the whole list."

Knowing when to cut his losses and walk away had served him well in the rodeo. It served now. For a long while he sat watching her, even in the muted light, and with lines drawn by exhaustion, she was lovely. As lovely as she was tough, as resilient as she was stubborn. A Benedict. A small smile flitted over his face. "Right."

The engine roared, the lights came on. "I suppose four out of five should be considered good odds."

As the truck turned, coming around half circle in the direction that would lead to the Rafter B, Hank nestled deeper into the hard backed seat. More asleep than awake, she muttered, "With a Benedict, two out of three would be good. Three out of four, amazing. Four out of five? A blooming miracle."

When their dust settled and the moon broke full over the rim of the canyon, Sandy Gannon rode out, with Black Jack trailing in his wake and a grin on his face.

Bonita sat dozing over the newspaper when the peremptory crack of a single knock roused her. The ranch and bunkhouse had long ago fallen into the hushed, desultory hour when inspection and repair of personal equipment were complete and conversation stuttered to a halt. Even the most gregarious cowboys had drawn into themselves, contemplating their day and welcoming the end of it.

Savannah would not knock, and no one else would come calling. Unless there was trouble.

Her chins quivering, Bonita jerked to her feet in alarm. Bare feet tapping over stone tiles, she hurried to answer a second knock, as sharp, as peremptory. Giving no thought to safety or her own protection, she threw the massive door open and peered into the darkness. "Yes?"

A hulking figure stood on the veranda. A tall and strange, misshapen creature. With a hand over a palpitating heart, she gasped a muffled scream and lurched back.

"Bonita?" The voice was at odds with the monster her native superstitions had conjured.

"Who are you? What are you?" Her mind told her there should be menace in the voice. Yet that she heard none did not still the fearful rush of her pulse. "What do you want?"

"You are Bonita, aren't you? Bonita, who makes fabulous bear sign."

"Bear sign?" Arched brows flew up, her chins drooped. "Señor Steve?" The little woman stared harder, her eyes growing accustomed to the darkness, seeking a man she'd heard much of, but never met.

One shape became two that merged. A tall and wickedly attractive man with a woman in his arms.

"Savannah!" Bracelets jangled as usually competent hands fluttered in panic. "*¡Dios mío!* Is she hurt? What happened? Where is Señor Sandy?"

"Shh…" Steve quieted the torrent as he stepped further into the light. *Savannah*. Sandy called her sis, and he, Benedict. Here, then, was another who avoided the masculine appellation. "Savannah's fine. She's only worn down. On the way home she fell asleep in the truck.

"I don't want to wake her." He advanced farther into the foyer, searching doorways and stairs as if each held the key to a great mystery. "Which room is hers?"

Bonita had been staring raptly at him, noting that this man who threatened the order of Savannah's life held her as if he would never let her go. Prompted by his question, she leaped into agitated action. "Her room is first at the top of the stairs. Señor Jake sleeps downstairs at the back of the house."

"He's in his room now?" Steve was acutely aware that it was a little late to be concerned with bringing Jake Benedict's curiosity and then his wrath down on his daughter. But until this moment he'd thought only of the woman he called Benedict, and her dire need for rest.

"He retired early," Bonita explained. "He pushed himself too much, and the day exhausted him."

"Family trait," Steve quipped gruffly, and ignored Bonita's questioning look. "I'll take her up now."

Bonita would have gone with them, but something in his manner warned her away. As he climbed the stairs with a strength that belied old and recent injuries, she stood by the first riser, her hand on the balustrade. A vigil she would keep until Steve Cody descended the stairs alone.

Her bedroom was large, but Spartan. The few personal touches were clustered unobtrusively on a small dresser. Pretty bottles of lotion and perfume, a tube of lip gloss, a brush and comb, reminding that Savannah Henrietta Benedict, who lived and worked like a man, was very much a woman. Incongruously, but perhaps not, in a separate place of honor lay a worn and stained boot heel with a star carved in its side.

A picture of a young woman much like Savannah stood on a table by her narrow bed. It didn't take a mastermind to determine this was Camilla Benedict, mother, wife, nemesis. Truant.

The familiar jut of a very determined chin sparked a smile in his dark eyes. There appeared to be no quit in the woman, yet she had. He wondered why.

Savannah stirred restlessly in his arms, reminding of his self-appointed guardianship. Crossing to the bed, he laid her on the thin, utilitarian spread.

As he backed away, considering what he should do next, Savannah muttered unintelligibly, shifted and turned to lie slightly on her side. One arm was thrown over her head, the other crossed at her waist. Her braid lay like a gleaming lariat at her breast.

Steve stood by the bed, looking down at her. For an instant, in a quirk of memory, the spare but lovely figure became a pale and helpless body, the wasted prison of a keen and gentle mind. More memories threatened, recollection burned into him, that could never quite be dismissed. With a jolt, he shook the remembrance aside and knelt by the bed to do what he could to make Savannah Benedict comfortable for the night.

First were the boots, falling with a soft thud on the bare floor. The belt followed as he slipped it expertly from the narrow waist of her jeans. He considered her shirt, worn and old, drawn taut over her chest and slender torso. One snap had pulled open, revealing a wisp of lacy lingerie and the creamy swell of a perfect breast. It would be simple to deal with the remaining snaps, and then the bra, releasing her from its restraint.

A part of him urged it. A part knew he should not. He settled, instead, for smoothing the fabric of her shirt and folding back a crumpled collar before slipping the tucked hem free of her jeans. Backing away again, acknowledging the peacefulness of her deep sleep, he realized there was little else he could or needed to do.

Even as the judgment was made, he was returning to her bed, sinking down at her side to gather the braid in his hands. Deftly he loosed the woven mane, combing his fingers through it, letting it slide like silk over his palm. There was no cause for what he did, except that he wanted it. He wanted the feel of dark, gleaming silk flowing over him, touching him.

As she lay, deep in sleep, a vital and enchanting woman, he wondered what he would discover wrapped in it, bound to her by it.

Steve smiled ruefully at the impossible thought. The attraction was there, drawing him to her and growing stronger. But no matter the prevailing truce, they were from opposite sides, rivals for the same prize. When it was resolved, one would win, one would lose. He would be foolish to think the attraction would survive.

"If I lose, I'll be gone." Threading his fingers through her hair once more, he watched as it drifted like a mist over the pillow. With the light from a single lamp falling around them in a circle of muted radiance, the scent of sun drenched roses enveloped him.

She loved the canyon and the old house as much as he. As surely as he lived he knew the repairs were hers, not gratitude from a roving cowboy. A gift, instead. Her gift, a labor of love. He found consolation in that as he stroked her cheek, remembering the first time he'd stepped into the house. The scent of roses, her scent, was his first memory. He wondered if it would be his last.

Savannah stirred and turned. Fearing that if he stayed longer, she would sense his presence and wake, Steve slid from the bed. Crossing to the door, he paused for one last look, reluctant to go, knowing that he must before he threw reason and caution aside and answered the clamoring demand of his body.

"You're a fool, Cody, she isn't for you. That was ordained before the cards were dealt. Once burned is enough." Words filled with steely determination, denying what he wanted most. Throwing open the door, he stepped into the hall, catching one last glimpse of her as it closed behind him.

The latch engaged with a metallic click. Savannah stirred, she smiled, caught in a memory or a dream, and was still again.

"She sleeps?" A worried question, mirroring Bonita's face.

"Yes." Descending the stairs, Steve caught her hand in his. "You'll see that she rests? Guard her from herself?"

"With my life." The dramatic statement came naturally to Bonita. Her fiery, motherly temperament was the bedrock of the resolve that kept her on at the Rafter B. For Savannah. And for Jake, as she endured his insults and ill temper. But she wondered if this young man knew what he was asking. If Savannah decided to rise within the hour, no one could stop her.

Unless it was this man.

"I will try," she promised again.

His finger at her chin lifted her face to the kiss he dropped on her cheek. "Thank you."

Then he was gone in a whirl, his steps echoing, then fading as another door closed behind him. Touching her cheek, Bonita stared after him, a look of awe in her eyes.

"The man could melt a heart of stone," she murmured, and wondered if he knew.

Chapter 12

Hank Benedict dismounted, stripped the saddle from the mare, then tossed the gear over a waiting sawhorse before leading her to water. As the long Romanesque muzzle dipped to the trough, she stood by the mare, stroking her neck, smoothing her mane.

"She's great, isn't she?"

The question was aimed at Steve, who paused to watch as he finished tightening a cinch. His response came drolly on cue, part of an unwritten script. "She's great."

They'd found a common ground for agreement, and over a period of days and weeks had even grown comfortable with it. Conversation remained spare, focused on horses, training, and little else. Safe subjects, keeping the door closed on things they'd rather not think or feel.

Workday matters, simple things, Steve mused wryly. All very proper, prudent, and clinically businesslike. But only a fragile and tenuous barrier for seething emotions and mercurial passions that were far from simple. Far from proper or prudent, and never more than a heartbeat from surfacing.

It was there, this nameless thing that wouldn't be denied, waiting to ignite. Temptation, building like a storm, needing only a careless and unguarded moment to break free.

She was as aware of it as he. He saw it in the depths of thoughtful silences, the unexpected tremor of her hands. He heard it in a faltering word, a phrase lost, then recaptured in an exasperated rush.

There was no help for it. It was a part of them, buried not nearly deeply enough. Smoldering. Waiting.

He watched her across the corral, as she petted and praised The Lady. Watched and admired the proud, straight back, the unerring and certain moves of a small woman who commanded rougher and bigger creatures out of knowledge and respect.

"Horses, cattle," Steve muttered under his breath. "Men."

Gitano snorted and pranced at his shoulder, impatient for the promised ride. "Quiet, boy." He ruffled the dark mane flowing over a bowed neck as he looped the reins over a rail. "I know we have time to make up, but you'll have your turn."

He'd been riding for two weeks. Since the day Dr. Bonner stopped by, looking more like Doc Holliday than a modern day man of medicine with his boots and hat and a heavy mustache drooping over his mouth. Eyes twinkling, drawing a stethoscope, not a gun, the medic had given Steve a clean bill of health.

Grateful to be done with enforced idleness, Steve had resumed training and exercising the other horses. But not The Lady, or Lorelei. The rapport between Hank and both mares continued strongly, the rewards were spectacular, to disrupt it would border on criminal.

Disrupting it would mean the end of her visits to the Broken Spur. He knew it would come someday, but he wasn't ready to face that time, nor to explore the reason he dreaded its coming.

"Thirty days," Hank declared, pleased with her progress.

Steve shook free of his distraction. "Thirty days?"

"The Lady's had thirty days under the saddle," Hank explained, speaking of the training she'd given the horse once it was broken to the saddle. "A solid foundation." Created in her patient way of asking, not demanding, reward, not punishment. "The major work from now will be reinforcing and refining what she's learned."

Running her hand down the mare's flank in a final rewarding gesture, she stepped away. "Pedigree, confirmation, ability, she has it all. With her willingness to learn and work, that makes her an exceptional horse."

Steve said nothing, wondering where this was going.

"Have you considered keeping her?"

He'd thought of little else since he'd first seen the mare on the same ranch that produced Gitano. "You forget, I have debts to pay, or there won't be a ranch for her."

"Maybe." Hank was pensive, her argument falling into place even as she spoke. "Maybe not."

Steve snorted impatiently, tossing away a sliver he'd torn from the fence. "Apparently our debts are as different as our lives. There's nothing indefinite about what I owe and when. Without a good price for the horse, I won't make it."

"Put her into competition. She'll be good in the ring."

"You're suggesting the prize money would cover what I owe?" His laugh scoffed at her. "Dream on."

Hank ducked through hewn rails to stand by him, catching his wrist. "It needn't be a dream. When other ranchers see what she can do, they'll be lining up for a colt bred out of her. The bank would extend the loan if she and Lorelei were offered as collateral. Better yet, some of the ranchers would pay for the sire to be a stallion of their own. Or, if you wish, in lieu of payment the stallion might be offered to stand at stud, adding to your bloodlines." Pausing for only a moment, she admitted honestly, "I would, and forgo the first colt out of The Lady in the bargain."

"You're joking!" He didn't move, didn't take his wrist from her insistent grasp. "You have to be, or you're crazy. What you're suggesting would take years."

"Of course it would, but I'm neither joking nor crazy." The idea that had been forming in her thoughts for days grew more exciting as she spoke. Taking her hand from his wrist, she gestured toward the rim of the canyon and its unstable terrain. "Think of the combination. The Lady's a cat. Black Jack is as surefooted as a mountain goat on steep trails. You've seen that for yourself."

To his own everlasting concern, the vision never left him. A beast more savage than tame, a fey and beautiful woman, galloping over treacherous ground.

Unmindful of his silence, fervor mounting, she persisted. "Imagine what it would mean. You have Gitano and Lorelei. Add to their colts those produced by Black Jack and The Lady and you have the makings of a unique breed.

"There are other stallions worth considering, bloodlines that could enhance your own." With astonishing ease, she ticked off the names of some of the best horses in the world, revealing a salient knowledge of horses and their breeding. "Titan, of the Rocking M, a strong Kentucky-bred thoroughbred standing better than seventeen hands. A good horse, better than good. Then there's Bailarin, a wonderful Arabian imported from Spain by Jubal. You know Jubal, you've seen his stock.''

The list grew. Horses Steve had only read about, and never expected to see. The best of their respective breeds, commanding astronomical fees for stud.

"Last, but far from the lesser," Hank continued her enumeration, "Midnight, a Morgan stabled by David Drescher. Fire and Ice, a pair of Norwegian Fjords from Hacienda Desierto. There are Andalusians, Manchesters, a Peruvian Paso. The list is endless." Pausing for breath, she smiled up at him, her face flushed, her eyes bright and fervent. "A veritable melting pot to choose from, or not. And when you have..." A graceful gesture offered him the ultimate prize. "The Cody Horse of the Broken Spur."

Steve tensed out of surprise. "Where did you hear that? What do you know about the Cody horse?"

"You told me." Lady ambled to the fence, stretching her neck over it to snuffle at Hank's shoulder. She was too intent on Steve to notice. "The Cody horse was one of a couple of things you were clear on when you were hurt."

A frown carved lines in Steve's brow. "We haven't talked of that anymore, but it seems I babbled my life history to you."

"Only disjointed words and phrases. An occasional name." One a woman's name. Angie.

"Words and phrases, but enough."

"It goes no further," she assured him.

"I didn't think it would." His plans for the ranch were no secret, just something he wasn't quite ready to discuss openly.

Hank was startled by the easy comment. "You weren't so trusting a short time ago. What made you change your mind?" Her gaze searched his face, looking for the catch. "Or have you?"

"Any man who witnessed you at work would have to be a fool not to believe in your integrity. He would have to be an even bigger fool not to know that it applied to all aspects of your life."

"Integrity?" She angled her hat back a notch and lifted a dubious brow. "Benedict integrity?"

"Yeah." She was her father's daughter in many ways. From the first acre of land acquired to the last, the Benedict empire had been predicated on a foundation of moral rectitude. Jake had capitalized on his neighbors' misfortune without conscience, but their troubles were never of his making. If Steve had learned little else in his days in and around Silverton, he'd learned that. Jake might fight tooth and nail for the canyon, but he would fight fairly. As would his daughter.

"Even an obstinate idiot has to admit the truth," Steve confessed. "Especially when it hits him in the face."

Hank chuckled, diffusing an undercurrent of tension. "You said that, not I."

"And you won't let me forget it." He ventured the prediction, hardly cognizant of it as the low, smoky sound of her laughter danced over him again, fanning embers so carefully banked.

"Never in this life." Her lingering smile was a flash of white in her tanned face. The guardedness was gone, the need for carefully worded conversation forgotten as caution was tossed aside in the excitement of her plans for The Lady. Invisible armor had fallen away leaving her vulnerable, touchable.

It would have been so easy to take her in his arms, answering needs of body and soul. Instead, he settled for a touch, a stroke of a finger, allowing himself a morsel when it was the feast every part of him demanded. Tracing the path of a shadowy blue vein that disappeared into her hair, he managed a hoarse comment. "I would be disappointed if you did."

Hank slanted a glance at him, meaning to toss a biting observation into the teasing fray, and found herself speechless. He had leaned close, so close she could brush his lips with hers by simply rising on tiptoe. She was shocked that she wanted the feel of his mouth, the taste, more than she ever thought possible.

His hand hovering at her temple, light, incredibly gentle, sent shock waves through her with the power of a hurricane. She tried to concentrate on what she'd meant to say, but the beat of her frenzied heart swept it from her mind. Mesmerized by him, wondering and bewildered, she saw a subtle change in the gold-spangled darkness of his eyes, and heard the swift shudder of his indrawn breath.

He leaned closer, as if compelled by a force beyond his control. The scent of him filled her. One move, the barest turn of her head, and his mouth would be hers.

Only one, she thought, wanting it desperately, but afraid. Her eyes closed, her head turned away in anguish. She was afraid. Not of him, but of herself.

His fingers curled, the heel of his hand and his knuckles resting against her cheek only a moment before moving away. He stood without speaking, without touching her, simply looking down at her. Beneath his searching gaze, without his touch, Hank felt lost and disappointed.

Disappointed. The thread of their conversation surfaced. She clung to it like a lifeline. Her voice was low and blue, rusty with unanswered needs. "I wouldn't want to disappoint you."

He smiled, but only with his lips. His eyes were dark, the golden light of laughter gone from them. "You won't."

Neither pretended to understand or misunderstand. Silence rent a chasm between them, a bittersweet reprieve. But only that.

Gitano pawed the dust, and flung back his rippling mane. The jangle of bit and stirrups set up a clatter recalling the real world. Steve was first to respond. "I'm being summoned. When there's a saddle on his back, Gitano expects to fly, not stand." Tucking his thumbs in his back pockets to keep from reaching for her again, he cast a glance at The Lady. "How about it? Are you up to a run?"

"No," Hank blurted. Riding with him was the last thing she dared. Spending another minute in his company was more than she trusted herself to deal with rationally. "I have to go."

"Do you?" Skepticism colored his tone. "Tell me why."

"I have chores to do."

"Sandy will see that they're done."

Hank shook her head. "I need to go home."

"But not to pressing chores." Something in him wouldn't allow her the luxury of the lie.

Catching her lip between her teeth, she stared out over the floor of the canyon. Grass, standing knee-deep, swayed in a current of air unperceived by human senses. She watched it dip and weave, a golden sea without ebb. From the early days of her childhood, she'd found escape from the turmoil of her life in this peaceful place. Now that peace was lost.

Rousing from her thoughts, she backed away. "I have to go. I have to think. This is all new to me."

"Is it?" Closing the space between them, he cupped her chin in his palm. "Can you truly say you haven't thought of this moment for weeks? Haven't we both known what was happening, and that this was inevitable? I want you, Savannah." His voice was uneven with passion. "I've wanted you from the first. Can you deny you haven't felt the same?"

"It isn't that simple." An adamant jerk of her head sent her braid tumbling down her back.

"Isn't it?" His thumb brushed over the corner of her mouth, and her lips parted in a muted gasp. His point made, his dark gaze commanding hers, he murmured, "Will you deny this? Can you?"

"It isn't that easy," Hank insisted doggedly. Spinning away from his touch, she faced him again safely out of reach. "There's more to deal with than desire, or lust."

"This is you and me. It doesn't involve the Broken Spur or the Rafter B. Run from it as long and hard as you like, but you can't hide. It will always be there. Always." His mouth quirked in a grim smile. "You and me, Benedict."

Shaking her head again, she backed further away, unable to deny his point or explain her own. "I need time."

"You're running."

"I've never run from anything in my life."

"Maybe not, until now. Admit it, Benedict, you're running from me."

"No!" she insisted, but found no words for more.

He laughed, a mocking note. "Just when I'd convinced myself you weren't capable of lying."

"I'm not running from you, Steve Cody. I'm taking time to sort what's between us in my mind. I'm entitled to that."

"How much time?" he wondered, mockery replaced by an even more infuriating indulgence. "How long will it take you to accept the inevitable?"

"A week," she shot back at him, choosing a measure of time arbitrarily, out of desperation.

"A week," Steve agreed. "In seven days, we'll meet here. You can tell me what you've decided over dinner. Eight o'clock?"

"Eight will be fine."

"If you aren't here in a week, I'll come to you."

"I'll be here," she flung at him. "Count on it."

She started to go. Catching her arm, he brought her back to him. Their bodies did not touch, yet the electricity between them was nearly palpable. "One more thing."

"Only one?" The look she tossed up at him was hot with anger.

"One." A short and clipped answer, his patience was nearly at an end.

"What would that be?" she drawled, pretending she didn't feel the charge, the hunger.

"Come as Savannah, if there's really such a person. I'm tired of the macho Hank Benedict." Making yet another point, he released her abruptly, as if the feel of her were abhorrent. "Now, go."

Ripping Gitano's reins from the rail, he vaulted into the saddle. Folding his arms over the pommel, reins dangling loosely from his fingers, he leaned down. "Seven days, Savannah. Be here, or on the eighth I'll be knocking on your door."

Before she could lash back at him, he wheeled the horse in a dancing turn. Ready and eager, Gitano needed no urging. Their red wake sifted down on her, and standing in the murky cloud, she watched until horse and rider vanished from her sight.

The cadence of pounding hooves faded, became an echo of itself, and faded again. Then there was a silence that seemed to close in on her. Hurrying from it, she sprinted for the truck, wishing she went to Black Jack instead. She needed a good, hard ride. One that demanded every bit of her concentration, leaving room in her mind for nothing but the rigors of the range.

When the door slammed with the hollow thunk that warned one day it would truly fall off, she gripped the steering wheel. "I'm not running," she muttered to a man who wasn't there. "Not from you."

A turn of a key and the engine fired. Hank made no move for the gears. Listening to the heavy, steady thrum, she faced an inescapable truth. She hadn't lied, she wasn't running from Steve Cody.

Reaching blindly for the gearshift she dragged it into position. Her boot stamped down on the accelerator, tires spun and skidded. The truck rocked and rattled, slipping over the road, gaining the traction to settle itself. One final fishtail to the right, corrected by one to the left, and she was in control, zeroing in on her destination.

She drove as she rode, too fast, too furiously, but asking no more of the machine than of herself. And somewhere on the bumpy ride to the Rafter B, she faced the truth. No, Savannah Henrietta Benedict was not running from Steve Cody, she ran from herself.

"Hell!"

Vibrating wire snapped from his straining grasp, writhing and lurching like something alive, retracting with a metallic screech into a remembered coil. Cursing under his breath, Steve stripped off his gloves, dragging a streak of blood over the top of his hand. An irritated glance determined the cut of a barb was only superficial, thanks to the glove and none to Steve.

He'd worked too long and done too much, pushing his body beyond endurance, hoping to quiet his mind. What he'd succeeded in accomplishing in seven days, in terms of the ranch, was astonishing. In terms of personal success? He laughed shortly. The list was meager, and far from successful. All he could tally were battered hands, a mean temper, and a mind filled with images of the woman who could have taken the canyon from him, and hadn't.

What did it mean? What did she want? What did he?

Questions that had no answers. Matters unresolved.

"Tonight," he muttered, ignoring his bleeding hand as he slipped on his gloves again. "Tonight decides it."

Struggling again with the wire, he wondered what the night would decide.

"Well, sis, I see you're still here."

Hank turned from her scrutiny of the horizon and the building storm to look blankly at Sandy.

"You're still here," he repeated in response to her vague reaction. "Seven days in a row you've stood here looking to the east, and Black Jack gets a little fatter and a little sassier every one of those days."

"It's going to rain."

"Maybe." Silver-streaked hair gleamed in the late afternoon sun as he nodded, scotching a circuitous argument. "Maybe even a boomer. Be a few hours yet, time for a ride."

"The rest won't hurt him."

"Nope," the foreman agreed in his usual mild fashion. Spinning his stained hat in callused fingers, he leaned a shoulder against a veranda support. "Won't do his temper any good, either. Being cooped up so long, I mean."

Hank raked a hand over her loosely drawn hair, smoothing back tiny tendrils curling riotously in the unusual humidity. She said no more, hoping for once Sandy would just go away.

Ignoring her pointed silence, the foreman launched into a rare one-sided discourse. "I considered having one of the hands exercise him, but that would only make him madder. And the guy who got elected would probably demand combat pay. It don't help that word got around that the last feller who tried to ride the stallion after a long layoff had a long layoff himself.

"Matter of fact, Holt still limps when it rains. Poor old hoss." A slow, considering shake of his head emphasized his sympathy. "I guess he'll just have to molder there in his stall. I 'spect he'll be chewing the bark off the rails before too long."

"There is no bark on the rails," Hank snapped, rising to the bait.

"Well, now, you're right, there ain't. But it don't change the fact that we have a mighty antsy stallion pacing the stable." Heavy brows lifted as he let an assessing look pass over her. "It appears we have a mighty antsy girl pacing the veranda too."

"I haven't been a girl in a long time, Sandy." Distant thunder rumbled, as the storm continued to build.

Sandy grinned and caught the end of her braid, ruffling the curling ends before letting it swing across her shoulders. "To me, when you're fifty, you'll still be that feisty young girl who met the world fair and square and never ducked."

"Never until now, you mean." Hank turned from the vista that had absorbed her for nearly an hour. "You think that's what I'm doing now? Ducking?"

"We both know who's out there, sis. I don't know what's got you moping and clinging to home like a calf without its momma, but I know what it ain't."

She almost smiled then. Her beloved Sandy was always most endearing when he lapsed so earnestly into his earthy, philosophical cowboy persona. "I suppose you're going to tell me what it isn't."

"I'm thinking on it. Been thinking on it nearly the whole week."

Sighing, Hank accepted the inevitable. "There's no better time than the present."

"Yeah, there was," the foreman said grumpily. "A week ago, before you stopped sleeping and eating, and skinnied down so bad."

"Ouch!" She tried for a smile and succeeded in a grimace. "Am I that bad? A skinny hag?"

"You ain't a bone yet, but you're getting close. And you ain't a hag. If you don't believe me, ask that feller down in Sunrise Canyon."

There, the subject was broached. "You think Steve is the reason for my mood."

"It ain't the horses. By now you should have them ready for just about anybody to put them through their paces. And it's for damn sure not the canyon. I know better than most that you have an attachment to the place, but I know just as well that if it wasn't for Jake, you wouldn't give a plug nickel for owning it. 'Specially not when someone has finally come in who could make it the spread it ought to be." Sandy paused in the unnaturally long speech before adding gruffly, "And he will, if he gets the chance."

"You think he should have that chance."

"I do." There was no hedging in the blunt statement. "Have from the first."

"Jubal shares your conviction."

"If you could pin Jake down, make him see beyond this obsession, he'd agree. Fact is, if he told the truth, he'd have to admit a speck of admiration for the boy. Grudging, mind you, but for real. Must be kinda like looking in a mirror that lops forty years off his age every time he looks at him."

Hank shot a pleading look at him. "What would you have me do?"

"I've had my say," Sandy demurred. "The rest is up to you."

"I don't know! My mind's in a muddle, I can't think!"

"Then follow your heart."

"That's no easier." Biting her lip, she turned her head away, but not before he caught the glint of tears.

His hardened palm brought her back to face him. "Maybe it ain't easy, but it's right."

Hank sighed, a tremulous note. "I'm such a fool, I don't know what my own heart is telling me."

"You will, once you put everyone and everything out of your mind. Be selfish for once. When you do, you'll hear your heart's voice. Then, if you're even half the woman I think you are, you'll go where it takes you. Choosing between love and old loyalties can be a terrible thing. But Jake made his choices a long time ago, and Camilla made hers. Now it's your turn.

"Listen to your heart, sis." Disconcerted by the poetic philosophy, he cleared his throat brusquely and touched her shoulder in a fond farewell. "I'd best be getting on in. Jake and I have some things to go over, tallies and such, before we get down to the real business of plotting who will capture whose knight."

"Sandy." Delaying him, she rose on tiptoe to kiss his cheek. "Thanks."

A blush tinged a rugged face already darkened and weathered by years on the range. Making a production of resettling his Stetson at just the right angle, he stroked the brim and cleared his throat again. "I didn't mean to meddle. One way or another, I just wanted to help."

"You did. Or you will have, once I'm thinking straight."

"Just don't think it to death. Impulse can be a wonderful thing." Another stroke of the Stetson's brim, and what was virtual loquacity in a taciturn man was done.

Hank watched him walk across the veranda with the curiously efficient stride of one who spent little time out of the saddle, and made the most of it. When the door closed behind him, she heard Jake's querulous greeting and tumbled into confusion again.

"What do I do?" she whispered to the sky, but the sky had no answer.

Pacing the veranda, changing one vantage for another, she found herself skirting the issue. Dodging the real question, unable to let her mind consider it. How could she make a choice, when she wouldn't allow herself to recognize the truth?

"Nothing," she muttered heatedly. Angry with her indecision, she made it a choice. "I decide to do exactly that . . . nothing."

With that, she hurried into the house and to her office. Barricading herself behind a stack of the old-fashioned ledgers Jake still insisted on keeping, she sought to immerse herself in the mundane facts and figures of the ranch.

An hour later, when Bonita tapped on the door, calling her to the late dinner that always followed one of Jake and Sandy's lusty games of chess, Hank was sitting as she had from the first. Gloom gathered in corners, behind doors and along bare walls, while the lamps remained unlit, the pen in her hand unused, the pages of the ledger unturned.

Peering into her sanctum Bonita asked hopefully, "Will you come to dinner tonight, Savannah?"

Hank looked up, frowning, and suddenly breathless. "Say that again. Exactly!"

Perplexed, but patiently, Bonita repeated her query. "Will you come to dinner tonight, Savannah?"

Savannah.

As if the key to all the mysteries of her heart were bound up in the name, everything fell wonderfully into place.

"No." Her pulse pounding, Hank rose from her chair. Her choice was made, it had been made all along. "Thank you, but no, Bonita," she repeated decisively. "I have a dinner engagement."

"At this hour?"

"Yes." Hank tossed down her pen and closed the ledger. "At this hour."

"Where? When?" Bonita babbled, thinking of the miles that separated the Rafter B from Silverton, or any of the closest ranches. "Surely by now it's too late."

"He'll wait."

"The storm, it comes." Bonita tried another argument. "It promises to be terrible."

Hank would have said the promise was wonderful, for she loved
the storms. The grandeur of summer thunderheads, the drama. The
howl of the wind, the sonorous and prophetic rolls of thunder. A
deep purple sky, rent by lightning flashing like the clash of the
swords of the gods. Silver rain slanting in the wind, uniting the
brooding heavens with the land. And when it was done, there was
silence as pristine as the newly washed land.

"I have time."

Silencing any other objections by throwing her arm around the
shoulders of the shorter woman, she walked with her through the
house. At the stairway, she took both of Bonita's plump hands in
hers. "Don't worry, I'll be fine. I promise."

"You go to the Broken Spur. To Señor Steve!" Bonita exclaimed in abrupt insight.

"It's something I have to do, Bonita. For myself."

"You're sure?" A patrician brow arched skeptically. "You won't
get hurt?"

"I'm sure." Not sure that she wouldn't be hurt by her decision,
but sure that, no matter the outcome, she would ultimately be fine.

"Then hurry." Bonita squeezed her hands, then shooed her up
the stairs. "Do what you must." Her expression grew thoughtful.
"And go with God."

Candles burned low, their flames casting a kaleidoscope of
dancing shadows against the walls of the cabin. The hum of the
battery driven generator was silent, the dinner prepared with the
energy it provided grew cold.

His back rigid, Steve sat at the table, seeing neither candlelight
nor shadows. A stormy breeze gusted through the open doorway, a
candle flickered, guttered, sending up a tiny wisp of hazy gray, then
rekindled. The scent of smoke and paraffin mingled with the fragrance of flowers.

A petal fell from the single rose held by a vase in the center of the
table. Like a leaf caught in a down draft it drifted forlornly. A
teardrop of satin, gleaming blood red against the bleached patina
of ancient wood. Catching it between his fingertips, he savored the
softness, the scent that held the secret of a thousand memories.

"Damn me for a fool!" The petal bruised beneath the pressure
of his regret, staining his flesh with its color. With a look of distaste he flung it away.

Lurching from his chair, anxious to be done with reminders of his
stupidity, he began to clear the table. Thunder rumbled amid the

rattle of dishes. Lightning flashed, illuminating his dusky world for a brief second. Once in the furor, in a mad moment, he thought he heard the cough of an engine, the grind of a gear. In another he imagined the shine of a light too constant, too unspectacular to be part of the storm.

Halting in his chores, he listened. Nothing. "Accept it," he growled. "She isn't coming."

But he'd been so sure. Sure she cared, sure she would come to him. There was no help for arrogant mistakes. Tomorrow was the eighth day, he wouldn't be going for her. The empty threat lay like dust on his heart. He'd never intended to go, for the choice had to be hers. "I thought I knew."

Steps creaked, a muffled tread crossed the porch. As he approached the sink he wondered what creature scurried by seeking refuge. The quiet rap came unexpectedly, taking him by surprise. Wheeling about, he found a storm shrouded apparition in the open doorway.

"What the devil? Who—?"

A woman too beautiful to be believed stepped into candlelight. A vision in a gown of creamy lawn and lace, with deep brown hair loose and flowing, curling riotously in the storm. Beneath the tumble of her hair, bare shoulders shone as darkly burnished alabaster. Her eyes, catching the reflection of a flame, glittered silver and gold, and solemnly held his.

She was slender, but not angular, the lines of her body planed and sculpted, but not hard. Her breath came in deep, silent shudders, and with each rise and fall of a daring décolletage, the curve and cleft of her breasts enticed, beguiled. Shimmering, lovely womanliness played hide-and-seek behind a lacy shield. Drawing his hungry gaze with wicked audacity to impudent nipples, tantalizing and unfettered beneath the clinging fabric.

In the wavering of a guttering candle, she was all he'd dreamed she would be. Never taking his gaze from hers, with an unsteady hand he set the last of the dishes aside, their discord fading into silence broken only by the rumble of thunder.

Lightning split the sky, a luminous backdrop for the doorway where she stood. Creamy lawn turned to illusory veil, drawing every curve of her naked body in perfect relief.

Steve's heart shivered, his chest jolted with a breath caught and lost. He was sure he would die from wanting her, and his voice was rough and raw, his words unexpected. "Tell me you didn't ride that devil of a horse in the dark of the storm."

His eyes narrowed, his manner commanded. "Tell me."

Her laughter was soft, sending ripples from his chest to the pit of his stomach. "Black Jack's tucked safely in his stall."

She was moving as she spoke, small and exquisite, with the long, supple skirt clinging and swaying around her. He realized only then that her feet were bare. As bare as her body beneath the pale gown.

She leaned to snuff out a struggling candle. Lace and gauze dipped lower, revealing, seducing. Steve's nails scored his palms, his arms shook with the force. Lips tightened over gritted teeth as he fought for control.

"Dinner ruined hours ago," he heard himself say in a voice that wasn't his.

She laughed again. The same smoky note, the same bewitching allure. "I didn't come for dinner."

"Then why?" She was only inches away, all he need do was reach out to take her. "Why are you here?"

Her throat arching gracefully, her eyes searched his. Witch eyes, seeing into him, finding desire that matched her own. "My name is Savannah," she murmured. "I came for you."

Passion detonated. The past and all its problems vanished. The future waited. He reached for her, his face grim, his touch gentle. He drew her close, burying his face in her rose scented hair. "Then God help me."

"No," she countered, turning her lips to his. "God help us both."

Chapter 13

He drank deeply of her, a solitary man who had never known true loneliness until Savannah. But now she was in his arms, and as the storm broke, wreaking the passions of heaven on the earth, another storm, one of heart and soul, wreaked its passion on Steve.

He was shaking, his chest heaving in a broken rhythm, as he drew away from a kiss that shattered every reservation and rational thought. Bodies inches apart, her skirt brushing the crease of his trousers in their only contact, he looked down at her. Candle flame and the flicker of lightning revealed to him a woman he'd never met.

Savannah, soft and inviting. A sultry wanton, alluring, seductive. Unrepentant.

The exigencies of the week marked her. Evidence of sleepless nights brushed like blue veils beneath a curtain of lashes. A body grown thinner bespoke hard, driving work meant to deter a troubled mind and quiet the restlessness of a tender heart.

The toll of every battle was there for him to see, yet the woman who looked at him with grave confidence in her smile was a woman undefeated. A woman who admitted what she wanted, what she must have, and would let nothing stand in her way.

With his eyes never wavering from her, he lifted his hand to her cheek, letting the back of it follow the delicate curving ridge, his nails scoring a path of fire and need to the base of her throat. Her breath faltered, ceasing, leaving her in utter stillness as the lazy drift of his fingertips traced the band of lace over the swell of her breasts to her shoulder. Slowly, with the curl of a finger, he slipped the fine lawn away, drawing it down to the bend of her arm.

Falling lace caught and clung, revealing the crest of a nipple clothed only in its intricate pattern. Delicate rose-brown, dappled by cream, mesmerized, enticed. A perfect and fleeting fit for the hollow of his palm, an instant before his grasp closed over the shielding band, baring her body to her waist.

As he took the weight of flawless globes in his cradling clasp, the breath trapped in longing shuddered from her. The stroke of his thumb over tender peaks drew a hushed cry. Her head thrown back, her hair fanning about her waist, her writhing body reveled in the caress she'd wanted and needed for so long.

A wordless sigh burst from her as callused palms moved with incredible tenderness over her midriff to her hips and her thighs. Drawing the gown from her, he let it fall like spilled moonlight in a pool at her feet.

She was beautiful. As beautiful as he'd dreamed. With a body made for a man's touch, she was the elegance of sweeping hollows, luscious curves and maddening secrets. A temptress daring that any delightful part be left uncharted, any secrets left unraveled.

Accepting the tacit dare, he began a silent, wandering journey through mystery and feminine loveliness. With tantalizing caresses he memorized the slope of her hip, the joining crease of buttock and leg; then, at the apex of her thighs, the texture of dark curls coiling into the gliding subtlety of his fingertips. Leaving the shielded treasure unplundered, his seeking, learning hand discovered the flat plane of her hard, lean belly; the curve of a narrow waist, a rippled rib cage too slender for her strength. At last, and again, the cleft and undercurve of her breasts.

He was fiercely aroused as he cupped their softness once more in his palm. A lover driven to the brink, quenching lusts of his own making, bent to take a taut, exquisite tip in his mouth. His suckling kiss, drawing the unashamed testament of her own lust to his laving tongue, sent spears of keening desire lancing through him. His heart pounded, wild and erratic, the furor of passion outstripping the furor of the ever descending storm.

Raising his head from her breast, he found her smoky, languid gaze upon him. "Benedict." Then, softly, "Savannah."

"Yes, Savannah." Her hands pressed against his chest, splayed fingers measured the race of his heart, glided to his throat and curled at his nape. With only a nuance of pressure she guided his mouth back to hers. Her naked body molded curve and plane of his. Drawing him closer, holding him harder, she teased his lips.

"For this night." She rose on tiptoe, bringing passion to passion, offering herself to him and to truth. "A night we knew must come."

Thunder boomed, and lightning turned the world to eerie fluorescence. The smell of ozone filled the air, and with it the sound of splintering wood as somewhere nearby a tree rent by the fiery bolt fell with a monstrous crash. The floor shook beneath their feet, cobwebs floated from ancient rafters. And while the earth still quaked and the pounding rain began, he swept her into his arms.

The door was kicked shut, closing out the storm, then the pad that was little more than a bedroll was at her back. Lying prone beneath him, with belts and buckles and rough cloth taunting her, she cried out in frustration.

"I know," he answered on a breath. His forearms framing her face, his fingers tangling in her hair, he lifted away only a little to feast on the wanton his caress had created. His words took on a soothing, consuming rhythm, its seductive cadence kept and marked by slow, lazy kisses. "I know, my love. I know."

When she would have protested that he couldn't know, that this madness must be hers alone, the tug of his teeth at the lobe of her ear, and more muttered words, scattered even that thought. When she grew restless and greedy for more, before her greed could be spoken, his mouth drifted here, there...the hollow beneath her ear, the base of her throat, the cleft of her breasts. One nipple, and then the other. Suckling, Sweet.

Wonder and agony.

"Steve." Only his name.

Pain and plea.

Pain he shared. A plea he answered.

Levering himself away from her, he stood by the bed, looking down at her in the flame of the one brave candle unvanquished by the winds of the storm. "I've wanted this." He kicked aside the slippers he wore instead of boots. "Since the first day I saw you on the streets of Silverton, I've wanted it.

"I knew then that you were dangerous. That somehow, because of you, my life would never be the same." The snaps of his shirt opened, each muted crack heralding another inch of his brawny chest revealed. When he shrugged it from his shoulders, his torso was dark. As dark as Bonita. *Indio* dark.

"Will anything ever be the same, Savannah? After tonight can it be?" His hand rested at his belt, but before he could deal with it, she was on her knees before him, fingers more nimble than his dealing with leather and buckle.

"For a quiet man, you talk too much, Steve Cody. You said that neither yesterday nor tomorrow mattered, and you were right. This is between us. Only us." Drawing the belt from its loops, she moved away. Kneeling on the crude bed, she folded her hands, her fingers locked.

"Only Steve Cody, Savannah Benedict, this night, and what we make of it." Silver eyes flashed in the swift glare of lightning, her chin lifted, turned. A move that sent her hair tumbling over one shoulder and down her back. As if it knew life and mischief of its own, a part coiled at her hips and brushed the soles of her feet. Another curled at her breast playing a winsome game of hide-and-seek. "What would you make of it, Steve?"

"This." The last of his clothing was gone as he drew her down with him to the bed. His long legs, muscular and naked, twined with hers. The dark pelt at his chest cushioned her breasts, as arousing as his suckling kiss. He drew her closer, his thrusting manhood hard against her belly, striking fire to fire, turning heated blaze to an inferno. "I would make this of it."

Then his hands and his kiss were everywhere, devastating with their bold touch, building sensation upon sensation. The last shred of logic and will deserted her. She was pliant and languorous, his to do with as he would. But even as she thought she would never need or want to move again, a new desire was stirring. A need to touch him, to know him as he knew her. Catching his wandering hands in hers, she drew them first to her breast, then to her lips.

"Let me touch you. I need to touch you."

Steve shuddered at the thought of her hands on him, the sheer insanity it would invoke. Turning with her, he held her close until she rested over him. Then he released her, touching only her throat and nape as he drew the wealth of her hair down on him. He wanted the silken web flowing over him, as with lips and hands and laughing witch eyes she cast her magic spell. "I'm yours, Savannah, to do with as you like."

Her caress was tentative, unpracticed and unskilled. If there had been any lovers before him, Steve knew it was not the lover a woman such as Savannah Benedict merited. But lack of expertise was no match for innocent delight. In a matter of minutes, as she discovered and explored his most vulnerable places, drawing from him responses he'd never encountered, he was shaking with an agony that was sweet, and terrible, and desperate all in one.

She was beginning again her delighted and delightful quest when he caught her hair in his hands, winding it around his palm, drawing her lips to his. "Enough," he snarled in a voice that was harsh, even as his kiss was gentle. "Unless you would make love to a lunatic, enough!"

Savannah hesitated, lying over him she was as still as death. *Love*. She'd never said the word, never questioned what force had brought her to him. Never faced the depth of her own true feelings. But she'd known. Deep in her heart, she'd known for a long time.

"What more would you have, Savannah?"

"You," she answered as she listened to her heart's voice and knew Sandy's words were words of wisdom. "I would have you."

"And you will."

As if she were a feather, as if he were not weak with desire, he swept her beneath him. He took one long, hard kiss, his mouth ravishing hers as tenderness fell from him like stricken armor. There was a fierceness in him as he caressed her, and more than a little madness as his body plunged into the crucible of hers.

She was hot and sweet and giving. And with the sweetness and the giving, knotted tensions eased, turning to fire. He heard the pounding of the rain, felt the rock of the howling wind threaten walls and roof, but he couldn't care. She was wine in his blood, breath in his lungs, the beat of his heart. And as he thrust into her, into softness that sheathed the length of him, as sensation after mounting sensation caught at him, she became his life.

Savannah reached out to him, her arms circling his shoulders, her legs clasping his hips. A turn of her head and her lips brushed his shoulder, her tongue tasted the clean salty flavor on him, and with it desire moved to another plane. Feeling, unfathomable, demanding, gathered deep inside her. Too much to bear, too powerful to control, too wondrous to believe. Nothing in her life had prepared her for the mind shattering pleasure that mounted in currents that never ebbed.

She wanted him closer, deeper. More. Grasping his hair she bore down, her nails cutting into his scalp as she met thrust with thrust. And in the midst of furor it began. A nuance. A whisper. The ripple of a stone in a quiet pool. Building, building, wave upon wave, until it became a cataclysm washing over her. A sea threatening to drown her in the bittersweet torment of passion and desire.

"Steve," she called his name hoarsely, and had no reckoning of the power of her cry.

The raw hunger in her whisper, the pulsing clasp of her body, catapulted him over the final edge of constraint. Slick with sweat and magnificent, he bucked and lunged, stroking the throbbing flesh that held him captive. Stoking the fires that licked at them, he took her further, spiraling down with her into dementia that could have but one end.

And when she convulsed in the throes of ultimate release, he reared over her, a grimace of victory distorting his face. He was primal man taking what was his. The pagan warrior crying triumphant possession over the prize of victory as he plunged savagely to the tip of her womb, and spilled his seed.

The storm chose that moment to unleash the worst of its wrath. Thunder pealed in a deafening roar, lightning fell through windows with a white, blinding glare. The earth shook, roof and walls groaned. But for Steve and Savannah the storm that both destroyed and resurrected had ended.

The cabin was serenity in the wake of passion, and darkness hovered as the valiant candle snuffed out. In peace and unshakable calm, he gathered her into his arms. With their bodies still joined, stroking the sweat of their mating from her, he kissed away her tears. And as he held her, as surely as he knew tomorrow must come, he knew his premonition had proved true—that from this moment his life and Savannah's had changed forevermore.

"Tomorrow." The harsh word fell like a stone in a sudden well of silence.

Drowsily she nestled against him. "Mmm?"

"Nothing, love." He kissed the top of her head and rested his chin on her hair. "Only thinking aloud."

Savannah heard, and understood, but said nothing. Drifting in the peaceful aftermath, surrounded by the essence of him . . . the scent of soap and leather and lovemaking . . . she knew he questioned, as she did, what transitions this night would bring.

One did not walk through fire and emerge unscathed. Nor face the truth of love and turn away from it. No matter what the future brought to them, Savannah knew she would carry the memory of this night, and the love, forever in her heart.

Her love. "Forever."

One word. A promise to herself. An admission of truth. With a wrench of her heart, she wondered if it was an omen that Steve spoke of a day and she of eternity. A frisson of fear for the unknown rushed through her in a shiver.

He drew away, grave concern in his expression. "Are you cold, love?"

Love. He called her love as he had before, but it was only a name. No more than dear, or honey, or, God forbid, good buddy. She wouldn't deny the sorrow of her loss, nor let herself regret it. The decision had been hers. He'd made no declarations, nor offered any promises, and still she'd come to him.

Her choice. No recriminations.

"I'm not cold." Gathering his hand in hers, she clasped it to her breast. "I'll never be cold when you're with me."

He moved to cover her, their joined bodies beginning to pulse with awakening need. "I know a wonderful way to warm you. If you were cold, that is."

Locking her arms around his neck, Savannah shivered again, not completely in pretense. "Gracious," she murmured lazily. "There must be a draft. A chilly one."

Smiling, he began to move within her. "A draft."

The sun was up. By rancher's standards the rain drenched morning was ancient, but neither Savannah nor Steve squandered a thought on time. The horses had water and grain. A late start, or even a day of rest, would do them no harm.

Lying in bed, a sheet drawn to his waist, his arms folded behind his head, Steve watched Savannah as she wandered through the cabin. She'd taken the time to slip on the gown before she began her exploration. So he amused himself imagining and remembering the exquisite form hidden and yet intriguingly revealed by the cling and sway of flowing lawn.

He found he liked the charming disarray. Tousled hair combed into little order by the rake of her careless fingers, face flushed by a subtle glow, eyes languid and dewy, heavy with contentment. As she wandered from place to place, learning about him from the clutter of personal items, she made no effort to disguise that she was a woman who had only moments before arisen from his bed and a night of making love.

Steve liked that about her. The honesty, the candor that left no room for coy pretenses. He chuckled, admitting he liked everything about her. Especially the way the banded lace dipped and swayed as she moved, the weblike threads brushing a rose-brown nipple in full bloom, then teasing it to a taut, irresistible bud. Even now, his mouth hungered for the taste of it, his tongue longed to curl around it.

"What?" Savannah stopped in mid motion, her silver gaze on Steve rather than the open book in her hand.

"Hmm?" Steve lifted a questioning brow.

"You laughed."

A wicked smile tugged at the corner of his mouth. "I did?"

"Yes." Snapping the book shut, she returned it to a shelf filled with other books with surprisingly eclectic titles arranged in no apparent order. "You laughed." Her hands were at her hips, lawn and lace pulled taut over her breasts. "And you were staring."

"Not staring." Delight sparkled in his eyes. "Admiring."

"Admiring? Me?" Before he could respond, raking her hands through her hair in a rare and enchantingly feminine gesture, she rushed on. "I must look a sight."

Steve leaned forward, stretching to catch her hand. "Leave it. I like it like that. A little wild, a little fey." More than anything he liked it flowing over him, wrapping around him, binding him to her.

"You're joking." She would have taken her hand from his, but he wouldn't release her. In her effort the gown slipped over the curve of one shoulder. "Either you're joking, or you're nuts."

"If it's nuts to like and admire you, then I guess that's the verdict. I'm nutty as a greedy squirrel." Linking his fingers through hers, he held her tighter. "Because I like everything about you. I like you more than you know, and I admire every inch of you. Every perfect, secret place, such as . . ."

It was Savannah's turn to lift a questioning brow. "Such as?"

"Ah . . ." He sighed and grinned. "I thought you'd never ask." Pulling her to him, stopping only when her knees touched the bed, he leaned to her, muttering huskily, "Such as this, and this, and this."

As if to torture himself, he made his journey over the smooth planes of her brow and cheek arduously slow and deliberate, with each of a hundred kisses a tiny taste of her. "Then there's this, and this." His teeth nipped at the lobe of an ear. His mouth brushed over hers, but he was too intent on his goal to linger. "This . . ."

Light kisses blazed a trail at the curve of her jaw, the arch of her throat, the cleft of her breasts. "And this." His mouth found the goal for which it yearned. His tongue, the taste it craved. The puckering nipple, with its dapple of lace, was like nectar to him. Desire lanced like chained heat from the tip of his tongue to the center of him, as his teasing went awry.

"Savannah." He lifted his head from her breast. "I didn't mean . . . I thought . . ." His look was stormy, sultry. "I can't back away." Releasing her, he stabbed his fingers through his hair, tearing at it as if he would punish himself for his folly. For awakening sleeping desire so soon. There was a desperateness in his look, his words. "I need you. But I won't . . ."

He would have turned away then, but Savannah wouldn't let him. Catching him by the shoulders she held him fast.

"Savannah?" A frown scored his face, and she caught a heart wrenching glimpse of the past, and a little boy whose innocent prank caused trouble he hadn't intended.

"Shh." She crossed two fingers over his lips, stilling the rambling that was half demand, half apology. "I know." A tender smile touched her mouth, a graceful shrug sent the gown falling to her feet. A lazy tug took the sheet from him in slow and maddening purpose.

"Cowboys aren't so different from lovers." The words were a whisper, a needful sigh. She knelt on the bed before him, her fingertips drifted lazily over his chest, tangling in the pelt that trekked in a narrowing vee from tense male nipples to ridged stomach and beyond.

"Sweetheart." He caught back a shudder as Savannah's roving fingers did a bit of teasing on their own. "I don't think your dance card's been full enough for you to know what the hell you're talking about."

Savannah laughed softly and teased again. "The fabled card is full enough that I know one special cowboy and one lover very well."

"What do you know so well?"

"That he finishes what he starts." Her hands slid over his chest, a slight push sent him falling back. Bracing her body above his, letting the tumble of her hair sweep over him, she sealed her fate. "I know that if, because of something he'd done, a lady really needed comfort, he wouldn't deny her."

"What would comfort you, my love?"

"You." As deftly as she mounted the stallion, she mounted Steve. "This." Recalling for him the mischievous journey he'd taken, she began to sway. "This." Her body glided over his. "This." Her voice was rasping, her cry hoarse as she leaned again to him, whipping him with the swirling strands of her hair, caressing him with the tips of her breasts. "And this."

She was a Cossack, an enchantress. The warrior's woman taking the booty of her conquest. No race through the desert was ever so wild. No horseman ever so fiery, no steed so hot-blooded.

And when she sank quietly into his open arms, no woman was ever more deeply in love.

"Only one more." Savannah rose on tiptoe to brush one last tangle from Gitano's mane. When she drew away, he snuffled at her shoulder and nudged her arm. Laughing, she patted his neck and stepped away.

Steve leaned against the stable door, watching a dangerous stallion behave like a puppy. "You've made a pet of him."

"Do you mind?"

"Surprised. He's done this once before, but I never expected it again."

Savannah faced Steve, her hand still on Gitano's neck. "The little girl in Mexico. The blind child who saw what he was."

"She believed in him."

Giving Gitano one last stroking pat, she stepped away. She'd learned much of Steve's life, but in casual bits and pieces, not soul searching conversations. She liked the naturalness of it, the comfort and growing friendship it proved. Her own life had revealed itself with the same ease. At the most natural moments she'd spoken of the parental contest waged over her, the first star for her boot, regrets for ambitions unrealized that were regrets no more.

Now she knew the matters, small and great, that shaped his life. He knew her better than anyone had, or ever would. He had become more than her love and her lover, he was a rare and trusted friend.

As they walked from the stables, the last chore of the day finished, his arm lay over her shoulders, his hand at her nape. Autumn was not yet a reality, gold and amber were only beginning to show among the trees and across the meadow. But soon their small world would be awash with glowing shades of captured sunlight. But for now the season manifested itself in subtle hints, and in days that grew shorter. And as they walked together in quiet communion, the first of twilight was falling around them.

"Will you be going back to the Rafter B?" Steve was first to break the silence, and only a slight tightening of his fingers on the tender flesh at the side of her throat betrayed that it was more than incidental interest.

"Tomorrow begins the final judging and culling for the Silverton Fall Festival, and Jake will be primed and ready long before dawn." The celebration that was more for show and bragging rights was just weeks away. Jake Benedict's body might be faltering, but his competitive spirit raged on. "If I'm not in the corral waiting and ready, along with every other hand he expects, there will be the devil to pay."

"And questions you aren't ready to answer yet."

There was no rancor in his observation, and Savannah looked for none. From the moment she'd faced and acknowledged the depth of what she felt for Steve, she'd acknowledged that love and loyalty could not always go hand in hand. For the summer, with help from Sandy and Bonita, she'd skirted the problem, drifting along, happy and content, reveling in first love. Now autumn was upon them. The time of harvesting what one had sown.

"Not even Sandy could head him off if I'm among the missing tomorrow. But..." Spinning about in his path, she caught him around the waist, determined to hold back the inevitable, preserving for a little while what they had. "There's no hurry now, is there?"

Tossing her Stetson and his away, he folded her in his arms. He would worry for her when she drove the rough road home in the pitch of night, but he couldn't send her away. "No hurry at all."

Music flowed over them as they sat together, watching darkness gather in the canyon in layers like drifting smoke. The hum of the generator didn't encroach on the peaceful moment, and nothing distracted from the strains of the adagio that was her favorite.

The day and her surprise when she'd found the player and the trove of treasured compact discs was her most discerning and touching discovery of the unpredictable man she'd been given to love. Her surprise wasn't that he liked music, nor even that Mahler and Martucci, and Grieg were among them. It was the origin of the music, its import.

Adagios. His mother's music, her favorite.

"How old were you?"

As always in the quiet times, when they were even closer than in the aftermath of making love, he followed her thoughts. "I was eleven when we realized the weakness was more than simply that she was not strong. Twelve when the diagnosis was confirmed. From then, the ALS moved swiftly." He used the initials for the tongue-tangling paralytic disease. Lou Gehrig's disease, ALS. By any name, a slow and excruciating death sentence for the body of a vital woman, the imprisonment of an intelligent mind that would stay whole. "At the end, when all voluntary motion was lost, when her body was a cage, these were her escape, her one salvation."

"And yours." Savannah took his hand in hers. "Because it was all you could give her."

"Until I was seventeen. Then nothing was enough."

In golden moonlight it was easy to imagine how he'd been at seventeen. How handsome, with the first look of manhood about him. She didn't need to be a mother to know a mother's pride in such a son. "As long as she could see and hear, the music and you were enough."

Martucci gave way to Grieg, and when the music ended darkness was complete. Autumn was in full tilt now and the celebration almost upon them. Knowing her schedule hardly left room for breathing, Steve walked with her to the truck, kissed her, murmured something into her hair and waved her on her way.

The road was an empty track before he turned away to the solitude of his night.

Humming as she worked, Savannah curried Lorelei until she shone like glistening black water. Steve had ridden out to repair a stretch of broken wire discovered along the way of their customary evening ride, and she was alone in the stable. The cough of an engine and the squeak of brakes went unnoticed as she launched into one of the more lively adagios.

Footsteps muffled by hay and her own exuberance stopped short of Lorelei's stable, as the clap of a single pair of hands announced an intruder.

Whirling in astonishment more than fear, speechless, Savannah stared into the loveliest blue eyes she had ever seen.

"Well, well," a femme fatale dressed in impeccably tailored Western garb spoke before Savannah could find her tongue. "Who are you?" Eyes that on second glance were too hard for real beauty swept over her. Assessing her, measuring her with calculated care. "You look more like a hired hand, but with a manicure and a little war paint, you could pass as one of Stevie's latest buckle bunnies."

"Stevie?"

"Of course." The woman stripped her gloves from her hands, baring blood red nails. A superior smirk further marred her beauty. Her cool stare raked over the disheveled Savannah, the practiced eyes noting the evidences of a recent tryst and a swim in the misty pool at the base of the small waterfall. "Don't pretend, and don't play innocent. Not with me."

Savannah bristled. "I'm not pretending, I never play innocent. And who the hell are you to walk in here asking questions and giving orders?"

"You don't know." Brows arched in a wicked cast. Artfully ruffled blond tresses tumbled down an elegantly clad back. "You really don't."

The woman paced a step nearer. Her bosom, straining against the tasseled blouse was generous, her leather clad hips were full, her legs long. "Are you too far in the boonies to know how to put two and two together?"

"I can add, if that's what you're asking." Enough, Savannah thought, to know that a few more pounds and the seams of the leather costume would burst. "That doesn't mean that I know who you are." Stepping away from Lorelei, she nodded at the figure standing in the gloom by the door. "Or your friend, either, for that matter."

"My name is Tad Jasper, ma'am." A man of the same cut as Steve stepped into the light. Hat in hand, he spun the brim nervously. "I'm an old friend of Steve's. We rode the circuit together."

"Mr. Jasper." Savannah acknowledged the introduction.

"No, ma'am," the nervous cowboy rushed in. "Just plain Tad."

Savannah inclined her head, an unconsciously regal gesture, as she turned back to the blonde. "That leaves you."

There was nothing beautiful about the smile that bared perfect teeth. A wave of her hand flashed red talons. "Then, by all means, let me introduce myself." Her pause for effect was almost laughable. "I'm Angie Cody."

"Cody?" The name was all that Savannah could manage as a coil of dread settled in her stomach like a serpent. "Angie Cody?"

"Ahh." The blonde was beginning to enjoy herself. "Perhaps you've heard of me?"

Savannah shook her head mutely.

"Not in the newspapers?" Angie Cody was obviously grieved that her fame had not preceded her to what she considered backwater country.

"Our local paper isn't exactly cosmopolitan. The society page consists of who is visiting whom, and what student made the dean's list at which college. Other than that, unless you raised a prize bull, or bred a champion horse, I doubt you would make news here."

"Then, perhaps, from Stevie?"

Savannah drew herself to her full height and moved to the stable door. "Steve has never mentioned any Cody other than his mother and father."

He hadn't discussed this woman, but Angie was one of the names he'd called in three days of delirium. Dread growing colder, coiling tighter, she waited for the dramatic revelation the blonde was building toward with malicious relish.

"Surely, being the honorable man he claims, he hasn't misled you. Surely he's mentioned me." Angie lifted a beringed hand and fluffed her hair again.

The theatrical concern only sustained Savannah's dismay, but she was too much the fighter to give this woman the satisfaction of her victory. "I have no idea who you are, or what you mean to Steve."

"Oh, my poor dear!" Angie Cody preened a bit, allowing herself a small, pleased smile. "I thought you would know! That Stevie would have the decency to tell you."

"Tell me what?" Savannah had endured all she intended of this woman.

The sharp knell of a river stone beneath a hoof preceded the splash and thrum of a racing horse. Steve, returning from repairing the fence. Perhaps concerned about the strange vehicle parked by the barn.

Perhaps not, Savannah thought, as she matched stare for stare with the hard but beautiful woman who bore his name.

Angie heard the beat of the hooves, and the masterful confidence took on a reckless tone. A frown marked a forehead rarely allowed to wrinkle. Brilliant nails curled into soft palms. Her game of cat and mouse ended abruptly as she rushed to deliver the blow she'd been savoring. "Surely you aren't so obtuse that you haven't realized that I'm Stevie's wife."

Wife. The word she'd suspected, expected. Dreaded. The knife thrust in her trusting heart twisted. Savannah felt as if she'd been dealt a killing blow, but none of her pain at her lover's duplicity was revealed on her face.

Gathering the tools she'd needed with Lorelei she put them away, then opened the stall door and stepped through. "My chores are finished and I should be heading home." Her voice was level and she was pleased by the cool, calm tone of it. "After such a long absence, you must be looking forward to a private reunion." Glancing at Tad Jasper, who seemed even more ill at ease, Savannah wondered at his role in this. "A reunion for just the two of you."

"I assure you I'm looking forward to seeing Stevie alone after so long." Angie ran a nail down Savannah's sleeve. "If you've kept him from being lonely, you really won't be needed anymore."

"What the hell!" Steve stood in the doorway, his stance militant, his eyes blazing.

"Steve!" Angie rushed to him, her arms outstretched as if she would embrace him. "Darling, you look marvelous."

She was a pace away when he caught her wrists, holding her away. "Angie," he spat the name. "What are you after now?"

Blue eyes blinked innocently. "Why, Stevie, I'm here because I'm you're wife."

He cut her short. "Ex-wife. Very ex."

"I know, darling. That was a mistake I've come to correct."

"The only correction I want you to make is to take your lap dog," a jerk of Steve's head was the first indication that he was aware of Tad Jasper, "and hightail it out of here before I throw you out."

"Darling, you don't mean that."

"Try me." Steve released the slender wrists that jangled with bracelets, and backed away.

"But, darling . . ."

Savannah had seen and heard enough. "This looks like a discussion that could take awhile. If you'll let me pass, I'll be going."

"Savannah." As she approached the door, Steve held his ground, blocking her way.

"Move, please." Stopping abruptly, she kept her distance from Jasper and both Codys.

"This isn't what you think," Steve protested.

"You have no idea what I'm thinking."

But he did. It was there in her eyes. The hurt, the betrayal. The mistrust. With an angry gesture he ceased his pleading and moved from her path. "Go, then. If you believe so little in me."

Oblivious of Angie Cody and Tad Jasper, Savannah stared up at Steve for a long while, searching for the man she'd loved and trusted. In his closed expression she found only bitter anger. After a moment she stepped past him and walked out of his life.

Chapter 14

"What the hell is this all about?" Steve's bitter words lashed through the baleful stillness of the barn.

Savannah was gone, lost to him. She'd walked out of his life with a hurt and stunned finality, driven away by a faithless and deceitful woman. A mistake from another life. His own guilt, his long, silent reluctance to speak of the past, only fueled his anger. "What now, Angie? What are you after this time?"

"You know as well as I, darling." Angie took a gliding, provocative step to him, raised a hand to his cheek and found her wrist caught in again a crushing grip.

Keeping her captive in his savage hold, in the murky light of the barn, Steve was a menacing specter as he glared down at her. His face grim with rage, his teeth clenched, he bore the look of a man pushed to the edge. A dangerous man, who could break her wrist with a snap of his own, and wish it was her neck.

"Damn you! Damn you for coming here." His voice sank to a growl. "For hurting her."

Blinded by his own distress, with innate gentleness fled from him, he bore down on the small bones of Angie's wrist. At her cry of pain, Tad Jasper made a move toward them. A swift, threatening glance from Steve stopped him in his tracks.

"Hey, man." Jasper backed away with a capitulating gesture. "I don't want any trouble."

"Then you picked the wrong company." Flinging Angie from him, Steve watched dispassionately as she fell in a heap on a bed of straw. "You don't want trouble, Tad? Put as much distance between yourself and Mrs. Cody as you can."

Jasper knelt by Angie, brushing straw from her hair. He touched her as a lover would, a man too truly snarled in a web of hypocrisy to recognize it. As if she were made of glass, he helped her to her feet. "I guess I'm in for the long haul. What Angie wants, I'll help her get."

"Which isn't me. The three of us know that." To Angie he said with deadly calm, "It was never me, was it? Once the glamour and the money were gone, other pastures were more enticing."

If he was honest, Steve knew he must admit the marriage hadn't lasted even that long. The ultimate break came when the final injury ended his chances for the national championship and his career at once. But it was simply a culmination of something begun months before. Angie wasn't cut out for the periods of unexpected solitude that were as much part of the rodeo as the excitement. She couldn't deal with injuries curtailing her social life. And she hadn't.

For months before the end of the short marriage, he'd coped alone, in whatever town, and whatever rodeo, while Angie caroused. She could always find the biggest and wildest party, like water seeking its own level. At first he felt it was innocuous, a lively woman searching for the excitement as necessary to her as life. In the end, he was glad when she elected to leave. Glad enough to give whatever she asked to make it happen.

That generous spirit vanished long ago.

When he looked at her carefully, objectively, there were cracks in the perfect facade. The sophisticated Western costume was an old one. There were worn and tattered places in the leather, a button dangled by a thread. Her makeup was little too heavy, her hair a little too brassy. The extraordinary beauty was slipping into the harshness of discontent. Perhaps that explained why the most striking of all the buckle bunnies, who once could pick from any number of champions, had attached herself to the less than illustrious Jasper.

Steve knew then why she'd come. He asked again, this time needlessly, "What do you want, Angie?"

"Why do I have to want anything?" Her shoulders were drawn back, her breasts thrust against clinging fabric. "What law says I can't visit you, just to see how you are? For old times' sake."

A laugh erupted from Steve. "You never cared in old times, why would you now?"

"I cared," Angie protested, disturbed that Steve was so thoroughly immune to her seductive ploy. "Wasn't I always there by your side when you needed me?"

"You were by my side, all right. In the winner's circle, and on the way to the bank. But when my ribs were smashed, or a shoulder displaced, you could be found at the nearest bar."

"She was young," Jasper interjected. "Too young to understand what it was like for us."

"Don't kid yourself, Tad. Angie was born old. She'd been around the circuit a time or two when I hooked up with her." Steve regarded her with low-keyed disgust. "From the looks of her, she's been around and down a time or two since."

"Damn you, Steve Cody!" Angie would have launched herself at Steve again, but this time it was Jasper who held her away.

"I was damned the day I met you, Angie." Steve didn't flinch, he watched her, as unperturbed as he would if she were a stranger. "But not anymore."

"You'll pay for that." Angie pulled away from Jasper, viciously tugging her clothing into order. "You'll pay with everything you have."

"Ahh." Steve crossed his arms over his chest. "We finally come to the crux of the matter. Money. That's what it all comes down to with you, isn't it, sugar?" The last was a long, soft drawl, the name one Steve knew she despised.

"It was certainly all you were ever good for," she flung at him. "There were men out there, real men, who made you look like a boy."

Steve smiled at the slandering of his virility. "You should know, sugar. You should know, as well, that I'm broke, so even the little I was good for isn't there anymore."

"No?" A wave of her hand encompassed the stables and the canyon beyond its walls. "A half million dollars on the hoof, and maybe more in land, what do you call that?"

"I call it a *potential* half million on the hoof, and an equal *debt* in land. With any profit to be realized in a far distant future. And, debt or profit, I call it mine."

"That's where you're mistaken." Angie played her trump card. "I call it ours. Half the stock and half the land you're standing on belongs to me."

"I'm sure you can't wait to tell me how you arrived at that conclusion." Jasper was forgotten as Steve's narrowed gaze pinioned the gloating woman. Beyond the wide door of the barn, Gitano stirred, the saddle creaking as he stamped and pawed restlessly in the lowering sun. He was the bedrock of every dream for the Broken Spur, and he was forgotten in a riveting moment.

"Arriving at the conclusion was simple." Glee became triumph. "When you and Charlie struck your bargain for the ranch, our marriage was very much intact."

"No." Denial was quick and sure, and wrong.

"Yes." Angie smiled, perfect teeth framed by lips too darkly drawn against the encroachment of petulant wrinkles. "You were still in the hospital when the papers were to be signed. It was a while before you could."

Steve remembered the transient aphasia, the weakness in his hands, resolved only shortly before he left the hospital. He'd signed a stack of papers at the time of his release. And though they'd been apart more than a year, one of them ended his marriage.

Chafing at legal delays, and then the delay by his year of rehab, she'd taken her awarded share and celebrated. He'd paid the debts of the marriage and his injury. Now she wanted more. "So you've come to stake a claim on the Broken Spur."

"Just my legal share."

"Only what you're due," Steve mused as if mulling over the possibilities.

"Exactly," Angie agreed quickly.

Steve's laugh was harsh. "In that case, what you're due is exactly what I said, half of a tremendous debt and a long wait."

A smug smile turned her face ugly. "What I have is half a stable of valuable horses, and half a canyon Jake Benedict would give his soul to own."

"The canyon isn't for sale."

"We'll see about that, won't we?"

"There's nothing to see. You've taken all from me that you're going to. The Broken Spur isn't for sale under any circumstance." Grim with anger, Steve turned from Angie to Jasper. "Get her off my land, Tad, and out of my sight before I throttle her."

"Oh, ho! Listen to him! A cuckold from one end of the rodeo circuit to the other, and never any show of spirit. But look at him now." Angie tucked her thumbs in the band of her trousers. Pleased by the success of her goading, she rocked back on the heels of her boots and laughed. "The pussy cat finally shows some claws."

"The claws were always there, sugar." Steve said quietly, reining in his temper. "You just never saw them before, you weren't worth the effort to unsheath them."

"How dare you!"

"I dare a lot when it comes to the Broken Spur." Without looking away from her, he spoke again to Jasper. "You don't need this scheming bitch, but if you want her and her pretty neck in one piece, take her away. Now."

Leaving Angie to sputter at the savage dismissal, and Jasper to stand with his mouth agape, Steve went to see to Gitano. He was sliding the saddle from the stallion's back when he realized Angie had followed him.

"You never cared." The words were thrown at him as she blocked his path to the shed where the saddles were stored. "You never loved me at all, and I knew it." A small quaver crept into her voice. "Did it ever occur to you that all I did was in the hope that I was wrong? That somewhere along the way you would say, stop."

"Frankly, no, it never occurred to me, and I doubt the idea ever occurred to you until now. But you're right about another thing. I didn't love you." His voice gentled, for even when he fought for a dream, he wasn't a cruel man. "My father had just died, and for the first time there was only myself, and the endless days and nights. I'd been alone, but never lonely, or in love."

He looked at her then with a mix of pity and remorse. "For my sins, Angie, I mistook what you brought to me as love, rather than the temporary ease of loneliness. For that, I'm sorry."

Her openhanded blow took him unprepared. His head rocked with it, and back again with the second. "You aren't half as sorry as you're going to be, Steve Cody!" Her shriek became a threat. "Or half as poor!"

"We'll see, Mrs. Cody—the ex—Mrs. Cody." He bowed mockingly over the saddle. "Remember, half of nothing is still nothing."

"Let's go, Tad. Our business here is ended, for now." Sliding her hand through the cowboy's folded arms, she steered him toward their car. "Just so you'll know," she called back to Steve, "we won't be very far away. Anytime you want to make a deal, we can be found at the Silverton Hotel."

"No deals, Angie."

"No? As you say, Stevie, we will see." The last of another threat was lost in the starting rumble of the engine. With a slam of doors and a punishing turn that barely missed the corral, Jasper drove toward Silverton.

"Whoa, boy. Easy." Steve settled Gitano with a croon. Music blaring from speakers positioned along the parade ground pounded the bordering stockyards with the throbbing beat of an old headache lurking in the brain.

"It's not as quiet as the canyon by a long shot, but we'll manage." He stroked the arching quivering neck of the high strung stallion as it crowded closer to the makeshift fence that separated them. "We'll do better than manage, and in three days we'll be home."

Silverton's Fall Festival was in peak form. From the look of the crowd, every cowboy and cowgirl from every ranch for miles around jammed the streets and festival concourse. Sprinkled among them were gaggles of children, a cosmopolite or two, families, tourists, city folk and farmers. And if luck was with him, more than a serious breeder or two.

As he'd always done, he stood apart, more observer than participant, his thoughts turned inward, his concentration centered on the contest at hand. Yet this time he hadn't been so completely unaware or so completely untouched by the mood of the crowd.

This time he'd listened and watched. Absorbed the atmosphere, and watched. And when he searched among the crowd, there was laughter on every lip, a twinkle in the eye, a swagger in jaunty steps. Finery shouted its stiff newness in a flash of gaudy colors, or announced treasured antiquity in a worn and muted sheen. But no matter the costume, or its age, one thing was clear, for native Westerners and tenderfoot alike boots and buckles and Western hats were de rigueur.

As were dust, heat, sawdust and sand. Adrenaline surged, excitement mounted, the scent and feel of them hovered in the air. Silverton named it festival, but by any name it was much like a thousand small town rodeos he'd ridden in a thousand times. The aura was always the same, and beyond the season he'd found little difference from his first day in town.

Except the face he searched for wasn't there.

"But no matter what, this time, we're part of it." A very different part, because he was different. He'd come with a sense of trepidation, wondering if he'd feel a stranger in a world that was once his life. He found instead that he liked this new role in which horse and rider would work together, rather than one struggling to conquer the other. "We'll work together, and we'll walk away with best of show in more categories than one."

In this quiet time, when the stockyards were oddly deserted and only he moved among the animals, he let himself admit winning wouldn't be quite the same without someone to share it. "But we'll manage in that, as well, Gitano. We'll manage."

He'd managed already, for Savannah had been conspicuously absent from the Broken Spur in the week following Angie's fiasco. Yet absence hadn't blinded him to the wisdom of her advice. On a dark and lonely night, when the canyon seemed more claustrophobic than tranquil, he'd changed the course of his plans. He would show the stallion and Lorelei, and enter The Lady in competition. If they won, the prize money would help ease the financial burden, the honor and exposure would do more.

"The Cody horse," Steve said simply because he liked the name. And because he'd begun to believe it might come to pass.

But would it be the same without Savannah?

He missed her. Every day he missed her. The emptiness she'd left in his life never lessened, not even when he accepted that it would be permanent. "We'll make it, Gitano." He stroked the stallion, assuring himself more than the animal. "It won't be easy, but we will."

Gitano's whinny, and the flick of his ears, warned Steve they weren't alone. Swinging around, he found himself face-to-face with the last person he expected.

"Savannah."

"I'm sorry." She was ashen, shadows still lay beneath her eyes. The surprise and malaise that swept over her face were quickly concealed. But not quickly enough. She backed away, half turned to go, yet she didn't. Still poised for flight, stammered excuses poured from her. "Sandy told me Gitano was here. I thought he was alone. I wanted to see him." Subdued, she made another apology. "Forgive me, I didn't mean to intrude."

"You aren't intruding. In a way, you have as much at stake in this as I." Black eyes, hungry for the sight of her, savored every detail.

She'd proven she was many women, and today she was yet another he'd never seen. Familiar and practical work clothes had been discarded for traditional Western garb. Handsomely tailored narrow trousers and a shirt in shades of gray fit her slender frame like a glove. A fringed vest of butter-soft leather draped loosely over the slight rise of her breasts. Only a belt of silver, inlaid with turquoise, revealed that pounds only recently recouped had been lost again.

She was beautiful and frayed at once, and he wondered if she was sleeping at all. From the underlying fragility he sensed, he suspected that she wasn't.

If things were as they should be, when the festival was done, he would take her to the Broken Spur. There he would kiss away her doubts, and hold her while she slept. And when the fatigue was gone, he would make love to her until she slept again.

But things weren't as they should be.

"Gitano missed you. So did Lorelei. The Lady went off her feed for a day or two." He searched for safer topics and found there were none.

"I missed them." She was becoming more ill at ease and more anxious to be away, but couldn't bring herself to leave without a word of encouragement. "I wish you luck with them."

"I don't need luck." Steve took a step toward her, drawn by a power stronger than he. "I had you." Flags of color brightened her cheeks at the tribute. He smiled ruefully. "In that, I was fortunate. Win or lose, Savannah, you made them champions."

"You would have done as well. Perhaps better, if it weren't for the Lawters."

"I owe them a debt of gratitude."

He was so close. His nearness, the familiar scent of him—soap and leather and captured sunlight—made her head spin. She wanted to run from him, she wanted to run to him. She wanted him to hold her and make her believe everything would be all right. Instead, she stood her ground, clinging to the little pride he'd left her. "The Lawters could have killed you. What debt could you owe them?"

"They brought you to me, and into my arms."

"Don't!" She backed away, giving ground she hadn't intended. "I'm not sorry I came to you. I would have done it for anyone."

"The Good Samaritan?"

"If you like, yes. The rest was a grave mistake."

"No!" He caught her hand in his, keeping her with him. "Nothing as right as what we shared could be a mistake."

"So right you forgot a little detail like having a wife?"

"Ex-wife," Steve said patiently. "You seem determined to forget that most important detail."

"All right, then, ex-wife." Savannah stood stiffly in his grasp. "One who clearly doesn't plan on remaining an ex for very long."

"She wants half the canyon and the Broken Spur, not me. You're a fool if you can't see that."

Savannah laughed. Even to her the sound bordered on hysteria. "You're an even bigger fool if you can't see she wants both."

"Dammit! You don't know anything at all about our marriage and what it was like, but just like that, with a snap of her fingers, you think I'm going to fall back into her arms?"

"She's a beautiful woman."

"So are you, Savannah."

Jerking back violently, she pulled from his grasp. "I don't want to hear this."

"Then go!" Simmering temper flared as Steve lashed out. "Nobody asked you to come here. Just as nobody asked you to come to the canyon. We would have muddled through then. We will now."

"But . . ." Inexplicably, she was reluctant to leave, when it was what she'd wanted only a heartbeat before.

"Go!" The word was a snarling command. He was convinced there was nothing more to say, yet when she made no move to comply, he sighed harshly, and heard himself offering explanations. "Okay." He shrugged in defeat. "Maybe you were right. Maybe I should have told you about Angie, but I didn't. Maybe I didn't want to sully what we had by bringing her into it. Maybe I forgot. Or maybe I simply didn't think she was an issue, any more than if you had some past lover hovering in the background.

"Hell, maybe I didn't think at all." His blazing gaze held hers. "I couldn't, you know, when you were in my arms."

With a shock, Savannah realized only then that in their quiet moments, when they spoke of more than ranching and horses, their discussions of the past had centered on childhood and family and ambitions. Beyond that, she'd thought no more clearly, and been no more forthcoming, than he.

Suddenly it seemed important that he know what he'd never asked. "Steve."

"What?" The word burst from him with the force of an expletive. A savage gesture underscored his tension. "What now?"

Her mouth was dry, she felt like a schoolgirl admitting she hadn't done her homework. "You never asked... I never told you..." She was babbling like that frightened schoolgirl, and didn't know why.

"What didn't I ask?" Anger abated, tensions eased as swiftly as they'd come. His was reflective, bemused. "What didn't you tell me?"

Her heart thudded beneath her breast, her throat threatened to close. Her lips barely moved in a whisper. "No lovers."

Two words that he didn't seem to hear, exacting a toll beyond their worth. Clearing her throat, and drawing herself erect, she repeated in a voice that was thankfully strong, "I've had no other lovers. There was never anyone before you." Staring down at her hands, unable to meet his look, she whispered almost too softly to be heard, "No one ever mattered as much."

Steve heard. Each time he'd heard her admission, but in his heart he'd always known. Just as in her heart she should know he could never settle for someone like Angie again.

If only she'd listened to her heart's voice…but that time was past. "Go," he repeated wearily. "There's nothing left for us now."

"There never was."

"You don't believe that!" His head reared back, the fire in him rekindled. "You don't believe it now, and you didn't then, or you would never have come to my bed."

"I don't know what I believed."

"Don't you?" His look touched every part of her, remembering the woman who had held him and loved him as fiercely as he had loved her. "You're asking me to accept that you crawled into my bed with no more concern than an alley cat in heat?"

The harsh analogy stunned her, but she made no effort to interrupt him.

"Jake Benedict's daughter wouldn't." His tone lost its hard edge. "Camilla Neal's daughter couldn't. Not for any reason save one."

"Lust or love," she spoke as thoughtfully as he. "Whatever the reason, does it matter anymore?"

He was silent for a long while. The brassy music blasting over the festival grounds changed, shifted moods. Trumpets and drums gave way to the mellow notes of a guitar strumming the opening chords of a plaintive Western ballad. Before the melody became apparent, the pure, sweet notes were reminiscent of a favorite adagio. A poignant, heartbreaking composition they'd listened to together countless times.

There was music. As the sun dipped behind the Western rim and darkness filtered through the canyon. Music. As storms of heart and body raged. Music. As her body curled into his, tender and trusting, and thoroughly loved.

Rhythmic cadences of a popular tune became more pronounced and definitive, his sense of déjà vu vanished. An ache for lost trust filled him.

There was music. As hope perished.

"You're right, Benedict. Lust or love, what does it matter?" He moved away, dismissing her. Little changed about his posture. His back was as straight and strong, his broad shoulders as stalwart. The tilt of his head beneath the brim of his Stetson was neither belligerent nor dejected. He'd put her out of his life, without a backward glance, accepting the emotional pain as stoically as he did physical pain.

Only the tiniest tremor in the hand that stoked Gitano's forelock betrayed him. And, if Savannah had been near enough to see, would have proved his cool rejection a lie.

Standing as she had, yet completely and firmly dismissed, she was bewildered by her continued reluctance to go. She shuffled her feet, her boots scuffing the straw strewn dirt. It was only a small move, but one that uprooted her from this place that seemed to hold her with a will of its own. And still she couldn't go.

"Steve."

He turned to her, his expression hard beneath the sardonic line of his brows. "Still here? When only a minute ago what you wanted most was to be gone from the unscrupulous rogue?"

She turned more than ashen under the windburn of her skin, and Steve wondered why he couldn't hate her for understanding him so little. Why he wanted to hold her and comfort her for the insult she'd paid him.

"I never called you either unscrupulous or a rogue." Her voice was halting, broken. Her hands were still locked before her, slender fingers twisted fretfully.

"One look was worth a thousand words, sweetheart."

The name that should have been an endearment crushed her with its rancor. They couldn't be lovers, should never have been, but she didn't want him to despise her. "I never meant it to be like this. This isn't how I wanted it to be."

"How do you want it, Savannah?"

"I was hoping we could be friends."

"Just friends?" Cynical disbelief swept through him. She thought they could be just friends, when even now, when he'd meant to turn his back on her forever, he still wanted her? Silently he damned her naiveté, while every part of him ached so badly for her he was like an maddened addict. An addict whose drug was Savannah. Whose craving was so great that, with the least provocation, not even the risk of intruders would stop him from dragging her down with him to the straw and making love to her at Gitano's feet.

The worst of it was he knew that once he touched her she wouldn't stop him. Then would come the hate. Until the next time.

"Friends? That's what you want from me? All you want?" There was a storm in his look, thunder in his voice.

"That's what I want," she answered, refusing to be daunted by his ferocity.

"There's a better than good chance I won't be here."

"You will. I'm sure of it."

"Madame Savannah and her crystal ball?" he mocked.

"I'm not Madame Anybody, and I don't need a crystal ball to know you're going to make a success of the Broken Spur."

"Why?" Steve refused to let her off the hook so easily. "What makes you so sure?"

Searching for a response, she found none but the truth. "I'm sure because of you." In the beginning, her answer was tentative, guarded, then spilled out in a rush. "I believe in the Cody horse."

Her lashes fluttered down, then up again with a slowly taken breath. His gaze waited for hers, and under its piercing intensity, the rest of her admission tumbled from her. "I believe in you."

"As a horseman," Steve said flatly. "But not a man."

"I..."

"Don't." He stopped her with a slashing gesture. "Don't say what we both know isn't true. Don't deny what can't be denied."

Savannah had no more strength to wrangle. She was uncertain, confused and vulnerable and made no effort to conceal it. As she stood across a chasm of her making, a small, sad smile touched his lips, recalling a memory. A memory so overwhelming that for a stunning, thoughtless instant, there was neither chasm between them nor earth beneath her feet.

The blast of music faded into illusion, becoming the splash and ripple of a waterfall. In its mists a man and woman stood entwined, lovers, lost in themselves, caring for neither time nor circumstance. Soon they would swim naked in the small pool carved by eons of rain and wind and streams rushing over stone. And when they mated, she would be soft and yielding as the water that embraced them, he hard and strong as the crucible of stone. The pinnacle of desire would be exquisite beyond measure, the culmination wild and fierce and absolute.

As it had been for them. For Savannah and Steve, who could be more than friends, but never less than lovers.

"Do you see, Savannah?" he asked, his voice hushed, as if he'd seen into her thoughts, lived a part of her reverie. "No half measures. Never for us. Do you understand?"

She nodded, her writhing fingers were still. There was nothing more to say, nothing more to do. It was time to go, and still she couldn't move. "I wish…"

"If wishes were horses, honey, the Broken Spur would be a five star gold mine." The raucous comment was bold and brash, like the woman who made it. Angie stood in the corridor that ran between temporary stalls. Better groomed this time, but still a mélange of brass and flash that made Savannah seem as inviting a shady glen.

"What do you want, Angie?" Steve hardly glanced at her as he watched hurt gather in Savannah's eyes. "I've told you there's nothing here for you."

"And as I told you, that remains to be seen." Sauntering past Savannah, she stopped a pace closer to Steve. "At any rate, Tad and I thought you might need a cheering section." Slim shoulders lifted elegantly, large breasts shimmied within the containing satin of a form fitting shirt. "A little encouragement never hurts."

"Coming from you it might."

"Ahh, Stevie, you don't mean that." With a sidelong glance at Savannah, she shrugged, including her in a tongue-in-cheek camaraderie. "Stubborn male pride! What's a girl to do about it?"

"I'm sure I wouldn't know." Savannah's reply was stilted.

"You realize this is all because I left him. I know now what a mistake it was, and Stevie must, too, but I just can't seem to get past his…"

"Stubborn male pride?" Savannah finished for her.

"Exactly!" Angie's mouth curved in delight at what she considered her success. "Then you do understand."

"Until just this minute, I didn't. Now I understand perfectly." Angie was a bad joke, a threatening nuisance. Savannah's eyes were bright as they found Steve's. "Stubborn pride, whatever the gender, can destroy something too precious to be lost." Her voice softened, dropped. "But only if we allow it."

Nothing changed in Steve's posture or his face. Only a breath half caught, then cut short, betrayed his questioning surprise. Savannah didn't wait for more. Or less, if that was to be the way of it. She wanted to know his response to her sudden clarity, but not here in a predator's company.

"I'm sure you both have a great deal to discuss." She turned to the woman who watched her sharply. "Angie." She didn't offer her hand, didn't use the surname she knew now was the only claim the woman had on Steve. "Meeting you again has been, shall we say, illuminating."

"Illuminating?"

Savannah turned a bright smile on her. "Very illuminating, when it shouldn't have had to be."

"It shouldn't?"

"Certainly not." Savannah patted a satin clad shoulder. "But you have business with Steve, and I'm keeping you from it."

"Yes." Angie bristled, suspecting that something significant had just occurred and she hadn't understood. "You are."

"But no more." With the grace taught her by a Southern lady, Savannah inclined her head and retreated.

Her journey to the entrance of the stockyards would be long and slow. Before she'd taken a half-dozen steps, the hiss and buzz of furious conversation began. The words were indistinguishable, the mood required no interpretation. Angie Cody was in fine form, switching from calculating seductress to calculating shrew on a whim and a heartbeat.

Steve's voice was quiet, and deep, but stronger. Angry words rang sharply through the corridor. "No more, Angie. Not one penny, or one grain of sand."

Angie laughed. So certain, so confident. So cruel, with greed stripping reason and humanity from her.

Savannah could see her clearly now, as if blinding scales had suddenly fallen from her eyes. She knew she hadn't before because she'd been waiting for the spoiler, expected it.

"All because it was too wonderful, I nearly threw it away." At the last stall she paused and looked back. Steve hardly moved as Angie gestured pointedly with her saberlike nails flashing blood red. "Maybe I did throw it away because of you, Angie. Then again," she smiled, a smile filled with hope, "maybe not."

There was little Savannah knew of love, except that it had a way of surviving. Steve loved her. He'd never said it, but she knew. Standing in the stockyard, with animals milling and lowing, and blaring music changing to an aching ballad, she knew.

Where there had been little trust, she would trust in love.

Lost in hopeful dreams, she continued toward the parade ground, managing only a distracted greeting for a stockman passing by. "Morning, Cactus."

"Morning, Miss Benedict." Cactus Poteat was sometimes a drifter, sometimes a cowhand, a state dependent on whether or not he was sober. Tipping his hat, he watched her furtively out of sight before stepping into the yard.

Eager to retrieve the bottle he had stashed in the Spanish stallion's stall, he hurried down the corridor. Eagerness curdled to anxiety when he found the stall occupied, and a ripsnorting argument careening along. No matter how desperate he was for a drink, there was little to do but wait. Creeping into the shadows, finding a pile of straw, he stretched out for the duration.

Quite into his cups already, he was just drifting off when he heard a slap and a woman's screech. Then the voice of the squatter from Sunrise Canyon thundered, threatened.

Footsteps rushed past his hiding place, and the yard was quiet.

"A pity," Cactus grumbled as he settled too comfortably into the hay to seek out his bottle after all. "A dang pity if a man was to truly break the neck of a woman as pretty as that." A snore rattled the back of his throat, and buzzed his lips. He snorted and stirred, rubbed the tickle of his mouth. Later he would search out the bottle, carefully hidden in the most perilous place he could conceive. For now, he settled into sleep again.

"Yesiree." His words slurred as he slipped over the edge. "A dang pity, for sure."

Chapter 15

"Well, now, aren't you a treat for eyes lonesome for the sight of you?" Caught up in Jubal's bearish embrace, Savannah could only hang on and hug back.

Leaving her with ribs that were one squeeze shy of cracking, he put her from him. Holding her at arm's length, his hands resting briefly on her shoulders, the massive man looked her over from head to toe. "It's been too long since I've been around to ride herd on this slave driver here." A slanting glance flicked to Jake and back. "And I can tell he's been working you too hard."

Jake snorted and whipped his chair around, giving them his back as he glared out over the festival grounds. The arena lay virtually at his feet, a natural amphitheater formed as the land was formed, by the forces of nature. This was the second day of the festival, the most important; in a few minutes the highlight of the festivities would begin. The showing of the horses, prize stock from some of the richest and best ranches, and from the working ranches, the shoestring operations.

Always a splendid gathering of horseflesh, no matter the source. But one, more than any other, captured the interest of Jake Benedict and every serious horse breeder alike.

Steve Cody's Spanish stallion would be strutting his stuff for the curious and informed in less than a quarter hour. If rumor could be believed, the stallion was the best of a spectacular stable, expected to sweep the show.

Jake hadn't been feeling so well lately, but not even gimpy legs and a herd of wild horses could have kept him away. "Nosiree," he groused aloud to himself. "No-sir-damn-ree."

"Jake's right, Jubal. He's worked me no harder than usual." Rescuing her hat from the precarious angle left by the exuberant embrace, she smiled her brightest smile, defending Jake as she wrongly interpreted his muttering. "Working the herds and the stock can be taxing for any of us this time of year."

"Working the stock and what else?" Jake brought his chair around abruptly. The look in eyes so like her own pinioned her with their question.

His remark took her by surprise, in all the months of her protracted days, he'd never commented on her absences. If he'd questioned Sandy or Bonita, each had sidestepped the truth adroitly and hadn't worried her with news of the inquisition. "It's true," she admitted. "I've been away some."

"Some!" Jake leaned forward in his chair, his elbows on the armrests, his fingers locked in a hard grip. "Gone more than she's home, and she calls it some?"

"She's a woman grown, Jake, wouldn't you think she deserves a little privacy?" Jubal intervened, casting a puzzled look at her.

"She wants privacy, all she has to do is go in her own room and shut the door. She'd be perfectly alone there. I damn sure couldn't disturb her if I wanted to."

The big man chuckled heartily. "Maybe being alone in her bedroom isn't the sort of privacy our Savannah would be wanting." His twinkling eyes swept over her appreciatively. "The range is as full of wranglers who'd like to spend time with her as it is jackrabbits."

In spite of an effort to the contrary, Savannah cringed. Jubal was trying to help, trying to tease Jake from his bad mood, but the direction he was taking was dangerous ground.

"It ain't wranglers. Hell, not even *a* wrangler." Jake snorted his distaste for a greater complaint. "It's those damn lawyer books."

A look of blank astonishment left her speechless as silver eyes flashed at her again.

"Don't act so surprised, either of you," Jake fumed, working himself into a rank mood. "Takes no genius to figger that when she sneaks off to whatever line cabin she's holed herself up in, it's to study on them dusty tomes. Making ready, so she can go back to finish what she started. Fact is, I expect any day to hear that she's decided to go back East.

"Deserting!" His mouth pursed, turned down in a grim line. "Just like her ma."

Savannah gaped at her father, wondering how he'd arrived at this theory. "Where did this come from? What prompted you to think I was considering returning to law?" Questions burst from her. "Did Sandy tell you?"

"Sandy told me nothing," Jake groused. "Fact is, he's made a career out of telling me as little as he could about you. 'Twas true when you were a little girl, and true now. And before you ask, Bonita's as closed mouthed where you're concerned."

Her relief was palpable, the last thing she wanted was for either Sandy or Bonita to jeopardize their jobs by lying for her. "Then all on your own you arrived at the conclusion that I was studying, planning to go back to Georgia after all this time?"

"Oh, I looked around for a likely fella first, and finding none, it wasn't a great stretch to make the conclusion."

"Not a great stretch!" It was Jubal's time to snort. "You take a flimsy thread and weave a whole cloth from it, and you say it isn't a stretch? Even if it were more than a thread, why would it be cause for resentment? The child has given you more than a father's due for more years than I can count. Even putting aside her own ambitions for you when you needed her. How could you begrudge her if she did want to continue her studies?" Jubal wagged a finger. "Mind you, I say *if*."

"She's a Benedict, a rancher, born and bred to it. She'd die of boredom locked in a courtroom listening to a bunch of legal prattle."

"If she were just your daughter, maybe." Jubal shifted his weight, his face alight as he mounted his fictional white charger to gallop full speed into battle. "You forget she's Camilla's daughter, as well. From a scholarly family peopled with doctors and lawyers, and judges and such."

Jake bristled, his head jerked up, slumping shoulders lifted. "It's not something I'm likely to forget, considering I have her image before me every day of my life."

Jubal rocked back on his heels, pleased by this rare chance to make a point that needed making. "And every day you miss her."

"I do not!"

"Do!"

Looking from one determined man to the other, Savannah was exasperated by the childish nature of their argument, but relieved their attention had been diverted from her. In a suspicious thought, she wondered if that had been Jubal's intention all the while.

"What do you take me for? A blathering idiot? The woman absconded, left me without a backward glance, why on earth would I miss her?" Jake was too bemused to be concerned by the stares of those who hurried by to take their seats before the showing of the horses began.

"She didn't abscond." If Jake was bemused, Jubal was completely oblivious. "There was nothing secret about her leaving, or the reason for it. She gave you every opportunity to ask her to stay."

"Every opportunity!"

"Yes, Jake Benedict, every opportunity. And do I think you're a blathering idiot? No." Aware or not, in any case, Jubal dropped his tone a degree. "Stiff-necked pride is your problem. Any fool but you would have asked her back, especially when you wanted her back so badly."

"You've become an expert, have you, Jubal Redmond?"

"Jake! Jubal! That's enough." Savannah had been content to remain a silent bystander, glad Jake's focus had switched from her. She always enjoyed this common and often comical sparing of old friends, but a warning flag had been raised. Temperament of the discourse had turned from heated to icy, and the use of full names signaled it was time to step in. "You sound like children."

"Don't." Jake practically bellowed the denial.

"Don't," Jubal echoed more quietly.

"You!" Jake stabbed an accusing finger in Jubal's direction, returning to the argument as if Savannah had never intervened. "You would have asked Camilla back."

"In a heartbeat, on my knees," Jubal shot back.

"You were always half in love with her yourself."

At her father's revelation, Savannah's jaw, which seemed eternally prone to drop today, dropped again. As if she were watching a fast and furious tennis match, her head swiveled from one graying giant of the West to the other.

"I was, and more than half." Jubal nodded, perfectly at ease with his admission. "A common condition among half the populace of the county—the half that isn't female—and you, Jake. You loved her then," he finished in a drawling flourish. "You love her now."

Jake Benedict tossed about in his chair, his fist drummed the armrests. "Where the hell did you get an idea like that?"

"From the best source. From you. What can you say to deny it?" He didn't embellish his proof with his own astute observations, or Sandy's. Jubal was too wise to bring him into this. The foreman had been fired too many times for too many reasons. Meddling in Jake's emotional ties to Camilla might be the one that stuck.

"I say we need to change the subject." Savannah stepped between them. "This isn't the place for this."

"There's no place for it." Jake glared up at Jubal, tossing the only insult he could think of at him. "Damn Kentuckian."

The announcer chose that time to make the last call for the show of horses. In his singsong voice he invited all who were interested to take their seats before the initial parade around the ring.

"We should go," she urged. "Sandy will be waiting for us."

"We should, and yes, he will," Jubal agreed. "All of us are anxious to see what young Cody has done with his stock."

"You mean you're anxious to see what he's done with yours," Jake tossed over his shoulder as Jubal grasped the back of his chair. "And I don't need your help."

"I won't deny I'm curious to see if my faith in the boy is vindicated." Jubal kept his hold firmly on the chair, slowing its descent down a ramp constructed for Jake. "What's more curious is the way you keep insisting you don't need help. All of us do, at one time or another."

"You're just hurrying me along because you're anxious to see that horse of yours."

Jubal accepted the rebuke calmly. "That's right, I am quite eager to see Lorelei. We settled that a minute ago."

The chair bumped down the incline, held in check by strong, caring hands. Reserved ringside seats, set apart from the others, waited for them. The Redmond and Benedict boxes were side by side, as they had been for years. Sandy, alone, waited in Jake's, while Jubal's spilled over with guests and acquaintances.

"Got your usual welcoming committee, I see." Jake's head was high, his scowl deep. "Hangers-on, waiting to see if you made a fool of yourself or not this year."

"Not hangers-on, Jake. Friends, who came to cheer my good judgment."

"Bosh!"

"Bosh?" Savannah repeated the odd comment.

"Bosh?" Jubal frowned and shuddered.

"Exactly," Jake declared as his friend and nemesis wheeled him into the enclosure where Sandy waited. "Is there an echo in here?"

"No more an echo than my judgment is poor."

"You'll be singing a different tune when the squatter falls on his face."

"I've made mistakes in the past, but not this time." Jubal paused before firing his next salvo. "He isn't a squatter, the canyon is his honestly and aboveboard."

"Damn you, Redmond! You want him to succeed. That's why you gave him the horse, and why you're championing him now." Jake huffed and puffed his indignation. "Some friend you are."

"That I am, believe it or not." Jubal set the brakes and backed away from the chair as Savannah slipped by to take a seat by Sandy.

"Then spare me from my enemies."

"Spare you from your greed," Jubal said bluntly. "You've coveted the canyon for nigh on to forty years, when you don't need it. Steve does. Given half the chance, he'll make it a workable operation. Ultimately his success will reflect on all of us and be a benefit."

"Next you'll be looking to pair him with a woman, to populate the entire countryside with Codys."

"The thought crossed my mind." Jubal's gaze strayed to Savannah. "He's a fine young man. Reminds me a bit of another rancher who came here nearly forty years ago with only his horse, his saddle, the shirt on his back, and a dream of the Rafter B in his head."

"Bosh!"

"We're back to that again?" Jubal rolled his eyes at a silent Sandy, who only grinned.

"You're such an expert, Jubal Redmond, you tell me what woman in her right mind would want the upstart?" Jake paused and shrugged. "Especially if he was like me?"

"Good question." Jubal paused, too, for effect. "Maybe there's a woman for him here. One with Camilla's sterling qualities." An eyelid dropped lazily over an eye. An infinitesimal move, but one that spoke more than a thousand words, and Savannah understood that everything Jubal Redmond had said and done in the friendly fire of his discourse with Jake had been calculated, and for her.

"You have one of your grand Eastern ladies all picked out for him, have you?" Jake's laugh was a deep chuckle that escalated to a shrill cackle as his merriment heightened. "I can see it now." Wiping a tear from his eye, he chuckled again. "The squatter in his jeans and boots, stinking of dust and horses, whilst the grand lady cooks over an open-hearth fire in diamonds and pearls, drenched in Oh de Paree.''

"Act the buffoon, if you will." Jubal's smile was tolerant. "I remember the grandest of ladies, who turned her back, not on diamonds and pearls or Oh de Anywhere, but on all she held dear to be your wife. Who are you to say Steve Cody can't find a woman of the same sort?"

"Camilla struck a business deal. Financial security for her impoverished genteel family, a wife for me."

"Maybe that's all it was in the beginning, but what kept her here nineteen more years?" Jubal shot back as a vanguard of horses began to enter the arena.

"Gentlemen." Savannah used the term loosely as she touched her father's arm. "The show we've all been waiting for is about to begin. This discussion would be better postponed for the time being."

"No need. It's settled." Jake swiveled in his chair to face her. "Jubal's going to find the squatter a woman he thinks will stick. Then we'll see if she does, any more than he will."

"That's where you're wrong," Jubal put in his two cents again. "He may be a young he-coon, but he's the same as you were. He'll find his own woman and, for him, she'll stick."

The speaker blared again, the announcer asked for quiet. Jubal settled in a seat between Jake's chair and Savannah, rather than joining his guests in his own box. He sat ramrod straight, his face bland as he stared directly ahead. Only a surreptitious pat on her knee offered Savannah a mix of encouragement and consolation.

Lights dimmed, a spot focused on the arch leading from the stockyards. In the end of the day the air was cool and crisp, but not cold. Twilight deepened, excitement arced through the theater like the spark of an electrical charge. The audience fell silent, holding its collective breath. A hoof struck stone where no stone should be, a stallion as black as the night, as iridescent as the stars, stepped into the arena and stood in the circle of light.

Gitano. Bold and majestic. An uncivilized creature tamed by his rider's touch only because he wanted to be, standing poised and cool, waiting for a signal.

Fifteen seconds passed. Twenty. Thirty, without a quiver or ripple of the magnificent hide. Steve lifted the reins, brushed the sleek flank with his spurs. A low murmur of awe rose from the crowd and Gitano began a slow, graceful canter.

"Damnation," Jake exclaimed in a strangled whisper.

''Not damnation!'' Jubal corrected on a lost breath. ''Bravo!''

''Amen.'' From his seat on Savannah's right, Sandy concurred. ''And hallelujah.''

''Yes.'' Her spellbound whisper was a prayer of thanks, and vindication. Without looking away from horse and rider, she reached out to clasp a hand of friend and foreman in each of hers.

''What did I tell you?'' Jubal clapped Jake on the shoulder as applause thundered and the lights came halfway up. ''A clean sweep for the Broken Spur. Best stallion, best mare of show, *and* best working horse. The Lady is something to behold, isn't she?''

''Which one?'' Jake asked sourly. ''The one that wore the saddle, or the one hanging on the squatter's arm?''

''Well, now, that depends.'' Jubal turned his attention back to the arena. A moment before Steve Cody had been standing apart, letting a stockman hold Gitano while rancher and breeder alike circled the handsome stallion. Now he'd been joined by a voluptuous blonde who preened in the edge of the spotlight, clinging to him like a limpet.

From a distance, she appeared young in dress and manner. Her hair was worn long in a girlish, fly away style. Her body gave the impression of being taut and controlled. A stunning woman, but to the connoisseur in Jubal the sum of her impression was all wrong. Puzzled, he glanced at Savannah, who hadn't looked away from Steve.

Leaning close, he murmured for her ears alone, ''Is this someone to be concerned about?''

Savannah didn't answer at once, as she watched Angie slide her arm through Steve's, hugging the bulging muscle against her breast.

More than comfortable in his natural silence while Jubal jousted with Jake and Savannah refereed, Sandy cleared his throat. Tugging his hat to a sharper angle, he offered a terse explanation, ''An ex-wife, looking for a few more bucks.''

Jake grinned. Jubal's brows shot toward his hairline.

''Came in a week ago,'' Sandy continued as tersely. ''Holed up at the Silverton Hotel with a two-bit cowboy on a short rein.''

''I repeat my question.'' Jubal's face was grave as he watched Savannah's expression turned as blank as stone. ''Is this someone to be concerned about?''

''I don't know what you mean by concern,'' Jake put in. ''But from the looks of her, she wants more than a few more bucks. I reckon any fool could guess that's what she wants most, but she'd sure take the squatter in the bargain.''

Sandy touched Savannah's shoulder, a subtle expression of encouragement. ''I reckon Steve will have something to say about that.''

Jake's laugh was a cackle. ''From where I sit, he ain't exactly fighting her off.''

''Would you have him cause a scene?'' Savannah asked softly.

''Steve Cody is a gentleman.'' With another pat on her knee, Jubal offered comfort to accompany his observation.

Feeling rather like a kicked puppy to be stroked and petted, but loving these tough, hard-bitten men who knew no other way of showing they cared, Savannah agreed. ''Angie's counting on it.''

Casting a worldly eye at the woman whose performance made her more tawdry than beautiful, Jubal grimaced. ''That is as obvious as the lady, dear heart, but even gentlemen have limits.''

''Not where she's concerned.'' Savannah raked an agitated hand down the long coil of her braid. ''Or so she thinks.''

At the low comment, Jake's head swiveled toward his daughter. ''You seem to know a mighty lot about this ex-wife of the squatter.''

''No.'' She stared into the distance, away from the arena, away from Jake's narrowed gaze. ''Not a lot.''

''If that was her ace card, she played it in the wrong game.'' Sandy's comment was almost a crow. ''The lady, and I use the term loosely, just got her comeuppance.''

Startled, Savannah looked down in time to see Steve peeling Angie's arms from his neck and setting her firmly from him. As she stood in the spotlight, face a ghostly rictus and breasts heaving in short, furious breaths, he lifted a forearm to his mouth to wipe a smear of lipstick from it. With a finality that needed no interpretation, he turned his back on the woman who had been his wife and walked from the arena.

''Damn you, Steve Cody!'' Angie's raging cry soared above the rumble of the crowd, silencing it. Every gaze was glued to her, mortified for her, but if she knew, she didn't seem to care.

''Damn you!'' she shrieked again as Steve walked without looking back. ''You'll pay for this. By God! I'll see that you pay. When I'm done, you'll have nothing. No ranch, no horses. Nothing.''

Her tantrum ended, all her allure exposed as tarnished and false. Angie stood awkwardly, pinned like a tattered butterfly in the unforgiving glare of the spotlight. No one in the audience moved, no one spoke. Then, in an act of compassion, some kind soul pulled the master switch, plunging the arena and the woman into darkness.

One by one the voices began. Gossip hummed like a tuning fork as the slow procession from the amphitheater commenced.

"Well, well, well." Jake chuckled and gloated. "Our all-American ro-day-o hero ain't so lily white after all."

"Shut up, Jake!" It was Sandy who snapped the command a second before Jubal could. And Sandy who fumbled in the dark to take Savannah's cold hand, offering the warmth of his own. "You don't know what the hell you're talking about, so for once in your life, just shut up."

She was dressed for the dance. Music throbbed in a rhythmic beat. Paper lanterns circling the wooden platform erected precisely for this special evening lent the night a festive air. But an hour of preparation in the Benedict suite at the Silverton Hotel couldn't wipe the tragicomedy played out in the arena from her mind. After deliberately dallying over her hair and makeup while Jake and Sandy joined Jubal's coterie for drinks, she walked to the dance alone, feeling anything but festive.

"Hey, boss lady!" A cowboy, cleaned up and slicked down after the afternoon and evening events, fell into step by her. "Save me a dance?"

Drawn from her wandering and her thoughts, she looked up, blinked owlishly, focused thought and vision. "Jeffie?"

"In the flesh."

"Good grief! You've grown, Jefferson Cade." Indeed he had. Taller, broader, more confident. Had she seen him in the months since the day the Lawters attacked Steve? Surely she had, but she couldn't remember. "You must be every inch of six feet."

"Yes, ma'am, Miss Benedict, ma'am."

Savannah almost laughed aloud. If she hadn't recognized Jeffie before, she would now. "Is this your first festival?"

"First as a real cowhand instead of a kid." He blushed a little and shoved his hands in his pockets, suddenly shy after his euphoric greeting. "I got my star."

"Already? Show me!" She stopped dead center in the walkway and, when he lifted the heel of his boot for her inspection, admired the perfectly carved star sincerely. "I suppose this means you don't belong to the saddle soap and neat's-foot oil brigade anymore."

"No, ma'am." Jeffie's blush deepened. "Fact is, I've sorta been filling in for you, what with you being so busy with Mr. Cody's horses and all."

"So busy—" Savannah cut short her comment. "How did you know that?"

"Well, ma'am, it wasn't a hard thing to figure, once I saw how it was between you."

"Once you saw what, Jeffie? When?"

She spoke gibberish, but it made perfect sense to the boy. "The day he first come to the barn at the Rafter B. I wasn't spying or nothing, but I saw how it might be. Later when he was hurt and you took out across the range like a bullet, I saw for true how it was. I ain't told nobody though. I mean, it wasn't any business of mine, so I didn't say nothing."

Savannah stared at him. Out of the mouth of a fledgling cowboy, she heard the facts of her life. What might be, what was, and couldn't be denied. Wouldn't be denied. So what was she waiting for?

"Jeffie." She caught his arm, her hand shaking but her mind set on its course. "I'll take a rain check on that dance." Framing his face in her palms, she rose to kiss his soft young mouth. "But we'll have it, I promise."

Spinning in a whirl of her skirt, she rushed down the walk. In another whirl she turned to walk backward. "Jeffie."

"Yes, ma'am."

"Nothing." Her laugh was giddy. "Nothing except, thanks."

"You're welcome, I'm sure." With his hand lingering over his mouth he watched her hurry on. A fingertip stroked the exact spot her lips had touched, and he wished he understood what he'd done, so he could do it again.

She was lost in the crowd when he ventured a guess at her new destination. A smile displaced awe. "Good luck, boss lady."

The stockyards lay in shadow, the still darkness broken by random bands of dim light filtering from the adjacent grounds. But she found him there, where she knew he would be. The stables were quiet, tired horses drowsed with drooping heads. Only Gitano stirred, handsome and glittering in a shaft of pale radiance as he snuffled at Steve's shoulder.

Savannah stopped beyond the arrow of light, her step muffled by fresh straw, her heart aching for this man who seemed so alone when he should be celebrating. Yet, she asked honestly, wasn't this where he should be, with his horses, where he was most at home?

Watching him, listening to his low croon, she felt like a trespasser blundering into a private moment. The elated conviction Jeffie had sparked wavered. She shouldn't be here, shouldn't intrude on Steve's joy or his pain. She'd lost that right weeks ago, thrown it away like a fool.

Daring not even a rustle of her skirt, she backed away, taking each step carefully. Retracing her steps in slow motion.

A noise, a whisper, a guttural sigh rent the quiet, freezing her in place. Standing as rigid as marble, she probed murky corners for the cause of the stealthy disruption. There was nothing, no more sound, no unfamiliar shapes, yet a subtle shifting in the air scratched at her nerves and prickled at the back of her neck.

Calming clamoring instincts, she looked down the corridor at her back, hoping the disturbance hadn't been another rancher checking his animals, or an anxious breeder stealing one more peek at coveted stock. Studying the empty passage, she prayed fervently the stalls were as empty, that she might yet retreat as unobtrusively as she'd come.

No one was there. She was certain, and scolded herself for being silly. Everyone was at the dance, only she and Steve . . .

A coughing grunt stabbed through her speculation. A thud and a muffled screech sent shivers lurching through her. She barely bit back a scream as a form as black as Hades burst from the gloom. Ears flattened, tail waving like a banner, the yowling creature scurried over her foot.

A cat! A mouser come to its own festival.

Laughing silently at her silly notions, she breathed a sigh of relief. Relief that was to be short-lived.

"Savannah?" Steve stood in her path, blocking her escape. "What the hell are you doing here? Why aren't you at the dance?"

Of course he had heard, of course he had investigated. She was an unthinking simpleton not to expect it. Looming over her, he was a fearful figure, but she was done with fear. Her chin angled a bit, her throat bobbed putting the last of paralytic fear away as she answered honestly. "I came because I knew you would be here."

"It wouldn't take a mastermind to make that deduction." The sharp rise of a night breeze carried the raucous cadence of a line dance to them. The deep, booming notes built to a crescendo, then easing and softening, segued without missing a beat into the poignant notes of ballad. The change went unmirrored in Steve.

There was no relenting in him, no ease, no softening. "You haven't answered my question."

"I came because I thought you might need me."

"Ah, you thought I might need a friend, and that you might be that friend."

His bitterness lay like a burden on her heart. She met his harsh stare with every shred of poise Camilla had instilled in her. "The thought crossed my mind."

Laughter as grating as a steel trap ripped from him. "I have my horses and a few trophies to set on a mantel, why would I need a friend? Why you?"

"Why me, indeed?" A sound of hurt too low to be perceived trembled in her throat. Bowing to it only briefly, she muffled a sigh. "I can see I was mistaken."

His look swept over her, no detail escaping him. Not the circular crinkled skirt falling away from a tightly cinched silver belt—filmy georgette, clinging to narrow hips as only georgette could. And certainly not the peasant blouse, its neckline gathered discreetly, then tied loosely over the swell of her breasts. A simple costume, but worn as Savannah wore it, a study in innocent seduction stronger than pain. Stronger than betrayal.

He never forgot how lovely she was, but each time he saw her was like a renewal. Even now, remembering how quickly she'd doubted, how easily she'd walked away, he wanted to touch her, to draw her into the flames of passion that consumed him.

Silence seethed, linking them across an invisible chasm neither could breach. In the play of light and shadows, his gaze was dark, unreadable. Yet she felt the power of it, sensed the barely controlled passion. But contempt could be as compelling as attraction, and hate as passionate as desire.

Hopeless regret crept through her in its relentless path to heart and soul, leaving her brittle and cold in the heat of the night. Fighting to hold back the pain, she turned her face away. Somewhere in the nether regions of the stockyard the displaced mouser scratched and huffed. From an even greater distance, too far to threaten, thunder growled and lightning flashed, dancing through the open portals of stalls like a half-hidden candle.

Savannah didn't see, she didn't hear, as she braved his stare again. "Coming here was a mistake. I seem to make the most and the worst when you're concerned." Unaware her battle to hide her agony had been lost, she bowed her head, speaking in a whisper as she turned away, "Forgive me, for everything."

"Wait." He touched her then, a hand at her shoulder, detaining her, not with its power, but with its need. "Which was the worst?"

She could have shrugged out of his grasp with only a move of her shoulders, and yet she didn't. "Does it matter anymore?"

"It matters." Thunder was a whisper now, the lightning too dim to discern, but he lifted his head, staring beyond her as if he would see. "There was another night, another storm." His gaze swung back to her, stark and piercing, as if he would see beyond civilized trappings. "Do you remember?"

"I remember."

"A night of mistakes."

"No." She moved from him, from his touch. "A night that made the rest of my life a mistake."

Intent on walking away for the last time and her heart caught in throes of grief, she didn't see his control snap, nor the hand that flashed out once more to spin her back to him, to hold her and keep her. "Stay."

It was shocking to see the fury in him. "I can't."

His fingers were brutal on her arm. "Tell me why." When she didn't answer, he shook her gently. "Tell me why you watched me from the rim of the canyon. Why you came to me the night of the storm, and tonight. Tell me all the whys."

Looking into his grim face, she knew there was but one answer. One answer for every question. One answer for a thousand questions, but her heart wouldn't dare the words. "It doesn't matter why. Not anymore."

"Stop sounding like a broken record! It matters to me."

"Why?" She shot back at him, and would have laughed at the insanity of the repetition, if she wasn't suddenly and completely convinced that her life as she knew it would change with his answer. "You tell *me!*"

"Dammit, Savannah!"

"Why?" She was implacable, and, all the while, trembling inside.

"Because I love you." The admission burst from him like an accusation. "For what it's worth, I never wanted it any more than you wanted to love me." Brooding anger fled from him, his brutal hold eased. Bringing her nearer, he cupped the back of her head in his palm. "You do love me, you know. You have for a long time."

Putting her from him, but only enough to frame her face in a shaft of light, desperation edged into mockery. "What?" He laughed softly. "No argument?"

She could only shake her head, her heart too full for speech of any kind.

"Then, stubborn woman," he shook her again, gently, "will you tell me what I need to hear?"

"No!"

"Yes." If she was stubborn, he took it to a higher plane. "I will have the words, if it takes all night."

"I can't. I won't."

"You can. You will." His fingers drifted from her cheek to her throat, lingered at the tie of her blouse. "Oh, yes, you will."

There was tenderness in his touch, and it was her undoing.

"All right, then! Yes! Yes, I love you. Damn you, Steve Cody! I love you!" She would have stepped away from him, run away, if he'd let her. "There, I've said it." She glared up at him. "Are you satisfied?"

"For starters." He ignored the stiffening of her body as he hauled her hard against his. "But I promise it will get easier with practice. Just as making love will get better."

Denial stumbled on her tongue as he nibbled at her lips. "It can't be. We can't be."

The tie of her blouse slid like silk through his fingers, its tiny bow unraveled. Gathered fabric slipped from her shoulders. When she would have struggled away to cover herself, he caught her wrists, shackling them in one hand. "It can. We can." He muttered, feasting on the sight of her heaving breasts, the budding nipples. "Let me show you."

His free hand covered her, caressed her, lifted a perfect bud to his kiss, and she was lost. "Show me." Surrender, whispered on a lost breath. "Please."

His hands skimmed over her until she writhed against him. His tongue laved and tormented, kindling hungry, raging infernos. There was demand, not surrender, when she tore from his curbing grasp, her fingers diving into his hair to drag his face to hers. "Show me!" She was wild and reckless, her voice rising, hoarse and urgent. "Damn you, Steve Cody! Show me now."

He laughed and swung her into his arms, stepping with her into the darkness. "Within an inch of your life, sweetheart." On a threat and a promise he strode to the deserted exit of the yard. "Within an inch of both our lives."

Drawn from his stupor, Cactus Poteat flailed about for the cat, before he realized it was the sound of voices that woke him. Angry voices, of a man and a woman.

Fumbling for a half empty bottle, he tilted it to his mouth, draining it. Coughing and sputtering as the rotgut seared his throat, he slumped back against a saddle, his strangling silenced as he heard a shout and caught a bleary glimpse of Angie Cody.

"Man oughta have better things to do with a beautiful woman."

As angry voices grew louder, he pulled his battered hat over his eyes and settled back into a makeshift bed of hay. A pity, he thought as he drifted and dreamed and sank deeper into an alcoholic fog. "A real pity."

Chapter 16

Cactus woke with a shaft of morning sun burning its way through his eyelids. Moaning, he threw an arm over his face, shutting out the penetrating spear that scattered in his skull and bounced like neon Ping-Pong balls against the back of his eyeballs.

"I need a drink." As he spoke his stomach lurched, his head swam with the promise of a monumental hangover. "I need one now."

Rolling from his back to his stomach, he rested a second then crept carefully to his hands and knees. Sunlight glancing off yellow hay was monstrous, but there was no help for it. He needed a drink, had to have a drink, before he could even get to his feet. *The bottle.* Turning his head cautiously, eyes slitted against the glare, he searched for the precious treasure, praying it might have an inch, or even a drop of the liquid his body craved. "Where is the damn bottle?"

Scrabbling over the hay, he found it safer for his stomach if his eyes were closed. Like a blind crab he slipped and slid, patting the slick surface, digging into prickly mounds, tossing handfuls aside. Edges like tiny knives sawed at his flesh, clung to his hair, wedged in his shirt collar to scrape his neck. Cactus didn't care. Cactus cared for nothing but the drink he needed.

He was so frantic, he almost missed her, and very nearly didn't recognize the feel of stiff, cold flesh.

"What the devil?" Forgetting the precarious balance of his head, recoiling, he sat back on his haunches, his eyes popping in surprise. Clouded vision cleared. "Hey, lady." Scurrying back to her side, he stared down at her. "Wake up. A barn ain't no place for a lady to sleep."

She was a sprawl of colors, slack limbed and shrunken. A tangle of blond hair streamed over her face, obscuring her features. With a tentative hand, he shook her gently, and swallowed a scream as her head lolled at an impossible angle. The mask of hair fell away, empty eyes stared from a distorted face.

"Lady?" The alcoholic clouds were dissipating, the sickness of fear replaced the sickness of his hangover. He prodded her again, gingerly, to test his suspicion. "Lady? Ohmigosh! Lady!"

She was cold, and very dead.

"Oh, gosh! Oh, gosh! Ohmigosh!" Lurching to a crouch and then his feet, he stood with his head hanging as the ghost of a memory clawed at him, ripping open a seam in the fog of drunken stupor. Then he was running, screaming. "She's dead! He killed her!"

"Whoa there, friend." Jubal Redmond snagged the scarecrow figure as it erupted from the stockyard and, in a split second of recognition, put a supporting arm around the wizened cowboy as his short bowed legs gave way. "Cactus! Is this some sort of joke?" Jubal sniffed and turned up his nose. "Or are you too drunk to know?"

"No joke." Cactus peered past a congregating crowd to the stockyards. "Not drunk." He took a heaving breath to steady himself, and a babble of disjointed words and phrases tumbled out. "She's dead, Mr. Redmond. He killed her. I heard the fighting, and now she's dead."

"When? Who fought, Cactus, and are you sure she's dead?" Jubal asked with forced calm. "Who is she? Where is she?"

"Last night, after closing. There." A bony, straw covered arm pointed to the stockyard, his shelter for a drunken night. "Cody's wife lies there, cold in the hay." He turned indignant. "Course I'm sure she's dead, I know dead when I see it. And Steve Cody done it."

The rustle of the crowd dwindled and died to shocked whispers. A phalanx of men peeled away, intent on investigating. Jubal's dour, barking command stopped them. Even Cactus didn't get too drunk to recognize death. "Nobody goes into the yard. If there's evidence it shouldn't be disturbed." In a quiet, rapid fire decision, singling out the most reliable, he took charge. "Shugarman, call emergency and the sheriff. Hollister, see to Cactus. Jeffie, you guard the entrance. Angus, see to the back. No one is to go in until the sheriff arrives.

"The rest of you get on about your business, unless it was in the stockyard." As the gaping crowd reluctantly dispersed, Jubal halted Sandy Gannon in a quiet undertone.

A frown etched Sandy's face, with an impatient hand he stroked his clean shaven chin. "What can I do for you, Jubal?"

"I was hoping that together we could find Steve Cody before some hothead from the crowd does."

"Finding Cody isn't the problem." Sandy's blue eyes were grave. "Saw him just a bit ago, having breakfast at the Silverton Hotel."

Jubal slanted a probing look at his old friend. Something was amiss. "If finding him isn't the problem, then obviously something else is."

"He's not alone."

"Oh?" Brows like silver arches asked the question.

"Sis is with him."

"Savannah?" Jubal groaned at the complication. "How long?"

The grim glare of Sandy's gaze turned icy, his expression closed. But only for an instant, as reason counselled it did no good to hide the truth, especially from Jubal. "From the looks of it, a long time."

"Mended fences?"

"I'd say so."

"Does Jake know?"

Sandy laughed shortly. "Have you felt the earth shake this morning?"

"Think she'll give Steve an alibi, with circumstances as they are?" It was a question Jubal had to ask, if only to confirm that Sandy's opinion concurred with his.

"If she is his alibi, nothing will stop her."

"Steve will," Jubal predicted. "Until it turns ugly. After that, our Savannah will do what her conscience says she must."

"Then the earth *will* shake." Sandy made his own prediction of disaster, as he walked with Jubal to the Silverton Hotel.

"Angie's dead?" Savannah's hand shook as she set her glass of water on the cloth laden table. "How? Why? Are you sure?"

Steve's hand covered hers, silencing her with its comforting grasp. There was regret, but no grief in his face. "Where was she?"

"Cactus Poteat found her in the stockyard." Jubal waved a waitress away, wanting no one overhearing their conversation.

"How did she die?" Steve eyed both men coolly from an ashen face, but there was fear hidden beneath his calm veneer. Not for Angie, who was beyond need for fear. Nor for himself. For Savannah, whose life could be destroyed by this, if he didn't stop it.

"You don't know?" Sandy tossed the question at him almost casually.

"Should I?" Steve turned from Sandy to Jubal, gauging their reaction to his evasion.

"Cactus says he heard the two of you quarreling in the yard. Twice. The second time was last night, after closing on the concourse." Jubal's response was mild, facts without accusation.

"We quarreled," Steve admitted. "It was a common occurrence with Angie. But only once in the yard, certainly not last night. I didn't see Angie again after the scene in the arena."

"He couldn't have seen her after closing..."

"No, Savannah." Steve stopped her with a look. "I don't think either Sandy or Jubal came to interrogate me. That's for the sheriff to do." He faced the two men who had believed in him, men he counted his first friends in Arizona. "I assume that's what this is about, warning me that the sheriff has been called, and what he will be led to believe."

"Billy Blackhawk is a good man." Sandy shifted in his seat, keeping his gaze firmly from Savannah. "He'll believe proven facts, not the crazy gibberish of a drunken old coot."

"I can give him facts." Savannah tugged her hand from Steve's, drawing it into a fist before her. "I can tell the sheriff exactly where Steve was most of last evening."

"But you won't." Leaving no room for argument Steve slid back his chair, addressing both Jubal and Sandy. "When Blackhawk comes, tell him he can find me in my room." Smiling crookedly at Savannah, denying his need to brush the tumble of her hair from her shoulders, he bowed slightly, with a touch of old-fashioned gallantry. "Thank you, Benedict, for allowing me to share your table."

Then he was walking away, as if they were little more than strangers. As if a night of love such as she'd never thought to know again hadn't happened. Her chair skidded back with such force it toppled over. "Wait."

The pleasant rattle of crockery and conversation stopped. Curious diners stared at her, but she didn't care. "You can't just walk away as if..." The cold stare he fixed on her had her stumbling, searching for words.

"As if nothing happened?" Before she could respond, he went on in a tone no one beyond their table could hear. "Nothing did, Savannah, but a most enjoyable breakfast between acquaintances."

"Nothing? Acquaintances?" Her fingers closed over the napkin lying beneath her hand, frail fabric threatened to tear. "That isn't true. You know it isn't."

"It's your word against mine, sweetheart. When it comes to resolving a murder, I wonder who will be believed. Sandy. Jubal," he didn't take his gaze from her, "make her see. Make her understand what she could be doing to herself and to Jake." To Savannah he said, "I won't pretend I have any love lost for your father, but can you live with yourself if you destroy him?"

"The truth won't destroy him," she insisted desperately.

"Won't it?" His grave smile became a small, defeated quirk. "You're all he has, could he survive losing you?"

"If he loses me, it will be his choice." She flung the napkin away, as if she would fling away the burden of her father's pride.

"It isn't an issue of choice." A shake of his head lent emphasis to Steve's point. "As Sandy and Jubal will vouch, he's been who he is and what he is too long to change."

Then he was walking away again. This time she didn't call after him, and this time he didn't turn back.

"Why?" she whispered as Jubal rose to lift her chair from the floor, then pressed it to the back of her knees, forcing her to sit. "Why is he doing this?"

"You know why, sis." Sandy brushed roughened fingertips over her white knuckles. "We all know."

Savannah knew. She had doubted Steve, not as a cowhand, but as a man. He repaid the hurt with love, and now sacrifice. "I can't allow it." With challenging bravado, she faced Sandy and Jubal, who had known her all her life. "I spent the night in his room, not in mine."

She met their gazes levelly, refusing shame where there was none. "I made love to him and with him. Neither of us slept, and he never left me."

"Sis, you don't have to do this."

"Yes, I do! Can't you see?" Her voice rose a frantic notch. "I can't let him be accused of something he didn't do."

"But can you live with what this will do to Jake?" Jubal made Steve's point again.

"I don't know!" She raked her hands through the loose flow of her hair, agitation turned to bewildered dejection. "I don't know." Looking to older, wiser heads, she pleaded for advice. "What do I do?"

Sandy said nothing. And for once the Kentuckian was at a loss, his expression bleak.

"Nothing, Jubal?" Her eyes were bright, glittering with unborn tears. "Have you nothing to suggest?"

His sigh was harsh, frustrated. "Only a caution that you weigh your options, choose the path that does the least harm to the fewest people." Massive shoulders shrugged as helplessly as Savannah's had. "And if you can find some magical crystal ball, maybe you can deduce the answer to that particular riddle."

"Sandy?" She paused, waiting for this man who had stepped in, playing the role of father many times when her own lacked insight.

In a pall of silence Sandy chose his words carefully. "We all know what you should do, don't we? The honorable thing," a hint of pride threaded through his voice, "and what you've intended all along." Taking her hand in his, he loosened her fingers from their tight fist, then wove his own through them. "Since the day you won the first star, you've determined the course, not of ambition and wishes, but of responsibility and honor, and, by God, you stuck to it.

"It was the same when you walked away from your studies in law. Your choice was made, in all the years you've never deviated, never bartered your honor. And I won't ask you to in this." A long speech for taciturn Sandy, and he hadn't finished. His fingers moved restlessly over the back of her hand as he made the decision he'd waited years to make. "I ask you, now, to wait, to give me time. There is a way. If it works, no one will be hurt. At least not irrevocably."

Savannah didn't ask his plan. If he'd intended her to know, he would have told her. Instead, she studied the strong, handsome face of her foreman and friend, nodding a tentative agreement. "How much time?"

"Three days. A week at most."

Sandy's succinct answer drew a surprised look from Jubal. "A plan that can rectify all of this, set into motion in so little time?"

"All it requires is a yes from the necessary person."

"And if the answer is no?" Jubal asked, almost certain he knew the direction of Sandy's plan.

"Then it's sis's bronc to ride," the foreman replied grimly.

A waitress hovered just out of hearing, needing to serve, or prepare the table for the next diner. Jubal held her at bay with an openhanded signal. Determining, as he did, that her tip would be more than adequate. "When will you begin?"

"Today."

"Make it three days, Sandy, and I'll agree to give your plan a chance." Hopes stirring, Savannah decided it was time she took a hand in planning her fate and Steve's.

"There could be problems," Sandy protested. "Delays I can't anticipate,"

"Three days." She was adamant. "By then Steve could very well be in jail. I won't let him stay there any longer than that."

"He'll be angry if you come forward," Jubal ventured.

"Then he'll just have to be angry." She dismissed the threat of it as unimportant in the scope of things. "I won't live a lie."

Neither Jubal, nor Sandy, nor Savannah, noticed it was never suggested that Steve might be guilty. The possibility of guilt never occurred to either of them.

Jubal looked from one friend to the other. "It's decided?" His concern settled on Savannah. "You'll wait?"

"Three days." Three fingers reiterated a timetable carved in stone.

"All right!" Sandy brought the discussion to a resounding end. "Three days it is, then."

"Go away, Savannah." Steve gripped the bars that separated them, then jerked away when she would have touched him. "I don't want you here. I don't need you anymore." He looked away, avoiding the hurt he knew he would see in her eyes. "Why won't you understand, I don't want you?"

Each word was evenly spaced, each a sharp stake he would thrust into her heart. Savannah flinched, but would have none of it. "Nice try, Mr. Hero, but you aren't going to drive me away with that." Her shoulders stiffened, her head lifted. "You aren't going to make me believe you love me in quiet times, then send me away when there's trouble."

"Go. Leave me in peace." His lips were tight, a rim of white betrayed the battle he fought as a man of little cruelty struggled to hurt and repulse. "I don't love you, I never did. The line always works.

It worked with the buckle bunnies, it worked too damn good with you. At least they were smart enough to know the love ended the minute they climbed out of my bed. I didn't have to shake them off, they knew to save both our pride by going away."

His eyes were dark and hard, without a hint of compassion. "Go, leave me alone."

"Oh, I'm going. You can count on it, but not in the spirit you want me to." Undeterred, she promised, "And I'll be back."

"I won't see you."

"I'll come anyway."

He tried to stare her down and discovered she was stronger than he. In the only defense he had, to make her believe, he turned his back on her in a gesture of dismissal and walked away.

Savannah stood as she was for long while, wishing she could reach him. Wishing she could make him understand she had no choice.

Her boots grated on the concrete floor of Silverton's small jail. The door that led to the sheriff's office squealed, protesting as she opened it. Pausing, she held her breath, hoping he would call her back. He didn't.

Sighing, she leaned her head against the splintered wood of the door. Her eyes closed against the burn of tears. It shouldn't be like this. She'd hoped Sandy's mysterious plan would be accomplished and she released from her promise before it came to this. Neither she, nor Sandy and Jubal reckoned with the speed of the sheriff's investigation. Neither expected Billy Blackhawk would consider the evidence against Steve overwhelming.

She hated seeing him here, a man locked away from the land he loved. A word from her and it wouldn't have to be. Soon, with a word from her, it *wouldn't* be.

Rousing herself, she went through the motions that would be unnecessary in another day. "Have you considered legal counsel?"

He made no show of hearing her.

That he had or hadn't was of little consequence, when she had only to honor her word and wait to prove his innocence. "I'll be back."

Hinges squealed again. The latch engaged, and on the other side a bolt shot into place, before he turned, before he muttered, "No."

The veranda lay in darkness. As usual, Savannah paced its length alone. Jake, after admitting he was still exhausted from the aftermath of the festival, had retired early with a book. By now he was sleeping with the book lying on his chest. Bonita had given up on coaxing her to a late dinner and had gone home. Sandy was nowhere to be seen. After being underfoot and hovering over her for a day, he quite simply disappeared.

He'd been gone since early morning, and none of the hands knew where, or why. Savannah wanted to hope it was in keeping with his great solution to her dilemma, but a day such as this sucked hope from her.

She hadn't reckoned with the tabloids or the press. Hadn't expected to see Steve in jail and his picture plastered over every paper. Each reporter seemed bent on creating the perfect catch phrase to describe Steve's involvement with Angie, and then the murder. One, in the epitome of bad taste, stooped to calling his ill-fated quest for the national championship a saddle bronc rider's trail of tears.

Tomorrow, when the three days had ended, she expected that same reporter would revise his copy to read triangle of tears.

Most saddening was the injustice done to Steve, and that in the brouhaha of reporting, no one thought to mourn for Angie.

"Unless Tad Jasper found it in his heart to mourn." Gripping a post, she lifted her face to a night touched by autumn. Tad Jasper swam in her thoughts, and she found herself wondering where he was the night Angie died, and where he'd been since. "You've made yourself scarce, haven't you, Jasper? I wonder why."

Drawing back from speculation when she knew too little for it, she let her mind drift where it would. Oddly, it drifted to Jeffie, a good young cowboy already, exhibiting the potential of becoming better than good. It was he she'd entrusted with the care of the Broken Spur and its prize stock.

Just until Steve was home again.

Tomorrow.

Brushing her hair from her shoulders, she let the weight of her hand rest on taut, sore muscles. The first sign that she wasn't sleeping nearly enough. Sighing at the futility of even trying, she cocked her head and drew a deep breath.

Dust. She inhaled dust. Enough that it tickled her nose and the scent of it permeated the still air. Someone was coming. Someone in a hurry, who drove at foolish speeds over the unpaved road that led to the ranch. It wouldn't be Sandy. He had too much respect for machinery of any sort to punish it in such fashion. Not Jubal. If he felt an urgent need for a hurried visit, he would come by chopper.

A frisson of excitement drew her to the front steps. A coil of fearful dread kept her from descending them. She was a reluctant welcoming committee of one, and wondered to whom she would be offering welcome. Or if she would.

There was little time to wonder more before the massive Suburban skidded to a halt. The notes of a classical piano reverberated from the open windows, and from his place in the passenger's seat, Sandy turned his head to toss her a weak smile.

The engine stopped abruptly, and with it the music. The driver's door swung open, and a sleekly coiffed woman climbed from under the steering wheel. In the moonlight she was slim and perfectly dressed for the occasion. If driving across the desert as if it were the Grand Prix was the occasion. Stripping driving gloves from her delicate hands, she tucked them casually into the belt at her waist. One quick gesture smoothed her silver-brown hair back to its low chignon before she moved into the glare of the Suburban's headlights.

Hands on slim, trouser clad hips, her booted feet apart, she flung out her challenge. "Well, Savannah Henrietta, are you just going to stand there?"

Savannah blinked, then blinked again, certain she imagined the whole scene.

"Is this how you greet me after four years?"

"Mother?"

"Who else scares Sandy out of a year of his life when she drives?"

Who, indeed? "What are you doing here? Why are you here?"

"Hey!" Camilla Neal Benedict opened her arms. "First things first. You may be only a year or so from thirty, but you'll always be my little girl. And I need a hug."

Savannah needed no second invitation.

"So." Setting a cup of tea before her mother, Savannah sat on the sofa by her. "Why are you here?"

Ignoring the steaming brew, Camilla covered her daughter's hand with her own. "My daughter needs me, where else would I be?"

"But how did you know?"

"Darling, Sandy told me." Camilla leaned back feasting her eyes on the woman her daughter had become. "He tells me everything."

"Then you know about Steve."

"And the canyon, and Jake's continuing obsession with it," Camilla finished for her. "But more than that, I know that you're in love with this young man. A man Sandy says is much like your father was forty years ago."

"He's as stubborn." In the slanting light of a lamp, Savannah's face was etched with worry.

Camilla slipped from her chair. Like a graceful wraith she prowled the enclosure that served as both family room and library. "I know what it's like to love a stubborn man." Her slender fingers stroked a small bronze of a horse and rider. "I made the mistake of trying to be more stubborn, of out waiting him."

Savannah watched her mother move from place to place, touching old treasures, discovering the new. "You're speaking of Jake."

"There's never really been another man in my life. What began as a business arrangement didn't stay that way for me. Jake, either, if he would admit it."

"But you fought. I remember how you fought."

Camilla laughed. "Fighting doesn't mean one doesn't love."

"But the baron, or the duke, or whatever he was!" With a flick of her fingers, Savannah dismissed the title, but not the man. "You were considering marriage."

"The count? A ploy. Trying to out Benedict a Benedict." A tinge of resignation colored the older woman's words. "It never works."

"You wanted Jake to ask you back?"

"I spent a long time wanting it." Camilla sighed at her own folly. "When he had his strokes, I hoped he would need me. He asked for you, so I didn't come. Like a fool, I played by his rules instead."

"But now you're here. For me."

"And for myself." In measured steps the older woman returned to the sofa. "I'm playing by my rules now. I would have been here a day sooner, but there were people I needed to see. Doctors and therapists and the like."

Savannah was instant concern. "You aren't well?"

"On the contrary, healthy as a horse." Pleased at her choice of words, she ran a hand over her hair in a gesture much like her daughter's. "A fitting analogy, in the circumstances, wouldn't you say?"

"Then why the doctors?"

"For Jake. We're playing by my rules now, remember? I'm going to get him out of that chair, back on a horse and, eventually, back in my bed." Taking up her cup, she chuckled wickedly, savoring the taste of tea and conquest. "The poor man isn't going to have a choice, and he isn't going to know what hit him. In fact, he's going to have his hands so full with me, he'll have neither the time nor the inclination to cause you and your young man too much trouble."

"Too much?"

"One can't expect him to stop being a stubborn Benedict altogether." The wicked chuckle became a wicked grin. "I wouldn't want him to." Setting the cup aside, she patted Savannah's knee. "It will take him a while to get over his mad spell when you go. Time is the key. Time, and a grandbaby or two."

"You're jumping the gun a bit, aren't you?"

"Only if it isn't what you want. Only if you really don't want this young man after all."

"Oh, I want him. But he's . . ."

"Stubborn?"

Savannah's smile was slow in coming, but there was the dawning of understanding. "Yes."

"Then play by your rules. Ignore him."

"What if it doesn't work?"

Elegant shoulders moved dismissively, tendrils from an elegant chignon teased the collar of an elegant shirt. But no one could question the strength. "Then what will you have lost that you hadn't already?"

Savannah spoke her respect for the unleavened wisdom. "When should I begin?"

"Why waste time? What about tomorrow morning?"

"I should tell Jake first."

"I'll tell Jake." Camilla declared. "Just as soon as he gets over the shock of seeing me. And after he realizes that this time I'm here to stay."

"You're going to bully him."

"Damn straight."

"Something only you could do."

"Ditto."

For a moment, Savannah regarded her mother silently. She'd never been more beautiful, and despite the fatigue of her trip, she seemed to grow younger by the minute. "You know, I think you'll do it. If he survives, before you're through Jake will be Jake again."

"Oh, he'll survive. I know you were jesting, but I've spoken with his doctor here on that matter." Taking Savannah's hand, she drew her from the sofa with her. "But I might not, if I don't get a little R and R before I fire the first salvo."

"Oh, dear." Savannah was embarrassed by her careless hospitality. "I'm afraid none of the rooms are ready for guests, but where would you like to sleep?"

"Darling." Camilla raised a lecherous brow. "If you hadn't slept with your husband in so many years, and his bed wasn't yet an option, where would you sleep?"

"As close as I could get, the adjoining bedroom."

"Exactly."

"It's dusty."

"Are you going to let a little dust stand in your way when you go to your young man? To Steve?"

"Not hardly."

"Then, like daughter, like mother."

"Shall I have Sandy bring up your bags?"

"Nope." Camilla caught up her handbag and fished a filmy wisp of a nightgown from it. "This is all I need."

Savannah choked a bit on that. "You're going to let Jake see you in that?"

"Sure, why not? A preview of coming attractions, so to speak. I'm told I don't look so bad for an old broad."

Startled amusement blooming into a laugh, Savannah flung her arms around her mother. Her tanned cheek was warm against the translucence of Camilla's. "You're no broad. Not an old one, at least. And no matter what happens tomorrow, I'm glad you're here."

Camilla hugged her back and kissed her. "Not one dab gladder than I."

Steve cradled his forehead in his hands. Without benefit of a mirror, he knew he looked as rough as he felt after a sleepless night. But as he lifted his aching head, how he looked was the least of his concerns. His eyes were slitted in concentration, his teeth ground one over the other rippling his unshaven cheek. When he drew in a long, shuddering breath, he had to fight to keep from drawing in another, and then another. Even the small window that only recently announced the dawn did nothing to ease a smothering sense of claustrophobia.

But it wasn't sleeplessness or claustrophobia, or even a charge of suspicion of murder, that had him swearing under his breath, pondering what the hell he should do. It was Savannah.

He groaned, or maybe it was a growl, when he thought of her and what he feared, no, what he knew she intended to do. He had no more desire to be accused and charged with homicide than the next cowboy, but he'd rather prove his innocence without dragging her into it.

"How?" How the hell did he go about proving he wasn't guilty of murder, when he was locked away? Raking his hands brutally through his shaggy hair, he tried to think logically. If he wasn't locked away, where would he start? Who in Silverton, where Angie was a virtual stranger, would have motive, or provocation, for killing her?

The answer to that was simple.

Steve Cody.

Only he was threatened by her. Only he stood to lose all he had. His were the dreams she would destroy. Only his. In his own mind evidence mounted against him, strangling all hope from his soul, while the little cell smothered the life from him.

Slamming a fist into the thin mattress that served as seat and bed in the tiny room, he refused to be the instrument of his own defeat. There had to be someone. A chance encounter. Perhaps, considering Angie's tarnished finery, an assignation—a quick roll in the hay for a few quick bucks—gone wrong. Life and death at the whim of a stranger. An old acquaintance.

"An old acquaintance! Good lord! That's it." Levering himself from the bed, he paced in excitement. "Tad Jasper."

The man was not a bad sort. In fact, he never seemed to mind that he existed on the fringes of the rodeo, picking up small change, taking second-rate rides. Not the sort the buckle bunnies flocked to. Not enough glamour, not enough money. Angie was a step up for him.

"Or was he her step down?"

No matter the case, the man was besotted. He wouldn't hurt her, Steve argued, playing devil's advocate. Unless...

"Unless he realized she was only using him." Steve stopped his pacing. The cell block was quiet, he was its sole occupant. The only ears to hear and judge the ebullient speculations were his own. "If she spurned him, if she only wanted him when she needed him, and didn't anymore... Would he be angry enough to kill her?"

He answered his own question, damning it with a shake of his head. Jasper wasn't a killer. "But if she made him angry enough, if he lost his temper. If he lashed out..."

Breaking off his vocal deliberation, he strode to the bars. Someone other than himself should hear his theory. If not a lawyer, then Billy Blackhawk.

"Deputy." He tapped the bars with a tin cup left with the clutter of the breakfast he hadn't eaten. "Deputy!"

"Yes, sir." The uniformed deputy who answered his summons would have been far more convincing dressed in a letter jacket, watching cheerleaders at the nearest high school, than he was as guard to an accused killer.

"I need to speak with the sheriff."

The boy scuffed his feet, if he'd said aw shucks, it wouldn't have been surprising. Instead, he blurted, "Sheriff Blackhawk ain't here."

Steve was frustrated, angry, each of which made his voice sharper than he would have wished. "Where is he? I saw him earlier."

"Yes, sir." Swallowing hard, the boy struggled with the speechlessness of lingering hero worship. "He had an early meeting, then the two of them rushed out. Said they'd be back in a bit."

"They?" Steve gripped the bars, the cup clattered to the floor, rolled to the corner and lay still. "Who was with the sheriff?"

"Official business, Mr. Cody, and not for me to say." Saying no to a hero was difficult, but the young guard knew his duty.

"When will he return?"

"I'm not privy to his schedule, sir."

"Will you tell him I need to see him the minute he comes in?"

"Yes, sir." The guard almost bowed, almost touched his forelock. "The very minute."

"Thanks." Steve's gaze dipped to the name tag on the boy's chest. "Thank you, Deputy Bridges."

When the beaming Bridges had gone, Steve felt deflated, anxious, as if delay would weaken his theory. He started to pace, realized it only reinforced his awareness of the confining space, stopped. But idleness was as difficult. He had no books, no papers, nothing to pass the time.

Sprawling on the bed, the back of his head resting on his folded arms, he stared at another ceiling. From beginning to end, in his mind he replayed every meeting with Angie, and with Tad. Tad was always there, standing on the sidelines, watching and listening as Angie made her plays. How much of it was too much? How much before he reached his breaking point?

Hours later, Steve was still pondering, still wondering, when the squealing door broadcasted the arrival of Billy Blackhawk.

"Sheriff." Steve lurched to his feet. "I have to speak with you."

"So our starstruck deputy told me. Many times."

"I have to speak to you, now!"

Billy Blackhawk was a young giant of a man, part Apache, all stoic, and one who never seemed to hurry even when he did. Utterly calm under the brunt of Steve's urgency, he lifted a staying hand. "I have every intention of hearing what you have to say, but I'm not a man who bides well in confining places."

As Steve questioned what few places the big breed wouldn't find confining, the key rattled in the lock, his cell door swung open.

"I'd prefer to have this conversation in more spacious surroundings. My office, for instance," Blackhawk continued with a casual ease. "Or, better yet, now that I'm off duty, the nearest open air tavern."

Perplexed, Steve stood before the open door. "What are you saying?"

Blackhawk grinned a rare grin, displaying dimples completely at odds with the roughhewn features of his magnificently chiseled face. "I'm saying you're a free man, Mr. Cody."

"What? How?"

"It's a long story that can be told in many words. But better in one."

"One?" Steve was completely mystified now.

The sheriff stepped aside, revealing that he wasn't alone, making an unneeded introduction with a natural gallantry. "Your alibi, Mr. Cody."

Steve's expression was grim. When he could speak, his voice rang hollowly in the small cell. "Savannah."

Blackhawk chuckled. "That's the word."

Chapter 17

Billy Blackhawk leaned back in his chair, propped his feet on his desk, folded his hands over his lean midriff and waited for the fireworks.

He didn't have to wait long, and his ex-prisoner didn't disappoint him. Before Savannah had time to settle into her seat, Steve was standing and glaring over her. "What the devil is this all about, and what are you doing here?"

Glancing up at him, then at Blackhawk, taking a page from Camilla's new rule book, she smiled a maddeningly unperturbed smile. "An unusual reaction, wouldn't you say, Billy? I didn't expect a brass band, but one does wonder whatever happened to 'Hello, how are you, it's good to see you again?'"

Steve overrode any comment Blackhawk might have made. "I haven't been in the mood for brass bands or etiquette for days, Savannah."

"No," she murmured. "Obviously not."

"I told you not to come here." His fingers opened and flexed in irritation, vexation, frustration, and countless other emotions he couldn't fathom. One he did recognize was the mounting need to yank her from her chair and kiss that unruffled, ladylike demeanor to hell and gone. "I told you I could manage alone. What the devil did Jake say about this?"

"I really have no idea." A delicate shrug sent one side of her blouse sliding from her shoulder. As his eyes widened, she hid another smile and left it as it was.

"You have no idea! What the hell does that mean?"

"It means what I said. I don't know what he's thinking because I didn't tell him."

Relief reeled through Steve. "I thought . . ."

"You thought I told Billy you couldn't have killed Angie because you were making love to me the whole night through?"

"Dammit, Savannah! You didn't."

"I did," she went on serenely, as if he weren't cursing with nearly every breath, or scowling at her as if he would gleefully throttle her. Casting a look at Blackhawk, she invited confirmation.

"Miss Benedict has sworn to me that on the night Angie Cody died, she, Miss Benedict, was with you in your room at the Silverton Hotel. She has further sworn that between the hours of twelve midnight and seven in the morning, neither of you left the room." Blackhawk stated facts as if he were reciting them, in a tone that offered no judgment.

"That's it?" Tearing his gaze from Savannah, Steve wheeled around to face the sheriff. "On a word from her, without proof, you swing the cell door wide and invite me to freedom?"

Billy's pale golden eyes glittered in his expressionless face. "It wasn't quite that simple, but yes."

"And you believed her?"

"I did. But a court might not, so I went with her to investigate an idea she proposed." Blackhawk's hands were still laced over his middle, his thumbs tapped one against the other in a lazy rhythm. "A hunch, a theory, call it what you like, but one that had occurred to me, as well."

"What theory?" Steve demanded.

"That Tad Jasper killed Angie Cody in a jealous rage." Nothing changed in Blackhawk's face, his bland manner revealed nothing.

It was gratifying to hear his own speculations echoed almost verbatim. But, despite his surprise that the sheriff had thought to look past him, given his strong motive and a preponderance of circumstantial evidence supplied by Cactus Poteat, Steve's attitude didn't change. "How did you go about checking out this mutual theory?"

Something that might have been the beginning of a grin but too minute to recognize, flitted over Blackhawk's sculpted face as his thumbs continued their tapping cadence. "I asked him."

Incredulous silence followed the casual comment as Steve stood apart, his stare moving from one solemn face to another. Weary from his long night, his sigh was harsh, irritable. "Ah, of course, you just asked."

Blackhawk's grin came out of hiding. "You know a faster way to get at the truth?"

"Of course not," Steve drawled. "Not when the suspect just couldn't wait to tell you he'd killed the woman he worshiped like a lovesick puppy." His fist slammed the desk. "Dammit, man, do you take me for a fool?"

"Well, now, Mr. Cody." Taking his feet from his desk and his hands from their repose, the sheriff leaned forward. "There are a lot of things I might take you for, but whether or not one of them is a fool remains to be seen.

"But," he lifted an emphatic finger, "to answer your question, as a matter of fact, Jasper was more than willing to talk. You might say eager. Said he didn't mean to do it, but didn't mean for you to take the blame, either. Asked me to tell you he would have been on down to make things right in a day or so."

Startled, annoyed, afraid to be relieved, Steve couldn't get past his wariness. "I can't believe this."

"Then I think it's about time you started."

"You were suspicious of Tad all along?" It would explain why Blackhawk was so quick to act on a hunch and a theory.

"He was a strong possible."

A gaze as dark as night bored into the golden stare of the sheriff. "Tad isn't really a killer."

"I know," Blackhawk agreed. "It doesn't require a degree in psychology to see he's really a mild, noncompetitive personality. But even mild mannered folk have their breaking point. Tad Jasper was quite simply the wrong man, in the wrong place, with the wrong woman."

Thoughtfully Steve admitted Angie's greed had made her the wrong woman for many people. For him, for herself, and most of all, for Tad. "Where is he now?"

"Angie's body has been released by the coroner. Since no family could be found, he wanted to make the final arrangements. I believe he said she was born in El Paso, and he felt she would want to be interred there." Blackhawk paused, allowing opportunity for objection or accord. When Steve's only response was a slight expression of acceptance, he continued in his same unruffled manner. "He'll be along when he's through. I left a deputy with him, as a formality, but I don't consider it was necessary. I suspect some sort of closure for Angie was all he was waiting for before he came in to confess."

"Confess! He was coming in to confess!" Steve swung around to Savannah, who had sat quietly during this strange exchange. "Then Savannah needn't have come in at all. There was no reason to expose herself to gossip and scandal."

"That isn't exactly what I said." There was the cutting steel of a rapier in Blackhawk's hard tone. "I wouldn't make light of what Hank did for you. Without her statement we just might have considered Jasper a crackpot looking for kicks by confessing to a crime. After all, what real evidence do we have other than his story?

"Should I remind you that Cactus saw you in the yard. He heard you threaten her." A steely gaze matched the steely tone. "You, Cody, and no one else."

Passing a hand over the aching muscles of his jaw, feeling the scrape of his stubbled cheek against his fingertips, Steve's mouth went dry. He needed no reminders of how near he'd come to disaster. "After days locked up in a box, I don't have to be told that I should be thankful, nor to whom I owe my thanks."

"I thought not." Blackhawk amended his observation tersely, "I hoped not."

The skepticism, however mild, rankled, but Steve wasn't to be swayed from his point. "Regardless of what happened, or how, the important point is that with Tad's confession you won't require Savannah's statement. You said the court might not believe her, so no one outside this office should be privy to her information."

"You keep putting words in my mouth, then twisting them." The sheriff complained, but without any show of the irritation expressed only seconds before. "All I can promise is that we won't use Hank unless Jasper's confession doesn't hold up. In which case, we won't be able to avoid bringing her into it."

Out of sheer perversity, because he felt Cody needed a short lesson in reality, Blackhawk didn't mention traces of skin found under Angie Cody's fingernails, a smear of blood on her palm and shirt. Signs of injury, but not to her, for other than a broken neck the pathologist had found no wound on her body. It was a natural deduction that Angie had fought with her killer, that the skin and blood were his. Steve Cody had no wounds. But it had taken only a glance to confirm that Jasper's face and hands looked as if he'd tangled with a wildcat. Blackhawk was confident DNA testing would substantiate the rest.

"There has to be some way you can insure you won't have to call her," Steve persisted.

"Said I'd try." Massive shoulders moved beneath the khaki uniform. "And I will."

"Trying isn't good enough, Blackhawk. *Do* it."

"Steve!" Savannah intervened in the verbal sparing. "It isn't your place to tell Billy how to do his job. If he said he would try to keep me out of this, that's exactly what he'll do—try. Beyond that, his hands are tied."

"It's okay, Hank, your man and I understand each other on this matter." Blackhawk leaned back in his seat again, folded his hands at his waist, but kept his feet on the floor. Cocking his head, he swept Steve with a probing look. "You know, Cody, you strike me as a man who needs to get his priorities in order."

"Yeah? What order would you suggest?"

Ignoring the sarcasm, Blackhawk took the question at face value. "Instead of fretting over troubles that might come to pass in the future, you would be wise to look at today and count your blessings.

"Hank just gave you back your life." Something like envy moved in eyes that burned like a tiger. "If I were you, I'd take her home, and I'd spend the rest of all the time she'd give me proving to her just how grateful I can be."

"You would, huh?" Steve said dryly.

"Yep."

"You know," his militant manner softened, his voice turned thoughtful, "you may be right. In fact, you are right, Blackhawk." Turning, he found Savannah watching him, a smile that defied interpretation on her lips. "But I think there's a problem with it."

"You think so?" Savannah asked before the sheriff could. "I wonder what it could be."

"For starters, one of us has some explaining to do, the other some apologizing." As she sat quietly, still maddeningly unperturbed, he added quietly, "Wouldn't you agree?"

"Perhaps." Her lashes drifted down, shielding her eyes as she thought of Camilla's rules, her own new rules. A tremor of anticipation quivered in her as she decided there would certainly need to be explanations, and, if he insisted, apologies. But later, much, much later.

Watching her, Steve found her so still, so peaceful, she hardly seemed able to cope with the real world. Yet he knew that she could, that she had, that she would, better than anyone he'd ever known.

She was lovely, sitting in a cracked leather chair in Blackhawk's austere office as if it were the most natural place to be. And, as he'd found she would always be, she was many women in one. The proper gentlewoman, with her skirt brushing to top of her boots and her hands folded primly in her lap. The sultry siren, with her hypnotic scent of roses and wild flowers drifting to him.

She was Savannah. A wonder filled, vexing mix of lady and hoyden, with her hair flowing wild and free, her calm silver gaze and her controlled little smile.

And all the while her blouse slipped further from her shoulder.

God help him! He wanted to forget ranches and canyons, and Jake Benedict, as much as he wanted to forget explanations and apologies. He wanted to kiss the curve of her shoulder so innocently bared, and touch his tongue to the special place he'd discovered would always leave her trembling and far from prim.

More than that, he wanted to take her in his arms and hold her, and make her his. This time forever.

The admission didn't surprise him. He knew without the words that it was what he'd wanted for a long, long time.

If he just hadn't thrown it away.

Touching her, feeling the heat of her flesh, letting his fingertips linger on that special place only for a moment, he lifted her face to his gaze. Beneath the serenity, he saw a flare of heat turn her eyes fierce and sultry. Heat that became blazing, hungering need before her lashes dipped again like a veil.

"Savannah," he murmured, and then again, because he liked the feel of her name on his lips. "Savannah, what are you thinking?"

Her hand lifted to his, holding his palm to her cheek. Then she was rising. "I'm thinking we've taken enough of Billy's time. Unless there's more to be done—papers to be signed, red tape to be cut—we should let him get back to his job."

"Sheriff?" Steve didn't trust himself to say more as he backed away from her, not daring even a look.

"There's nothing," the sheriff assured as he left his own seat, honoring a tradition his mother had drummed into him, standing when a lady stood. And Savannah Benedict was a lady. He'd never doubted that she was. Now he knew she was one hell of a woman, as well. "You're free to go, Cody, with nary a scrap of paper to be signed, nor an inch of red tape to cut."

"Thanks," Steve extended his hand. They were were much alike. Men who could be friends or continue as careful antagonists. He thought that they might be friends. "I owe you a great deal."

"You owe, *compañero*." As callused palm slapped callused palm, the sheriff looked down on Savannah. "But nothing to me."

From its place in a corner, a clock from another era ticked down the minutes of another day. Men who could have lived as well in the time when it was new put aside differences that caused the crossing of their paths. Their handshake was strong and firm, building a bond, signaling a beginning.

"I wonder—" Blackhawk began, and stopped abruptly.

"If I know what I've been given?" Smiling his first real smile, Steve took Savannah's arm. "I know. Oh, yes, I know."

As Steve Cody escorted Savannah Henrietta Benedict from his office, Billy Blackhawk didn't call the customary warnings after them. Didn't suggest that Steve should stay close, or caution that he not leave the country. Intuition, common sense and an old-fashioned gut feeling predicted the so-called squatter of Sunrise Canyon wouldn't be going anywhere. Not for a long, long time.

Drawn to the window, brushing motes of dust from the pane to clear his vision, Blackhawk allowed himself an uncommon idle moment. A moment of watching a rare and beautiful woman. Steve Cody had love, fidelity, and valor walking by his side. No man could hope for more.

"This is your second chance, friend." Another chance for something Blackhawk knew, too well, many men never had once. "This time, don't screw it up."

The streets of Silverton were eerily deserted. Ranchers, shoppers and tourists had scattered to attend chores and obligations put aside for the days of the festival. Merchants scurried within their establishments, never looking out their quaint storefront windows as profits were tallied, shelves restocked and inventories refurbished. Steve and Savannah walked alone. Unseen and, at last, un-watched.

It all seemed so easy in Blackhawk's office, but in their isolation they were ill at ease and restive. Together, yet alone. Friends who had lost their way. Lovers with no idea how to begin healing the breach, and less of their destination.

Turning from the main thoroughfare, as a matter of habit, Steve took her arm as they stepped together onto the aged, boarded walk that led to the lot where his confiscated truck had been stored. Boot heels tapped in unison over creaking wood, resounding like reveille through the alley as the shade of buildings engulfed them.

Savannah's calf length skirt billowed and swirled around her as he drew her to an impatient halt. They were so close he could feel the heat of her, see the sudden rush of her heartbeat throbbing in the hollow of her throat, smell the scent of roses rising from her hair.

So close. So far. Drawing his hand from her arm, he let it fall heavily to his side. "What now, Savannah? Where do we go from here?"

There was agony in him, and that she regretted. But there was also need, and in that she found her beginning. "We go home." Fingers that had ached to touch him drifted over his stubbled cheek and curled into his hair, bringing him down to her, down to her kiss. She whispered against his lips. "We go home."

If she'd intended to say more, it was lost in the explosive passion that ravaged Steve at the first touch of her lips, the sweet, rough glide of her tongue. In a swift, fluid move, he backed her into the alcove of a doorway, pinning her against the wall. Then his kiss descended, hot and greedy, on her mouth. Whatever breath the slamming blow of his body hadn't knocked from her was stolen by an overpowering stab of desire.

She couldn't breathe, couldn't think. She didn't fight. She didn't want to fight. Not even when she felt herself go weak and dizzy with her body's demands for the ease not meant for public streets or private alleys. Her arms closed tighter around him, one foot braced against the wall, allowing him access. As he caressed her, shamelessly she cradled his trembling body with her own.

Steve sank deeper into the magic of her kiss. Touching her, feeling the buck and shudder of her hips as he stroked her, sending passion and longing spiraling into urgent, demanding desperation. She was a temptress, a sorceress stealing sanity from him, drawing him into the dark, sweet madness of enchantment. He wanted her naked and wild beneath him, her body arching to take him. He wanted her as mad as he, crying his name as softly and plaintively as she cried when his seeking hands left her breasts to tangle in her hair.

Clinging to him, she cried out again. "Please."

"No." Tearing himself from her with every shred of strength he had left, staring into her dazed gaze, he found himself falling again under the spell of witch eyes. "No! Dear God, no! I want you, Savannah, so badly I'm not sure I can survive you. But not here."

Backing away, he let his hands slide from her hair, to her shoulder, to her breasts. Cupping a perfect, naked globe in his palm, succumbing to temptation more powerful than reason, he bent to suckle. And for his folly was nearly lost to reason and propriety as the soft rosy bloom of a nipple tightened to a taut, pebbled bud against his tongue.

"No." Marshaling every ounce of discipline, he said again, "Not here." Drawing her blouse over her, covering the beguiling nipple, he didn't turn from her sorceress's gaze. "Not in a doorway in an alley like a tart.

"We're going home, Savannah." He took her hand, folded it in his. "Home to the Broken Spur."

Savannah woke heavy eyed and languid. Purring as contentedly as a kitten, she stretched gingerly, testing each muscle, savoring every delicious ache of her body. Touching her face, she found it not unpleasantly tender from the scratch of Steve's beard. Her own fault, she remembered, for not giving him time to shave following the bath they'd shared.

Silently she blessed Jeffie for filling the water tank, starting the generator to heat it, and leaving the music playing. The small bouquet of autumn wild flowers hadn't been a bad touch. "Jeffie," she murmured. "A romantic, who would have thought it?"

Stretching again, finding new and sweeter aches that needed soothing, she slipped from the bed. Winding the sheet around her, she went in search of the only one who could offer the ease she needed.

Her search didn't take her far. She found him, barefoot, dressed only in jeans, sitting on the front steps. As he looked blindly out over Sunrise Canyon, shades of twilight slowly deepened into night.

"Hi," she murmured as she slid close.

"Hi, yourself." Steve didn't turn from his deep study, didn't look at her.

"Hey!" Touching his chin, turning his face to her, she recognized the troubled look in his eyes. Her heart plummeted, her throat constricted. "Second thoughts?"

Steve couldn't deny he was troubled, he didn't try. "Some."

"About me?"

"Second thoughts for you and what I've done to your life, not about you."

Savannah smothered a sigh, wondering when he would realize no one person was responsible for the upheaval in their lives. A part of the blame was Jake's, for being obstinate about the canyon. A part was Angie's, for her greed. A part, she admitted with brutal honesty, was her own. "I'm sorry."

"Sorry?" A frown etched the lines between his brows a degree deeper. "Sweet heaven, what have you to be sorry for?"

"For doubting you."

"Doubting isn't a cardinal sin, sweetheart."

"Isn't it?" Sliding her arm though his, she leaned her head on his shoulder. "If I'd been stronger, surer, and stood by you, maybe none of this would have happened. Angie might be alive, and Tad Jasper a free man."

"What happened to Angie had nothing to do with you. She was trouble looking to happen. It happened to her. Hopefully, with the extenuating circumstances, Tad will only be facing a charge of manslaughter."

"I'd like to think that."

For a while they sat companionably, her head still on his shoulder, troubles quieted, if not resolved. Steve roused from his thoughts, touched her cheek and made a decision. "Maybe we should leave the canyon."

"What?" Savannah jolted from her own reverie. Sitting rigidly erect, she asked more calmly than she felt, "Why would you leave when this is everything you've wanted? When this is where you can make the Cody horse a reality?"

"I said maybe *we* should leave, love. Maybe the canyon was everything I wanted, but not anymore." Taking her hand in his, he raised it to his lips. "I want you, more than the canyon, more than the Cody horse, more than anything in the world. If we go, if we leave the canyon to Jake, I hope in time he'll accept me, that we belong together. And you can be happy."

"I'll be happy wherever you are, but we'd both be happiest here. I doubt Jake will be spending much time thinking of the canyon. Before my mother is finished with him, I don't think he'll have the time or the inclination to bother."

"He's wanted the canyon for a long time."

"She's going to prove to him he wants her more." Savannah planted a trail of kisses over his bare shoulder. "In time, she'll convince him to be magnanimous and forgive me for defecting."

"Is that what you did? Defect?"

"No." Rising from the step, she stood before him taking both his hands in hers. "I fell in love, and, as a wise man told me I should, I listened to my heart's voice."

"Your mother, is she strong enough to convince Jake of that?"

"At the moment, she's invincible." Drawing him to his feet, with her lashes dipping to her cheek, then rising to let her steady look meet his, she smiled her sorceress's smile. "But no more than I."

"Ah?" The lift of his brow was an unspoken challenge. "You're certain of that?"

She laughed softly. And in the twilight, with her languid gaze, her mouth swollen with his kisses, and her hair falling to her waist in a dusky tangle, she was irresistible.

"Cocky, aren't you?" he whispered hoarsely as his voice failed him.

"Am I?" She took a small step back. "You tell me."

A flick of her hand and the sheet was falling. Before it hit the ground she was in his arms, and he was striding up the steps, across the porch to the bed that waited.

The room lay in near darkness. In the little light their bodies gleamed with the sweat of battle, of loving, of exhaustion. As her hands locked about his wrists, holding them above his head, her hair swept over his chest, blunt cut tips teasing and tantalizing, seducing him again. His gasp and a stifled groan sent ripples of pleasure quivering and sweet, low in her belly. And as she felt his captured body's response, she began to move again, slowly, leisurely savoring the pleasure she took, the pleasure she gave. Then, as his breath quickened, her teasing and her mood changed. One wicked, one wanton, as she watched and played a silent game of waiting.

His breaking point was prefaced by a cry and a thrashing, rearing turn. His body still immersed in hers, he crushed her beneath him. Dragging her arms above her head, holding her captive as she had him, he set out to conquer as he'd been conquered.

"Drive me mad, would you?" he growled in her ear.

"Mad, yes," she admitted. "As mad as I can."

"Two can play the game," he promised, or perhaps he threatened.

"No." Thrashing against him, straining away from his hold, she turned her head to catch his lips. Hungering for them, dying for them, she found herself engulfed, devoured, as the rhythm of his probing tongue matched the endless pounding thrust of his body.

Paroxysms of pleasure too glorious to bear splintered through her, threatened to destroy her. Tearing her wrists from his grasp, she clawed at his hair, wrenching her mouth from his. "I can't. I can't."

His rhythm didn't slacken, nor, for all her protests, did hers. Convinced she would die if he didn't stop, certain she would die if he did, she found herself cleaving to him, battling him, matching thrust for thrust, shudder for shudder, cry for cry.

Tension escalated. There was pain, there was euphoria, there was regret, and joy. Deep inside her the one small part she thought would only be hers, loosened. And loosened again.

"No," she whispered, wanting to hold on, wanting to let go.

"Yes." Understanding her conflict, fury swept from him. When he had been fierce, he was gentle. But in his gentleness there was no relief for her.

"I can't." Her nails pierced his shoulders, her teeth scraped his skin. "I can't."

"You can. You must. We must." Brushing her hair from her face he looked into her fevered eyes. "Let me show you," he murmured, sighing softly against her cheek, drawing away from her as if he would leave her.

Her scream was a wild ululation as her body lunged to keep him. "No! No! No!"

"Yes." With a return of fury, he plunged deeper, farther, taking the part she would keep, claiming all of Savannah as his own.

And as their world exploded, filling hearts and souls with the brilliance of a shower of a thousand falling stars, Steve gave to her as much of himself.

"Savannah?" She lay so still, so quiet, Steve was frightened. Rearing over her, by the light of a harvest moon falling through the window he searched her face. Teardrops shimmered on her lashes and spilled in shining paths down her cheeks. "What is it? What's wrong?"

She didn't move, didn't seem to hear. He grew frantic. "Dear heaven, sweetheart, did I hurt you?"

"Hurt me?" she mused. Drawn from her reverie, meeting his tortured gaze, she said solemnly, "You could never hurt me."

"Then why these?" He caught a tear on a fingertip. "Why the tears?"

"Because I didn't know."

"How it would be to love completely?"

She looked away, afraid of what she might see in him. "You must think I'm a naive simpleton."

"What I think," he declared as he brought her back to him, "is that you're wonderful. And if you're naive or simple because you've never felt like this, my dearest love, my first love, then so am I."

"Dearest? First?"

He kissed her and smiled.

"Love?" He'd said it before many times. She needed to hear it again.

"Love most definite."

"Before," she faltered and swallowed, and moistened dry lips. "Before, when you asked if I would leave the canyon, were you asking me to marry you?"

"No." Too quickly for pain or disillusion, he said gently, "It wasn't a proposal, but only because that wasn't how I wanted it to be. Neither is this, but what the hell!!"

Laughing, he scooped her up and tumbled her on top of him. "Savannah Henrietta Benedict, with your hair like pale midnight and your eyes like new silver, will you marry me?"

A look of mischief flickered in her solemn face. "Do you think I should?"

"Considering the magnitude of what just happened, for the sake of our future generations, I think you'd better."

Mischief turned to grave wonder. "Could it truly be . . . do you think . . . would you mind?"

As gravely as she, he considered. "In reverse order, would I mind? No. Do I think you might have conceived my child? A definite possibility. Could it truly be?" He drew a long, slow breath, considering again. "In case it isn't, we could always try again."

"Now?"

"Do you know a better time?"

Peering through the gloom to see if he was teasing, she realized he was not. "You'd have to be an iron man."

"Maybe I am, sweetheart, and the fault is yours."

As simply as that, in a move as smooth as silk, he spun with her, covered her, made good his speculation, proved his accusation.

Chapter 18

"Nervous?"

"As a filly looking at her first bridle."

While he struggled with his tie, Steve bent to kiss Savannah's cheek in the blaze of the not so newly installed electric lights, in the not so newly remodeled and enlarged ranch house. Gently he chided against her fragrant cheek, "And you're the one who's been assuring me that everything is going to be all right."

Savannah laid down her brush. "I'm sure it will be. It's just that I haven't seen my father in over a year."

Saying nothing, quietly Steve let her convince herself.

"Mother says he's fine. Sleeping with her often and quite lustily. Riding horses, bossing the hands, arguing with Jubal, and in general, driving Sandy nuts and firing him regularly."

"He would."

A frown marred the smooth plane of her brow. "She said he still limps a bit and cramps when he's done too much."

Steve sighed and gave up on his tie. "Do you think Camilla, martinet that she is, would let him do any real harm to himself?"

Savannah folded her nervous hands in her lap. "Of course not."

"Sweetheart." Kneeling behind her, Steve pressed his face to hers, watching her in the mirror of her dressing table. "He's going to take one look at our little girl and fall madly in love. Then he's going to be so proud of you for producing such a wonderful combination of Benedict and Cody, he won't be able to stay mad at you.

"After that, he's going to size me up. He'll think about it for a minute, then come to the only conclusion he could." Patting her stomach, he grinned and kissed her ear. "He's going to think I'm one helluva guy for putting our little bundle in you in the first place."

Laughing as he intended she should, Savannah swatted his hand away. "In your dreams."

Rising, Steve gathered her shoulder length hair in his palms. "Stranger things have happened." Things like a bucking horse called Shattered Dreams, who'd given him the best dream. And men like Charlie and Sandy, who would never admit they were in cahoots, but had played at long-distance matchmaking. And, finally, a half-breed sheriff, who believed in a woman so strongly, he helped her save the man she loved.

Bending again, he buried his face in her fragrant neck, wondering what it was about the Benedict women that made so many men fall in love with them. As a faceless count, and Jubal, and Sandy, and Jake had with Camilla. As Lawter, and Jeffie, and Blackhawk, had with Savannah.

And I, he thought as he breathed in the fragrance of her skin. "I," he murmured, "most of all." Leaving a trail of open mouthed kisses from her ear to her nape, he ministered most deliberately to the vulnerable spot at her shoulder. "By the way, Mrs. Cody," he whispered as she shivered beneath the lave of his suckling tongue. "I like your new bob."

"It isn't exactly a bob, but thank you, Mr. Cody." When he moved away, to steady her hand she picked up the brush to finish one hundred strokes.

Watching her, familiar yearnings reborn, he traced a pattern of lace down her arm and back again. "If you weren't dressed . . ."

Her eyes met his in the mirror, languid and soft, and her voice was low and bluesy. "Dresses come off."

Steve groaned and cocked his head to listen. "And babies wake. I suppose one of us should see to her. Since I've finished dressing and you haven't, I surmise it should be me."

Savannah saved her smile until he was gone, knowing perfectly well that if he hadn't been dressed, he still would have seen to the baby. He spent every minute he could with his daughter.

She was six months old, her name was Jakie Camilla Cody. And though she'd never seen her first namesake, she never lacked for attention. Camilla and Bonita were regular visitors. Sandy and Jubal fought constantly over who would hold her, when, and how long, and who took unfair advantage of a sneak visit. Jeffie, who had left the Rafter B to work for Steve during Savannah's pregnancy, proved that he was not only a top hand, but a topnotch baby sitter in a pinch.

"Now," Savannah whispered as she put the finishing touches on her makeup, "if Jake will just find her as irresistible."

Snapping shut a gold compact and dropping it in her purse, she went to discover what Steve and Jakie thought was so funny.

"This is it." Savannah let her gaze range over the house and grounds. She hadn't seen the Rafter B in over a year, but with the exceptions of certain feminine touches, it had changed little.

"Ready?" Steve held Jakie in one arm and linked the other through Savannah's.

"As ready as I'll ever be."

Dinner was a stiff and stilted affair, and not exactly a success. Though Camilla was the impeccable hostess, Jake was sullen and quiet, Steve withdrawn, and Savannah simply miserable and heartbroken.

After dinner, coffee and brandy on the veranda proved no better, until Camilla took the situation in hand by asking Bonita to bring the baby to her.

"Look, Jake, isn't she beautiful?" Camilla offered the child for his inspection.

"A baby's a baby," he groused, and refused to look.

"Not this one," Camilla persisted. "Ask Jubal or Sandy, or Jeffie for that matter."

Interest tweaked, Jake grumbled, "What the devil would either of those old war horses know about babies?"

"More than you do," Camilla declared, and before Steve and Savannah's astonished eyes, she plopped the baby in its grandfather's lap. "Jake, it's time you met Jakie."

For what seemed an eternity, the two of them stared at each other. Jake looking as if he were holding a basket of soap bubbles he mustn't pop. Jakie puckering to howl like a banshee at any second. By design, or instinct, or perhaps out of mortal fear, Jake bounced his knee and the threat of the banshee howl became a bell-like giggle.

Just for the sake of experiment, Jake tried it again. The baby giggled again. A third time brought a third giggle, and a bouncing demand for more. "Smart little squirt, aren't you?" he observed. "And bossy, like your gramma."

As if it had just dawned on him, he lifted his narrowed gaze to Camilla. "What did you say she's called?"

"Jakie," she repeated with no little satisfaction. "Jakie Camilla Cody."

"Jakie." The stubborn man tried the name on his tongue. "Jakie." A smile cracked the stern lines of his mouth. "Well, I'll be damned."

Something in his voice, or in his manner, struck the infant as comical. Her laughter was infectious, and even Steve and Savannah, who had watched the exchange in wonder, had to smile.

"You think that's funny do you?" he demanded, and bounced his knee again.

Jakie hiccuped and laughed again until she was limp. When Camilla would have taken her, Jake snatched her from reach. "We don't need your help. We're doing fine, aren't we, Jakie girl?"

"Jakie girl?" Steven muttered in an undertone to Savannah.

"Works for me," she responded.

"Me, too, I guess."

"Why did no one tell me?" Jake's voiced carried like shot over the veranda. "Why am I last to know this girl bears my name?"

Savannah set her coffee cup on the table by her chair and straightened her skirt before she answered. "I suppose because none of us thought you would care."

"If you thought I wouldn't care, why did you give her my name?"

Wondering how she could explain, Savannah gathered her thoughts and opted for the truth. "I wanted her to have something of her grandfather. Even if she might never know him, I thought it was important."

"Important to whom?" Jake demanded.

"To me," Savannah replied.

"And to me," Steve added.

"Why?"

Without hesitation, Savannah answered, "Because I love you."

For a fleeting instant, Jake had no answer, but in the next he was snapping at Steve. "What about you? Are you going to tell me *you* love me?"

"No, sir, I'm not." Laying his hand over Savannah's, smiling at her as he laced his fingers through hers, he replied without bothering to look back at Jake. "But I love your daughter. If naming our daughter after her own father makes Savannah happy, then I'm happy with it.''

''You are, are you?''

''Yes, sir, I am.''

Tense seconds ticked by, Jake cleared his throat. ''You got sand, boy. Coming in here pretty as you please, after taking the canyon and then my daughter from me.''

''I didn't take anything from you,'' Steve rebuked mildly. ''Neither the canyon nor Savannah were yours to have.''

''You arguing with me?'' Jake scowled and dandled the hiccuping baby on his knee.

''It won't be an argument unless you make it one.''

''Oh, ho. You're a smart one, aren't you?'' Before Steve could respond, he was rising from his chair and fending Camilla's helping hand away. ''We're all right, Miss Camilla, my legs will hold us both long enough for Jakie girl and Grandpa to take a little walk, and have a little discussion. But don't worry, we won't go far, and I sure as hell won't drop her.''

''Hallelujah,'' Camilla said in a tone of awe as Jake moved out of range. ''It's really true that wonders never cease. She's got him. Hook, line and sinker, she's got him.''

''What does that mean, Mother?''

''It means, my darling, that it will be a while before he admits it, but the war is over.''

''How can you tell?'' Steve asked.

Camilla smiled a smile he'd seen too often on Savannah's face, and each time he lost a discussion or an argument. ''I have my ways. Shh,'' she whispered, ''here he comes.''

Jakie was laughing again, and had a death grip on a lock of Jake's hair, but he didn't seem to mind. No one presumed to know what he might say, but no one expected his comment.

''You've cut your hair.''

Savannah's mind had been too full of worry to remember that her father hadn't seen her with the new cut. ''Yes.'' She wondered if he would guess that, because of Steve, she didn't need reminders that she was a woman. ''I have.''

He looked at her as if he were only just seeing the woman she'd become. The mother of his grandchild. ''I like it,'' he pronounced after his long study, adding the name no one had ever heard him say. ''Savannah.''

''Thank you,'' Savannah said when she could.

Their collective shock went unnoticed by Jake. "We've had our discussion," he announced, equally oblivious of the baby's tugging. "Considering that we've lost six months of each other's company, Jakie girl and I have arrived at the conclusion that the situation should be corrected. After all, she'd got good genes in her, and stubborn ones to boot. She'll need all of us to guide her. So, we'd best let bygones be bygones."

He looked to Savannah. He didn't say he loved her, or that he was proud of her, but it was there in his face.

"That's what I hoped for." Her voice shook with pent-up emotion. "That's why we came."

Jake nodded abruptly, and swallowed noisily.

"You're welcome at the Broken Spur anytime." With that, Steve made his peace.

"I just might take you up on that, son. In fact, Jubal tells me there's a horse I should see."

"Yes, sir, there are a lot of horses, but there's one special one, a colt. The first Cody horse. Without Savannah, I would be a rodeo has-been with nothing to show for it but a pair of broken spurs. And he would still be only a dream."

"The Cody horse," Jake mused. "Has a nice ring to it, doesn't it, Jakie girl?"

Jakie girl only hiccuped again.

Camilla smiled and laid a hand on Jake's shoulder.

Steve Cody drew his wife into his arms, kissed away her tears and whispered four words that would define the rest of their lives.

"I love you, Savannah."

* * * * *

Who can resist a Texan...or a Calloway?

This September, award-winning author
ANNETTE BROADRICK
returns to Texas, with a brand-new
story about the Calloways...

SONS OF TEXAS

Rogues and Ranchers

CLINT: The brave leader. Used to keeping secrets.

CADE: The Lone Star Stud. Used to having women
fall at his feet...

MATT: The family guardian. Used to handling
trouble...

They must discover the identity of the mystery
woman with Calloway eyes—and uncover a
conspiracy that threatens their family....

Look for **SONS OF TEXAS:** Rogues and Ranchers
in September 1996!

Only from Silhouette...where passion lives.

The Calhoun Saga continues...

in November
New York Times bestselling author

takes us back to the Towers and introduces us to
the newest addition to the Calhoun household,
sister-in-law Megan O'Riley in

MEGAN'S MATE
(Intimate Moments #745)

And in December
look in retail stores for the special collectors'
trade-size edition of

THE
Calhoun
Women

containing all four fabulous Calhoun series books:
COURTING CATHERINE,
A MAN FOR AMANDA, FOR THE LOVE OF LILAH
and *SUZANNA'S SURRENDER.*
Available wherever books are sold.

MILLION DOLLAR SWEEPSTAKES
AND EXTRA BONUS PRIZE DRAWING

FORTUNE'S Children™

Bestselling Author
MERLINE
LOVELACE

Continues the twelve-book series—FORTUNE'S CHILDREN
in September 1996 with Book Three

BEAUTY AND THE BODYGUARD

Ex-mercenary Rafe Stone was Fortune Cosmetics cover girl
Allie Fortune's best protection against an obsessed stalker. He
was also the one man this tempting beauty was willing to risk
her heart for....

MEET THE FORTUNES—a family whose legacy is greater than
riches. Because where there's a will...there's a *wedding!*

A CASTING CALL TO
ALL FORTUNE'S CHILDREN FANS!
If you are truly one of the fortunate
few, you may win a trip to
Los Angeles to audition for
Wheel of Fortune®. Look for
details in all retail Fortune's Children titles!

As seen on TV!
Free Gift Offer

With a Free Gift proof-of-purchase from any Silhouette® book, you can receive a beautiful cubic zirconia pendant.

This gorgeous marquise-shaped stone is a genuine cubic zirconia—accented by an 18" gold tone necklace.

(Approximate retail value $19.95)

Send for yours today...
compliments of  *Silhouette*®

To receive your free gift, a cubic zirconia pendant, send us one original proof-of-purchase, photocopies not accepted, from the back of any Silhouette Romance™, Silhouette Desire®, Silhouette Special Edition®, Silhouette Intimate Moments® or Silhouette Yours Truly™ title available in August, September or October at your favorite retail outlet, together with the Free Gift Certificate, plus a check or money order for $1.65 U.S./$2.15 CAN. (do not send cash) to cover postage and handling, payable to Silhouette Free Gift Offer. We will send you the specified gift. Allow 6 to 8 weeks for delivery. Offer good until October 31, 1996 or while quantities last. Offer valid in the U.S. and Canada only.

Free Gift Certificate

Name: _____

Address: _____

City: _____ State/Province: _____ Zip/Postal Code: _____

Mail this certificate, one proof-of-purchase and a check or money order for postage and handling to: SILHOUETTE FREE GIFT OFFER 1996. In the U.S.: 3010 Walden Avenue, P.O. Box 9077, Buffalo NY 14269-9077. In Canada: P.O. Box 613, Fort Erie, Ontario L2Z 5X3.

FREE GIFT OFFER   084-KMD
ONE PROOF-OF-PURCHASE
To collect your fabulous FREE GIFT, a cubic zirconia pendant, you must include this original proof-of-purchase for each gift with the properly completed Free Gift Certificate.

084-KMD

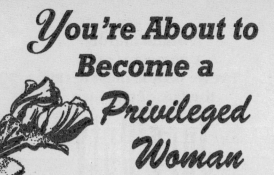

You're About to Become a *Privileged Woman*

Reap the rewards of fabulous free gifts and benefits with proofs-of-purchase from Silhouette and Harlequin books

Pages & Privileges™

It's our way of thanking you for buying our books at your favorite retail stores.

PROOF OF PURCHASE
Offer expires October 31, 1996

SIM-PP171

Pages & Privileges ™

Harlequin and Silhouette— the most privileged readers in the world!

For more information about Harlequin and Silhouette's PAGES & PRIVILEGES program call the Pages & Privileges Benefits Desk: 1-503-794-2499

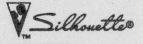

Silhouette®

SIM-PP171